NURSE KITTY'S
UNFORGETTABLE
JOURNEY

NURSE KITTY'S UNFORGETTABLE JOURNEY

Maggie Campbell

ORION

First published in Great Britain in 2021 by Orion Fiction,
an imprint of The Orion Publishing Group Ltd
Carmelite House, 50 Victoria Embankment
London EC4Y 0DZ

An Hachette UK Company

1 3 5 7 9 10 8 6 4 2

A CIP catalogue record for this book is
available from the British Library.

ISBN (Mass Market Paperback) 978 1 4091 9180 3
ISBN (eBook) 978 1 4091 9181 0
ISBN (Audio) 978 1 4091 9182 7

Typeset by Born Group
Printed and bound in Great Britain by Clays Ltd, Elcograf S.p.A.

www.orionbooks.co.uk

This book is dedicated to the doctors, nurses and auxiliary staff in NHS hospitals who have risked their lives to save those of others during the COVID-19 pandemic.

1949

Chapter 1

'Mam, are you sure you haven't got any vanilla extract?' Kitty asked, dropping her spoon. She leaned her tired arms on the baking bowl full of margarine and sugar, disappointed that her efforts at creaming the contents together still hadn't resulted in anything resembling 'light and fluffy', as the recipe suggested. Her fingers were slippery from greasing the cake tin.

There was no answer from the parlour. Small wonder her mother couldn't hear her above the rhythmic click-clack of the treadle sewing machine's mechanism as the belt revolved with every step on the footplate. Kitty could hear the needle thumping home, sending thread into the fabric of the garment her mother was working on. It was her father's cough that truly drowned everything out, however – a barking cough that rattled ominously deep inside his chest.

With slippery margarine-fingertips, Kitty levered a kitchen cupboard door open. Even in June, the paint was sticky with cold in the perpetually icy maisonette. Damp was climbing its way up the wall at the back of the cupboard in peppery mildew blotches, claiming the contents of the cupboard over time and by stealth. The bag of flour, at least, was still untainted. Kitty's mother was a reluctant baker, so Kitty had bought the flour herself only last week, on her day off.

'This will put hairs on your chest, Dad!' she shouted through to the parlour, chuckling to herself and anticipating

3

some witty, lippy come-back. 'Or maybe feathers on your bum!' She cracked an egg into the baking bowl. 'Real eggs, Dad!'

Her father's answer took the form of a spluttering cough that turned into veritable rolling thunder.

'Ooh, eh, our Kitty!' her mother cried. 'Your dad!'

Kitty wiped her hands on her apron and hastened into the parlour to find her father coughing blood into an inadequate white lady's handkerchief, held to his mouth by her mother. The red was so vivid against the snowy white, it hurt Kitty's eyes. 'Oh, you're kidding!' She whipped the tea towel from her shoulder and gently pushed her mother aside. 'Don't worry, Mam. I've got him. Listen, do us a favour! Can you nip to the corner shop and ask them to phone for an ambulance? This isn't right.'

Her father shook his head violently, trying and failing to speak. He grabbed the tea towel off Kitty and wiped his blood-stained mouth. The coughing fit started to calm as he breathed heavily through his nose. 'I'm fine! I'm fine, Elsie! Don't go calling the cavalry, for Christ's sake.' He coughed again, but this time, there was only blood-streaked mucus.

Kitty offered him his mug of tea. 'Drink this. Come on, Dad. Wet your whistle.'

She smoothed his Brylcreemed hair from his furrowed brow, noting how grey and clammy his complexion was and how bloodshot and rheumy his eyes were – no longer attributable to the booze, since he had long since stopped trying to make it to the pub. 'Let me see the back of your throat, Dad. Maybe you've ruptured a little blood vessel from coughing.'

Her father seemed encouraged by this and opened his mouth to reveal four lonely molars and three front teeth, all yellowed from smoking. There were no false teeth today, despite it being his birthday. He closed his mouth. 'You've seen enough. It's not a matinee. If you're not careful, I'm going to start charging. Shilling a pop.'

Feeling the grip of her mother's hand on her forearm, Kitty studied the expectant looks on her parents' faces. 'There's no obvious rupture, but I suppose it might be lower down in the gullet. Honestly, Mam. We're going to have to get him to a doctor.'

'Not to-bloody-day, you don't!' her father bellowed, coughing anew, though it was a short-lived outburst. 'It's my birthday and I want this cake you promised me.' He grabbed his walking stick and shooed her away with it. 'Our Ned's going to be here later. Your brother's not going to want to get off a boat after weeks at sea and hold my hand in some doctor's waiting room, is he? I'm fine.'

'You're not fine, Bert,' Kitty's mother said. 'This has been going on for weeks.'

'I'm all right, I said!' He reached for his packet of Woodbines, tapped out a half-smoked cigarette and lit up the remnants. Red sparks dropped onto his prosthetic leg as the burning-hot tobacco shards fell from the end of the loosely packed dimp. 'There we go. That'll do the trick.' He coughed and blew out a cloud of foul-smelling smoke, but there was no more blood, at least – just that ominous rattle and wheeze.

Kitty exchanged knowing looks with her mother. 'Leave him to it, Mam,' she said. 'There's no talking sense to him, right now. I'll get James to give him the once-over when he gets here. He'll be able to make arrangements for him to be looked over in clinic by the hospital's chest man. Let's pray it's not TB.'

The crow's feet at the corners of her mother's eyes had deepened of late. What had once been a fine line between her brows was now a deep cleft. Caring for an invalid while working long hours at the sewing machine was clearly taking its toll. She nodded and treated Kitty to a weak smile. 'Thanks, love. You're a good 'un.'

Throwing open the window to let a refreshing blast of Salford air in, Kitty turned to appraise her father. A pale and shrunken facsimile of the formerly handsome, notorious jailbird Bert Longthorne was sitting in a second-hand chair that had belonged to a dead woman – fitting, since Kitty's father looked like he was trying death on for size. He reached out to crank up the cricket commentary on the wireless. She felt a pang of sorrow for the happy life that her family could have had, if only her father hadn't frittered away his prime years, stealing anything that hadn't been nailed down and then paying his overdue taxes with his very liberty, doing stir at Her Majesty's pleasure. Semi-legendary and well loved among the city's criminal fraternity he might be, Kitty mused, but that was no compensation for the anguish he'd put his own wife and children through over the years.

She turned to her mother, who was standing at her father's side, still clutching the bloodied tea towel expectantly. 'And you're nothing short of an angel, Mam. Putting up with his nonsense! I don't know. Maybe our Ned should take you to Barbados with him, when he goes back. A month in the West Indies, listening to the breaking waves instead of Dad's nonsense, would do you good.'

For a moment, the long-suffering Elsie Longthorne flushed pink, perhaps at the thought of feeling the sand between her fingers on a picture-perfect tropical beach. No disabled husband. No freezing-cold maisonette. No cramp in her fingers from tirelessly sewing the garments she'd taken in for piecework-pittance. The blush faded. 'You'd best get on with that cake, our Kitty. And I'd best get back to my work. Flights of fancy won't put bread on the table in my house.'

With a sinking feeling, Kitty returned to her baking bowl to find that the egg had curdled with the margarine and sugar.

'Oh, I don't believe it!' she told the peeling wallpaper. 'The only time James manages to get hold of fresh eggs, and I make ash and blotty of the recipe. Kitty Longthorne, it's a good job you're a nurse and not a cook!'

'Pipe down in there!' her father shouted. 'I can't hear what's being said.'

Kitty pushed aside her worries about her father's worsening health and her mother's despondency to beat the mixture with renewed enthusiasm. Before long, the salvaged mixture was ready and the cake was in the oven. She could feel the fatigue tugging at her eyelids as the last week of gruelling shifts at the hospital reminded her that she was overdue a proper rest. There was no time for a catnap on the spare bed, however. At any moment, James would knock on the door, and Kitty wanted to be ready for him.

Peering in the cracked mirror that was propped on the mantelpiece of the tiled fireplace in her parents' bedroom, Kitty carefully applied soot to her eyelashes with an old toothbrush. Then she put on a little red lipstick, smacking her lips together. She patted the tiniest amount onto her cheeks and rubbed and rubbed until she looked fresh-faced enough to pass muster as the fiancée of Park Hospital's leading plastic surgeon.

'You'll do,' she told her reflection. 'You're no Hedy Lamarr, but you scrub up all right.'

There was a knock at the front door. Kitty's heartbeat picked up to a gallop. James. She held in her growling stomach, primped her hair one last time and fixed a smile on her newly reddened lips.

She emerged from the bedroom as her mother was opening the door. 'Hello, love. Come in. We're not proud.'

James locked eyes with Kitty immediately and grinned. He took off his trilby as he stepped inside and handed a parcel to Kitty's mother. 'Elsie, you look lovely, as ever. I've brought a little something for the table.'

Kitty's mother took the large object, wrapped in newspaper. 'Oh, get away, you rum pig! Now what's this?' She opened the wrappings and smiled. 'A chicken! Hey! Look at this, Bert! A fresh chicken, big as a turkey!'

'Dispatched, plucked and dressed this very morning,' James said. 'I've just finished treating the veteran son of a gentleman farmer in Dunham Massey. He dropped it into my clinic as a token of his appreciation, would you believe it?' Reaching into the deep pocket of his camel overcoat, he took out a bottle-shaped gift, wrapped in tissue paper. 'And this is for you, sir.'

He proffered the bottle to Bert, who tore off the wrapping. He perched a pair of new tortoiseshell NHS reading glasses on the end of his nose. 'Single malt? Well, I say! That'll do nicely!'

'Happy birthday, Bert.'

James then swept Kitty into his arms and kissed her tenderly on the cheek. 'I'm afraid I ran out of pockets, so all I have for you is my heart. Will that do, Kitty?'

Kitty chuckled and batted him away, almost embarrassed by the uncharacteristic show of affection in front of her parents. 'Pack it in, James! What on earth has got into you?'

8

Her fiancé shrugged. 'Good day at work. I won a battle with Cecil at a board meeting and . . .' He pulled an envelope from his inside pocket and waved it at Bert. 'I got tickets to see the match at Old Trafford for me, you and Ned. How about it?'

Her father's eyes brightened. 'England versus New Zealand?'

James nodded. 'Third test. Brian Close and Les Jackson are making their debuts. If I can't treat my soon-to-be father-in-law to the best seats on his birthday, when can I?'

The excitement brought on yet another rumbling, rattling coughing fit, but this time, there was mercifully no blood. Kitty could see from James's furrowed brow, however, that he could hear something amiss inside the old man's chest.

Later, as she and James set off alone in his Ford Anglia and headed out towards Liverpool, Kitty broached the subject of her father's health. 'Do you think it's TB?'

Peering through the windscreen at the flat marshland that flanked the Mersey to their right, James shook his head. 'It's impossible to know. I'll arrange X-rays and blood tests for him, first thing on Monday morning. Get your mother to bring him in. I'll have a word with Galbraith, too. He needs to see him as an emergency.'

'He's stubborn, my dad. He hates doctors. Especially after the printing press.' She remembered seeing her father, pinned beneath the giant piece of machinery, in a deep pit made by a V2 that had come to rest beneath a bakery in Stretford. The unexploded bomb had just been waiting to decimate the entire district, and Bert Longthorne, Manchester's coupon counterfeiter, had woken it from its slumber with his idiotic antics. Kitty sighed.

'Leave it to me, darling.'

James drove the length of the Port of Liverpool to find where Ned's boat had docked. The *Tradewind* had already arrived and its passengers were disembarking in droves, like a colony of ants spreading out to find new territory. Kitty's breath came short with excitement as she searched for her twin brother among the mainly Black passengers, who were dressed in their Sunday best, all carrying cardboard suitcases and clinging to their hats in the stiff Merseyside breeze.

'He won't be hard to spot!' Kitty said. 'There can't be anyone else on board with a face like *that*.'

'Steady on, Kitty,' James said, scanning the crowd of disembarked travellers. 'I think I did rather a good job on your brother. He's quite the handsome chap, these days.'

They waited and they waited, standing there on the dock until all the passengers had gone and Kitty had started to shiver. James tried to put his coat around her, but she pushed him away when she spotted a man in uniform making his way down the gangplank. She ran up to meet him.

'Excuse me. I'm looking for my brother. Ned Longthorne. He was a passenger on this ship, but he's not got off. I'm worried he's still on board. Maybe he's fallen asleep. Can you check?'

The man looked at her impassively. 'Everyone's off, madam. It's only staff on board now.'

Kitty could feel tears stabbing at the backs of her eyes, but she willed them to dissipate. 'That can't be right. He's coming home for my dad's birthday. We've got a chicken in the oven. I baked a cake!' The words of blind panic were tumbling out of her mouth at speed.

The officer agreed to check the roster, but when he returned, he was shaking his head. He spoke to James.

'I'm sorry, but Ned Longthorne never sailed on this ship. He booked a ticket, but we have no record of him boarding in Bridgetown.'

Chapter 2

'Now, Longthorne,' Matron said, reviewing her notes, attached to a clipboard. 'I want you overseeing casualty this morning. We're inundated with the Royal Infirmary's overspill.'

'What's happened?' Kitty asked, checking her starched nurse's cap was securely attached.

Matron's lips thinned. 'They've sent us three delightful gentlemen, fresh from a bare-knuckle brawl.' She gesticulated with her pen towards three occupied cubicles. In two of them lay two man-mountains, whose faces and knuckles were a mess of blood and swelling. In the third, a Black man lay asleep, or perhaps unconscious. It was difficult to see the extent of his injuries, as he'd been heavily bandaged. 'Heaven knows why they didn't keep them there, patch them up and kick them out.'

Kitty nodded. 'I presume they've been sent for Dr Williams's plastic surgery ministrations.'

'It would seem so.' It was unusual to see Matron so obviously disconcerted. Ordinarily, she was the swan of the nursing staff, gliding along, no matter how rough the waters, guiding her cygnets in the subtle art of swimming while all around them sank. 'They need to be assessed and sent to a ward. And that's all very well, but I'm three nurses short to begin with and Doris Bickerstaff is off sick. I know it was your father's birthday at the weekend,

Kitty, but you took half of Tuesday off to accompany him for some tests, didn't you? Could your mother not have sufficed as moral support?' She didn't wait for a response. 'Really, I'm going to have to cancel any time off from now on. Look at them! We're overwhelmed.' She peered over her heavy-framed glasses at the walking wounded of Davyhulme, Urmston and Stretford, who were packed into casualty's waiting room. 'This is what happens when you say, "Come one! Come all!" to Manchester's sick and dying. The National Health Service is a free-for-all, in every sense of the word.'

'Not before time, though, eh?' Kitty said, eyeing work-worn women in jumble-sale coats and undernourished children wearing clothes that were too big, or else too small. Everybody looked older than their years. The post-war period was proving quite a trial.

The Longthornes had problems of their own, however. Though Kitty had been plagued by worry about Ned since leaving the Liverpool dockside without him, she'd still not managed to send him an angry telegram. Working unbroken shifts, from sun-up to sun-down, and chaperoning her father to the hospital had taken precedence over any trip to the post office. Today, she would still have to wait until her break – *if* she got a break. 'Leave it with me, Matron. If maternity's quiet, I'll get Schwartz to pitch in.' Kitty knew she could rely on her old friend and nursing compatriot Lily Schwartz, who was one of the only nurses remaining from Kitty's days as a trainee.

'Good girl.'

Matron continued on her rounds, leaving Kitty to marshal the two junior nurses who were tending the patients in the worst condition. She sent for Lily Schwartz.

Within an hour, Lily joined her, and together they entered the cubicle with the first of the men who had been sent from the Royal Infirmary.

'Good morning,' Kitty said to the man on the narrow bed. 'I'm Nurse Longthorne, and this is Nurse Schwartz.'

The man turned his bloodied pulp of a face towards them both. Though his left eye was nothing more than a slit in a swollen mess, his right eye was uninjured. He fixed Lily with a chilling stare. 'Nazi or Jew?' he asked, balling his busted fist, apparently feeling no pain. It was clear from his accent that he came from the other side of the Atlantic.

'Nurse, since you're asking.' Lily seemed in no mood for verbal abuse, but she kept her voice friendly and even. She looked down at the man's notes. 'Yank?'

The man grimaced. 'Canadian, and proud of it, *missy*.'

'You're a long, long way from home, then. The war's over, Mr Morgan. Didn't anyone tell you?'

The man was silent.

Kitty took over the conversational reins. 'It says on your records that you and your compatriots were fighting at the Band on the Wall. But that's a music hall, isn't it? A note here says you were brought into the Infirmary, accompanied by two police officers.'

'What's it to you?' the man asked, turning towards the curtain that separated his cubicle from that of his opponent.

'If our plastic surgeon is to treat you, Mr Morgan, I think he ought to know the circumstances surrounding your injuries. Don't you?'

'I've done nothing wrong, ma'am. Police left, didn't they?'

'What were you doing at the Band on the Wall? These wounds have all the hallmarks of a bare-knuckle fight. Broken nose. Bust-up eye. It looks like your Black friend's head has been used as a football. He doesn't have any wounds to his knuckles at all, I'm told.'

The man sighed. 'I work at the club. I'm a barman. Sorta. So's Jim.'

'Don't make me fetch the police again, Mr Morgan. I've got other patients waiting. How about we start with a dose of the truth?'

Morgan rolled his good eye and gasped. 'We sometimes have a fight. Lunchtimes at the club. There's a bit of boxing, you know? The guys from the market come and watch. It's no big deal.'

'Bare-knuckle boxing. For money.' Kitty turned to Lily. 'Is that legal?'

Lily shrugged. 'How should I know? Jews don't box.'

Kitty stifled a grin. 'So, let me guess. You and your pal, Jim, have stayed on since the war ended, carting barrels and crates for the club owner.'

'Yes, ma'am.'

'And you supplement your wages with a bit of bare-knuckle boxing in the backyard? The boss takes bets.'

Morgan shrugged.

'So what's the story with the Black man?' Kitty had already read his notes. There was something that didn't quite sit right with the boxing bout story. The third patient had artists' hands, for a start, and was a good three or four stone lighter than the two white men.

'I can't speak for him. It was all good, clean fun, though. Boys being boys.'

Lily stepped on Kitty's foot and the two retreated from the cubicle. When they were out of Morgan's earshot, she whispered, 'Those two have beat the other one up. I'd put money on it.'

Kitty nodded. 'Bullying?'

'Did you hear how he spoke to me? Nazi or Jew? That's not a tolerant man, in there, and our Black patient only has defensive wounds. I'm going to take on Jim the giant. You see what the story is with their friend.'

With a deep intake of breath, Kitty swept aside the curtain that concealed the Black man. He seemed to be out cold, but he stirred when she touched him lightly on the arm.

'Hello, there. I'm Nurse Longthorne.' She took his notes from the end of the casualty bed. 'And you're Mr Chambers?'

The man turned towards her. Could he even see her? His bandaged head put her in mind of Ned, when he'd hidden in plain sight on a ward, masquerading as a badly burnt American GI. Was this man concussed? Kitty needed to shine a light in his eyes to see if his pupils dilated, but she couldn't even see beyond the lacerations, bruises and swelling. His face was reminiscent of offcuts of stewing steak she'd seen in the butcher's. She felt suddenly nauseous at the very idea.

'Lloyd, miss,' the man suddenly said. 'Me name's Lloyd Chambers.' He spoke haltingly, as if he'd bitten his tongue. His Jamaican accent was still pronounced, though.

'You're in a bad way, Lloyd. Does it hurt?' She looked for information about any analgesics he'd been given at the Infirmary.

'Me face feel like I been trampled by the four horses of the Apocalypse. But me hand . . . I'm worried that it doesn't hurt enough. Can't feel it at all, nurse. Can't bend me fingers.'

He reached out to her, and when she unwound the loose bandaging around his right hand, Kitty could see that there were no cuts to his knuckles from throwing a punch, but it was possible he had several broken fingers. Had his hand been purposefully crushed?

'Were you X-rayed at the Infirmary?'

He shook his head. 'I got to play trumpet, nurse. I'm in the house band at the club. It's my livelihood. Please fix me hand up.'

'What happened to you, Chambers?' Kitty lowered her voice to a whisper. 'You can tell me. Did the men in the other cubicles – the men you came in with – did they beat you?'

Lloyd pursed his split lips and grimaced. 'I got in the way. That's all.'

She frowned at him, sensing that there was more to his story than he was letting on. What kind of a place was the Band on the Wall? Its notoriety had started during the war years, when drunken soldiers on leave – particularly Canadian airmen – would go there to dance and drink far too much. The place was in a part of the city that Kitty wasn't familiar with. Oldham Road and Ancoats. That wasn't a Hulme girl's stomping ground and, in any case, her evenings off as a young nurse had always been few and far between.

'Well, let's clean you up first, so the doctor can see what he's dealing with,' she said. 'Then we need to get you X-rayed.'

Kitty was just about to tell him that Park Hospital had an outstanding and renowned plastic surgeon on site, called James Williams, when a hue and cry erupted from the direction of the casualty entrance.

Drawing the curtain across the cubicle to shield her Jamaican patient from the hubbub, Kitty hastened to the double doors to find a woman trying to drag a man out of a black cab, single-handedly. 'Help me! Help! He's bleeding to death.'

Chapter 3

'Stretcher! I need a stretcher! Bring a wheelchair! Anything!' Kitty shouted, hoping her cry for help would fall on her nursing compatriots' ears. 'Quickly!' There wasn't a single nurse or auxiliary free, however. She yelled at the cab driver. 'Give us a hand, for heaven's sake! We're short-staffed.'

The cab driver rolled his eyes and nonchalantly opened his door. While he hitched up his trousers, Kitty and the woman cracked on with the task of manoeuvring the wounded man out of the cab.

'What happened?' Kitty asked, staring at the man's midriff. His shirt was blood-soaked. There was a patch, about an inch wide, where a wound oozed blood that was almost black, as if all hell had broken loose inside him.

The woman's cheeks were flushed. Her hair hung loose as she heaved at the man's legs. 'He was cleaning the bedroom window and he fell off the ladder, onto railings. The only set left in Stretford after the war, and my Tommy's skewered on them!' She let out a loud, anguished sob. 'Will he live?'

The man groaned. His eyes rolled back in his head.

'Stay with us, Tommy!' Kitty said. She looked over her shoulder at the cabbie. 'Are you going to help, or what? Get a damned wheelchair! Go and find a nurse or a doctor or both. *Now!*'

The cabbie adjusted his trousers again. 'This has buggered my shift. I'll have to go home and scrub the back of the cab out.' He shuffled off into the casualty waiting area, grumbling about stained leatherette and lost earnings.

Kitty turned back to the injured patient, who started to slide off the back seat. He was out cold.

'Look, I'll get in,' she said, gingerly trying to push the man back onto the seat so she could climb in beside him. He was a dead weight. 'I'll grab him under the arms and pass him to you. All right?'

The woman nodded.

'Come on, Tommy. Let's get you into the hospital.' As Kitty grabbed the heavy man under the arms, she noted with dismay that the cabbie had not returned. 'You pull. I'll push.' Shuffling forward, slipping more than once in the man's lifeblood, Kitty and the woman somehow managed to get the wounded man out of the cab. 'You take one arm. I'll take the other. Wrap his arm around you, like this. Shove your shoulder into his armpit.'

'It's like the *Marie Celeste*,' the woman cried, peering into the packed waiting room that was devoid of any medical staff. 'I got a neighbour to ring for an ambulance and I waited. Not a soul turned up. Where's all the flaming ambulance men and doctors?' Her knees were almost buckling beneath the weight of her unconscious husband.

'Don't ask.'

Finally, the cabbie appeared, pushing a wheelchair. Lily was at his side.

'What have we got?' Lily asked, taking charge of the wheelchair and putting the brake on. She eyed the man's wound with a raised eyebrow and gestured to the cabbie to relieve the struggling wife.

'This is Tommy. He's had a tumble onto iron railings.' Kitty didn't need to tell Lily that the man was haemorrhaging and had sustained terrible internal injuries. She turned to his wife, who stood, shaking from adrenalin and wringing her bloodstained hands. 'You go and take a seat, love. Leave this to us.'

The woman shook her head. Her teeth clacked together when she spoke. 'Not on your nelly. I'm staying with my Tommy. He came back to me from Normandy. I'm not letting him out of my sight now.'

'Nurse Schwarz! Take Mrs . . .?'

'Travis.'

'Take Mrs Travis to the reception desk, will you? Mrs Travis, Nurse Schwarz, here, needs you to get your Tommy booked in. Please. We're professionals. Let us look after him.'

Kitty locked eyes with Lily momentarily and then looked pointedly towards the sign that gave the directions to the emergency operating theatre.

Lily nodded. 'Come with me, Mrs Travis. Let Nurse Longthorne take your husband to the doctors. No queuing for him!'

Without waiting to see if the woman would comply, Kitty whisked her patient off in the direction of the theatre, as fast as she could without breaking into a run. 'Come on, Tommy. Stay with us, chuck!' She was doubled up, leaning forward to put pressure on his wound while she pushed the wheelchair down the corridor. His pallor said he didn't have much longer. 'Don't you leave us, Mr Travis! Nearly there.'

She pushed past ambling outpatients and visitors who ogled the sight of the bleeding man in undisguised horror. 'Excuse me! Move aside! Make way! Coming through!'

On the way to the theatre, she didn't pass a single nurse.

Finally, Kitty arrived at the doors to the theatre. She turned the wheelchair around and wedged the door open with her bottom. 'Emergency coming through!' she said, trying to keep the panic out of her voice.

A junior doctor came out to meet her, smiling. 'Nurse Longthorne! You're a sight for sore eyes. Are you here to assist—?' He looked down at ashen-faced Tommy, lolling in the wheelchair. 'Ah.' He reached out to feel his neck. 'We've got a weak pulse.'

'He's fallen onto railings. He's lost a lot of blood. Can I leave him in your capable hands?' Kitty asked. 'Casualty's overrun.'

Professor Baird-Murray, Park Hospital's most senior surgeon, was at the sink, scrubbing the previous patient's blood from his forearms. He turned around, eyed the junior surgeon as he and the anaesthetist manoeuvred the patient onto the operating table, and smiled at Kitty. 'Longthorne! Jolly good. You've got theatre experience, haven't you? Be a good girl and assist us, will you?'

'But, professor, Matron told me to—'

'Nonsense. Nonsense. Matron will understand. We're two theatre nurses short, thanks to one wedding and one mutiny. It's a damned nuisance. The theatre's in bally disarray. Get cleaned up, and let's tend to this gentleman. There's a good girl.' As if he didn't for a moment expect dissent, he turned his attention back to his junior surgeon to give orders.

In the strict hierarchy of Park Hospital, the professor was king and emperor. What option did Kitty have but to scrub her hands and arms, put on a gown and pitch in? Matron would simply have to understand.

It didn't take long to prepare for surgery, and soon, Kitty was handing the necessary implements to Baird-Murray, as he opened Tommy Travis up to see the extent of the internal damage.

The heart monitor that Tommy had been connected up to beeped feebly, even as Baird-Murray clamped this artery and cauterised that vein. Kitty heard the roar of the blood rushing in her ears as she held her breath. Would they be able to save this unfortunate man?

Suddenly, there was a gurgling sound, as Tommy started to choke and spit up blood.

Chapter 4

'We're fighting a losing battle, here, gentlemen,' Baird-Murray said. 'With this much transabdominal damage and haemorrhaging, we are mere dogs barking at the moon.'

The heart monitor's beeping changed to one final, sad, continuous note.

Tommy was gone.

Kitty bit her lip. Having a patient die in her care was by far the worst part of her job, yet deaths at Park Hospital were not as infrequent as they should have been, considering they were in peacetime. She now thought of Tommy Travis's poor wife, sitting in casualty, wondering when she'd be able to see her husband.

The professor stepped away from the operating table and the dead patient, holding his blood-stained hands in the air. 'Shame. He came to us too late. Why on earth was it down to you to wheel him in here, Longthorne?'

Feeling a failure, Kitty shrugged. 'His wife . . . God knows how she got him off those railings.'

Baird-Murray looked up at the ceiling. 'It would have been far better if she'd left him in situ, so the fire service could have cut out a section of the railings. Mr Travis should have been brought in, in an ambulance, railings and all. Poor man might not have bled to death. This was a case of too little, too late.'

'His wife said she waited and waited for an ambulance

that never came,' Kitty said. 'So, she ended up flagging down a black cab. And there were no orderlies or spare nurses in casualty. Just me. It was do or die, so I grabbed the first thing with wheels that I could and hot-footed it down here.'

Baird-Murray nodded, solemnly. 'You did well, Longthorne. Now, I have a tonsillectomy arriving here at any moment and a rather involved eye surgery after that, so do me a favour and notify the man's family, will you?' Without waiting for a response, he turned to his junior to discuss removing Tommy Travis's body to the mortuary.

Kitty scrubbed her hands under water that was as hot as she could bear, facing the tiled wall so that the doctors wouldn't see the tears that silently rolled down the sides of her face. Being a nurse had always been a rewarding but hard job. Of late, however, it had got even harder.

Why had Tommy Travis's story had to end in tragedy? As she gulped down her sorrow, she realised that the answer to that lay in the myriad military cemeteries up and down the country – there were now insufficient working-age men to work as ambulance drivers and hospital porters. Perhaps the greatest challenge to the quality of the NHS's care, however, was the exodus of nursing staff, who had chosen family life over a vocation that often demanded too much for too little pay. The edict that nurses should remain unmarried was not every girl's cup of tea. 'How do we even get through each day?' she quietly asked her own reflection in the tiles.

Making her way back to the casualty waiting area, Kitty spotted Mrs Travis among those waiting to be seen. She was gazing into space. Instinctively, Kitty hung back. Informing relatives of a death was something doctors or ward sisters normally did. Feeling that she needed to buy herself a few more minutes to come up with words that would convey such devastating tidings sensitively, she ducked into a cubicle before she could be spotted.

In the bed, an elderly woman lolled against the wall. Her eyes were glazed, her face utterly drained of colour. She had a cut to her left temple and the beginnings of a nasty bruise. Kitty realised that this frail-looking woman might have had a nasty fall and banged her head.

'Nurse, I think I'm going to be sick,' the old woman said, slurring as she spoke. Kitty held a bowl under her chin. 'Here you go, love.'

'Where's the doc—?' The woman vomited with gusto, then accidentally knocked the bowl flying.

'Deary me,' Kitty said. 'What a to-do! Not to worry. Let's get you cleaned up.'

She glanced out at Mrs Travis through a gap where the cubicle curtain didn't quite meet the wall. Kitty was torn. On the one hand, she urgently needed to tend to this elderly lady. On the other, her freshly scrubbed forearms itched uncomfortably at the thought of leaving Mrs Travis wondering about the fate of her husband one moment longer than was necessary.

The curtain to the cubicle was swept aside suddenly. Matron peered in. She seemed unmoved by the strong smell of vomit and the mess on the floor.

'Longthorne. There you are. There's a little girl with suspected peritonitis just been brought in. She's in cubicle seven. Prep her for theatre, would you?'

Kitty opened and closed her mouth, willing the desperate words to come out in the correct order. 'Tommy Travis. A haemorrhage case. I need to tell his widow, but this lady, here . . .'

'We're swans, Longthorne. Swans.' Matron smiled blithely. She made a flapping motion with her hands, representing the ferocious paddling that went on beneath the proverbial gliding swan, out of sight of the world above the water's surface. 'I have every faith in you.' She was gone before Kitty could respond.

Kitty hastily cleaned up the old lady, dashed down to the child in cubicle seven, readied her for surgery, alerted a junior doctor to the old lady's head wound and the possibility of a bleed on the brain, and finally found breathing space to face Mrs Travis.

She approached the unwitting widow.

'Mrs Travis?' She laid a hand gently on the woman's arm, feeling her husband's blood dried into the fabric of her sleeve. 'Would you like to follow me? I need a word.'

Mrs Travis smiled up at her, hopefully. Her smile slid, as if the truth of the matter dawned on her. 'It's bad news, isn't it?'

Kitty ushered her into an empty side room. 'I'm so sorry. I don't know how to tell you this, but—'

'He's dead. My Tommy's gone, isn't he?' Mrs Travis bit her lip. Tears welled in her eyes and rolled onto her cheeks in fat beads. She looked down at her shoes, watching the tears fall onto the blood-stained leather.

'I'm afraid there was nothing we could do. And we gave it our best shot, honest to God. We had our most senior surgeon on the job, but your husband's internal injuries – he'd just lost too much blood, and by the time he got to us, the damage was beyond even Professor Baird-Murray. I'm so, so sorry.'

Mrs Travis sobbed like a lost girl. Kitty put her arms around her. Offering a shoulder to cry on was the least she could do for this accidental widow.

Despite calls on her expertise from various doctors, fellow nurses and impatiently waiting outpatients, Kitty didn't leave Mrs Travis until she'd put her in touch with the mortuary staff to retrieve the body of her husband and had ensured that Mrs Travis's sister could come to pick her up from the hospital and take her home.

'Oh, God bless you, Nurse Longthorne,' Mrs Travis said, as she headed to the exit, arm in arm with her sibling. 'You've been so kind. From the minute we pulled up in that cab.'

Kitty shook her head. 'Us nurses always try to do our best for all of our patients and their families. I just wish . . . If only . . .'

Mrs Travis regarded her through red-rimmed eyes. She nodded. 'If ifs and ands were pots and pans, eh? You tried. And I'll remember you for that, lovey.' She rubbed at her eyes with fingers that still bore traces of her husband's blood in the cracks of the skin and beneath the nails. 'Ta-ra.'

Kitty's heart was so heavy as the newly bereaved woman walked out of casualty that she wondered if she'd be able to carry on with the shift. Yet, the rest of her working day sped by in a blur of wound-cleaning and the application of dressings. Kitty supervised the admission of another case of appendicitis, two women with advanced kidney infections and four suspected cases of TB.

She thought of her father, coughing at home, and made a mental note to chase an appointment with Galbraith, the heart and lung specialist, as soon as she could. First, though, she had to slip away to the post office to send that telegram to Ned. What terrible fate could have befallen her liability of a twin brother? Was he in trouble with some Barbadian gangster or else with the police? As she felt for the pulse on an old woman, she wondered what the prison was like in Barbados, or if, indeed, they even had one on the island.

When the large clock on the wall told Kitty she had a twenty-minute window of opportunity, though she was reeling from fatigue and her head pounded, she slipped on her nurse's cape and made briskly for the main entrance.

'Longthorne!'

Kitty turned around to see Matron standing behind her. She was wearing an unforgiving expression.

'Matron? Is there a problem? I've managed to get Schwartz to—'

'I've just bumped into Mr Galbraith. He asked me to tell you he has an opening at the end of his clinic for your father.'

'But I must nip—'

Matron looked down at her nurse's watch, pinned to her uniform. 'You have less than an hour to send word and get your parents up to the hospital. Galbraith is a busy, busy man. I'd hurry, if I were you.'

Chapter 5

'Now, Mr Longthorne. You went for X-rays and blood tests a few days ago.' Mr Galbraith ran his hand over his shining bald pate and fingered his pencil moustache. His stern expression gave nothing away. 'Dr Williams impressed on me that yours is an urgent case, so I've looked at your results at the earliest convenience.'

Kitty stood at her father's side, holding his only remaining hand. Her mother was seated next to him on the far side, looking wan and ragged at the edges but nowhere near as frail and visibly diminished as the once-strapping Bert Longthorne.

'Go on, doctor. Is it TB?' Her father coughed ominously.

Galbraith shook his head. He stood and switched on the lightbox on the wall, then fixed two X-rays over the bright light. Kitty immediately spotted the problem and stifled a gasp.

Using a long ruler, Galbraith pointed at the mass next to her father's spine. It was the size of an apple. 'There's no easy way to say this, Mr Longthorne. It looks very much to me like you have a tumour.'

'No!' Kitty's mother cried out. She reached for Kitty's father's prosthetic leg and looked up questioningly at Kitty, then at Galbraith. 'How can you know for sure?'

'I don't. Not at this stage. There's an outside chance it may be scarring from a former infection. I won't know until

I've performed a biopsy. That means taking a sample of the mass and studying it.'

Her father coughed and choked until he brought up blood. Kitty held a clean rag under his chin and dabbed at his mouth. In the bright light of Galbraith's office, she could see the illness in her father's eyes. She was almost overwhelmed by a sudden wave of guilt that she'd spent so long hating and bad-mouthing Bert Longthorne – a convicted thief, a spendthrift of his ill-gotten gains when he was on top and a miserly layabout and drunk when he inevitably sank back to the bottom. He was, after all, only human, and he was, for better or for worse, her father. She stroked his freshly washed grey hair.

'Oh, it's so distressing watching him, doctor,' her mother said, weeping quietly into a snowy-white man's handkerchief. 'All I want to do is make my Bert better, but I feel powerless.'

'Let's get the biopsy done, Mrs Longthorne. We'll admit your husband today. He needs help with his breathing, for a start. By the end of the week, we'll know what we're dealing with.'

Eventually, her father's bout of coughing settled with a few sips of water. 'I'm dying, aren't I?'

Galbraith folded his arms tightly over his white coat and pressed his thin lips together. 'Do you smoke, Mr Longthorne?'

'How long have I got? Six months? Will I make it to Christmas?'

'I suggest that you stop smoking immediately. That's probably what's behind your suffering.'

'Rubbish!' There was still a streak of defiance in the indomitable Bert. 'Everyone smokes.'

'*I* don't smoke.'

'No offence, but you look like a Wills's Capstan! Maybe a smoke would do you good.'

'Dad! Don't be rude!' Kitty felt her cheeks glow with embarrassment.

Her father, however, seemed to be enjoying himself, in spite of the worrying prognosis. 'Everyone knows that cigs are good for relaxing and watching your weight.'

'Sadly, Mr Longthorne, they're poison for just about everything else, and there's going to be a paper published next year, exposing the dangers of tobacco consumption. I've contributed to a large study, myself.'

Galbraith glanced up at Kitty and held her gaze. It was the same resigned expression he'd worn when she'd assisted him in the do-or-die surgery on a patient called Dora Mackie – a woman Kitty would never forget. She knew then that Galbraith didn't hold out much hope for her father's situation. It felt like fate was catching up with the old man.

The wards were so understaffed that Kitty had to pitch in with the admission of her own father. Though he remained belligerent, denying that he was suffering from anything more pernicious than a chest infection, Kitty willed the tears not to fall, for the sake of her mother.

'Will you keep an eye on him, Kitty, love?' her mother asked. She was folding Bert's clothes while Kitty helped him into a gown until pyjamas could be fetched.

Kitty nodded. 'I'm on this ward anyway. We're so short on senior nurses like me, so I'm having to work double shifts, God, help me! I spent the day shift on casualty. How I'm staying awake is anyone's guess.'

'Ooh, hey, I'm worried about you, our Kitty,' her mam said, rubbing her back. 'I've already got one who's laid up. I don't need another. And then there's Ned . . .'

Realising that her mother was so beset by woe over her father that she couldn't cope with any more bad tidings or worry, Kitty put her arm around her mother's thin waist. 'Don't you fret about me, Mam. I'm made of stern stuff.' She turned to her father and pointed to the desk from which she'd be overseeing the ward's activities on a moment-to-moment basis. 'There's nowt gets past me, so you'd better watch your step, Dad.' She patted him on the shoulder and pushed aside her exhaustion and any feelings of grief and regret.

It was going to be a long few days.

Chapter 6

Two days and nights had passed, and Kitty had snatched a grand total of seven hours' sleep. With so many demands on her time and so much on her mind, only strong tea and determination had stood between her and collapse. Now, with the nurse who worked under her on the ward standing before her, awaiting instructions at the start of a night shift, Kitty stifled a yawn, willing the fatigue away.

'Right, Nurse Taylor.' She looked down at her notes. 'We've got a new admission in bed six. He's post-operative and needs his chest-drain checking every—'

'Ah, Nurse Longthorne. There you are!' Galbraith walked into the ward and strode with purpose towards Kitty, his heels click-clacking on the hard floor. He was clutching a clipboard. 'Good. Good.' His grimace said matters were anything but good, however. He smoothed his hand over his bald head and tapped his neat moustache. 'Could we have a word in private, please?'

Dismissing her subordinate, Kitty led Galbraith to the ward sister's makeshift office which doubled as the ward's infrequently used bathroom. The desk was a polished wooden tabletop laid over the bath – a far cry from the offices of the consultants. Seeing that the sister was speaking to a newly admitted patient, Kitty offered Galbraith a seat, feeling her hands slick with sweat. This was it. The results of her father's biopsy.

'I prefer to stand, thank you.' Galbraith glanced down at his notes. 'Now, this is highly irregular, giving these results to you, rather than to your father. Really, you shouldn't be the one overseeing his care.' He twitched his moustache and clicked his heels together. 'But I realise that needs must and all that.'

Kitty pursed her lips and visualised her father, lying three beds down on the left, staring dolefully up at the ceiling as he gulped oxygen through a cumbersome mask. He'd tried to engage the neighbouring patients in conversation about the cricket. The fact that he'd quickly run out of steam bore testament to just how ill he was.

'No. I think you need to tell both of us. Together. It's bad enough that it's not visiting time. My mam should be here, by rights. But tell us together, sir. Please.'

'As you wish.'

They left the office and made their way towards Bert's bed.

'Kitty, love!' her father said as she and Galbraith approached. His words were garbled beneath the mask. He patted the bed. 'Come and sit with your old feller, while bald Clark Gable, here, reminds me what a low-life I am, and how I'm going to pay for it.'

'Behave, Dad. Come on, now. Mr Galbraith has your best interests at heart.' Kitty drew the curtain around the bed.

'Very true, Nurse Longthorne.' Mr Galbraith sat in the visitor's seat and smiled fleetingly.

Kitty sat on the bed next to her father, feeling light-headed and nauseous.

'Out with it, doc. I'm man enough to take bad news. Let me guess. You had a look inside and couldn't find a heart.' Kitty's father wheezed with empty laughter. 'Or am I just gutless? I've been accused of that a few times.'

'Shush, Dad!' Kitty took her father's hand.

'There's no good way to say this, Mr Longthorne.' Galbraith's Adam's apple rose and fell inside his thin neck like a bagatelle ball. 'I was right, I'm afraid. You do have advanced lung cancer. And it's spread to your lymph nodes.'

It was no use. The sob inside Kitty pushed its way out and resounded around the ward. She shoved her knuckle in her mouth to stem the tide of grief.

'Are you all right in there, Nurse Longthorne?' the junior nurse, Hettie Taylor, asked on the other side of the curtain.

'I'm fine. Carry on with your duties, Nurse Taylor,' Kitty said, hearing the wobble in her own voice.

At her side, her father lay perfectly still. The oxygen hissed down its tubing, but he seemed to be holding his breath.

Kitty squeezed his hand. 'Do you need Mr Galbraith to repeat that, Dad?'

The once-formidable Bert Longthorne removed his mask and perched it on his forehead. He wheezed as he spoke. 'How long?'

Mr Galbraith looked down at his shoes. 'There are some experimental treatments available involving nitrogen mustard. A sort of mustard gas. The initial study was only published three years ago, but . . .'

'No.'

'Or last year, this chap in America – Sidney Farber, a very well-respected pathologist at Harvard – he's been experimenting with folic acid and leuke—'

'Can you cut it out of me?'

'I'm afraid not. It's too big and it's spreading.'

'Then that's that. I don't want no mustard-gas poison inside me, doing God knows what to what's left of my lungs. I want to be left in peace to die. So, I'll ask again. How long?'

Galbraith touched his moustache. 'Four months. Five,

35

at most. I advise you to put your affairs in order. I'll make pain relief freely available to you.'

'I want to die at home.'

Kitty thought about her mother having to juggle a demanding job as a piecework machinist with tending to her father. 'No, Dad. You'll need round-the-clock care. I'm working, and Mam can't do it on her own. No.'

Her father turned to her and scowled. 'Are you going against a dying man's wishes, Kitty Longthorne?'

Kitty looked at his downturned mouth and the grey hue of his skin. With that one question, she saw her mother's sanity, her own professional reputation as being one of the most reliable nurses in Park Hospital and her fiancé's marital aspirations evaporate clean away. That didn't matter, however. There was no postponing death. In nursing her father to the end, she would inevitably let the matron down at a time of dire need, but Kitty knew she had no option but to put her duty as a daughter above her duty to Park Hospital. If she didn't, her mother would surely buckle under the strain of providing palliative care herself.

I should leave now, she thought, *hand in my resignation, marry James now, so Dad can walk me down the aisle. It's the right thing to do.*

She shook her head regretfully. 'I wouldn't do that, Dad. If you want to die at home, in your own bed, then that's the way it'll happen. I promise.'

With a heavy heart, Kitty sought Matron out. She found her on the maternity ward, admonishing the night-shift nurses for a cleaning misdemeanour.

'Ah, Nurse Longthorne! Just the woman!' Matron said. 'I have news.'

'So do I,' Kitty said, swallowing hard.

Chapter 7

'Good Lord, man! The decree has come from the Government. We must swell our ranks, and the Commonwealth is the place to provide the labour!'

The following morning, when Kitty walked into the foreboding boardroom that normally hosted the hospital's board of directors and was closed to the nursing ranks, she found James shouting at Professor Baird-Murray. Baird-Murray was seated at the head of the gleaming long table, flanked by his acolytes, the Chief Radiologist, Sir Basil Ryder-Smith, and the head of Orthopaedics, Dr Derek Swanley. Kitty recognised some other consultants who were on the board. Judging by their expressions, she'd interrupted a heated debate. Baird-Murray's usual pallor had given way to flushed cheeks; his fastidiously Brylcreemed hair was dishevelled. Was she perhaps point three or four on a long agenda of things to rail against?

Standing up, pointing his cigar at James with a shaking hand, the most senior consultant surgeon in Park Hospital retorted in a thunderous voice. 'Too much change too quickly is bad for morale, Dr Williams. The NHS is only one year old, for heaven's sake. And now, we're to recruit staff from the colonies? Are we to have *that lot* running riot in the junior nurses' accommodation?'

Kitty held her hand to her mouth. Baird-Murray's attitudes were hardly anything new. She'd seen a few lodging houses on the way to her mother's bearing the signs, 'No Dogs, No Blacks, No Irish'. It was abundantly clear that Manchester's great unwashed were mistrustful of the new arrivals from Ireland and – mainly – Jamaica. What was unexpected, however, was that an educated man like Baird-Murray should hold such unsavoury views. Kitty had met a number of first-generation Irish immigrant and West Indian patients on the wards and had found them no different from their Manchester-born counterparts.

She looked to James, hoping that he'd dare to put the senior consultant in his place. James merely shook his head.

'Times are changing, gentlemen,' he said. 'Our great nation needs assistance in rebuilding the economy, and the Government calls on us to recruit nurses and auxiliary staff from the colonies. We are to become a rich tapestry of peoples, whether you like it or not.'

Sir Basil Ryder-Smith suddenly caught Kitty's eye. 'Cecil. We have ladies in our midst.'

Matron took a step forward and cleared her throat. 'Gentlemen, you asked me to call on one of our senior nurses to give an account of the staffing shortage and how it affects them.' She beckoned Kitty to take a seat at the end of the long table. 'I'm sure many of you know Nurse Longthorne.'

James locked eyes with Kitty and winked, though his expression remained stern. He ran a hand over his gleaming black hair and shifted position in his seat, eyeing the other men to see if they'd registered the exchange.

Kitty felt her heart pounding against her ribcage. Matron's 'news' the previous evening, that Kitty was to be the mouth-piece of the hospital's nursing body in a board meeting, had come as a shock. Kitty had been about to hand her notice in, but instead, her superior's pronouncement had left her blushing and tongue-tied. Now, she was facing the reality of having to report on the staffing crisis to a room full of privileged and powerful consultants. Matron may as well have pushed her into the spotlight on a theatre stage in front of an audience full of the harshest critics.

'Isn't this your fiancée, Williams?' Swanley asked James.

'Nurse Longthorne is here in a professional capacity, I assure you,' Matron said. 'She's no puppet for Dr Williams and his progressive views, Derek. Longthorne has a mind of her own, and it was I who decided she should be the one to tell you what it's like on the wards.' Matron laid a hand on Kitty's shoulder. 'Tell them, girl.'

'Well, we're run off our feet,' Kitty began. How honest should she be about conditions that were trying during the war but which had, of late, become dire? She could feel that her hands were clammy, but the consultants weren't to know that. Beneath the table, she surreptitiously wiped her hands on her skirt, swallowed hard and began. 'During the war, it was shocking. We expected it, though. All those wounded GIs being admitted in droves with the most appalling injuries. It was par for the course. But now . . .'

The consultants were smoking their pipes and cigars, appraising her with their hawk-like gazes, she could tell. Were they listening to what she was saying, though, or merely judging how attractive she was? Kitty reasoned with some regret that it was probably the latter.

'Since the start of the NHS, the wards are constantly full,' she continued. 'You all know this. The health of the nation was in the doldrums to begin with, and poor living conditions and continuing poverty have definitely made it worse.'

'Yes, dear. We *do* know all this. We're only too aware,' Baird-Murray said, relighting his foul-smelling cigar. 'Tell us something we don't know.'

'It's the nursing profession that's the problem, Professor.' Kitty could hear the blood rushing in her ears. 'Women have to leave if they want to marry. And the girls – they're overworked, underpaid. It's hard. Gruelling. The men have come back from war and most nurses want to marry and start a family. Working longer and longer shifts to accommodate more and more patients and to compensate for dwindling numbers of nurses just isn't conducive to womanly aspirations. That's why the Government's recruitment drive hasn't rung the bell for our British girls. They're not daft, I'm afraid.'

'And you?' Baird-Murray pointed his cigar at her. 'Why haven't you left and married Williams, here? He's losing his matinee-idol looks, isn't he?' The senior consultant started to guffaw at his own joke. 'Or perhaps he's *too* namby-pamby and you were hoping for some strapping young registrar in gynaecology who understands the mysteries of a woman's body.'

The others erupted into fits of unkind laughter.

'Steady on, Cecil! I'll not stand for your nonsense!' James said. His words of protest were drowned out by his colleagues' mirth.

It was Matron who restored order. She thumped the table. 'Professor! Kindly control your puerile impulses. Your deportment is most unbecoming in a medical man of your stature.' Her voice was so loud and authoritative that the consultants fell silent at once. She glared at them all, one by one, until they sat straight in their seats and studied their fingernails or notepads with sudden interest.

Kitty was bolstered by her daring. 'I won't discuss my personal arrangements or plans with you, Professor. James and I are both entirely committed to treating the sick. I've worked hard to get to the level that I am now, and I take nursing very seriously.' She exhaled slowly. 'I am well aware, though, that it's a hard, hard career path. The long hours, restriction of our personal freedoms and low pay are going to be the death of the profession. There just aren't enough of us to do a good job. This week, we've lost several patients – in no small part thanks to short-staffing. So, if there are qualified nurses and willing auxiliaries in the colonies offering to swap palm trees and tropical breezes for Manchester drizzle, honestly, you should be grabbing their hands off.'

Finally, Baird-Murray looked calm and contemplative, nodding slowly while dragging on his cigar. The other consultants were scribbling notes on their pads.

James locked eyes with Kitty again. She could see from the way in which his brown eyes crinkled up at the corners that he was smiling. He was proud of her. She felt a surge of love for him, manifested as a warm feeling in her chest and heat in her cheeks. Oh, to finally have the heart of the man she'd been in love with for years, after almost losing him to that turncoat, Violet Jones! Just for a moment, Kitty forgot about her father and Ned. She felt like the luckiest woman in the world. She felt guilty, however, for having spent months dodging the issue of naming a date. For some reason, despite her deep love for this brilliant and complex man, the prospect of becoming the doctor's wife had been terrifying. Perhaps Kitty hadn't wanted to give up the career she'd fought for. Perhaps Kitty was worried James would jilt her at the altar, as he had Violet. Perhaps Kitty merely felt she wasn't good enough to marry into a family of substance. At least her father's request that he die at home had brought her a step closer to leaving Park Hospital and to tying that knot. And yet . . .

'How will you recruit nurses?' Kitty asked. An idea had taken root inside her and was quickly sending up shoots. 'Will you have representatives go out there? To the West Indies, I mean. You know, to vet them and that; vet the nurses?'

Sir Basil Ryder-Smith pursed his lips. 'Yes. In actual fact, I'm sure I laid eyes on a consultation document from the Ministry of Health about sending emissaries from our domestic nursing body to recruit new staff.' He leaned towards her. 'Why do you ask, Longthorne? Are you putting yourself forward?'

Glancing at James to gauge his reaction and seeing that his olive skin had blanched, Kitty spoke in a small voice. 'Maybe. Yes.' She thought about the trips she'd had to Blackpool and the Lake District. Kitty hadn't even been to London, and yet Ned had been a Japanese prisoner of war, escaping and – if his tall tales were to be believed - against all odds, walking all the way back through the war-torn Orient, navigating parts of the old Silk Road to return to rainy old Manchester!

She felt stirrings in her belly – butterflies at the thought of boarding a great ship like the one she'd seen docked in Liverpool. The *Tradewind*. Might such an impressive vessel carry plain old Kitty Longthorne across the high seas, if not to find fortune and adventure, then at least to track down her missing brother and see what exactly he'd been up to in Barbados for the past couple of years; to tell Ned that their father was dying and to bring him home to Manchester to say his goodbyes? It felt too good an opportunity to pass up.

'Kitty! I mean, Nurse Longthorne,' James said, 'do you think we might have a chat about this? In private, I mean.'

Blinking hard, Kitty tried to dispel the absurd fantasy. She willed the jungle and white sand and bleached-out colonial buildings to disappear from her mind's eye. Yet they remained there, framed by a Caribbean Sea that glittered with promise.

'Longthorne and I will discuss it,' Matron said, bringing the matter to a close. 'I'll report back to you, Professor. In the meantime, take it as read that life on the wards for the nurses is tougher than it's ever been. If we're to help you doctors do your jobs properly, we need to swell our ranks urgently. Mark my words. Without adequate nursing care, the NHS will founder before it reaches its fifth birthday.'

Matron grabbed Kitty by the shoulder and squeezed, indicating that it was time to beat a retreat from this emergency summit. Given the way James's nostrils were flaring with indignation, Kitty had never been so relieved to part company with her fiancé. What had she done?

Once they were standing in the corridor, beyond the earshot of the men in the boardroom, Matron turned to Kitty.

'Are you serious about wanting to go to the West Indies on a reconnaissance, Kitty? It's quite an endeavour, and I could see Dr Williams's look of consternation, when you said—'

'Barbados,' Kitty said. The word had forced its way out of her mouth as though it had a will of its own. 'Not Jamaica or the Virgin Islands or any of those other places. Barbados. My twin's there. My Ned. He's in trouble. I can feel it in my waters. And our dad's dying. I need to bring Ned home. Please, Matron. If you can make this mad, mad dream a reality, I can kill two birds with one stone.' She grabbed Matron's meaty arm, almost giddy with her newfound rebellious spirit. 'I promise you won't be disappointed. I'll bring back the brightest and the best nurses that Barbados has to offer.'

Matron withdrew her arm and patted Kitty on the hand. 'Leave it with me, young lady.'

Chapter 8

'Are you going to say anything at all?' James said, staring resolutely through the windscreen of the Ford at the winding road ahead.

Those were the first words that had been spoken since they'd passed the outermost fringes of Bolton. The first peaks of the Lake District were already showing up ahead on the stormy-looking horizon.

Kitty shifted uncomfortably in the passenger seat, wishing she'd succumbed to the soporific whine of the windscreen wipers and dozed off before they'd breached Lancaster's outskirts. 'I don't know what you want me to say, James. It's a chance-of-a-lifetime opportunity for me. Sailing to the Caribbean. I've never been further than the Lakes!'

The tendon in James's jaw flinched. He blinked repeatedly. 'We're supposed to be naming the date and getting married! You won't commit to our wedding, but you will volunteer for *this* without thinking to consult me?'

Biting her tongue and swallowing the lump of upset back down, Kitty watched the sheep scud by in the surrounding rain-soaked fields while she considered her answer. *Consult me.* Perhaps he had a point. Weren't they a couple? An engaged couple, at that. Shouldn't she have discussed her idea before acting on impulse? Yet, Kitty was closer to thirty than twenty. She was a fully grown woman, able to know her own mind.

'Look, I love you, and I'm committed to our marriage,' she said, gripping her woollen gloves tightly. 'But the fact is, I had a career and a family before I met you.'

'Are you saying you care more about nursing and your family than me? Than us?'

'Hear me out, James! You asked. Now, listen to my answer, will you?'

He exhaled heavily, misting the windscreen somewhat. 'Sorry. Go on.'

Kitty bit her lip and rubbed his arm encouragingly. 'I love nursing, and I know I'm going to have to stop it the moment we're married. How would you feel if you had to give up your life's work overnight?'

James shook his head. 'It's not the same. I'm a consultant. I help people—'

'*I* help people!' Without pausing for thought, she slapped him on the shoulder with her gloves. 'Is that what you think about the nursing profession? Are we just the rubbing rags and you're the big wheel?'

'That's not what I meant at all, Kitty, and you know it.' His jaw was flinching again. 'I mean, I have a highly specialised—'

'I'm the first person in my entire family to have a skilled job. It's all right for you, coming from a family of Eton-educated toffs. You lot know your worth in the world. You're top of the heap. You can afford to have expectations and get them met. But me . . .?'

James indicated and pulled up at a bus stop on the almost-deserted country road. He brought the car to a standstill and switched the engine off. Staring dolefully into the hilly distance, he merely sighed.

'What is it? Why have you parked up?'

Kitty leaned back against the window, wondering which turn their argument would take. Just being in such close proximity with her dream man still made the blood rush in her ears and her breath come short. Yet, she knew the truth of who she was to marry now. James Williams, for all his brooding good looks, intelligence and gentle manner, had a tendency towards the sullen. Unless he was sparring in the hospital staffroom or boardroom, he seemingly thought it better to clam up than to engage in conflict. Time and again, Kitty was left agonising over what her fiancé really felt or thought. She knew, by now, that whatever narrative she'd created for him would invariably be wrong. 'What have I told you about letting the silence speak for you? Come on, James. Out with it!'

Finally, he turned towards her and took her hand. 'I love you, Kitty. I understand that you're devoted to nursing, but I desperately want you to be my wife. I want you to be devoted to me – to any children we might have. You can still help people. A doctor's wife can do good charitable works.'

'Ha! Doling out goodwill and patronising the poor, while I swan about in a mink coat and pearls?'

He flashed her a dazzling smile that lit up the dreary interior of the Ford and almost chased the smell of hot plastic away. 'I think you'd look rather dazzling in a mink and pearls. Is that what you'd like?'

Kitty batted him with her gloves again – this time, more playfully. 'That's not the point I'm trying to make. I'm a working-class girl, James. I like getting my hands dirty! I want to be the best nurse I can be before I hang up my cape and apron for good. And if that means I get to sail to Barbados and drag my brother back home, in time for my father's funeral, so much the better.'

His smile slid from his handsome face. 'A telegram won't suffice?'

'You think I haven't tried? I've sent two already and haven't heard a dicky bird.'

He turned the key in the engine and set off again. 'It's nice to know our future family comes second to Ned.'

'What did you just say?'

'Nothing. I didn't say a word, Kitty.'

As the miles scudded by and the countryside became more rugged, Kitty tried to engage James in lighter-hearted conversation about jazz and whether rhythm and blues was better than the likes of Frankie Laine and Perry Como – anything to pull the man she loved closer to her on what had been intended as a hard-earned romantic weekend away. She talked about the bare-knuckle fighters that had been sent from the Infirmary to Park Hospital. The Black musician, Lloyd Chambers, had since been referred on to James for reconstructive surgery.

'What do you think was going on there, then?' she asked. 'That Lloyd certainly didn't strike me as the sort of man who'd risk his livelihood as a musician to make a few quid in a fight.'

James's mood seemed to brighten. 'He's a fascinating case,' he said, taking the road towards Windermere. 'I worked on a Black American airman during the war, but it was a skin graft on his neck and I must say, he did scar quite badly. I haven't performed facial surgery on black skin before. I wonder how our friend Lloyd will heal. Poor chap. He does seem quite a gentle fellow, and his hand is a terrible mess.'

Finally, as Lake Windermere spread before them like a sheet of gleaming foil, and James pulled into the car park of the grand drystone-walled Victorian villa that was their guesthouse, Kitty felt the knots in her shoulders dissipating. When he opened the passenger door for her and helped her out, she drank in the icy, crystal-clear air.

'Ooh. Smell that!' she said, closing her eyes and savouring the smell of damp pine needles and wet bracken.

'A far cry from dirty old Manchester, eh?' James put his arm around her and kissed her gently on the cheek. 'Are you ready to be Mrs James Williams for the weekend?'

Kitty nodded, feeling a thrill of excitement as well as apprehension. These romantic trysts were never without risk, after all. 'Lead on, Macduff!' She turned her engagement ring around so that it looked like a simple wedding band.

When James booked them in at reception, Kitty felt the heat in her cheeks betray her marital status. Dr and Mrs Williams. The pretty young receptionist smiled coyly at James and then less enthusiastically at her, perhaps imagining what it might be like to be a doctor's wife; to be married to a man with status, power and film-star looks, tempered only by a Harris tweed suit. Would Kitty spend all of her married life looking for the next Violet, who might brazenly set her sights on luring James away with glamour and seductive qualities that Kitty simply didn't possess?

'Are you quite all right, darling?' James stroked her cheek and frowned quizzically.

Kitty flashed a pained smile at the unwitting receptionist. 'Perfect.'

'Oh, this is glorious!' Kitty said when James opened the door to their room.

A four-poster bed was the focal point of the room. The heavy, ornately carved oak was softened by a salmon-pink satin bedspread that looked like something from a Hollywood movie set.

With gleeful abandon, Kitty kicked off her shoes and flung herself on the bed, running her fingers along the grain of the silky fabric. She could feel the comfortable bed claiming her, as though it knew how bone-tired she was after back-to-back shifts, spent on her feet, and disturbed nights, trying to snatch a few hours' sleep on her lumpy single mattress in the nurses' home.

'Come and see the view, darling! It really is balm for the soul.'

James was standing at the full-length window, the Lakeland light picking out the promontory of his brow and his high cheekbones. He opened the metal doors and let the fresh breeze whip inside.

Reluctantly, Kitty hoisted herself off the bed and padded over to him. 'What a view!'

The guesthouse was nestled in the hillside above the lake. Below them, the road was relatively quiet, with travellers driven indoors, thanks to the bruising skies. Only the occasional fell-walker trudged by, wearing woollen socks, stout walking boots and a sou'wester hat, as though the winter had never ended.

'Storm's rolling in,' Kitty said, pointing to the phalanx of dark grey in the sky that was creeping over the water towards them. The low-hanging clouds that clung to the hillside above the far shore put her in mind of old army blankets, rain-soaked and heavy.

'Oh, drat. I thought we might have a romantic stroll to a lovely pub. Work up an appetite and then come back for dinner. The landlady's renowned for her flair with fish.'

Kitty put her arms around his waist and nestled her head

against his chest. 'I know another way we could work up an appetite . . .'

James tilted her chin and looked into her eyes. 'I love you, Kitty Longthorne. Go to Barbados! Have an adventure to tell our children about. I'll be waiting for you when you get back. And we'll name the date when you're good and ready. How does that sound?'

Showing her approval with a passionate kiss, Kitty yelped as James swept her up into his arms and carried her to the four-poster bed.

They undressed with urgency, throwing their clothes to the ground. Kitty felt the thrill of James's cool, skilled hands on her hot skin. She drank in the scent of his aftershave and the hard musculature of his arms, anticipating their two bodies becoming one. Just for a moment, she paused, staying his hand as it wandered to her thigh.

'Be careful,' she said.

'I will. I promise.'

By the time they were seated in the dining room for dinner, the sun had come out.

'I love summer evenings,' Kitty said. 'I love how it stays light till nearly eleven. It makes you feel like anything's possible.'

James chewed his plaice thoughtfully. 'It makes it a lot easier to work late into the evening if you know it won't be dark when you arrive at the hospital and dark when you leave. You know, when we're married, I'm going to try to cut my hours a bit.'

Just as Kitty was toying with her chips, imagining how it would be to rattle around a large house on her own or with a child all day long, waiting for a husband to come home from work, the landlady approached their table.

'So sorry to interrupt,' she said. She had a little notepad in her hand.

'Is everything quite all right?' James asked.

The landlady had Kitty in her sights, however. She spoke with a heavy Cumbrian accent. 'Mrs Williams. I'm not sure if there's some kind of mix-up, but there was a lady on the phone just now, asking for a Kitty Longthorne. She said you were here with a Dr Williams, so I—'

Kitty's chips suddenly lost their savour. She swallowed them down with a sip of water. 'It's my maiden name. Who was the—?'

'Said she was your mother. It doesn't sound good, I'm afraid. She said your dad's bad again. Urgent, like. And she doesn't know what to do. She wants you to come home straight away.'

Chapter 9

'Whatever is the matter?' Matron asked, ushering Kitty into the maternity office, where she shooed the on-duty sister out to allow them privacy. She closed the door. 'You're white as a sheet. Are you well?'

Kitty sat on a birthing stool in the corner of what was little more than a large store cupboard. 'I'm fine. Just a little nauseous. Look, Matron. I'm afraid—'

'Professor Baird-Murray has approved your trip to Bridgetown!' Matron was beaming. It was rare that this serious-minded, formidable woman ever smiled. 'You are to be our representative in the Caribbean, Kitty! Our very own recruiter, bringing back Barbados's brightest and best!' She clapped her hands together. 'Isn't that tremendous?'

Kitty's half-hearted smile faltered. 'I'm so sorry, Matron. I don't know how to tell you this.' She bit her lip. Her eyebrows bunched together. 'My dad's dying. He's back on the lung ward, as you know. Mr Galbraith gave him months, but he seems to be deteriorating fast. My mam can't cope. I had to come home from a weekend away and found the both of them in a right two-and-eight. It's not just coughing up blood – and there's more blood than before. He's started . . . soiling himself. That's why he was readmitted. Galbraith wants to find out if there's anything else going on. But Dad can't stay on the ward till the end.

What he needs is professional nursing care, at home. Me. I'm going to have to hand in my notice.'

'What?' Matron's cheeks flushed red. She stepped back and leaned against the sister's desk. 'Notice? But Kitty, my dear, the trip's agreed. When you come back from Barbados, I guarantee you'll be promoted to Sister, if you swell our nursing ranks.'

Shaking her head, Kitty looked down at her sensible flat lace-up shoes. 'I would have had to give up work anyway, when I marry Dr Williams. At least this way, I'm getting ahead of the game. I won't be letting anyone down by having to pull out of the Barbados trip at the last minute.' She laced her fingers together and shrugged. A tear tracked its way to her jawline and plopped onto her starched uniform.

Matron took off her glasses, set them down on the desktop carefully and rubbed her face with well-scrubbed hands. 'Kitty, Kitty, Kitty.' She put her glasses back on. There was defeat on her tired, ageing face instead of the usual chipper veneer. 'After all the obstacles you've hurdled to get this far up the ladder? My girl! You've succeeded in spite of significant odds. And I've always seen something of my younger self in you. Would you really throw all your achievements away to nurse a man who left you and your mother in the lurch?'

Kitty frowned. She felt a duty to defend her father, but knew that Matron had been there when a dirty, dishevelled Bert Longthorne had turned up at the nurses' home in the middle of the night, fresh out of prison and steaming drunk. He hadn't cared a fig about his daughter or his son, incarcerated in a Japanese prisoner-of-war camp, or the wife he'd left behind. He'd wanted nothing more than money.

'The timing's right. James wants to marry. I've been putting it off. I didn't want to . . . I didn't feel ready . . .'

Looking over her shoulder, as if she were about to reveal some terrible secret, Matron lowered her voice. 'To give up your calling? To abandon your professional aspirations and any adventure in favour of motherhood and routine domesticity?'

'We love each other.'

'Yes. And that's a real gift. Not everyone gets that.' She looked wistful for a moment, but she blinked, and the whiff of regret over lost love was gone. 'But at what personal price to *you*?'

Matron walked towards her, knelt with cracking knees and took Kitty by the shoulders. 'Listen, young lady. I've never had much in my life apart from my work. I am the matron. The matriarch. The hospital has always been my family and you nurses have been my children. And now, I'm close to retirement. When I go, I want to make sure the girls coming up through the ranks have the same determination and dedication that I had. It's the most worthwhile line of work, but being Matron isn't an easy job, Kitty.'

Kitty nodded silently. 'I know.'

'I have to bite my tongue. How many times a day do I get talked down to and ordered around by doctors who are young enough to be my sons? And then, there're the patients. It's always the men, telling me how to do my job, as if they had a clue.' She raised her eyes to the ceiling and stood with a grunt. Her knees cracked again.

'My point is,' she continued, 'even with all the long hours and aching feet and bad backs and the embarrassments and humiliations and horrors and disappointments – even with all of that, this job is worth it.' She clenched her fist. 'You have something real, Kitty Longthorne. You are succeeding in your vocation, and the sick and injured need you. You're like me. I see it in you. You love your job. So, why should you throw all of that endeavour and potential away for men? James gives up nothing to be a family man. Not a single thing. Your father will be dead and buried, but you – you'll have lost something precious.'

'I'll gain a family.'

'You still have time.' She waved her hand dismissively. 'In five years, you'll still be able to bear children, and the rules may change by then. You might be able to be both, Kitty. Imagine that! A mother to children and a mother to the hospital.'

Over the years, Kitty had heard the younger nurses and the male doctors sneeringly calling Matron a 'bluestocking' behind her back. Wherever possible, Kitty had spoken in defence of the stern but fair woman who had given her a chance and often taken her side in tricky staff conflicts. As she sat on the birthing stool, listening to the wailing of a woman in labour in the ward beyond, Kitty remembered how, as a trainee nurse, she had looked up to Matron. She'd always set out to garner her approval whenever possible, regarding this most senior woman in the hospital with a mixture of fear and admiration. What she was saying now was absolutely right, but . . .

'It's my dad. Whatever I think of him, he's family, and family comes first. If I don't look after him, my mam will end up wearing herself out, trying to juggle her job and him.'

'Your mother is a manual worker. She'll pick up more work when he's gone. You're a skilled woman, Kitty – a senior nurse at a time of dire need!'

'I'm engaged to a doctor, though. If I stop working to look after my dad, I'll have a wealthy husband to lean on. If my mam downs tools, she's got nobody else to put food on her table and keep the roof over her head.'

Matron shook her head and exhaled heavily. 'Your father has been given four months to live, five at best. I really do advise against you giving up your career, Kitty. The NHS needs you. But if you insist, I want you to work a notice period so we can prepare for the hole you'll inevitably leave. One month.'

Nodding, Kitty forced a smile. 'One month.'

Kitty's night shift came to an end not long after the sun had risen. Satisfied that her father had spent a reasonably comfortable night on the ward, Kitty approached his bed and watched his eyes moving beneath his eyelids as he slept. She checked his notes hooked over the end of his bed. His discharge home was planned for that afternoon. Discharged home to die.

She bit her lip. Her mixed feelings for him had been supplanted by grief. Hooking the notes back onto the metal frame, she returned to the head of the bed.

'One month,' she whispered to him, wrinkling her nose at the smell of carbolic soap and stale cigarette smoke as she kissed his forehead. 'One month, and I'm all yours to the end.'

Pulling on her cape, Kitty checked the clock to see if James would be in clinic. He regularly arrived early to read through patient records before his consultations began.

She made her way through the draughty hospital corridors to his plastic surgeon's fiefdom and sat on a waiting-room chair. Though the night shifts were generally less hectic than the day shifts, her feet still throbbed. Kicking off her shoes, she gathered her cape around her, hunkered down on the chair and, before long, fell asleep.

A kiss on the lips released her from troubled dreams of nursing her father aboard a sinking ship.

'You're a sight for sore eyes,' James said, smiling down at her. He took the vacant seat beside her.

'I must have dozed off.' Kitty looked at her nurse's watch and saw it was almost half past eight. 'I'm exhausted.'

'Hardly surprising.' He stroked her cheek, took her hand into his and kissed her knuckles. 'You work far too hard. Now, how's Bert? Has he been running you ragged?'

With the morning sun streaming into the waiting area, Kitty had momentarily forgotten her news. The truth erased the smile on her lips and seemed to snuff out the light. She pulled her cape tighter. 'I don't like the look of him. I'm not sure he'll last five months. Galbraith's worried about secondary tumours on his spine, maybe causing the incontinence.'

She told James her plans for leaving and acting as her father's nurse. 'It means I won't go to Barbados.'

'Oh, Kitty. I am sorry.'

Was he sorry? she wondered. He looked rather relieved for a man who was sorry her dreams of international travel had been dashed. 'Ned'll eventually read the telegrams I sent. He'll turn up like a bad penny. He always does. No, my dad's got to come first. And there's a bright side for us.'

James beamed at her. 'You're ready to name a date?'

She nodded and let him enfold her in a hug. 'Ooh, eh! Mind how you go! If you squeeze me any tighter, you'll have a string bean walking down that aisle!'

Kitty left Park Hospital's grounds as the first outpatients started to arrive for their appointments. She made her way to the local post office, desperate for sleep and feeling light-headed, but determined to send another telegram to her brother.

Thinking about the tumultuous few months that lay ahead, she tried to picture herself as a bride, dressed in ivory satin, perhaps with her face covered by a veil, gossamer fine enough to smile up at her father as he slowly led her to the altar. The bittersweet image kept fading, however, giving way to undulating waves and a featureless horizon.

'How can I help you, lovey?' the lady at the post office asked.

'If I sent a telegram to Bridgetown, Barbados, how would I find out if it wasn't delivered, please?' Kitty studied the face of the postmistress, wondering if she had ever left the windswept shores of the British Isles for somewhere more tropical. 'Only, I've sent two to my brother over there, and we've heard nothing back.'

The postmistress pushed her horn-rimmed glasses up her nose. Her lips thinned to two lines. 'I can guarantee you, he'll have got his telegram if he gave you the right address. The post office delivered millions of letters and parcels to the frontline during the war. Millions. It's nowt to get one telegram delivered safely to Bridgetown in peacetime, love.'

Kitty nodded. 'Well, can I send another, then? I'm trying to get hold of him. Our dad's – anyway, I'm worried about him. My brother, I mean.'

The postmistress's expression softened. 'Most folks, what go overseas, go for a reason. They want to run away from something here, or maybe they want to be someone completely new and just don't want the past reminding them who they really are. Have you tried getting in touch with Bridgetown police?'

Ned, in trouble with the police yet again. It was highly likely, but Kitty didn't want to tell that to the postmistress. 'I'll give it one more go with a telegram.'

She dictated her message.

Dad has cancer STOP Few months to live
STOP Getting married in just over month
STOP Please come home STOP

Kitty paid the postmistress but felt the walls of the post office keel at a strange angle. The light seemed to fade. She gripped the countertop.

'Are you all right, lovey?'

She was dimly aware of the postmistress raising the hinged flap on the countertop and coming round to the front. Then, the morning faded to black.

Chapter 10

'You've been overdoing it, darling,' James said, holding Kitty's feet against his knees. 'When was the last time you ate?'

'What are you doing here?' Kitty asked.

'I think you must have a guardian angel,' James said. 'One of these customers recognised you and kindly dashed over to the hospital to find me. So, here I am. Your knight in shining white coat!'

'Help me get up,' Kitty said, all too aware that several women and an old man were standing close by, watching as though she was a side-show at a cheap fair. 'I'm fine now. Honest.'

He helped her to her feet. The postmistress produced a chair from her living accommodation at the back. 'Here you are, lovely. Get sat down. I've seen how you nurses run yourselves ragged.' The postmistress blushed when she shifted her focus to James. 'I'll get her a glass of water, shall I? How about a boiled sweet?'

James beamed at her. 'Perfect. Good for the blood sugar.'

'Is that doctor's orders?' Kitty asked, breathing in and out slowly to stem the nausea that suddenly had her in its grip. She waved her hand in front of her face, feeling that every last drop of blood had drained from her head.

The postmistress offered her a humbug from a tall jar behind the counter. 'Treat yourself to a jaw-breaker.'

Kitty waved it away, however. 'Actually, I'm dizzy as a kitten. I'll give it a miss. I'll make a bacon butty when I get back to the nurses' home. Ta.'

'Come on, nurse!' James said. 'Let's get you home.'

'There you go. I've made you a nice cup of tea to go with the sandwich.' James carried a steaming mug towards her as though he had a Fabergé egg in his hands. 'Drink this!' He disappeared momentarily and returned, smelling strongly of fried bacon and bearing a sandwich on a side plate. 'Right, my darling. I'll have to be off.' He checked his watch. 'My first patient is due – ha! Four minutes ago!'

He smoothed the hair from her face. Kitty was almost overwhelmed by his simple acts of kindness. 'What have I done to deserve you? Now, go! Go, before there's bedlam in your clinic, or they'll all be demanding a brew and a butty.'

Saluting, he blew her a kiss from the door. 'As soon as I get a break for lunch, I'm going to ring the church about a date.'

Kitty could feel the bite she'd taken from the sandwich threatening to come back up her gullet. 'Great. Love you!'

She forced the tea down but pushed the sandwich away, wondering about the nausea and the fainting episode. Had their tryst in the Lakes put her in a predicament? James had been careful so far, but Kitty knew his method of restraint wasn't foolproof. Many a Catholic family with eight or more children, despite the parents' best efforts to stick to three, could attest to that.

With tears rolling down her face and into her tea, Kitty remembered the girls she'd seen on the wards – victims of backstreet abortions who had thought they, too, could run the gauntlet and get away with it.

She let out a shriek and kicked off her blankets. 'Stop feeling sorry for yourself, Kitty Longthorne. You've got nothing to moan about. If push comes to shove, and you've got a bun in the oven, you've got no one to blame but yourself. Be thankful you've got an eligible dreamboat of a man, who's already planning the wedding. It doesn't get any better than that.'

Her self-flagellation ended in wracking sobs. Tears for her dying father; tears for missing Ned; tears for herself, as she prepared to say goodbye to a parent and her career; tears for the baby that might be growing inside her – a baby she wasn't sure she was ready for just yet.

Kitty's father was discharged and sent home, entrusted to the care of her long-suffering mother. The next three weeks passed in a blur of long, long shifts while she trained her trusted friend Lily Schwartz to take over her workload.

There had still been no word from Ned. Kitty had sent a telegram and a letter to the police station in Bridgetown, but the response had come back that they were well aware of an Englishman called Edward Longthorne, who had a disfigured face and went by the name of Ned, but that he had neither been arrested nor reported missing.

With three days to go before she left for good, Kitty was sitting in the Sister's makeshift office, going over the rota of nursing staff with Lily.

'Now, I want you to watch Molly Henshaw,' Kitty said, looking at the meagre list of qualified nurses. 'She's a good nurse, but she can have a sharp tongue. I've had the odd trainee in tears.'

'Oh? One of those.' Lily raised an eyebrow ruefully. 'Yes. We know all about her sort, don't we?'

Kitty didn't need to be reminded of the dreaded Sister Iris, who had plagued the wards some years earlier, singling out Lily in particular for bullying because of her German-Jewish roots.

'Well, as I say, keep a watchful eye on Molly. We're buckling under the strain of too many patients and not enough staff as it is. We don't want her scaring off the trainees and juniors. Matron will have a fit!'

Lily nodded. 'Don't worry. The days of letting bullies run rings around me are well and truly over.' She checked the watch pinned to her chest. 'We need to be in the staffroom in five minutes. Come on! Let's go.'

When she stood up, Kitty eyed her suspiciously. 'We? In the staffroom? Why?' She took her pocket diary out and shook her head. 'I'm seeing Professor Baird-Murray in five minutes. I'm meant to report to him in clinic.'

Lily smiled and winked. 'Change of plan. He told me earlier that you need to go to the staffroom. I'll walk you there, because I've got business with Matron.'

The butterflies in Kitty's stomach told her something was amiss, but she batted her misgivings away and followed her friend through the hospital's draughty corridors towards the staffroom.

'You're up to something, Lily Schwartz. I can feel it in my waters.'

'Rubbish!'

Though Lily was facing away, glancing up at the notice-board outside the TB ward, Kitty could tell by the swell of her friend's cheeks that she was grinning.

They arrived outside the staffroom, immediately identifiable by the smell of cigarette, cigar and pipe smoke seeping under the door.

Lily went in ahead and ushered Kitty inside. The normally busy, buzzing room was totally silent and empty of life. Baird-Murray's leather armchair was unoccupied. No sign of Matron, either.

'Where on earth is everyone?' Kitty asked.

'Surprise!' A gaggle of hospital staff suddenly emerged from behind the door, behind armchairs and the curtains, all shouting in unison.

Kitty gasped, clasping her hand to her chest. She giggled nervously. 'Ooh, you bunch of rotters! I nearly had a heart attack. Now, what's all this about?'

Professor Baird-Murray stepped forward, bearing a large gift, wrapped in brightly coloured paper. With his cigar wedged in the corner of his mouth, he chuckled. 'You didn't think we'd let you go without a send-off, did you? Silly gal!'

'There's a card too!' Lily said, producing a large envelope.

'Oh, you shouldn't have!' Kitty could feel her cheeks ablaze with embarrassment. She took the gift and allowed herself to be shooed into the most comfortable armchair, close to the window. Sitting down with the gift on her lap, she surveyed the gathering of her colleagues properly. She spotted five nurses, seven young doctors and a handful of consultants – presumably all on their break. No James or Matron, though. Perhaps they were busy on the wards.

'Go on! Let's see what you've got,' Alice Timperley, the paediatric nurse, said.

Unwrapping her gift, Kitty found a lovely green woollen dressing gown and matching fur-lined slippers. There was also a small box beneath the layers. 'Oh. Nice dressing gown. And those slippers look really comfy.'

'We thought you could enjoy not having to get up at the crack of dawn anymore,' Lily said. 'Or go to bed when everyone's getting ready to start the day, for that matter. You can sit in front of the fire in this lot and enjoy breakfast at your leisure!'

Kitty bit her lip and grinned shyly. She'd been wearing a man's old dressing gown – a jumble-sale find that looked more like an army blanket than bed attire – since she'd started at the hospital as a trainee. 'Smashing! Ta. But what's this?' Kitty opened the box and gasped. Inside was a dainty gold watch with a slender leather strap. 'Oh, you shouldn't have!'

'It's twenty-two-carat gold plate,' one of the junior doctors said. 'Swiss.'

With wide eyes, Kitty tried on the impossibly luxurious watch. The leather strap was burgundy crocodile. It gleamed under the lights. 'I-I don't know what to say.'

'That's a first!' Molly Henshaw shouted out.

Everybody laughed.

The leaving party continued for another ten minutes. A fine-looking cake had been baked by Baird-Murray's wife and was shared out among the attendees. There was lemonade in mugs. The wireless played a jolly jitterbug. Kitty didn't try to stem the flow of the odd tear of gratitude and regret.

Everything was going swimmingly until the door to the staffroom opened and Matron stepped inside. She looked flushed and strode over to Kitty with purpose. As Matron approached, James also walked in, bearing a bunch of flowers. He beamed at Kitty and winked, mouthing, 'I've booked the church.'

Matron's stony expression looked anything but celebratory, however. Kneeling at her side, Kitty's superior placed a hand on her shoulder and whispered in her ear. 'I've sorted everything out, young lady.' Suddenly she winked.

Kitty could barely hear her over the hubbub. 'Pardon?'

'I've found a reputable palliative nurse for your father. One you can afford. She's recently retired. Mildred Thorpe. Very good woman. Willing to start tomorrow. Oh, and I might have failed to cancel your ticket to Barbados.' She grasped Kitty's hand between hers. 'Will you stay, Kitty? What do you say?'

Glancing from the beatific face of her fiancé to the matron, a disbelieving Kitty opened her mouth to give her answer.

Chapter 11

'What a wonderful send-off, Kitty,' James said. 'And nothing less than you deserve.'

He met her outside the nurses' home after her shift had ended and she'd changed out of her uniform. Taking from her the bag containing her leaving gifts, he grabbed her around the waist with his free arm and swung her around. 'And I've taken the liberty of booking the church! We, my dear, are to be married in the most perfect little spot in the whole of Cheshire, on the twenty-fifth of August. It's a Thursday, before you ask. All the Saturdays were fully booked, I'm afraid.'

'So soon?'

James's smile faltered. 'It's what you asked me to do. We talked about this at length. You wanted the wedding to fall in the next couple of weeks, before your father gets too weak to travel.'

Kitty held his face between her hands and kissed him squarely on the mouth. 'You're such a catch!' *Tell him what Matron said, Kitty, for heaven's sake!* her conscience cried out. *Nip this charade in the bud before things get out of hand.* A wave of nausea threatened to knock her off her feet yet again and she staggered.

'Are you quite all right, darling?' James asked, putting her swag in the boot of his car. He came round to the passenger side and opened the door for her. He felt her forehead.

'You're not going to faint again, are you? You're as white as a sheet. A bit clammy too. Perhaps you're coming down with something.'

Pushing him away gently, Kitty glanced up at the love of her life but couldn't look him in the eye. 'I'm fine, love. We'd better get going if we're going to get to Mam's for a late tea.'

The car journey was a merry affair, with James talking ten to the dozen about their plans.

'I think we should start looking at houses as soon as possible, darling,' he said, his handsome face completely transformed by the delighted smile he wore. 'I hope you don't think me presumptuous, but I've already been out to Hale and Bowdon on a little drive. There are some lovely places there. Big enough to bring up a family in. Some of them are quite newly built. Late thirties, early forties. Lovely inside bathrooms with pistachio fittings. Sinks in the main bedrooms. Formica counters in the kitchen. Nice gardens. You'll fall in love with the area. Oh, Kitty. It's so green, and right near the countryside of the Bollin Valley.'

She'd never seen James so happy, except, perhaps, when he'd made some new plastic surgery breakthrough. Yet she still didn't feel able to tell him what Matron had said.

'And in a week's time, once you're footloose and fancy free, you'll have time to go shopping for a wedding dress. I imagine that will be quite exciting. Don't show anything to me before our big day, though! Bad luck and all that!'

Matron's whispered words grew louder and louder in Kitty's memory, but every time she opened her mouth to tell James about Mildred Thorpe, the retired palliative nurse, and the valid ticket to Barbados, nothing came out. *I'll meet this nurse later in the week,* Kitty thought, *vet her myself. No*

point in prematurely telling James I'm having second thoughts.
He'll never speak to me again.

They pulled up outside her parents' maisonette. Kitty was surprised when the net curtain didn't twitch. The door was on the latch as usual, though. She carried the gift of the dressing gown and slippers inside with her.

'Sorry we're late, Mam! We got here as soon as we could,' she shouted through to the parlour.

Hanging her raincoat on the peg in the hall, she sniffed the air. Kitty realised that things didn't smell quite right in the Longthorne residence. In place of the usual pungent stink of overcooked white cabbage, she drank in the aroma of something utterly delicious. Stew, perhaps, but not her mother's. It was the kind she'd tasted once when James had taken her to a French restaurant in town. *Boeuf* something. It had had pickled onions in it, which she hadn't been sure about, but the rest of it had been mouth-watering. Even if she'd known how to prepare it, her mother couldn't afford the ingredients for such a rich dish!

'What are you cooking, Mam?' She opened the sticky door to the parlour, expecting to see her dad on his own. At this time of the evening, he'd normally be sitting in his armchair, looking dishevelled in his string vest and trousers, smoking and listening to the wireless.

'What's got into you?' Kitty asked, eyeing her immaculately turned-out father, who was wearing his Sunday-best trousers, by the looks of it, and a smart brown cardigan she'd never seen before. Slippers had appeared on the scene, perhaps for the first time in his life – leather ones, at that. All of his clothes seemed to drown him, however.

Her father rolled his eyes and shrugged. He gesticulated with his nicotine-stained thumb towards the scullery. 'Ask *her*.'

'Mam, you mean?' Kitty stood in the middle of the parlour, holding the bag that contained the new green dressing gown and slippers. 'Have you had a visit from the priest?'

Her father chuckled mirthlessly.

'Ah, there you are. Good to meet you, Nurse Longthorne!' A short, stout older woman, with white hair styled into a veritable helmet of old-fashioned demi-waves, emerged from the scullery. In her left hand, she held a wooden spoon. Her right she stuck out to shake hands with Kitty, like a man.

Kitty obliged, momentarily glancing beyond the woman to her mother, who was standing in the doorway, smiling. 'And you are?' She had already guessed exactly who the woman was, of course.

'Mildred Thorpe. Retired Sister. Your Matron and I go back a long way. She thought it best we meet.'

'Mildred's a marvel in the kitchen,' Kitty's mother said, wide-eyed and grinning like she'd fallen in the proverbial divi ticket at the Co-op. 'You should see how she's whipped up a feast for us. And our Bert's all clean and smart, like a band box. I can get on with some piecework, later! In fact, I might just put my feet up.'

James raised an eyebrow and looked enquiringly at Kitty. 'My word. *What* a send-off! I knew Matron always thought highly of you, but I hadn't realised she also had a soft spot for your parents. An evening off for your mother and dinner for us all. What a lovely gesture!'

'Oh, it's not a one-off,' Mildred said. 'Providing Nurse Longthorne and I see eye to eye and can agree terms.'

'Terms?' James asked, fingering the cuffs of his starched shirt and blinking far too quickly. He turned to Kitty.

Kitty toyed with the diamond in her engagement ring. It normally sparkled beneath the parlour ceiling light but, today, its brilliance was dimmed, as if the tense atmosphere in the room had sucked the very shine out of it. 'It's lovely to meet you, Mildred. Matron has nothing but good words to say about you. I did want to arrange a rendezvous for later in the week, but it seems you've beaten me to it.'

Mildred raised her spoon and smiled. Her face became immediately warmer, and the formidable exterior gave way to something more approachable and motherly. 'Efficiency and reliability. Those have always been my watchwords, Nurse—'

'Please, call me Kitty.'

'And you shall call me Mildred, dear gal, in the name of mutual respect. We are both nursing professionals, are we not? And your reputation proceeds *you*, too!' She trilled the R in 'reputation' – her speech more reminiscent of a melodramatic hunt-master from Buckinghamshire than a nurse from Manchester. She waved the spoon in the air as though she was cracking a whip. 'Come now. Your father is clean and medicated for his pain. Dinner awaits.'

Kitty handed the new dressing gown and slippers to her mother, pecking her on the cheek. 'Here you go, Mam. A little something for you. They're brand new from Kendal's.'

'Ooh, hey!' Elsie rummaged in the bag and pulled out her haul, holding the dressing gown against herself for size. She kicked off her shoes and pushed her feet into the slippers. 'What did we do to deserve all this? Your Matron sent the new clobber for your father. There was a lovely note. She's a good'un, that one. And now I've got a new rig-out, too! Aren't you the limit, our Kitty? Green. I love green, me.' She folded the robe up and, together with the slippers, put the lot back in the bag, setting it on the settee like a guest of honour, as if a brand-new garment was too good for wearing. She mouthed the name, *Kendal's*, with raised eyebrows.

As Kitty ushered her father to the scuffed table and they took their seats, James glowered at Kitty. The tendon in his jaw was flinching yet again.

'Look here, Kitty,' he said over a bout of coughing from her father. 'I don't know what's going on, but you obviously do. Don't you think it's time you let me in on your little secret arrangement with Matron?'

Kitty was about to answer when Mildred and her mother entered the parlour, carrying large bowls of fine-smelling stew.

'Matron has asked me to nurse your future father-in-law,' Mildred said, setting a bowl down in front of James with a flourish. 'So that your fiancée doesn't have to give up her life's work and travel plans just yet.' She turned to Kitty. 'She told me all about it, you know.'

Feeling her cheeks burn with embarrassment at her duplicity being served up at the table, like bread for the stew, Kitty polished her spoon on her skirt. 'I'm sorry. I only found out at my leaving party. Honest, James. Matron whispered it in my ear just as you came in with the flowers and the news about the church. How could I tell you?'

James set his cutlery down and spoke through gritted teeth. 'You've made the decision to stay? After making a song and dance about handing in your notice so we could tie the knot and you could look after Bert, here?' He raised his eyes to heaven.

At his side, Bert pushed his food around, sniffing a small spoonful with apparent mistrust. 'Kitty's got a terrible bedside manner. I'd rather have Mildew, here.'

'It's Mildred, Bert! Don't be rude,' Kitty's mother scolded him.

'Ay. Mildred. She knows one end of a bed bath from another. I can tell. I already feel more human after a good strip wash.' He put the spoonful of food in his mouth and nodded. 'And this stew doesn't taste half bad, neither. Your fiancée can't cook. You know that, don't you, Jimmy Boy?'

'I'm not marrying Kitty for her culinary skills, Bert! I'm marrying her, not just because she's beautiful, but because she's intelligent and – I thought she had integrity. Now I see you all know Kitty's mind before I do, I'm not so sure.'

Tears forced their way out of Kitty's eyes. They were hot and angry, plopping into her food as they had done when she'd been a child and Ned had said or done something unspeakably cruel. She pushed her food away and ran outside.

Not really knowing where to go, Kitty walked a few yards along the street, in the direction of the docks. It was warm outside, and the drunken patrons of the pub on the corner of the street were spilling onto the cobbles, slurring at each other convivially.

'Damn you, James Williams,' she said beneath her breath. A wave of nausea hit her anew. She placed an accusatory hand over her belly, beneath which she imagined a baby growing. 'And *you* can pack it in, and all. You all think you know what's right for me, don't you?'

She sat on the low wall outside a terraced house, hoping that the occupants wouldn't shoo her away.

'Kitty! I say, Kitty! Hold your horses!'

Looking up, she saw James striding towards her. His face was a picture of concern and contrition – or perhaps it was hurt and irritation?

He took a seat next to her and looked down at his shoes. 'Have you changed your mind, Kitty? About us, I mean?'

Kitty wiped her tears away forcefully with the back of her hand. She glared at him. 'No. *I* haven't.' She put her hand on his, but his palms remained fixed on his knees. 'Like that, is it?'

'Like what?' He looked straight ahead, as though she wasn't sitting right next to him.

'Well, you were sharp with me in there. And I didn't deserve it.'

'Oh, really, Kitty?' Finally, he turned to face her. There was no softness to his brown eyes, but the pain was apparent beneath the flintiness. 'Ever since we got engaged, you've been dragging your heels about naming the day. When, I'd finally resigned myself to the longest engagement in history, you then spring the news on me that you want to leave work and get married, fast. My head was spinning when you dropped that bombshell! I felt like I was being corralled into a shotgun wedding, though I was hardly going to complain! So, I embraced the opportunity and booked the church, thinking our happily-ever-after was finally within sight. But no. That wasn't the end of it, because while I was grinning like a fool in the staffroom – in front of *my colleagues*, I hasten to add – beaming like a berk for having booked the church, you're sneaking behind my back with Matron! It feels rather like being cuckolded, but less straightforward.'

Kitty took a deep breath and exhaled heavily. 'Until break-time today in that staffroom, I was still getting married to you, come the end of summer. I was still leaving next week. I *didn't* lie to you. That was my plan. Still is, technically. I'm leaving. I'm going to let my dad walk me down the aisle and then I'm going to nurse him to the end. That's it.' Her tears fell anew. 'I'm not r-running around behind your b-back. Don't punish *me* for M-Matron's . . .' She searched for the right word. 'Subterfuge.'

James stood and straightened his trousers. He didn't look at her again. He merely stared blankly at the terrace on the opposite side of the road. 'I must bite my tongue, Kitty. I know you're going through a lot at the moment, and I mustn't say something that I'll regret.'

He started to walk away.

'Where are you going, James Williams?'

'I'm going to get off, Kitty. I'll see you at work.'

Kitty leaped to her feet and swooned, feeling her cheeks prickle as the blood drained away in fear. 'You're leaving? You're going back without me?'

He didn't answer. She followed him down the street, back towards the car, but still, he didn't turn around.

Kitty felt anger well within her. She shouted after him. 'Just you listen to me, James Williams! I'm nowt more than a bottom-of-the-barrel Longthorne! Let's face it, the only time you ever wheeled me out to your parents, they were quick to make *that* much clear. I was flattered by Matron. I *am* flattered! And she's right. There's none so selfish as the dying. Dad's making demands of me, and it's no odds to him. He'll be dead and gone in three, four months. But I've got the rest of my life to live. And we've got the rest of our lives to get married. Why shouldn't I have one last adventure? Barbados, James. I've never been past Penrith!'

Her words seemed to fall on deaf ears. James kept walking and didn't turn back.

Chapter 12

I'm on my way STOP Ship docks in
Bridgetown in a month STOP

As Kitty watched the wake of churning sea streak behind the giant ship, she thought about the telegram that she'd sent to Ned. It was a moot point whether it would get to him at all, let alone ahead of her arrival. Still, they'd heard nothing from her errant twin brother and, still, her mother was fretting that he had been locked up or worse.

'Oh, Mam. Look after your poor, tired heart.' Kitty dabbed at her eyes as her mother became smaller and smaller on the dockside – still waving, though Kitty must have been no larger than an ant to her by now, dwarfed by the size of the boat and the grey Irish Sea.

Liverpool, once the north-western toast of industrial Britain, built on the proceeds of the Empire and bullish trade, served as a sorry backdrop to this drama. James was sitting in his Ford Anglia somewhere, refusing to join his future mother-in-law on the quayside, though he had, at least, driven them there, albeit in a rush. He'd wished Kitty a bon voyage by way of a mealy-mouthed truce.

'Will he still be here when I get back?' Kitty asked the liver birds, still breathless from her sprint up the gangway.

They had no answer for her. Today, they felt like carrion birds, waiting to pluck out her broken heart.

With one, final, hearty wave, Kitty turned around to face forward, where the sun was setting on England. This was the start. Adventure beckoned . . .

She picked up her cardboard case and pushed her way through the crowds, five or six people deep, hoping to find that Matron had booked her a cabin with a sea view. The other passengers seemed to be a mix of British subjects and people from the West Indies – mainly men – whom she imagined to be returning home to visit their families. Everyone was dressed in their Sunday best, judging by their formal clothes and well-tailored overcoats. Out on deck, the men wore trilbies, pressing them close to their skulls against the Irish Sea wind. The women sported silk scarves, tied simply beneath the chin, or else clutched at small millinery confections, better suited to a summer Sunday morning in church than the gusts that were coming in off the Atlantic.

The Atlantic. Kitty registered a thrill of excitement pass through her as she thought about her undertaking. She'd had to borrow money from Matron to replace the dressing gown and slippers that the leaving-present whip-round had afforded her, but it had been a small price to pay to see her mother in clean, new bed attire and to count herself as a transatlantic globetrotter!

'Can I help you, miss? You look lost.' A fresh-faced, uniformed member of the crew was suddenly standing before her.

Kitty clasped her hand to her chest. 'Blimey. I was miles away. Yes. Yes please.' She set her case down at her feet and produced her ticket from her hard-framed handbag. 'I'm looking for my cabin. I'm a nurse on the NHS's official recruitment drive, you know.'

The crew-member smiled blankly at her. 'Always good to have medical people around. Welcome aboard, miss.' He checked her ticket. The smile faded. 'You're below deck. Follow the signs.'

With that, she felt summarily dismissed as the lad gravitated towards a finely dressed woman clad in a mink coat and her dapper husband, who exuded power. Feeling disgruntled but curious all the same, Kitty watched as the lad doffed his cap to the couple and ushered them towards the sea-facing cabins, all smiles. She noticed they weren't carrying their own cardboard cases.

'Did I overhear you say you're a nurse?' a voice came from behind her.

Kitty turned to see a woman, roughly her own age, dressed in a bright red, velvet-trimmed coat that was a good couple of sizes too big for her. Her feathered hat looked like borrowed finery, too.

'I'm Ida,' she said. 'Ida Marks. Sister at the Manchester Royal Infirmary.'

'Kitty Longthorne. Pleased to meet you.' Right then, it felt like somebody was watching over Kitty, as the shores of everything she'd ever known faded to grey in the distance and only the unknown lay ahead. 'I'm a senior nurse at Park Hospital.'

'Davyhulme? Lovely! Are you going to Jamaica on the recruitment drive?' Ida linked arms with her and led them both along the crowded deck, weaving between excitedly chattering fellow passengers.

'Actually, I'm heading for Bridgetown. Barbados.' The name sounded terribly dashing. Kitty failed to stifle a giggle. Who was she – a simple girl from Hulme – to be gadding about on the high seas, heading for the palm-fringed shores of a tropical colonial outpost? 'My brother's out there, would you believe? But that's just a coincidence. Park Hospital's desperate for more nurses.'

'Oh, the Infirmary is too. It's the same everywhere.'

'Well, when the matron lined me up with this job, I could hardly say no.'

'Me too! I've only ever been to Blackpool and once to the Big Smoke, years ago.'

'Blackpool and the Lakes for me!' Kitty chuckled. 'What cabin are you in?'

Ida's brow furrowed as she fished in her handbag for her ticket. She pulled it out with a flourish and read the deck and cabin number aloud. It sounded familiar. Kitty checked her own ticket.

'We're in the same cabin!' she cried. 'I can't believe it. Two nurses from Manchester, bunking up in the same room.'

'How about that, then?' Ida said, steering Kitty towards the staircase that led to the lower deck. 'Fate's thrown us together. What fun we'll have on the high seas for a month!'

When they located their cabin, several floors down, it felt rather like they were in the bowels of the ship.

'You can hear the blooming engine!' Ida said, flinging her case on a lower bunk.

'Can I have the top bunk?' Kitty asked. 'I always had the top bunk as a little 'un.'

'You got any other sisters and brothers?' Ida asked, hanging her coat neatly on a hanger and hooking it onto the footboard of the top bunk.

'Just my twin brother,' Kitty said, remembering how she and Ned used to talk and talk after lights out when they'd been eight or nine, finally tiring and falling silent in the small hours. They'd run their mother ragged, necessitating constant empty threats in a bid to shut them up. She smiled at the memory. 'He's supposed to be in Bridgetown, running a hotel, so it's as much a family errand as an NHS mission. I feel very lucky.' She glanced over at the two vacant bunks that were fastened to the opposite wall. 'Who do you think we'll be sharing with?'

Ida shrugged. 'Maybe other nurses? It wouldn't surprise me if there's some central NHS booking system. Who knows? Whoever they are, I hope they're trustworthy.' She locked her passport inside her suitcase and slipped the key into her bag. She slid the case under the bunk and hid it behind a rolled-up blanket. 'There's lots of Black folk on board. We could get anyone. Make sure you keep your stuff safe.'

At that moment, the door opened and a tiny older woman entered with a much taller, much younger woman – she was not much older than a child. They looked like they were from one of the Caribbean islands.

Kitty found herself staring at their dark skin and old-fashioned clothes. Privately, she chastised herself for being rude and smiled at them. 'Hello. I'm Kitty. This is Ida. We're nurses.'

The tiny woman smiled uncertainly at her. 'Hello, dear. My name's Mrs Lewis. This here's my youngest, Joyce.' She spoke with a heavy accent. 'We sailing back to Bridgetown. You?'

Together, Kitty and Ida explained their mission. Throughout, young Joyce remained coy, merely sitting on the bottom bunk with her hands folded primly on her lap. Mrs Lewis, though, was an animated character, who revealed they'd been visiting her husband.

'My George be an engineer. He be working on a building site in Manchester, trying to fix the bomb damage to the Free Trade Hall.'

'Is he enjoying his stay?' Kitty asked, expecting to hear a glowing report on all that post-war Manchester had to offer.

The old woman made a strange sucking noise. 'Never seen weather like it. He'll be coming back home with webbing between his fingers like some frog. Me bones are killing me with all that damp.'

'Never seen no sunshine all the time we were there,' Joyce said, unpinning a cloche hat. 'And the food – what was the food like, Mumma?'

'Like eating cardboard.'

Kitty blushed, thinking of her mother's tasteless grey sausages, filled more with rusk than with meat. 'Well, we are still at the mercy of strict rationing.'

Ida raised an eyebrow, clutching her handbag defensively against her stomach. 'And there was me, thinking you lot were coming to Britain to find a better life. The way you talk, Barbados is paradise. Maybe you should have stayed at home.'

Mrs Lewis smiled, though Ida's condescending tone had chilled any warmth behind the woman's eyes to a hard frost. 'Huh! You got plaster fuh evah sore! Our menfolk have come to England to find work. Fair day's work for a fair day's pay. *You* lot need them as much as they need jobs. They don't owe no one no flattery.'

Ida grabbed Kitty by the elbow. 'Come along, Kitty. I think the air's a little stale in here. Let's go for a turn around the top deck. Look at the stars.'

Kitty was glad to escape the tense atmosphere. She sensed animosity, anger and disdain – almost visible in the air as flashing colours of red and green. As they were leaving, she mouthed 'Sorry' at the two Barbadian women, careful that Ida shouldn't see her. It wouldn't do to be anything but neutral in such an awkward situation.

'Don't you think we'd better be nice to Mrs Lewis and her daughter?' she said as they climbed the stairs. The air noticeably freshened.

'Why? What on earth do we owe two of *them* in bad clothes?'

'We're sharing a cabin with those ladies for the next month. They seem perfectly nice to me. I'd really rather not antagonise them. It doesn't seem like a good idea to pre-empt cabin fever.'

Out on deck, twilight had yielded to night, but the stars were hidden behind thick, low-hanging cloud.

Kitty grabbed the handrail on the starboard bow and looked down into the inky waters below. Her heartbeat quickened, as she felt a strong and illogical urge to throw herself overboard. She took a step back, feeling the deck spin, and tottered slightly, though the sea had only just begun to churn and roll ever so slightly. She knew there'd be worse to come.

'Are you quite all right, Kitty?' Ida asked.

Kitty took a deep breath and exhaled slowly. 'Long day. I forgot to eat.'

They made their way to the second-class dining room. Nobody had dressed for dinner, here. Kitty spooned three small roast potatoes onto her plate and poured a spoon's worth of gravy on top. She couldn't stomach any more. Ida, on the other hand, piled her plate high, as if it were her last meal.

'All that sea air gives me an appetite,' she said. 'What about you? Are you rationing yourself?'

Kitty shook her head. She could taste acid at the back of her throat. She was unsteady on her feet. 'I just need something plain. I don't want to—'

Feeling the colour drain from her face, Kitty dropped her knife and fork onto her plate with a clatter that made other diners look round. She shoved her napkin on the table, stood abruptly and sprinted out of the dining room, making for the side, though she could barely run in a straight line. As the ship lurched into the pitch and roll of the Atlantic, Kitty brought her potatoes back up with a vengeance.

'You should eat something, dear,' Mrs Lewis told Kitty, stroking her hair off her forehead. 'Then at least you got something to bring up.'

Kitty groaned and pulled the thin blanket tightly around her shoulders. She was sweating but oh, so cold. Her stomach was cramping as though she'd been poisoned. 'As long as I drink water, I'll be fine.' She'd swapped bunks with Ida so that she was now on the bottom with easy access to a bucket, placed on the floor close to her head. It reeked. 'I'm so sorry about this.'

'Seasickness be nothing to worry about.' Mrs Lewis waved her hand dismissively. 'When I first sailed to Britain, I turned my insides inside out.' She chuckled. 'This whole ship be full of puking passengers right about now. First class too. Money can't buy you sea legs.'

'Ida's already over the worst.'

Mrs Lewis curled her lip, opened her mouth to say something, then seemingly thought better of it. 'Here you go, dear. I'll empty your bucket.'

She returned minutes later with a rinsed-out, fresh-smelling bucket and set it by Kitty's bunk. There was something about the careful way she seated herself by Kitty's feet that implied she had a delicate question to ask. She laced her fingers together and placed her hands on her lap. 'Don't take this the wrong way, Kitty, but could you be . . . in the family way?' She raised an eyebrow.

If Kitty hadn't been feeling so ghastly, she would surely have flushed red with embarrassment. The question had taken her by surprise. Tears welled in her eyes. 'It's possible,' she whispered. She gagged suddenly, but nothing came out.

'When was your last monthly, dear?'

'I-I don't remember.'

'You don't put it on a calendar? Keep track? You got to keep track, girl!' Mrs Lewis looked at Kitty's engagement ring, reached out and touched the diamond gently. 'When did you and your man last have relations?' Her tone was utterly matter-of-fact and non-judgemental.

'A few weeks ago. We were careful. I think. My fiancé's a doctor. He knows—'

Mrs Lewis scoffed. 'He know! He know! Men don't know nothing when they be excited. They only thinking about they own pleasure. A woman have to take responsibility for her own body. You a nurse. You should know that.'

Kitty nodded ruefully. 'Don't tell Ida. Please.'

'There's nothing to tell.' Mrs Lewis winked and patted Kitty's feet affectionately. 'Just keep drinking water and make sure you get something salty down you. I'll bring you something on a plate. Nothing greasy. If it's seasickness, you be feeling better soon enough. If you carrying a child, you'll know by the time we dock!'

'Is it usual to get dizzy?' Kitty asked. 'When you're – you know.'

'You the nurse!' Mrs Lewis laughed out loud.

'But I've never been pregnant before and I'm not a doctor. I can't know everything.'

Mrs Lewis pressed her lips together and frowned. She shook her head. 'Dizzy? No. Not really. Never happened to me.'

The door opened. It was Ida, grimacing and waving her hand in front of her nose. Kitty wondered how much of the conversation Ida had heard. Would she press matters further?

'Poo! What a stink!' Ida cried. 'I'm going to leave the door open to let some air circulate. Is that all right with you, Kitty?' She started to wedge some toilet paper beneath the door.

'If Mrs Lewis and Joyce don't object,' Kitty said, relieved that Ida's mind was now elsewhere.

Her fellow nurse strode over to her, forcing Mrs Lewis to retreat to her own side of the room, given how cramped the cabin was. She felt Kitty's forehead. 'You're burning up. You've got an infection.'

Could that be what was making Kitty sick?

Ida took her suitcase from its hiding place beneath the bottom bunk. She snapped open the locks and lifted a folded jumper off the top to reveal an array of medical implements below. Kitty spied a thermometer, a stethoscope, several bottles containing various pills and potions, bandages . . . even suturing needles and some thread.

'I thought you said you were a nurse on a recruitment drive like me!' Kitty said, as Ida wielded an otoscope and looked down Kitty's right ear.

'Sister. Yes, I *am* going on the recruitment drive, but I'm also training to be a doctor. It's going to take me years, doing it part-time, but I don't think the men should get all the fun, do you?'

Kitty looked at Ida with new-found respect. 'You're an inspiration! Why did you bring all this equipment, though? Medicines and that! How on earth did you get hold of prescription medicines?'

Ida tapped the side of her nose and winked. She sat up straight and shoved a thermometer under Kitty's tongue. She took out a stethoscope and listened to her heartbeat. 'You don't think I'd venture out to the West Indies without taking some essentials, do you? The infant mortality rate for babies under one in Barbados alone is about one in three.'

Mrs Lewis made the sucking sound with her cheeks and teeth and shook her head. 'That don't surprise me. You English – you lording it over the colonies for centuries, taking what you want from the land to make money. You take our men to build your cities, but you leave us with scraps from the table. Our doctors be good, but the clinics be too small and crumbling. You wait till you see what *our* nurses have to put up with. People in the country, in the villages – if they get sick, they die. English hospitals and doctors and all that National Health Service free treatment be worth braving the terrible weather and chips for breakfast, dinner and tea.'

Ida blinked hard at Mrs Lewis. Her lips thinned to a line. She turned back to Kitty and smiled ruefully. 'You've got an ear infection.'

'What? I haven't even had much earache. I thought I'd got water in my ear when I last washed my hair.'

'Well, you have.'

'Is that why I've been dizzy?'

Nodding, Ida took a small brown bottle of pills from her case. 'Almost certainly. Balance is controlled in the middle ear. If you've felt dizzy, it could be caused by anaemia or bad nerves. But your ear canal is like an inferno and you've been vomiting for Great Britain. You're undoubtedly a bit seasick, but my guess is the ear infection's behind the severity of your vertigo.' She pulled out the cotton wadding that stoppered the neck of the bottle. 'I want you to take this penicillin. It'll be gone in no time.'

Within three days, Kitty was able to walk steadily, despite the constantly undulating motion of the boat, ploughing its way through a rough patch of weather. Her temperature had broken, she'd stopped being sick and the cabin mercifully smelled fresher, but she was still suffering from passing bouts of nausea.

The other women were off playing chess in the second-class lounge. As she took a moment to clean herself up and change her underwear, Kitty looked at the gusset of her old panties. There was still no sign of her period.

Under her breath, she looked up to the ceiling and prayed silently to God that her delayed time of the month would finally show up. She thought about James, sitting in his Ford, waiting for her mother while she waved goodbye to Kitty on her own. The love of her life – so handsome, so devoted, yet so distant, cold and demanding.

When Kitty was dressed, she took her precious stash of photographs from her suitcase and ran her finger over one of James – a professional portrait, taken by the *Manchester Guardian*, when they'd run an article about his pioneering plastic surgery techniques. He was more dashing than Clark Gable, more intellectually impressive than Einstein, but still, the way he'd sulked and refused to see the trip, her family's needs and her career from her perspective rankled Kitty.

'I love you, James Williams, but I'm not prepared to lose myself entirely to you,' she told the photo. 'And you're selfish to expect me to give up my dreams and commitments just to wash your smalls and pander to your ego. Kitty Longthorne's not a doormat for any man, mister!'

There was a sudden change in temperature in the cabin.

'Hey, what are you doing down here?' The unexpected sound of Ida's voice jerked Kitty out of her reverie. 'Are you in the doldrums, Nurse Longthorne?'

Kitty stashed the photos of James and her family back into the suitcase. 'I didn't hear you come in. How long have you been standing there?'

'Long enough to know that you need a change of scenery. Come with me!'

Ida led Kitty to the second-class lounge, where she'd saved her a seat at a table with Mrs Lewis, Joyce and three other women – teachers from the Virgin Islands. It was blowing a hooley outside, but there, in the clammy, packed lounge, Kitty was delighted to see a band of musicians playing jazz for the other passengers.

'We've got a trumpet player at Park Hospital. A patient called Lloyd,' she explained to the others. 'He plays at the Band on the Wall.'

'Music is life,' Mrs Lewis simply said. 'These lot be from Jamaica, I be guessing. We got the best musicians in the world. Come and dance, Kitty Cat.'

With that, she and Joyce stood to join the jitterbugging, jiving passengers on the makeshift dance floor in the middle of the tables and chairs. She held out her hand towards Kitty.

'Are you coming?' Kitty asked Ida.

Ida shook her head. 'You must be joking. I'm not making a show of myself in front of this lot. Besides, I've got two left feet. But you go. You look like you could do with letting your hair down.'

Kitty laughed, and it felt like a release. She wended her way through the crowd of passengers – English people, Jamaicans, Barbadians, other white people and Black people from the Caribbean islands. As she joined the Lewis women to dance, she felt the rhythm of the drums vibrate through the soles of her feet; she felt the thump of the double bass as it somehow made the air feel thick with excitement. Though she was wearing ugly flat shoes and wrinkled ankle socks and though her stomach was still raw from days of being ill, she let down her mousy blonde hair, started to dance and immediately felt like Lana Turner in *Two Girls on Broadway*.

Chapter 13

'What I'd give for a walk on terra firma,' Ida said, leaning against the railing near the prow of the ship.

'I know,' Kitty said, gazing out at the flat calm. Gently undulating water of the deepest azure blue had replaced the terrifying waves that had towered over the ship during the worst of the squalling weather. 'Look at that!' She gazed ahead, turned to her left, then turned to her right and took in the view of the blue skies and featureless horizon. 'Nothing as far as the eye can see. I've never known anything like it. Bit different from Manchester, eh?'

The two laughed.

'It's baking, too,' Ida said, taking off her lightweight cardigan and tying it around her waist. 'Must be in the high seventies. I swear I'm getting a tan like a navvy on a building site in July.'

Kitty looked at the honey colour of the skin on her arms and hands. It was true. They were both catching the sun. The tropical warmth seeped into her bones and made her feel invincible. It was more than welcome after her grim experience of seasickness, made ten times worse by the ear infection. She was still suffering from bouts of nausea, but somehow, the sunshine and Mrs Lewis's tip about chewing on a fresh piece of ginger, pilfered every morning from the kitchens, made everything a little better.

Feeling the hot sun on her face, Kitty closed her eyes

and inhaled deeply. At the front of the ship, she could only smell the tang of brine, carried on the slight headwind that they were sailing into. 'No chimney smoke. No car-exhaust fumes. No cigarettes or pipes or smelly cigars. Do you know, if my old dad had only ever had a lungful of this fresh air and had never started smoking, he'd live forever.' She felt the memories of her family tug at her heart. Dad, preparing for the end; Mum, run ragged with caring for a dying man, balancing the books against the odds and churning out labour-intensive piecework in poor light; Ned . . . 'My brother's in Barbados, like I said. Runs a hotel. Allegedly.' She didn't bother to keep the scepticism out of her voice.

Ida leaned over the railings to watch a school of dolphins following the ship. 'Is that why you put in for the job?'

Kitty smiled at the sight of a dolphin as it leaped from the water, twisted in mid-air and splashed back beneath the surface. It seemed to smile at her. She consigned it to memory. 'Partly. I need to tell him that our dad's not got long. But I'm worried about him – my brother, like. I haven't heard from him in months. He was supposed to come home and never sailed, even though he'd bought a ticket.'

'Brothers always turn up like bad pennies,' Ida said, turning around to face the length of the boat and stretching her arms wide along the rail. 'I've got five of them. Five! They give my folks merry hell – out on the prowl all night like alley cats, using up a few of their nine lives, no doubt. They always land on their feet. Men are built for adventure.'

'And women aren't?' Kitty felt a sudden urge to strip off her dowdy clothes and dive into the deep blue water to swim with the dolphins.

'Well, *we* certainly are.'

'I'm an intrepid traveller!' Kitty shouted to the open ocean and the seagulls that wheeled above them.

She laid a hand on her stomach. A cramp in her abdomen and a sudden, fleeting wave of nausea reminded her that, intrepid she may be, but she was still at the mercy of an embryo that in all probability had claimed ownership of her body. She tried to bat that prospect aside and chewed with renewed enthusiasm on her piece of ginger.

'Is anything the matter?' Ida asked.

Kitty shook her head. 'I think maybe the drinking water doesn't agree with me. I'm still not quite right.'

Ida nodded. She seemed convinced.

Together, they set off for a stroll down the length of the deck and were invited to play cards by a group of three young men and two women from St Lucia. Ida resisted, at first, but when Kitty reminded her that they were spirited adventurers and when Ida learned it was a game of poker, she relented.

'I've never played poker before,' Kitty said. 'That's more my brother's sort of thing.'

'There's nothing to it, and we're only playing for matches. Come on. It's a cinch!' Ida said. 'Follow my lead, and remember, give nothing away!'

For the first time in her life, Kitty found herself sitting next to a man called Clyde in the glorious sunshine on the high seas.

'So, what do you do, Clyde?' she asked as he dealt her cards.

Clyde pushed his hat back on his head and chewed thoughtfully on a match. 'Bricklayer,' he said. 'Back in St Lucia, I'm a qualified dentist, but in England, I'm laying bricks in pre-fabricated panels for new houses.'

'You're a *dentist*?' Kitty asked, bemused.

He nodded and laughed dryly. 'I know. I know. A dentist working on building sites, right?' Shrugging, he picked up his cards.

At his side, his brother, Henry, grinned at Kitty and leaned in conspiratorially. 'I'm a geography teacher back home.'

'Really? How interesting. Any idea where we are?'

Henry shielded his eyes as he looked into the sun. 'I'd say we're slap bang in the middle of the Bermuda Triangle right about now.'

Wide-eyed, Kitty considered the exotic ring that his words had. She wished, how she wished, that her mother was a fly on the wall at that minute, watching her daughter, plain old Kitty Longthorne, playing poker on board a ship in the Bermuda Triangle. Then she remembered the stories about it and felt panic creep in. 'Is the ship likely to disappear?'

Henry and Clyde both laughed heartily at her and waved her concerns away dismissively.

'Guess what I do in England,' Henry challenged her. He took a swig from a hip flask and offered Kitty some. 'Rum?'

Kitty shook her head and blushed, wondering if he was trying to flirt. 'Not for me, thanks.' He was certainly grinning rather exuberantly. 'What would a geographer do if not teach? Work at the Ordnance Survey? Something to do with weather forecasts? Really, I've no idea.'

'Bus driver in Birmingham! Maybe they thought I'd learn the routes quicker.' He raised an eyebrow and made the sucking noise with his teeth.

'What are you all doing on board the *Tradewind*, then?' Ida asked, arranging her cards. 'Have you thrown in the towel?'

'We're going home to our family for our mother's sixtieth birthday and our niece's christening,' Clyde said. 'Back to the green Pitons and palm-fringed beaches.' He sighed heavily. 'Trying to persuade them all to come to Britain, would you believe it?'

'Yeah, man,' Henry said. 'We can all pile into one room in the only lodging house we could find that didn't have a "No Dogs, No Blacks, No Irish" sign pinned to the door!'

'Why on earth would you give up good jobs in paradise and move to England where you don't feel welcome, and it's always raining? I don't understand.'

'One word,' Clyde said, sipping from the hip flask. 'Opportunity.'

'There's nothing back home,' Henry said. 'If you don't work on a plantation or fish for a living – even on the bigger islands, like Jamaica – it's all crumbling in the towns. I'd rather take my chances in England for a few years, earn some money and go back home a rich man. Send money home in the meantime.'

Henry leaned towards her and reached out to touch her hair.

Kitty balked. 'Whatever are you doing, Henry? I'm an engaged woman!'

She expected him to sit up straight and apologise, but he didn't. Instead, he took a lock of her hair between his fingers and rubbed gently. He shook his head slightly, as if in disbelief. Only when he was satisfied with his investigation and she'd swatted his hand away did he retreat. The girls in their group shot him a withering glance, but he merely smiled their way and won the hand.

'You looked at my cards!' Kitty said.

'I was entranced by your golden hair.' Henry nudged her playfully.

Rolling her eyes, Kitty threw her cards into the middle of the small card table, said her farewells and left Ida to it.

It had been an enjoyable afternoon, and Kitty couldn't believe the high time she was having now that her nausea had abated, soaking up the sunshine in the Bermuda Triangle with young St Lucians. She couldn't wait to tell James all about it. Then, she remembered she was annoyed with him. Perhaps she'd write to him. Yes, perhaps she'd write but wouldn't send it!

She retrieved some thin airmail writing paper that she'd packed in her case and found a quiet corner of the upper deck, close to the lifeboats. She started to write.

Dear James,

I hope you are well and missing me. I confess, I am missing you, despite my best intentions. I'm still quite cross that you acted like such a spoiled little boy before I left. They say that absence makes the heart grow fonder, so maybe this trip will be good for the both of us.

As I write, we have sailed into tropical waters off Bermuda, according to a St Lucian geographer who just beat me at cards, would you believe it?! Can you imagine your Kitty playing poker for matches with a band of strangers? With a bit of luck, we'll make it through the Triangle alive.

I've met another nurse here. Her name is Ida and she works at the Infirmary as a sister, though she's training to become a doctor. I admire her pluck. She actually knows of Violet through a friend of a friend, but I didn't push her for too many details. I wouldn't want to spoil the journey!

My dear James, I do realise that I am not entirely blameless with regard to the tension between us before I left. Of late, I excel in saying one thing and then doing another. It's a side-effect of trying to meet everyone's needs

*and keep everyone happy, my own happiness usually being
last on the list. I'm so very sorry you had to cancel the
church just as you'd booked it. I hope when I return that
you'll forgive me and greet me with open arms. My heart
is still full of love for you.*

*I've been meaning to tell you that, for a while now,
I've been worried that I'd fallen pregnant with our
child. I have had an ear infection and a large helping of
seasickness, but I find a little nausea is still with me until
lunchtimes, and my time of the month has not materialised.
I daren't give it too much thought! I'm not sure I'm quite
ready to be a mother.*

At that point, Kitty paused to read what she'd written and
tried to see the contents from James's perspective.

'No, no, no!' she scolded herself. 'The tone is all over
the place, you daft ha'peth. Stop begging for forgiveness,
for a start.' She scribbled out the sentence where she'd
admitted fault. She imagined she heard Matron's voice,
ringing in her ears, offering words of wisdom. 'Show some
self-respect, girl!' Then, she struck through the mention of
Henry the geographer and the revelation about her feared
pregnancy. 'One minute, you're a doormat. Next, you come
across as nothing but a heartless hussy who doesn't want
her fiancé's baby. Kitty Longthorne! You're just rubbing
your new-found independence in James's face. Oh, it's no
good! None of it.'

She screwed up her first draft and was poised to begin
again, when she heard a commotion coming from the other
passengers on the deck below.

Gathering up her paper and fountain pen, she approached
the rail and looked for the source of the hullabaloo. It was

one of the passengers from first class – a finely dressed gentleman in his fifties or sixties who was peering through a pair of binoculars.

'Land ahoy!' he shouted, passing the binoculars to his wife. 'Look, darling. Look to the horizon.'

'What is it, Gerald? What exactly am I supposed to be looking at?' the man's wife asked, as she peered through the binoculars. Her beaded gown shimmered in the late-afternoon sunlight.

'Search me, darling!' he said, slurring his speech slightly as though he'd started early on the aperitifs before dinner. 'Could be Florida. Could be Bermuda. Surely we're not approaching the Bahamas yet. But whatever it is, it's bally land, I tell you! We're nearly there.'

Chapter 14

'Passengers for Kingston! Attention all passengers for Kingston!'

Kitty was queuing with Ida on the stairs up to the deck, straining to hear the announcement being shouted through a loudhailer by one of the crew. The rest of his words, however, were swallowed by the excited chatter of passengers. It seemed as though three-quarters of the souls on board the *Tradewind* were all squashing together on one narrow staircase, waiting to disembark.

The boat juddered as the engines were thrown into reverse thrust so that it could dock safely.

'This is it, Kitty!' Ida said. 'Jamaica, here I come!'

'Oh, you lucky beggar,' Kitty said. 'You're going to be off this tub within the hour, basking in the sunshine and ready to start your adventure proper.' She gripped the banister to steady herself as the boat lurched sideways. It wouldn't do to fall headlong down the stairs onto the crush of people below. She put a protective hand over her belly, then removed it before Ida noticed.

'I've packed all the wrong clothes!' Ida chuckled, glancing down at her armpits. They were ringed with sweat. 'I hope they have a market in Kingston. I'm going to have to ditch my normal togs and dress like a native in a grass skirt and coconuts.' She laughed with a little too much gusto.

'Oh, I say,' Kitty said, glancing furtively at the scores of Black passengers standing within earshot. 'Ida! Really!'

One of the women standing two stairs above them turned around and gave Ida a stern look, but Ida seemed blithely unaware that she'd said anything untoward.

Kitty looked down at her feet, wishing she could escape to the top deck to wave everybody off.

'Do promise you'll look me up when you're back.' Ida clasped Kitty by the hand.

'Absolutely.' Kitty squeezed her hand, then gently pulled herself free. 'We'll be changed women after this! Especially now you own a fortune in matches.'

Ida threw her head back and laughed. 'Poker Queen. It's my new nickname.'

The wait for Ida to disembark was stiflingly hot and uncomfortable. When the queue had inched forwards and the gangway was within sight, Kitty prepared to bid her shipmate farewell.

'Do look after yourself,' she said. 'I hope Jamaica lives up to your expectations. Come back with lots of nurses, won't you?'

Ida embraced her stiffly. 'I just hope I can get a decent cup of tea!'

Kitty was surprised by a lump of sadness lodged in her throat. 'It's going to be a bit drab without your company.'

Before she could say anything more, Ida was whisked away from her as the crowd surged towards the gangway.

Though the sun was already high in the cobalt-blue sky, goosebumps stood proud on Kitty's tanned arms. Butterflies were on the wing inside her. She was totally alone for the first time since the voyage had begun.

Climbing up to the top deck, she leaned against the railing alongside the remaining travellers headed for Barbados. They all exchanged shy smiles with one another. For the British among them, there was trepidation and anticipation in their eyes. For the Caribbean-born seafarers, Kitty saw only relief that they were almost home.

'Kitty! Nurse Kitty Cat!'

Hearing a familiar voice, Kitty turned her focus away from the throng of passengers spilling out of the belly of the *Tradewind*, onto the Kingston dockside. She was surprised to find Henry standing before her. Dressed in a bright green shirt and a rather dapper black waistcoat, he was chewing on a match and grinning widely. He tipped his hat to her.

'Isn't it exciting?' Kitty said. 'We're almost there.'

'Feel that warmth in your bones.' He jostled his way to the railings and stood next to her. Unbuttoning his cuffs, he rolled his shirtsleeves up to the elbow. His movements were easy and languid. 'Look at all that green.' He pointed to the mountains that rose beyond the turquoise waters, beyond the busy harbour and beyond the rooftops of the bustling capital.

'It's green in England,' Kitty said. 'Haven't you been to the Lakes or the Peaks?'

Henry shook his head. 'I'm always working.' He moved in closer and locked eyes with her. 'But I've always been a fan of a nice view.'

'Oh, Henry! That's quite enough, thank you. I'm very flattered, but I'm an engaged woman.' Startled by quite how forward he was being, Kitty took a step back and trod heavily on somebody's foot.

She turned around to apologise, only to find, much to her relief, that it was Mrs Lewis.

'De higher de monkey climb, de more 'e show 'e tail, young man!' Mrs Lewis folded her arms across her ample bosom and narrowed her eyes at Henry. 'This passenger vexing you, Kitty?' she asked.

Henry straightened up immediately, muttered some-thing apologetic-sounding beneath his breath and scarpered without even saying goodbye.

Kitty wasn't entirely sure what to make of the scene, but Mrs Lewis threw her head back and laughed raucously until she wheezed and tears appeared at the corners of her eyes. 'That boy! If I had a shilling for every girl I seen him trying to sweet-talk on this journey! You better watch yourself in Bridgetown, Kitty, with that golden hair of yours and your trusting ways. High wind know where ole house live.' She laughed again.

Wondering what on earth her cabin-mate meant about an old house, Kitty smiled with bemusement. She wasn't used to being the focus of men's attention now that she had that all-important ring on her finger. For a fleeting moment, however, she did revel in having been blatantly pursued by a man who was surely her junior by some five years.

Kitty kept herself to herself for the rest of the journey, which passed without incident. The night before they were due to dock, she packed her case. Carefully, she folded her clothes, which she knew would be utterly inadequate for the tropical heat. Capitalising on the fact that Mrs Lewis and Joyce were at dinner, she took out her precious photos. She had but five of them.

First, she stared at the formal posed portrait of her parents. It had been taken in 1938, before her father's arrest, when her mother's face had been plumper and full of youthful vibrancy. Elsie Longthorne had worn her Sunday best for the occasion. The work-worn drudge Kitty had always known was nowhere to be seen, replaced by a fair-haired siren, whose prominent cheekbones and expressive, long-lashed eyes transported Kitty all the way to Hollywood. Her father had stood behind her mother, holding her by the shoulders with strong-looking hands and clean fingernails. With a twinkle in his dark eyes, he'd looked proud to be by her side. His deportment had bordered on the elegant; his thick black hair had been clipped and tamed like a toff's. Kitty realised her father had been handsome back then. At some juncture in the past, her mother had thought Bert Longthorne a catch. She chuckled at the idea. Then the realisation that her father was a broken man, preparing for his grave, snuffed out her mirth.

She took a deep breath and moved on to the photo of her and Ned, playing in a makeshift sandpit as toddlers. It was a delightful image of them building a sandcastle in what had effectively been an old bathtub full of builders' sand, stationed outside their house in Hulme. There was more sand surrounding the tub than inside it. Their father had equipped them with the rig-up to keep them happy on a hot summer's day, much to the neighbours' chagrin. Kitty and Ned had been naked, but for their underwear, and almost indistinguishable in appearance at that age. She couldn't remember the precise details of the photo, but she recalled that a professional photographer had been capturing images of Manchester's terraced streets and its working-class inhabitants in the mid-twenties. Her mother had somehow got hold of a copy. It felt precious.

'Dear God, please let our Ned be well,' she said quietly.

She cocked her head to the side, wondering if she'd be able to feel instinctively if Ned had come to harm or not. Her twin's instincts seemed not to work any longer. She wiped a tear away.

Finally, she looked at the photo of James and inhaled sharply. Her pulse quickened. Her cheeks flushed hot. Here was her matinee idol. The man of her dreams. Dr James Williams was also one of the most demanding people she'd ever met and a prodigious sulk when the mood took him.

She clasped the photo to her chest and closed her eyes, allowing the tumult of emotions he inspired in her to wash over her. She slid the photo into her breast pocket, resting over her heart.

As she closed her case, Kitty was full of worry and regret. She shouldn't have left Manchester. She was risking too much. What if her father died before she returned home? What if James broke off their engagement because he'd had his head turned by some younger, more vivacious, less changeable girl in Kitty's absence? What if she really was carrying James's child and the trip jeopardised her pregnancy?

The door to the cabin opened and Mrs Lewis's daughter Joyce came in.

'You been crying, Kitty?' she asked.

Kitty wiped her eyes roughly with the back of her hand. 'Nope.'

'Homesick?' Joyce climbed up to her top bunk, where she slept above her mother. 'My father gets homesick all the time.'

'It's not that.' Kitty placed her clean smalls in a corner of her case. 'I'm just worrying about my fiancé, that's all.' She showed James's photo to Joyce. 'We were supposed to be married, but now, he's having to wait because I so desperately wanted to make this trip. I'm just worried . . .'

Joyce nodded slowly at the photo. 'Nice-looking, if you like that sort of thing. But why you worry, Kitty? You think you missed your chance? Don' rush de brush and trow 'way de paint. That's what my mother says. Making him wait a bit longer might do him good. You'll be a long time married. I'm certainly not rushing. You wait till you see all those handsome boys in Bridgetown!' She giggled.

Her optimism was infectious. Mrs Lewis and Joyce kept Kitty's spirits high until they docked in Bridgetown. They exchanged addresses and stood by the gangway in a huddle, laden down with their cases.

'You keep in touch,' Mrs Lewis said. 'If you don't find my niece, Gladys, at the Black Rock hospital, write me.'

They embraced and Kitty turned to take in the view of her final destination. There was nobody waiting to meet her, but it hardly mattered. Bridgetown spread out before her – the busy harbour, full of fishing vessels bobbing on the Atlantic and larger vessels, like the *Tradewind*, being loaded with sugar cane, bound for Europe and America. Beyond the harbour, she could see the city itself – more of a town compared to Manchester. Its white buildings dazzled in the sunshine. In the distance, she was sure she could make out the vast expanses of green where tall sugar cane swayed in the breeze. Flanking Bridgetown, she glimpsed a coastline fringed with palms, punctuated by the odd fishing village, perhaps.

'Crikey. This is something like!' she muttered beneath her breath.

As she disembarked the old tub that had been her home for the past month, she forgot all about her seasickness and the stink of the smoke that belched out of its giant funnels. She forgot about the cramped conditions in the cabin and Ida's snoring. She thought only of the jewel colours of this new world – the azure of the ocean, the emerald green of the fields in the distance, the blinding white of the crumbling colonial buildings. Most of all, however, she thought of Ned.

Jumping on a windowless bus that took her into the centre, Kitty dodged the sandy cars with their honking horns and pushed past locals who ambled slowly down busy streets that, in some cases, were nothing more than compressed earth. With the dusty ground still undulating beneath her, as though she were still on board the *Tradewind*, she followed her hand-drawn map to the hotel where Ned allegedly worked. Her mouth was dry. Her clothes stuck to her body, but on she walked, her suitcase feeling heavier with every yard she travelled.

She found the Hotel Bajan on the corner of a street in a part of town that was less than salubrious. Ragged net curtains billowed through open windows. The paint was peeling. The sign was crooked. It didn't surprise her in the least that Ned was the manager of a place like this.

Walking up the creaking steps into a reception area that was cooled by a rickety ceiling fan, she found a young girl behind the dark wooden reception counter. The girl was rocking in a wicker armchair, fanning herself with a single sheet of paper.

'Excuse me,' Kitty said, setting her case on the ground. 'I'm looking for the manager of this place, Ned Longthorne.'

At first, the girl didn't respond. Kitty wondered if she'd spoken loudly enough to be heard over the clickety, clackety fan. She raised her voice, though her throat was raw with thirst. 'I'm looking for Ned Longthorne.'

The girl's movements were unhurried and nonchalant. She sat up and leaned forward. 'Everyone be looking for Ned. You better get to the back of the queue.'

Chapter 15

Having been sent packing by the girl on reception and told to come back later that afternoon, when the owner might be there, Kitty made her way to the hotel that Matron had booked for her. As she stared up at the crumbling façade of a lacklustre, utilitarian-looking establishment, Park Hospital seemed a world away. After her odyssey, she was almost too exhausted to take another step. The prospect of collapsing onto a comfortable bed in a room that she wouldn't have to share was the only thing that spurred her on to climb the stairs.

'Kitty Longthorne,' she told the clerk on reception. She handed him her passport.

The smartly dressed, handsome young Black man checked her credentials and then treated her to a welcoming smile. 'Is this your first time in Barbados, miss?'

'Ooh, I'll say!' She fanned herself with the passport that he had handed back to her. The blades of the ceiling fan were spinning around but they only pushed out more warm air. 'Can't you tell?'

He reached into one slot among a large bank of pigeon holes behind him and withdrew a large Bakelite hotel keyring with a single key on the end. He also took out a note and passed both to her.

'Thank you.' Kitty took the key and read the note.

Frank Springer from the *Barbados Advocate*
is running an hour late.

'Is everything all right, miss?' the clerk asked.

Kitty smiled. 'It's fine. I'd made an appointment with a journalist, but he's running a little behind. Can I order something long and cold to drink, please? For my room?'

'We don't have room service here, miss.' He seemed to be appraising her as she wiped rivulets of sweat from her forehead and the sides of her face. 'But don't worry. I'll ask one of the bar staff to bring you a big pitcher of something. You look like you could use it.'

When Kitty turned the key and opened her door, she found a small room with a single bed positioned in the middle of a tiled floor. There was a battered coffee table with a vanity mirror on it and an old armoire that looked as though it had seen better centuries. Most importantly, however, it was clean and quiet.

Heading to the shared bathroom, Kitty was delighted to see that this was scrupulously clean and sported a deep cast-iron bathtub. She locked herself in and poured a cool bath, almost to the rim.

'An extra hour to play with. This is luxury!'

As Kitty sank below the water's surface, revelling in the womblike comfort of being submerged and hearing only her heartbeat, she tried to cast off her worries about James and her family and her missed period. She put her hands on her belly, certain that it was already starting to swell. Suddenly, the burden of her probable pregnancy seemed to weigh her down and leech out the remaining air in her lungs until fear of drowning gripped her and she saw stars. She sat up hastily, spilling water over the rim of the bath, onto the floor. She rubbed her face and smoothed her hair back.

'Pack it in, Kitty,' she counselled herself. 'Remember why you're here. You're representing Park Hospital. You're a capable, sensible woman. Deal with the here and now. If you're in the pudding club, you can cross that bridge when you come to it.' She patted her belly and turned her attention to bathing.

When she returned to her room, she poured herself a tall glass of fruit punch from the pitcher that had been left on her nightstand in her absence. She sniffed it for signs of rum but deemed it alcohol free. She lay on the bed in just her clean underwear and fell asleep.

Insistent knocking roused her sometime later.

'Visitor for you in reception,' came the man's voice from the other side of the door.

Kitty was nonplussed. Then she remembered the journalist from the *Barbados Advocate*. 'Coming!' she shouted, leaping off the bed and dragging some clean clothes out of her suitcase.

Once dressed, she hastened downstairs to find a young man sitting in reception. He introduced himself as Frank and took out a notepad.

'So, Kitty Longthorne. Right?' He smiled at her, pencil poised against his pad.

His green eyes were dazzling. His light skin told Kitty he had one Black parent and one white. She wondered briefly how difficult it must be to sustain a relationship between a white landowner and a Black Bajan.

'Yes,' she said. 'I'm representing the National Health Service, and we want your readers to know we're recruiting.' Her heart suddenly felt bigger in her chest, swollen with pride. 'We want your nurses. Your brightest and your best. And we're offering them enviable career opportunities in British hospitals. Tell your readers that!'

The lad noted everything down, nodding and smiling. 'What happens when all the nurses get on a boat and sail to England?' he said. 'What will Barbadians do when they need help? Who will tend our sick and injured if everyone's gone to London and Manchester and Birmingham?'

For a moment, Kitty stared blankly at the young journalist. Of course, she'd never given that a second thought. She'd agreed to come here for King and country. It had never occurred to her that in doing so, she'd be leaving an already poor colony impoverished even further.

'Well, the beauty is that the trainee nurses can study to become State Registered Nurses in Britain, and when they come back home to Barbados, they'll be fully qualified. They'll train with the very best medical staff, and get top-notch experience.'

The journalist scribbled in his notepad, nodding. 'But you're talking about already qualified nurses going over there, too.'

Kitty hadn't expected this sort of reception. She realised she was an ambassador for Park Hospital, but she hadn't bargained with having to show diplomatic skills, too. 'Well, of course, they'll be able to send money home. The wages for a State Registered nurse in Britain are modest, but I understand nurses' wages are among the lowest of any civil servant, here.'

She could see him scribbling furiously. What was he going to put in his article? The NHS was paying for advertising space in his paper, but local women whose interest had been piqued by the advert would read the accompanying story with a keen eye.

'Travelling thousands of miles to Britain on their own is quite an undertaking for our women,' he said. 'What happens when they get there? Where will they live? We've all heard stories of the signs on lodging houses – "No Dogs, No Blacks, No Irish".'

'Oh, there won't be any trouble with that kind of unpleasantness. Nursing accommodation is provided,' Kitty said. She smiled, relieved that this was something she could talk about with authority. 'I've been living in a nurses' home for years! It's comfortable. It's got all the facilities you need, and it's nice to have the camaraderie of the other nurses.'

The journalist scratched at his chin, looked at her with a raised eyebrow and continued to scribble in his notepad, while shaking his head. Would winning the hearts and minds of the islands' nurses be rather trickier than Kitty had imagined?

Chapter 16

'What do you mean, "Everyone's looking for him"?' Kitty asked, looking for a lie in the girl's impassive face. 'This is the address he gave. He told me he works here!'

With the heat still bouncing up at her from the sun-baked, dusty roads, Kitty had returned to the place where Ned was supposed to be working – the Hotel Bajan – as soon as her meeting with the journalist had finished. She'd found the same insolent girl sitting behind the reception desk.

From the counter, the girl took up a long drink in a frosty glass that dripped with condensation. The sight of it made Kitty's mouth water. The girl slurped the pink liquid inside through a straw. The ice in the glass made a tantalising tinkling noise. She set the glass back down, observing Kitty closely. 'You want to book a room?'

'No. I want to find my brother.'

Her indifference was replaced by curiosity. 'You're his *sister*?'

'Not just his sister. His twin.'

The girl's eyebrows shot up. She pointed to Kitty's face. 'He used to look like *you*?'

'Before the war. Yes.' Dizziness suddenly whipped the inside of Kitty's head around like a spinning top. She slumped against the counter. 'Oh, dear. I feel—'

'Miss Cynthia! Miss Cynthia! Come quick.'

Kitty felt two strong sets of arms lift her up. She was half dragged, half frog-marched past reception and into a dining room of sorts that was set up with sticky-looking tables and mismatching chairs. In the far corner was a bright pink velvet chaise longue.

'Lay her down over there. We need to get her legs higher than her head.' The voice belonged to an older woman. Miss Cynthia, apparently.

'I'm fine!' Kitty protested, trying to shake herself loose.

'Stop struggling, now,' Miss Cynthia said. 'Let us lay you down before you fall down.'

Again, Kitty tried to shake off the wooziness and the women. 'I'm perfectly capable of—'

'Are you now? I don't think so. It does tek one hand tuh feel a lice, but two tuh tek it out.' Miss Cynthia triumphed, strong-arming a very wobbly Kitty onto the chaise longue. She scrutinised Kitty's face and made her open her mouth and stick out her tongue. 'Get this woman a drink, girl.' She waved the receptionist away dismissively.

The girl sucked her teeth noisily and flounced off.

While she was gone, Miss Cynthia raised Kitty's legs on some cushions and perched on the edge of the chaise longue, staring intently at Kitty's face. 'Did I hear right? You're Ned Longthorne's twin sister?'

Kitty nodded. 'My boat docked this morning. He was supposed to come home a month ago.'

The girl returned, carrying the same kind of long drink she had been sipping in the reception area. Kitty allowed Miss Cynthia to prop her up and savoured the sweet, cold drink.

'Ah! This be what you need. When did you last drink?' The older woman said something in rapid-fire patois to the girl and she left.

'I had a glass of punch at my hotel. But that was hours ago.' Kitty started to gulp the drink down greedily.

'Easy now. Not too fast. You'll wind yourself.' Miss Cynthia tried to take the drink from Kitty.

Kitty held on firmly. 'I'm dehydrated. I know. I'm a nurse, would you believe it? I should know better.' She chuckled and drained the dregs of the drink, swallowing a piece of ice, and silently praying that the water it had been made with wouldn't give her a bad stomach.

When she'd handed back her glass, Miss Cynthia sat with her hands folded on her lap, expectantly and with an eyebrow raised. 'What did you say your name was?'

'Kitty. Kitty Longthorne.'

Miss Cynthia nodded sagely. She rose from the chaise longue and took a sheaf of paper from a heavy old sideboard that stood against the opposite wall. She waved the paper at Kitty. 'You're the one been sending these telegrams all these weeks.'

'So they did get here! I tried to get in touch with the Bridgetown Police because Ned never responded, and I was worried about him.' The sense that something had gone terribly amiss gnawed in earnest at the back of Kitty's mind. 'How come you never contacted me?'

'I got better things to do with my time and money than answer telegrams for Ned Longthorne. 'Specially after how he done me wrong.'

Kitty shuffled up the chaise longue, now that she was feeling more herself. She kicked the cushions away and tucked her feet under her skirt. 'Did you wrong? How? What's Ned done now?'

'I own this hotel. It's not much, but it's mine. I left your brother in charge, thinking a white man – a British man – would be able to bring custom in from abroad. Respectable, God-fearing customers who just need a clean bed for the night and a simple meal. His face . . .'

'He was blown up on a ship in the Indian Ocean during the war,' Kitty said.

'Well, respect due to a dog, as we say here. I felt sorry for him. That was part of it. And I could see he was a charmer. That man could charm the birds out the trees. He'd been on this island a while, working in a fancy bar just off Trafalgar Square, and his reputation come before him. Nobody got a bad word to say about the Englishman with the heart of a saint and the face of a devil. So, I gave him a job as manager, and he took over running this place while I went to Florida in America to see my sister. She having some trouble over there. Health matters. So I had to stay a couple of months.'

Looking at the empty glass, Kitty frowned. 'Sorry your sister's ill.'

'She fine now. She better than me, because *she's* not had her livelihood ruined.'

Kitty pictured Ned in her mind's eye, and couldn't quite imagine him entering guest details into a ledger and organising the char lady, the porter, the kitchen staff. She covered her face with her hands. 'Tell me. Tell me what happened.'

'I came back to find him running this place as a whorehouse. I kicked his ugly red-leg ass out of that door faster than you can blink. I'm a Christian woman, and your brother had half of the farepikas in Bridgetown selling themselves in my bedrooms, all putting their ill-gotten gains in your brother's pocket!'

Kitty clasped her hand to her mouth. 'He wouldn't.'

'He could and he did!'

'Where is he now?' Tinnitus started to ring in Kitty's ears. She was breathing too shallow, too fast. This news was beyond any Ned-like misdemeanour she'd imagined.

Counterfeiting coupons and running up gambling debts had been bad enough. If Ned really had been living off the immoral earnings of the islands' most desperate women, he'd sunk to a new low.

'I don't know and I don't care.'

At that moment, a bell dinged in the reception area. It dinged again.

'Where is that idiot girl?' Miss Cynthia asked. She rose to her feet, taking the empty glass with her.

Kitty was alone. She swung her legs round and sat on the edge of the shabby old chaise longue, wondering what shenanigans had come to pass on it. Scantily clad girls in feather boas cavorting with fat old white visitors to the island was an image she hastily blinked away.

'Miss?'

Who did that little voice belong to? Had she imagined it? Kitty looked around but saw no one. It must have been the dehydration talking.

'Miss?'

Yet there was the voice again.

'Hello?' Leaning forward, she peered beyond the doorway to what might have been the kitchens, judging by the smell of stale cooking that emanated from the shadows. 'Is anyone there?'

Fatigue wasn't playing tricks on her. A tall, whippy sapling of a young boy stepped into the light. He looked around, as if checking that Miss Cynthia or the surly girl on reception were nowhere to be found.

Kitty beckoned him forwards. 'Don't be shy. I won't bite.'

The lad looked no more than fifteen, judging by the wispy suggestion of a moustache above his top lip. He was wearing a striped apron that was covered in old brown bloodstains.

Beneath the apron, his trousers and hopsack top were old and darned in places. He bowed slightly.

'What's your name?' Kitty asked.

'Lionel, miss.' The lad kept looking in the direction of the reception desk.

'Lionel, you can call me Kitty. Look, do you know what happened to Ned after he left? Where did he go?'

He pressed his lips together, as if grappling with a moral conundrum. His silence made the air even hotter and more sluggish.

'Please! I need to find my brother. Can you tell me anything about what he might be doing now?'

Finally, the lad locked eyes with Kitty. 'Last I heard, he's running a bar.'

Opening her handbag, she reached in to retrieve her purse. 'Let me compensate you.'

Lionel shook his head and held his hand aloft. 'No need for that. I don't need your charity, miss. I'm just doing Ned a favour. I liked him. He was kind to me.'

She smiled as much as her taut, tense facial muscles would allow. 'Good. Good. Thank you, Lionel.' Straining to hear what was going on in reception, Kitty was certain that Miss Cynthia was still booking her new guests in. Hopefully, the surly young girl was with her. 'Tell me. Was Ned as bad as Miss Cynthia made out? Was this place really a brothel?'

The lad retreated into the shadows.

'Please! I need to know. He's my twin. Was he bad?'

Biting his lip, Lionel exhaled heavily. He was just about visible now, in the shadows that led to the kitchens. 'Worse. There was girls and gambling and drinking. Men came here to buy stolen things. Finery. Stuff robbed from the plantations and rich white men's houses. Ned had a real

Sodom and Gomorrah going. But he was kind to me. He was kind to the girls and paid them better than the other whorehouses. He's not all bad. He be a tainted dollar, but he still be gold beneath the dirt.'

'Where is he, Lionel? I think you know but you're not telling me. Did Ned ask you to keep it secret?'

The lad's left eyelid started to twitch and he wiped his hands on his apron.

'You really don't need to keep something like that quiet from me, you know. I'm his twin sister. I've sailed thousands and thousands of miles to find him. Ned would want me to know. Please, Lionel. Imagine if your own sisters or brothers had sailed the oceans, just to check you were safe and sound . . . and to tell you your father was dying.'

Miss Cynthia was audible on the other side of the wall, giving her new guests their key, by all accounts. It was only moments before she'd reappear.

Lionel glanced furtively behind him and spoke in a whisper, with quick, precise consonants. 'I think he's gone up the coast to Holetown. That's what one of the girls said to me.'

'Do you know where?'

He shook his head. 'Bet there's only one white man like Ned in Holetown. My guess is, he shouldn't be too hard to find.'

Kitty nodded, committing the name to memory, wondering if the place lived up to its name. *Holetown*. If Ned was there, she'd find him.

Chapter 17

Kitty's sleuthing trip to Holetown had to wait. The following morning, after a fitful night's sleep when she had tossed and turned, thinking about Ned and still feeling the bed undulating beneath her, as though she was at sea, she ate a light breakfast and promptly brought it all back up. Gripping the toilet bowl in the shared facilities on her landing, her head pounded.

'Come on, Kitty,' she told her reflection in the open lid of the highly polished black toilet seat. 'You can't let everything get to you. Not Dad, not Ned, not James, not work, not this pregnant business. You're a medical professional and you've got an important job to do.'

She flushed the toilet, slid to the side and leaned against the cubicle wall for a moment. She wiped her mouth with her hand, not wanting to get newsprint all over her face from the square sheets of old newspaper that were hanging from a piece of string nailed to the wall.

Finally, stealing herself to get to her feet, have another wash and clean her teeth, she made her way back down to the lobby of the hotel.

'Nurse Longthorne?' An authoritative woman's voice resounded through the warm air of the lobby.

Kitty turned to see a tall, elegant white woman striding across the space to greet her, hand already outstretched. She was dressed formally in an impeccable blue linen ensemble, wearing a felt hat, though it was already in the eighties and as humid as a heated indoor pool.

Kitty shook the woman's hand. 'Very pleased to meet you, Matron.'

'Call me Winifred.' She was more like a film star than a head of nursing staff. She spoke with a slight Barbadian accent.

'And I'm Kitty, senior nurse at Park Hospital in Manchester.' Kitty took out her notepad and pen. 'Tell me about the nursing on the island, Matron – I mean, Winifred.' She couldn't help pondering how different this woman was from the short, stout, formidable matron at Park Hospital.

'Our nurses are wonderful,' Winifred said. 'All highly trained, but you know, they're up against it, because the health of the islanders is very bad. Very bad indeed.'

'Everybody's health has suffered because of the war. We've still got rationing in Britain, as I'm sure you know. I was lucky to get fresh eggs for my dad's birthday cake!'

Winifred seemed unmoved by Kitty's tale of the motherland's suffering. 'The Germans had submarines watching our coastline. We couldn't get supply ships in with deliveries. It's been horrendous. Add to that, no general hospital on the island – just a few clinics.'

'I'm planning to travel round the island to see for myself how people cope. I'm down to see your Bayley Clinic tomorrow afternoon – if you'll have me – and I've got an appointment at Black Rock Psychiatric Hospital arranged for the day after. If I can, I want to travel to the villages to see what medical provision they have.'

Winifred snorted with derision. 'Provision! Ha. Don't set your expectations too high.'

'I'm sure it will be an eye-opener.'

'Take whatever you British think is a bad state of affairs and multiply it by three – no, four. But when you're back home, don't expect those with power to be interested.' Shunting to the edge of her seat, Winifred cleared her throat. She had a secretive air about her when she spoke. 'I heard that the British Chief Medical Officer, Dr Humby, asked a photographer from the *Barbados Advocate* to take a photo of malnourished children on the island. When Grantley Adams, the head honcho, found out, know what the reaction was?' She leaned forward and raised her eyebrows. 'Humby was given his marching orders.'

Kitty grimaced.

'Nobody wants the rest of the world to know what goes on here, and Westminster's clearly not interested. We've got the highest infant mortality rate in all of the Caribbean islands.'

Having worked on the maternity and children's ward in Park Hospital many times over the years, Kitty tried to imagine a nursing environment where there was so much death. 'I was used to soldiers dying on me during the war, but losing newborns and infants on a regular basis . . . I don't think I'd cope very well, emotionally.'

'It certainly takes its toll,' Winifred said.

'Well, surely you need as many nurses as you can get!' Kitty said.

Winifred shook her head. 'Our problem isn't a nursing shortage. It runs deeper than that. Our problem is poverty and no investment in the island's infrastructure. My girls work incredibly hard. They're bright. They care about the patients. But they can't live on fresh air. I understand that.'

'So you're happy for me to speak to them?' Kitty asked.

'Absolutely. If they have a chance of working alongside

world-class doctors and earning what a British State Registered Nurse gets paid, they'll be bringing money and expertise back to Barbados.'

With her second official appointment over, and nothing planned until the following afternoon, Kitty finally had her window of opportunity to visit Holetown. She made her way to the bus station and found the correct bus stop. A rickety-looking charabanc was already waiting there with its engine thrumming away.

'A return to Holetown, please,' Kitty told the driver of the already-packed bus.

She paid her fare, hesitating over which of the unfamiliar coins to give him. While he picked the correct amount from her open palm, she surveyed the other passengers. They were all staring at her. Two old ladies near the front seemed to be having an entire conversation about her, as though she was the most interesting thing they'd seen all week. 'Will you let me know when we get there? To Holetown, I mean.'

The driver looked her up and down. It was clear that he too had never before seen a white Mancunian woman, dressed for ten degrees and drizzle in the blistering Barbadian sunshine. He chuckled to himself. 'Sure thing, miss.'

A young woman with a wriggling, complaining toddler stood to let Kitty sit next to her on the inside of a double seat. Hers was a pained smile. She must have been a good ten years younger than Kitty – little more than a child, herself – but she wrestled with the sturdily built, wilful boy, pleading with him to behave.

One of the old women who had been gossiping about Kitty turned around and fixed the toddler with a look that could have melted the seat's upholstery.

'Sit still and do as your mother tells you, boy!' Her castigatory, teacher-like tone made Kitty jump. 'Or you'll get a beating!'

The boy suddenly fell silent, looking at the old woman with startled, wide eyes. Tears welled instantly, but rather than bawling heartily, as Kitty expected him to do, he stuck his thumb in his mouth and let the tears track over his chubby cheeks in silence.

Unsurprisingly, the old lady used the opportunity of turning round as an excuse to ogle Kitty. Kitty tried to look out of the window, but like the bus she'd taken from the harbour, this had no glass in the windows. The curtains had been drawn to shield the passengers against the worst of the midday sun. The stiff breeze from the sea, however, blew the dusty, scratchy old fabric against Kitty's face and made her cough. At her side, the toddler kicked out and planted his meaty little foot squarely in the middle of her thigh – hard enough to bruise. It was going to be a long, possibly fruitless journey. The ground was still undulating beneath her and now her stomach was audibly rumbling.

After a while, as the bus jerked and jolted over potholes on the coastal road that led north out of Bridgetown, Kitty was aware of a man watching her intently. He wore an eyepatch over one eye. Unexpectedly, he rummaged in his shopping bag and pulled a small brown object out of a paper bag. He stretched across and offered it to her.

'Eat!' he said. 'Your stomach so noisy, it be giving me a headache.'

Looking at the brown ball with alarm, Kitty wasn't sure what to do. 'Oh, it's very kind of you, sir, but—'

'It be a bake.'

'Oh, like a bun?'

'Try it.' He waved the small brown ball at her again, spreading the smell of yeast, hot oil and sugar all around the bus. 'Everybody like bake. Go on! Eat!'

Smiling timidly, Kitty took the bun. Its texture was reminiscent of doughnuts, though there was no sugar on the outside. Her stomach growled so loudly, then, that the little boy, who was starting to doze off, jolted awake momentarily. 'Thank you so much,' Kitty whispered. She bit into the ball. Though she was still parched, her saliva seemed to flood in from nowhere. She could taste sugar, oil and spices – nutmeg, maybe cinnamon. 'It's delicious,' she told the man, not caring that she was still chewing as she spoke. 'I've eaten barely anything today.'

He laughed and offered her another.

'I couldn't possibly!' Kitty said, wondering if the man could afford to be handing out his food to perfect strangers.

'You can, girl. Take it. It be a bun, not lost treasure from the seabed!'

Taking the mouth-watering delicacy, Kitty thanked him again. 'It's honestly the tastiest thing I've eaten since 1938.' She giggled, feeling the life flowing back into her – warmed, not just by the sun's rays permeating the curtains, but by the kindness of these Bajan strangers. 'You really are too kind.'

They struck up a conversation, and Kitty learned that the man had flown during the early years of the war in the Royal Airforce's Volunteer Reserve.

'There was only a handful of us,' he said. 'Me, my pal Errol and his cousin, Gordon. Ten or so other men. We went to England full of hope and righteous anger, knowing if Hitler won, we'd be slaves all over again.'

'How brave,' Kitty said. 'Did you see much action?'

The man nodded thoughtfully. 'I bombed that Jerry. We went on raids that would make your toes curl. Dangerous work. But I never made it past Aircraftman Number Two Class.'

'Why ever not?'

He lifted his eyepatch and showed her a mass of terrible scarring in answer.

'Were you shot?'

Chuckling, he repositioned his patch. 'Bird strike!' he said. 'I was coming in to land and a bird smashed through the windscreen of my plane. Beak went straight in my eye.'

Kitty clasped her hand to her mouth. 'I'm so sorry,' she said. 'How terrible.' She explained how she'd spent the war years, tending the war-wounded and, later, American Air Force soldiers. 'If I'd treated you, though, I'd have remembered!'

One of the old ladies turned around at this point and harrumphed loudly. 'You such a liar, Eugene Livingston! Everyone know you lost your eye because you stuck yourself with your own cutlass during cane harvest.' She turned to Kitty. 'How he managed that, nobody know. He was the clumsiest boy on the plantation.'

Eugene shot the old lady a furious look. 'Wait till you trough an' put bubble in it, Mabel Johnson!' He turned to Kitty. 'Don't pay no heed to her, dear. That old woman wouldn't know a war hero if he came and sat on her lap.' He tapped his eyepatch. 'I was the Royal Air Force's secret weapon. This here be my medal for bravery.'

The bus erupted into a highly entertaining but heated argument between the old people. Though she struggled to understand some of the Bajan dialect, Kitty discovered that a German U-boat had torpedoed a Canadian merchant ship just beyond the coastal waters of Bridgetown.

'We went hungry,' Mabel told her. 'The Germans cut

off our trade routes. You English think we had it easy over here. But it was bad in a different way. When you can't get no sugar for your tea in London, we can't put food on the table in St Philip. You take a look around the island, girl. People be scratching a living.'

Eugene interjected with some more outlandish boasting, just as the neatly planted fields started to become punctuated by roadside shacks made from corrugated iron. Shopkeepers were serving cool drinks to locals through windowless apertures. Some vendors sold pineapples from tables. People walked along the edge of the road, carrying large loads on their heads or driving laden-down donkeys. The men were dressed shabbily. The women wore brightly coloured outfits. Some wore sandals. Others didn't, but trod the dusty road with bare feet.

'It's another world,' Kitty said, staring at a woman whose baby was tied on her back by a length of cloth. Her stomach churned, and not just from hunger. It dawned on her that she was in the midst of the adventure she'd so desperately wished for – bumping down the road less travelled in a bus with no glass in the windows; the only white woman on board, gazing out at tropical trees she'd never seen the likes of before. Thousands of miles from the familiar drizzle of Manchester and entirely alone but for Ned, out there – somewhere. Kitty Longthorne was a daring adventurer. She smiled at the thought.

The shacks and roadside stalls were soon supplanted by simply built single-storey buildings with additional streets beyond, visible between the houses.

'Next stop, Holetown!' the bus driver yelled.

'Well, it was lovely meeting you all,' Kitty told her fellow passengers.

'You look after yourself!' Mabel shouted, as she alighted.

'Watch out for liars and thieves – like Eugene!' She cackled with mischievous laughter.

As the bus pulled away, leaving Kitty in a blizzard of dust, she waved and then turned to face her next challenge.

'Right, Ned Longthorne,' Kitty said. 'I'm coming to get you.'

Chapter 18

'Excuse me,' Kitty asked a middle-aged, smartly dressed man. He was hastening somewhere, carrying a briefcase. 'Sorry to bother you. I know it's a long shot, but do you know of a bar, run by a British man?'

He looked at her with undisguised curiosity. 'No, miss. I don't go to bars. I don't drink.' Then he went on his way.

Wondering how on earth she'd track down her brother in the small town before the last bus left for Bridgetown, Kitty found a post office and went inside. She remembered that she had a small, battered photo of Ned in her purse, taken in Blackpool when he'd been reunited with her mother, after his spell in a prisoner-of-war camp.

'So sorry to bother you, madam,' she asked the woman behind the counter. 'I'm looking for my brother. I'm told he runs a bar here in Holetown.'

The woman balked visibly at the photo. 'Lord have mercy.' She was about to hand the photo back when a somewhat younger woman, who was stacking stationery on shelves, stepped down from her little stool and grabbed her associate's hand.

The younger woman looked at the photo and her expression crumpled into undisguised fury. 'I know this bougeley come-ya. He got kicked out of his job in Bridgetown, I heard, and we had nothing but trouble since he came here.'

'Do you know where the bar is please, miss?'

'Why? You want a job there?' She made the sucking sound that Kitty now realised was an insult. 'You some red-leg farepika?'

'I don't understand.' Kitty looked at the older post mistress for clarification.

'She mean, are you a lazy prostitute looking for work, dear?'

Kitty balked at the insinuation. 'I beg your pardon!' She pointed to Ned in the photo. 'This is my twin brother. I'm looking for him. I'm not a—'

The younger woman crossed her arms and treated Kitty to a disparaging scowl. 'I live across the road from where your brother working. That place full of rummies making a rucka-tuk. Shouting and laughing, full of drink at all hours of the day and night. They there for the girls.'

Kitty's smile faltered. 'You mean, it's a brothel?'

'See for yourself.'

The woman gave Kitty instructions for how to find the little bar, tucked away in a residential street. Yet, when she got there, it was anything but discreet. It was indeed rowdy. A fight was spilling out of the front door as Kitty approached. Four drunken men were slurring at each other. Two women looked on from an upstairs window, shouting encouragement. They were dressed in corsets and feather boas.

'Oh, Ned. You're incorrigible.'

For the second time since she'd arrived on the island, Kitty entered a run-down establishment and was told what a rotter her brother was.

'He not here,' the bartender said. He was a man of about sixty, who looked world-weary, judging by the droop of his eyelids and his shoulders. He was cleaning a glass with a filthy rag. He wore a tan leather apron covered in stains.

'If you see him, tell him Benjamin McKenzie be wanting to have strong words with him. He owe me money for the extra hours I been putting in, covering for his absconding white ass.'

'Well, don't you know where your own boss is?' Kitty asked, putting the photo of Ned and her mother back into her purse. She didn't want even the image of her mother to be privy to the disappointing conversation that she felt certain was about to ensue.

He laughed ruefully. 'He been gone for five weeks, now. Just went off one night with a truck full of girls to a plantation house in St Philip. Running gambling and all sorts of bacchanal down there for the owner's son or something. They come back but he didn't.'

'Didn't the girls say why he hadn't?'

'I serve rum, not pussy. I don't speak to those women.' He spoke with disgust licking at his every syllable.

'Do you have an address?' Kitty asked. 'For the plantation house, I mean.'

He nodded and wrote something on the back of a beer mat. 'I been working here a long, long time, miss. Your brother took a job I wanted and deserved. He give the owner good references, you know. Told us he been a prisoner of war. Got an award for valour. No way can old Benjamin compete with an exciting war veteran, even if he got face like a donkey been in a fight with a truck. So, the owner decide to give an ugly Englishman a Bajan's job. Since Ned been gone, I did some digging. I got some friends in Bridgetown say his references be a fiction. He got kicked out of his last job! Small wonder he turned this bar into a whorehouse. Your brother is a liar and a bad man.'

Sitting down heavily on a bar stool, Kitty rubbed her face.

'Oh, Ned, Ned, Ned!' Exhaustion washed over her and she had to steady herself on the bar. Momentarily, she felt a griping cramp in her abdomen. With a sharp intake of breath, she put her hand on her belly. The painful twinges passed.

'You all right?' Benjamin asked, setting his filthy rag down.

She shook her head. 'I only docked yesterday after a month's sail from Liverpool. I've nowhere near drunk enough for this heat and I've barely eaten. What I did eat at breakfast, I brought back up within minutes. I feel like I'm still at sea! I've got a brother who's left a trail of devastation all over the island, apparently – well, just in the two places I know of, so far! I'm supposed to be over here recruiting nurses to come to England. But instead, I'm scrabbling around like a headless chicken, trying to find my idiot of a brother.' She didn't even try to keep the sob inside. Kitty wept for her exhaustion and her disappointment and her exasperation and for the worry about the fragile life in her belly.

'Here now, young lady!' Benjamin put a placatory hand on her shoulder. 'Before you go running off to St Philip on a fool's errand, let me fix you something.' He poured her a large glass of ginger beer and disappeared into the back. Moments later, he brought out a plate of food.

Kitty looked down at the dish, wondering what the various golden-brown offerings were. It certainly smelled appetising. Her stomach rumbled loudly in assent. Checking the cutlery Benjamin had given her for cleanliness and deeming it more sanitary than the glass he'd been rubbing away at, she took a bite of something battered and deep-fried. It was instantly recognisable as cold fried fish, except it had an unusual flavour. 'Mmn. This isn't cod. What is it?'

Benjamin smiled. 'It be flying fish.'

She set the plate down, alarmed. 'Flying fish? You mean, actual fish that fly?'

'What else?'

'Oh, I, er . . .'

'National Bajan dish. Eat up. Nothing wrong with that. These be leftovers from lunch. My wife cooked them for me. She the best cook in all of Holetown.'

Kitty pushed a fork into the gloopy mass next to the fish on the plate. 'And what's this?'

'Macaroni pie. Go on. Get it down you. You look like a good meal could kill you, girl.'

'I *was* fairly poorly at sea. And I've not been marvellous since.' Kitty pulled at the waistband of her skirt, realising for the first time that her heavy, perspiration-soaked English clothes, woefully ill-suited to a tropical climate, were now a couple of sizes too large for her, regardless of the swollen feel of her abdomen. 'I suppose a spot of pie is just what the doctor ordered.'

Without further delay and ignoring the stares of the male drinkers who were sitting at the far end of the bar, playing cards, Kitty gobbled up the simple meal. She washed it down with the glass of delicious ginger beer. 'Please tell your wife she's a talented woman. I think she may have saved my life!'

Taking her purse out of her bag, Kitty put some money down on the counter.

'I don't want that,' Benjamin said, waving his hand as if the money was a bad smell. 'Put it away. This was me doing a good turn for a girl in need, far away from home. If it was my daughter in England, I'd hope someone would do the same for her.'

'I insist,' Kitty said. 'Please. After all Ned's put you through, paying my way for my dinner is the least I can do. The Longthornes owe you. Not the other way round.'

Benjamin took Kitty's money, but he repaid her honesty by arranging a ride out to the plantation house. He gave her two bottles of ginger beer and a parcel.

'What are these in aid of?' She took them, bemused.

'There's a slice of cassava pone and some Bajan black cake to keep you sweet. My nephew, Philbert, has agreed to take you to your brother. He got a delivery to pick up from the cane factory out there. But I warn you, the going's not easy. You looking at a good three or four hours' journey time.'

Trying to hide her disappointment, Kitty looked through the open door to the street outside. She glimpsed wheels, but they didn't belong to a car. Perhaps Philbert was parked across the street. 'It's really no trouble to make my own way there, you know,' Kitty said, feeling suddenly awkward at the prospect of a four-hour-long trek across country with a strange young man. 'I could get the bus.'

'It be an imaginary bus, then.' Benjamin chuckled and turned to serve a customer. With a rum bottle in his hand, he glanced back at her. 'Go! Your chariot awaits.'

Emerging from the dark and stale air of the bar, Kitty blinked in the still-brilliant light. Sundown was a couple of hours away, meaning she'd be arriving at the plantation house in the dark. She looked for a car or a truck, parked close to the bar. The street was empty but for a rough, uncomfortable-looking cart, pulled by a donkey who brayed at her as if the sweat stains beneath her arms caused it mortal offence.

She was just about to go back in to tell Benjamin that his nephew had driven off, when the young man holding the donkey's reins hopped down and doffed his straw hat.

'Miss. You want me to help you up onto the cart?' he said.

Kitty blinked hard, her brow furrowing. 'Sorry, I don't . . .'

'Philbert,' he said, extending his hand for her to shake. 'I be taking you out to the plantation house. Pleased to meet you.'

Chapter 19

'It's very kind of you to let me hitch a ride,' Kitty said, gripping the side of the cart for all she was worth, terrified that the donkey would drag them into a rut in the road and send her flying into a cane field.

'No problem at all,' Philbert said. 'Any friend of my uncle be a friend of mine.'

Kitty was glad that they were heading out of town and into the countryside, though the children who cycled battered old bicycles along the road stared at her as they passed, crying out something unintelligible to one another in their Bajan dialect. Was their curiosity aroused because she was a stranger in town, or was it because she was a white woman, sitting in a donkey cart with a Black man? She knew there were some white people in Barbados. She'd read about the ruling 'plantocracy' before she'd left, and she assumed the son who'd hired Ned's immoral services was one of the white ruling class, where the family's money had been made from sugar cane plantations and slavery. Observing the looks of incredulity on the children's faces when they saw her in the cart, though, she did wonder if there was the same level of segregation in Barbados as there famously was in America. *Should I ask Philbert?* she thought. *No. It might be impolite. Come on, Kitty. Think of something else to talk about!*

'What takes you out to the plantation, then?' she asked.

Philbert rummaged in a bag on the seat beside him and pulled out a fat green stalk. 'Here, miss. Have a chew on this. It be sugar cane.' He shoved a stick of cane in his own mouth and made encouraging noises.

Kitty tentatively took the cane he'd given her and sucked on the end. It was powerfully sweet and sent a shiver down her spine. 'Crikey! So this is where sugar comes from?'

Philbert nodded. He pointed to the field they were passing. It was one of the few where the tall canes had been cut to stubs. In the middle of the flat expanse, children were flying brightly coloured kites on the sea breeze. 'We in crop. That mean the cane be ready to harvest. I bringing jars of molasses into town to sell, so I got to drive there and back to the factory. I take you past there on the way. You never smelled anything so good in your life, miss.'

'Please, do call me Kitty.'

'Yes, Miss Kitty.'

Kitty looked down at his left leg and noticed, now he was sitting, that his trouser leg had ridden up to reveal a leg iron and cumbersome boot. It was clear he had suffered from polio as a child. Kitty wondered that she hadn't noticed it when he'd helped her into the cart.

'I've just noticed your leg,' she said. 'You poor thing!'

'No big deal,' Philbert said. 'At least I alive and working. Keeping the family fed. All this mean is that I drive a donkey cart instead of digging cane holes for five hours a day. That's tiring work. And then, the reaping. All back-breaking work, so I'm not complaining that I get to sit in my cart and enjoy the sunshine and the sea.' He pointed to the glittering Atlantic in the distance. It was a thick turquoise band beyond the flat green of the land – God's own playground, met by the majesty of the almost royal-blue sky. 'Beautiful. I bet England be very different.'

Kitty chuckled. 'I think I last saw the sun in 1942!'

They rode in companionable silence for a while. The sun had started to dip, painting the late-afternoon sky in fiery red, pink, orange and purple, when she spotted a large house some way off – almost the same vibrant yellow as turmeric, with white shutters on every upstairs window. A sprawling two-storey pile, fringed by tall palms, even from a distance it was clear that it dwarfed any of the modest little buildings and shacks they'd passed so far. Kitty squinted to make out the detail: the colonial façade boasted a large white colonnade at raised-ground level with a grand, centrally placed staircase that swept down to the gardens. 'Is that it?' she asked, feeling her heart pick up pace at the thought of finally finding her brother.

'Yes, Miss Kitty. That be the plantation house.'

In the fields surrounding the house, workers were still busy hacking away at the sugar cane. They paused briefly to straighten up, grabbing at their lower backs with one hand, nonchalantly dangling their long machetes at their side in the other. Men were loading giant bales of cane onto the backs of carts, just like the one Philbert was driving. The workers waved to Philbert, their enthusiasm faltering when they caught sight of Kitty at his side.

'They wondering what I'm doing with you. Tongues will be wagging.' He chuckled.

The donkey plodded on and on through the vast acreage belonging to the plantation house's owners. Now, whenever the cart struggled over a rut or a large stone, Kitty no longer felt every jolt in her tired bones. She was beyond discomfort. Her bottom was numb. She had been travelling for longer than she'd thought was humanly possible and, laughably, right at the end of her odyssey, when she needed to be alert, sleep was trying to claim her. *Wake up, Kitty!* she told herself. *You've got to stay awake for Ned.* The sun was setting in earnest, however, telling her to sleep, sleep, sleep.

Caught in the twilit world between wakefulness and sleep, with her eyelids drooping in earnest, she barely noticed the manicured gardens as the cart trundled up to the house. She paid little heed to the maid at the upstairs window, drawing the curtains. Nor did she really notice the high-pitched whine of the mosquitoes that buzzed around her in anticipation of a sundown feast.

'You be itching in the morning,' Philbert said. 'Make sure you rub some lemon juice on you when you get a chance. Those mosquitoes love British blood.'

Kitty was wide awake then. She slapped at her arms, suddenly feeling every tiny sensation as a mosquito sucked at her blood. 'Mosquitoes! Of course! Oh, dear. I haven't brought a net with me and it's dark.' She felt the blood drain from her cheeks. She'd checked the malaria risk before travelling and had discovered that it hadn't been a problem on the island since the twenties, but this didn't dispel her blind panic. 'Does the lemon work?'

Philbert pulled the cart up outside the house. 'Not really. But I bet they got citronella candles inside or some of that new fancy DEET.'

'I don't even know what I'll do for a bed for the night, if my brother's not here. I didn't think any of this through. Darn it!'

Helping her down from the rough, unforgiving old cart, Philbert shrugged. 'You be white. They gonna give you a bed for the night, all right. No problem. But if it come to the worst, you come and find me at the cane factory. I'll sort out some real Bajan hospitality. It might not be fancy, but the welcome be genuine warm.'

'Thanks, Philbert,' Kitty said, shaking his hand. 'I'll not forget your kindness.'

The cart trundled off. With the sound of crickets trilling all around her and the honeyed smell of night-scented flowers on the air, Kitty ascended the stairs and rang the bell to the plantation house. Was this a fool's errand? She cursed her lack of forethought. She had to be back in Bridgetown by the following afternoon, for more exploratory meetings with community leaders and a doctor who ran his own small, private clinic. Yet, here she was, alone and standing on the doorstep of strangers, being eaten alive by mosquitoes.

The door was opened by a Black maid in full uniform. 'Can I help you?'

Where should she begin? 'My name's Kitty Longthorne. I'm looking for my brother, Ned. I was told this is the last place he was seen.' Her heart pounded against her ribs. Beyond the maid, she caught sight of a shining marble floor and a splendid crystal chandelier hanging from a double-height atrium. Ceiling fans whirred away alongside it, making the lush palms in large planters nod in the breeze. Even at a glimpse, the place reeked of opulence on a scale she'd never witnessed before. 'He's the manager of a bar in Holetown. British. Disfigured face.'

The curl of the maid's lip told Kitty all she needed to know. 'You better come in, miss. I'll announce your arrival.'

Kitty was asked to take a seat on a lavish gilt chair, the likes of which she'd expect to see in some French chateau. Still, she was relieved to be sitting on something that wasn't bone-hard and being pulled by a truculent donkey. Even with the fans a-whir above her, Kitty was compelled to fan herself with an old copy of *Vogue* that had been lying on the occasional table next to the chair. Her hair clung to her clammy forehead. *What a fright I must look*, she thought, trying to catch sight of her reflection in the gleam of the marble floor.

Beyond one of the tall doorways, dinner was being served by two young maids, overseen by a formally dressed butler.

These people live like kings, she mused. *What on earth is our Ned doing here, rubbing shoulders with the likes of plantation owners?* More to the point, where *was* Ned?

Presently, a young man came out to greet her. He was dressed in a tuxedo as though he'd stepped straight off a movie set in Hollywood. He took her hand and kissed it. 'My dear. I'm charmed. Ned never told me he had a beautiful sister.'

'Where is—?'

'Do forgive me for leaving you to your own devices, no doubt wilting in the heat.' Her host snapped his fingers and a maid appeared from the dining room. 'Fetch our guest some lemonade,' he told the maid.

She bobbed deferentially and returned to the dining room.

Kitty craned her neck to see who was inside. Might Ned be there? 'You have a lovely home, and you're very kind, bringing me lemonade and all. But tell me, Mr . . .'

'Humphrey Buchanan. You can call me Humphrey. Humph to my friends.'

'Of course. Humphrey, I've travelled six thousand miles to find him. Please tell me where my brother is.'

At that moment, there was a squeak of wheels coming from the direction of the dining room. A leg appeared first, covered in a thick white cast. Then, the front wheels of a wheelchair. Finally, the invalid came into full view – half dressed in a claret-coloured satin dressing gown with his arm also in plaster, being pushed by a beautiful young Bajan girl.

'Ned!' Kitty cried.

Chapter 20

'Where the hell have you been, Ned Longthorne?' Kitty yelled, trying to make sense of the sight of her brother: encased in plaster like the war-wounded, yet carrying a large glass of red wine in his good hand, as though he'd been about to toast the good life. 'We waited for you at Liverpool docks. I stood, like a berk, until the last passenger got off the boat. Then, I find out you didn't even get on the blinking thing. Dad won't get another birthday, you do realise that, don't you?' Balling her fists, Kitty felt like flames might erupt from her mouth and sparks might fly out of her eyes. Instead, tears burst forth, causing her to hiccough and splutter as she spoke. She could feel a flush of angry red spread across her skin to her very hair follicles.

'Kitty!' Ned passed his wine glass to the Bajan girl. Despite the heavy scarring to his face and having one expression-less glass eye, the shock at seeing his twin sister there was clear. His remaining good eye was wide with surprise. The tendons in the back of his free hand were taut and white where he gripped his thigh. 'I never—'

'No, you never. That's right. You never think about anyone but yourself. You never get in touch unless you want something. You never.' Her anger started to subside, and Kitty was overcome by relief. 'Thank God you're alive!' She ran to his wheelchair and collapsed onto her knees, embracing him as best as she could. 'You idiot!'

'What on earth are you doing in Barbados, Kitty?' Ned asked. There was embarrassment in his voice.

Kitty got to her feet, aware once again that she was in somebody else's very grand house, surrounded by strangers. She wiped her cheeks hurriedly, noting the look of amusement on the owner's face and the awkward body language of the Bajan girl. 'Don't think I just came looking for you, Ned Longthorne! Although I thought you should know, Dad's dying, and I did want answers when *none* of the telegrams I sent to you in Bridgetown got a response. I even tried the police.'

Ned blanched. 'Oh?'

'They'd heard nowt. You can breathe easy.' She sniffed. 'Maybe some things are better discussed in private, eh?'

He nodded and then smiled. 'Let me introduce you, Kitty.' He pointed to the man in the tuxedo. 'This is my friend and patron, Humphrey Buchanan.'

'Yes. We've met.'

Humphrey bowed in dramatic fashion. 'At your service, miss. It's a pleasure to have you in my humble home.' He gestured towards the dining room with a well-manicured hand. 'I hope you'll allow me to show you some true Barbadian hospitality. If you've come all the way from England, you must be famished.'

Kitty's stomach rumbled loudly at the suggestion. She'd eaten nothing since the last slice of cake, hours ago, and then, she'd shared it with Philbert, giving him the lion's share. 'Well . . . that sounds very . . .' If Benjamin were to be believed, this Humphrey had been carousing with Ned's whores. What kind of a man was he? What kind of a woman would that make Kitty, to consort with his type? And what kind of girl was tending her brother? She quickly appraised the modestly dressed Bajan and then turned back to her host. 'It sounds just the ticket. Thank you, Humphrey.'

Humphrey took her hand and kissed it. 'My pleasure.'

'And who's this?' Kitty asked, smiling at the girl, trying hard to hide her cynicism and suspicion. 'Are you nursing my brother, or did he sustain these wounds fighting for your . . . ardour?'

The girl opened her mouth to respond, but Humphrey had wrested the wheelchair from her grip and spun Ned around to face the other way. He pushed Ned into the dining room, shouting over the girl's timid answer. 'Dinner awaits, fair Kitty! Follow me!'

'I'm Grace,' the girl said. She was still clutching Ned's glass of red wine. 'Grace Griffith.'

She spoke so quietly that Kitty had to read her lips to decipher what she was saying. 'Grace? Griffiths?'

'Griffith. No "S" on the end.'

Kitty desperately wanted to ask her the unthinkable, but common decency and her gut instinct told her that there was more to Grace's story than her simply being a prostitute. Prostitutes didn't wear calf-length home-sewn dresses that looked like hand-me-downs from the 1920s. Prostitutes didn't wear their hair in severe braids, with low-heeled, simple sandals on their feet. Was it possible that Ned had a Bajan girlfriend? 'And how come you're pushing my brother's wheelchair? In fact, why is my brother in a wheelchair?'

'I think you'd better ask him yourself,' Grace said, looking at the gleaming marble floor. She clasped her hands together, tugging awkwardly at her own fingers. 'I'm just looking after him.'

'Are you coming, Kitty?' Ned shouted through to the hall.

Kitty had no option but to follow, if she was to unravel the mystery.

The dining room was filled with light and delicious smells. The long rosewood table was groaning with tureens and domes – a feast fit for royalty. Kitty's mouth watered almost uncontrollably.

'My word. Is it somebody's birthday?' she asked.

The other guests – white people in their twenties and thirties, seated around the table and dressed to the nines in evening wear – laughed at her comment, but their laughter sounded superficial, and they exchanged knowing glances with one another. Or was that the fatigue taking over?

'Kitty, allow me to introduce my friends,' Humphrey said. He trotted out a list of upper-class-sounding names that Kitty would never remember. 'My father's away in New York on business. While the cat's away, Humphrey and chums do play!' He snapped his fingers at the butler. 'Music, Beresford!'

Beresford, whose short, curly hair was peppered with white, perhaps marking him out as a long-serving member of the plantation's domestic staff, put the needle of a gramophone on an old seventy-eight. The crackling, tinkling sound of jazz permeated the room.

Humphrey started to click his fingers. He took Kitty's plate and clumsily piled it high with food, humming and waggling his head in time to the music as he did so. When he presented the plate to her, he did so with a flourish, scatting along with the vocalist on the recording. He waved the food under her nose.

'Scoobidadoo, dabadoo, ladidaa . . . the maids usually do this. Can't you tell? Ha ha.' He slammed the plate down. 'Here you go, my dear. Beaujolais? It's not French, but it's still drinkable.' Without waiting for a response, he made to fill an enormous glass. As he did so, his gaze lingered on her chest.

Kitty put her hand over the glass just in time. 'I'll stick to the lemonade, if it's all the same to you.'

Was he hospitable and eccentric or merely mad and trying to humiliate her in some way? Kitty couldn't tell. She was so ravenous, it didn't matter. She looked down at the array of glittering silverware carefully placed around her plate, wondering which set of knives and forks to use. A couple of other guests started to snigger. Stuff them, if they were sniggering at her! She didn't care. Opting for the largest knife and fork, reasoning they were probably for the main course, she took a mouthful, chewed thoughtfully and turned to Ned. 'Now, how about you tell me why you're here and how you got in that state?'

Ned dabbed at his mouth with a napkin. He looked at the other guests, as if considering whether it was safe to talk about the circumstances around his broken limbs. He blinked repeatedly and returned his gaze to his plate. 'I arranged a party for Humphrey, here.'

I can guess exactly what sort of a shindig that was, Kitty thought. She kept her assessment to herself, however, and glanced again at Grace, though she kept her words for Ned. 'Go on. And try looking me in the eye while you tell me all this. I've sailed thousands of miles. I think it's the least you can do.' She kept her voice low, not wanting the other guests to be privy to his revelations.

Finally, Ned turned to her and looked at her chin.

'Hey!' She snapped her fingers. 'Up here.' Kitty pointed to her eyes.

'I fell out of a window,' Ned said. He shook his head and smiled wryly. 'Anyway, what's this about Dad? Last time I saw him, he was right as rain.'

'Cancer.' The smile slid from her brother's face, but she

went on. 'Now stop trying to change the subject. You fell out of a window – how, exactly?'

'High jinks. What can I say?'

'The Buchanan Plantation is a damn sight more comfortable than being laid up in a clinic in Bridgetown with the great unwashed,' Humphrey added. He took a large slug of red wine. When he spoke, his tongue was black and his teeth were dark grey. 'Our Neddy boy had drunk his body weight in rum, hadn't you, you rogue?'

Ned grinned, though the sheen of sweat on his forehead and the twitch of the fork in his good hand said he was nervous. 'I wanted to look at the full moon.' He shrugged. 'I ended up studying the flowerbeds at close quarters.'

Through gritted teeth, Kitty said as quietly as she could, 'When this lot are gone, I want the truth from you, Ned Longthorne.'

'And I want to hear about Dad.'

'Later. I'm not doing the Longthorne dirty washing in front of this lot.' Within earshot, she responded, 'And who patched you up?' She noted the professional-looking cast on his arm. It didn't look like an amateur had done it.

'Gracey, of course. Our little Grace has hidden talents.'

On his far side, Kitty could see Grace smiling coyly. She whispered something to Ned.

Kitty leaned backwards to speak to her. 'Surely you haven't reset the bones!'

Grace set her cutlery down. 'Oh, yes. It was no problem.'

'How come? You're not a doctor, are you? I thought you were—' Kitty stopped herself just in time. She realised that Grace was not a feather-boa-wearing call girl, even if she had been working in a brothel.

'A barmaid,' Grace said. She chuckled. 'And a croupier, when there's a game on. Lord knows, I'm not suited to bar work and gambling. I don't drink, I think gambling's a tax on the stupid and I hate staying up past ten! But I was a qualified nurse before I started working for Ned. The only reason I left the clinic where I trained was—' She bit her lip and looked down at the napkin she'd screwed up tightly in her hand. 'My father died in a terrible accident. He worked at the cane-processing factory.'

'Oh, I'm so sorry for your loss,' Kitty said. 'How long ago?'

Grace shook her head and met Kitty's gaze. Her eyes were glassy with sorrow. 'Not long. Not long at all. My mother needed help with my brothers and sisters during the day, so she could go out and work. I just wasn't earning enough as a nurse, and we needed the money. I come from a big family. Ten children!'

'Ten!'

The girl's smile returned, though a veil of sorrow seemed to fall over her delicate features and dim its brilliance. 'Unbelievable, isn't it? My mother could earn more as a cook in a bank manager's house than I could as a nurse. I'm definitely earning more as a croupier!' She dabbed at her eyes. 'Ned tells me you're a nurse.'

'I am. But I'm not sure I could reset broken limbs and put them in plaster – especially not out in the country, where there's no proper medical facilities.'

'Humphrey has the means to get anything he likes brought to the house.' Grace glanced at Ned and then gave Kitty a look that implied much. 'And on an island where people outside of the towns are left to their own devices, you soon learn to do all sorts of things above your station. Dealing with broken bones is just one of them. Working in the cane fields and the processing factory is dangerous. I've seen some terrible things in my time.'

Ned had noticed that he was being left out of the conversation. 'Are you ladies gossiping behind my back? Literally!'

Slapping his good shoulder playfully, Kitty wagged her finger. 'Lady-talk. Mind your own beeswax. She spoke over Ned to Grace. 'Before I head back to Bridgetown, let's have a chat about nursing, shall we?'

When the meal ended and Humphrey had made it clear that Kitty *simply must* stay as long as she liked and could take the guest suite in the pool villa, Kitty fought off exhaustion to corner Ned.

'Right, I want that word with you. In private.'

He was struggling to light a fat Havana cigar one-handed, speaking with it wedged between his teeth. 'Can't you see? We're in polite company.' He looked over to the other guests. 'These are all potential clients of mine.'

'What? For when you take your den of iniquity on a tour of the island?' She grabbed the handles of his wheelchair and pushed him out of the smoky drawing room, where the butler was serving port.

'Where are you taking me?' Ned asked. 'Stop this. You're being daft!'

Kitty pushed him through tall French doors onto a colonnaded veranda at the back of the house. It was screened to stop mosquitoes getting through after dark, though she could still hear the chirrup of the cicadas in the garden beyond. The veranda smelled of the citronella candles that flickered in the balmy evening breeze. Out here, the furniture was all dark-stained rattan with fat, white linen cushions. Kitty sunk into an armchair so that she was level with Ned. 'I want answers,' she said. 'Why did you miss the boat, and why the hell are you running brothels and gambling dens out here? I want the truth or I'll have a word with the police! I mean it.'

Ned puffed on the cigar, blowing the smoke up to the ceiling. 'I missed the boat because I fell two storeys out of a window and broke my arm and leg. I'm sorry. I don't trust the clinics here. They're – anyway, Humphrey offered to get Grace whatever she needed to look after me at the plantation.'

'Why? Because you keep him supplied with prostitutes?'

Her brother looked offended. 'I'm just meeting a demand. I saw an opportunity and I seized it, Kitty.'

'But you already had a good job, managing that hotel. I met the owner. She was lovely!'

'There was no money in it. She wanted me to bring in British custom, and when I couldn't do it, she threatened me with the sack.' He pointed to his face. 'Have I got a face that drums up custom, Kitty?'

'You could charm the birds out of the trees, Ned. I've seen you do it. The minute you open your gob, people forget what you look like.'

Ned looked at the glowing embers of his cigar. 'I tell people what they want to hear, and I give people what they need. When my old boss went off for a while, I turned that place around. She just didn't like my methods. Neither did old Ben. But he's a blinking hypocrite, because he likes the extra money well enough.'

'You're living off immoral earnings, Ned! You're a common pimp! For heaven's sake! If Mam knew—'

'Mam knows nothing, and that's the way I want it kept,' Ned said, leaning as far forward as he could. 'Anyway, never mind the interrogation. Tell me about Dad.' He was close enough for Kitty to smell the port and tobacco on his breath.

'He's got advanced lung cancer and a secondary tumour on his spine. Doctor's given him four more months, at most, but I'll be surprised if he makes three.'

'Jesus.'

'You should have come home for his birthday, instead of leaving me standing at the docks like Piffy on a rock bun.'

'I fell out of a window, Kitty.' He knocked on his cast. 'Not much I can do about that. What's done is done.'

Kitty rubbed her face and groaned. 'You bring a gang of prostitutes out to a plantation for a night of highly paid debauchery and gambling. You get so blind drunk that you fall out of a window and you think that's an excuse for not sending a telegram? If Humphrey can set up an impromptu fracture clinic in his guest bedroom, do you think he wouldn't arrange to pick up your post and for you to send a poxy telegram to England, explaining that you're injured and can't sail? We've all been worried sick – even Dad, who's got enough on his plate as it is. Saying sorry would have been better than nowt!'

'I do what I can with the humble means God gave me, Kitty. I'm not whole and I'm not wholesome. The war saw to that. But you wouldn't understand what life's like for me, because you can't see the bottom of the barrel from up there on your high horse.'

'Go to hell!' Kitty shouted. She stood abruptly and marched back into the house.

'I'm already there!' Ned's unapologetic voice drifted after her.

As Kitty retraced her steps back to the drawing room, she bumped into Grace. 'Were you eavesdropping?' she asked, in no mood for niceties.

Grace clasped her hands to her chest. 'No, Miss Kitty. I was worried about Ned. That's all. I wondered where you'd both got to.'

Kitty narrowed her eyes, studying this prim-looking girl in her simple dress and plain sandals. Respectable working women from Hulme like herself and her mother had never been to a casino, but Kitty had seen one on Pathé News, in a feature on Monte Carlo. There had only been men working at the roulette tables. She tried to imagine this girl, dolled up in an approximation of a croupier's uniform or some glamorous dress. 'Are you hoping to bag my brother as a husband, thinking he has money?'

Grace's face crumpled into a glare. The warmth of her demeanour suddenly frosted over; her words were sharp as an icy winter morning in Manchester. 'I'm not the sort of woman you think I am, Miss Kitty. I'm proud. I don't need no man keeping me. I don't sell myself to nobody and I'm not planning on giving myself for a ring and a promise either.' She looked at Kitty's engagement ring and pursed her lips. 'And if you think I'd be after your brother's wealth . . . well, that's the biggest joke of all. Don't let this planta-tion and his fancy company fool you. Your brother doesn't have two dollars to rub together. He's only got rich friends, expensive tastes and big bad debts.' There was a dangerous look in her eyes.

Kitty clasped her hand to her mouth and shook her head. 'I didn't mean it like that,' she said. She reached out to take Grace's hand, but Grace took a step back. 'I was trying to warn you. I thought you might be soft on him. I mean – you seem to have a good heart, and I know some girls like a man who needs saving. I just wanted to warn you off him. Ned's a lot of things, but a good catch he isn't. He'd eat you up and spit you out.'

Grace pushed past her. 'You underestimate me, Kitty Longthorne.'

Repairing to the guest villa, Kitty was feeling more than a little on edge. Things hadn't gone at all well with Ned. She'd managed to insult her first potential nursing recruit. She was in the middle of nowhere, surrounded by nocturnal tropical wildlife she couldn't even see. The clicks and whirs of the creepy-crawlies and the hoots and hollers of the other creatures rang through the night. Was that a bat she spied, flitting from the canopy of one tree to another? She picked up her pace and was relieved to come across the swimming pool. The kidney-shaped pool was artificially lit, and the turquoise water looked heavenly beneath the star-studded sky.

'Good evening, madam.' A man's voice made her jump.

It was the butler. He was tidying spent champagne glasses from the little tables by the loungers. There were at least two overflowing ashtrays that Kitty could see.

'Oh, yes.' Kitty placed a hand over her fluttering heart. 'Good night to you, too. Thank you for—'

'Of course, madam. Sleep well.' He turned his back to her and started to stack the glasses on a tray.

Kitty continued on down the winding path but then she thought about her commitments the following day. She walked back to the butler.

'Sorry to be a bother, but I need to get to Bridgetown tomorrow, and I don't fancy another uncomfortable journey on a donkey cart, if I can help it. Is there a bus I can catch nearby?'

He shook his head. 'Tomorrow? No, madam. No buses coming this far out. Not till next week, at any rate. Next Wednesday. Only four days to wait, madam.'

Kitty swallowed hard. She was going to miss the appointments Matron had made with the leading medical professionals on the island!

Chapter 21

'What's that noise?' Kitty woke, splayed like a starfish across the double bed in Humphrey Buchanan's pool house. She wiped her mouth, looking up at the circulating ceiling fan.

Caw, caw. Something was making a terrible din outside. She checked her watch, still feeling the pinch of being four hours behind Greenwich Meantime. Five in the morning. At home, it was already nine. Outside, the sun was already up. *Caw, caw. Twit, twit, twit.* The birds were so much noisier in the West Indies!

Pulling her sweaty blouse away from her skin and downing the glass of water next to the bed, Kitty padded to the window and tugged aside the net curtain that covered it.

'Blimey.'

She glimpsed the manicured tropical gardens at close quarters for the first time. Just outside the guest villa, a peacock was hooting for all he was worth, shaking his magnificent petrol-and-green plumage, seemingly just because he could. The call of a pea-hen came from further away. Tiny, brightly coloured birds flitted to and fro, darting to a giant fan of foliage, the likes of which Kitty had never seen before. Was it a palm? What was the tree next to it? What were those fruits hanging from its boughs?

Perhaps her morning sickness knew it was only five, because it hadn't put in an appearance yet. Feeling curiosity draw her like a magnet to the world outside, Kitty pulled on the silky green guest robe she found in the bathroom and stepped outside, wearing her shoes with the buckles undone.

She stood only yards from the villa and looked around in wonder. Through the trees to her right, she glimpsed the sea. To her left, a winding path led through the most heavenly gardens she'd ever seen. The path was lined with hibiscus hedging, neat as a pin and covered in tomato-red blooms. Clip-clopping in her unfastened shoes over to a bush, she plucked a flower and pushed it behind her ear. Beyond the hedging was thick-bladed grass, ringing a bed full of candy-pink flowering shrubs. In the middle was a thicket of broad leaves sporting purple and orange flower spikes. She studied them intently.

'Birds of Paradise. That's what they're called.'

Kitty jumped, wondering who the voice belonged to. 'Grace!'

It was her brother's carer. Kitty was surprised to see her up at such an early hour, dressed like a school ma'am in a blouse and long skirt; flats on her feet. There was no sign of Ned. 'I was in a world of my own. You gave me a shock.'

'I'm staying in another guest house further down the path,' Grace said.

'But I thought—'

'Whatever you thought, you've been thinking wrong. I told you last night. There's nothing between me and your brother. And he might have been selling girls to these people, but I was never one of them.'

Kitty grabbed Grace's hand. This morning, she was pleased to see the girl didn't shake her loose. 'I know you're not. I absolutely didn't mean any disrespect to you last night, and I apologise if I caused offence. I can see you're a professional. I can see you're respectable. I just think – well, if I'm honest, I think you're too good to be keeping company with my gadabout brother.'

Grace nodded. 'He was suffering. And once a nurse, always a nurse.'

'Speaking of which—' Kitty raised a finger. 'Wait there. Let me throw some clothes on. 'Don't wander off. I need to discuss something with you over breakfast.'

Five minutes later, Kitty had rubbed her teeth clean with the corner of a towel, had had a hasty strip wash in the sink and was standing back on the path in yesterday's clothes. 'Shall we?'

She and Grace walked past the jewel of a pool and up to the house. The deep yellow of the exterior glowed amber in the early-morning sun, and the heat of the sun was already bouncing up off the pale stone flags that paved the poolside and paths. A maid greeted them, bobbing in deference to her employer's esteemed guests. Kitty and Grace were seated on the veranda at a large hardwood table, looking out over the gardens with the sea in the distance. All the insect screens from the previous evening had been rolled up, and a fresh sea breeze cooled them.

'If you knew the sort of place I come from, Grace—' Kitty said, allowing the maid to unfurl a thick, brilliant-white napkin on her lap. 'I've never seen colours as bright as this. We get stormy days in Manchester, and when the sun comes out against the dark grey skies, it's spectacular. Well, I thought it was, until I came here.' She exhaled deeply. 'How do you live in paradise? How do you get anything *done*?'

Grace chuckled. 'This is no paradise, Kitty. Don't be taken in by a bit of sunshine and a rich man's playground. This isn't the real Barbados. Humphrey's family made their money from the profits of slavery. There's centuries of African blood making this soil rich.' She didn't lower her voice. The maid, standing to attention in the background, seemed to be listening intently. 'Barbados is a breadbasket for Britain, but the locals go hungry. We're abandoned children of the motherland, taking scraps from the table in a crumbling empire. Why do you think a qualified nurse is pouring rum in a whorehouse to make ends meet?'

'I feel ashamed,' Kitty said. 'I've sailed for six thousand miles and I know nothing about this place.'

'You wait till you've been here a week; till you get a feel for the real Bridgetown,' Grace said, spreading butter on a freshly baked cob. 'You won't believe your eyes.' She took a bite and chewed thoughtfully. 'Mind you. You're white. I doubt you'll get to see the *real* Barbados.'

'Show me,' Kitty said. 'Come back with me to Bridgetown. I've got meetings with local big-wigs and medical people, but I want to see the truth. How the locals really live. You can be my guide.'

'Why me?'

'I think you should come to England to be a nurse,' Kitty said. 'I have a good feeling about you, Grace. The way you've tended Ned's broken bones. The quality of your knowledge and care. I want you to be my first recruit. Will you consider it? A fresh start in Manchester. Park Hospital, where I am – it's a lovely, friendly place. Think of it! Guaranteed work in the National Health Service. Money to send home . . .'

Suddenly Kitty remembered what the butler had said about the transport situation. 'Oh, blast! I don't think there's a bus to Bridgetown until Wednesday, and I've got appointments this evening.'

'Rearrange! I'm sure Humphrey will let you stay,' Grace said.

The maid poured them both a glass of orange-coloured drink. 'Mango and pineapple juice, madam,' she said, as if spotting Kitty's enquiring look.

'It's no good. I've *got* to be in Bridgetown later,' Kitty said, savouring the heavenly taste of the juice. 'Much as I'd like to live high off the hog here for a few days, and catch up properly with that daft brother of mine, I'm here to work. I've got a big job to do. If I can't thumb a lift, I'll have to walk it.' She put her hand on her belly and felt ripples of nausea start to wash over her.

Grace laughed. 'You're going to walk for four hours?' She glanced at her watch. 'Well, you'd better set out now!'

Tearing a piece off her bun and examining it cautiously, Kitty realised the ludicrousness of her suggestion.

Her plans were interrupted by the squeaking of wheels. Ned rolled through the French doors, pushed by a maid.

'Ned!' Kitty said, standing to greet her brother and wondering if the tension between them would have eased overnight.

Grace took the handles of the wheelchair from the maid, almost pushing her aside. 'I'm so sorry, Ned,' she said. 'I didn't think you'd be up this early. We never usually see you before eleven.' She wheeled him alongside the table, fussing over him proprietorially.

Ned fixed his eye on Kitty, waving Grace away. 'I barely slept. My leg was itching like hell beneath the cast, but that was the least of it. What was it Mam said when we were kids, Kitty? Never go to sleep on an argument. Well, thanks for the sleepless night.'

Sipping from her juice, Kitty considered her words carefully. 'It takes two to tango, Ned.'

'Unless you hadn't noticed, I'm out of commission. Tangoing is the last thing on my agenda right now.'

'Stop acting like a kid. Be a man, for once! Our dad's on his last legs, and here's you, cracking jokes!'

'Guess Dad won't be tangoing either, then.'

Kitty fought a strong urge to throw her napkin at her brother's head as she might have done when they were children. A cramping pain in her abdominal region reminded her that she needed to keep calm and not let him get to her. Beneath her napkin, she placed a placatory hand on her belly. 'Don't get cute with me. You stood us up – left me standing at Liverpool docks in the freezing cold.'

'Yes. You already said that.'

'I had to tell Mam and Dad that their prodigal son hadn't returned. And not a word of explanation or apology from you. You're not on. If I can sail for a month, take two buses and sit for over three hours on a donkey cart to get here, you can certainly ask Humphrey to organise a trip to the post office in Bridgetown to send a lousy telegram to Manchester.'

'Yeah. And you said that and all.'

Kitty ignored her brother's flippant responses. He needed to hear what an inconsiderate berk he'd been. 'Well, I'll keep saying it until you actually listen. If Humphrey's workers are shipping cane in trucks, are you telling me he hasn't got a car?'

'A Rolls-Royce, actually.'

'Right. So there's no excuse. You're just plain selfish. You always have been.'

Swigging from a cup of coffee that Grace had poured him, Ned continued to eye Kitty. Despite James having given him a new face, against terrible odds, there was still so much scar tissue from his burns that it was difficult for Kitty to discern his expression. Was he angry? Was he on the cusp of conceding? Was he remorseful? She decided to take a mouthful of bacon and let the silence absorb the tension between them. The air was thrumming with it. Even the maids were fidgeting awkwardly in the background.

'Is Dad suffering?' Ned finally spoke.

'He's on oxygen. He's coughing up blood and he can't control his bodily functions. We got the diagnosis just after his birthday.'

'And there's nowt they can do?'

She shook her head.

'He's got four months, you say?'

'Three now, I reckon, like I said. A couple of months at best, by the time I get back. If I'm lucky. I'm running the gauntlet, coming here.' Finally, they were communicating.

Ned lit a cigarette with his good hand and exhaled a plume of smoke. 'Lung cancer. Who'd have thought it?'

Kitty pointed to the cigarette wedged between Ned's fingers. 'Doctor reckons it's the cigs that do it. There's a study coming out next year. If I were you, I'd jack those in.'

Dragging hard on his foul-smelling cigarette and expelling two plumes of smoke through his nostrils, Ned scoffed. 'What do I care if I go early? What exactly have I got to stick around for? A face that could curdle milk, no home of my own, sod all prospects, no wife and kids . . . let's face it, what woman would have me? There's better-looking gargoyles hanging off Manchester cathedral.'

Suddenly realising that her twin was in pain beyond that from his broken limbs, Kitty shelved her grudge. She rose from her seat, moved around the table and, leaning in from behind, she put her arms around Ned and pressed her cheek against his. 'Daft apeth.'

'Get off me, you dozy sod!' He tried to slap her away.

Despite his best efforts, she held onto him as she had done when they were small – whenever Ned had woken in the middle of the night, plagued by night terrors. 'You *can* have a normal life, you know. You just need to forgive yourself.'

'I'm not a good man, Kitty.'

'But you can be. All you have to do is start acting like one.' She released him from her embrace and took her seat again. Those ripples of nausea became more insistent. She pushed the bacon away.

'Your sister's right,' Grace said. 'You've got a good heart, Ned. You've just got to stop hating yourself.'

Ned thumped the table. 'Shut up, the pair of yous! Stop telling me what sort of man I am. You two know nowt about me. You don't know what goes on in here.' Still holding his cigarette, he poked at his head. 'You don't know what I've seen; what I've been through; what I had to do to get back from Japan.'

'Give over, Ned! *Stop* feeling sorry for yourself,' Kitty said. She could feel hurtful words pushing against her lips. She thought of her mother, slaving away in an engine factory in Trafford during the war, now having to sew garments in the poor light of the parlour, while caring for a dying man. She thought about the millions who had been slaughtered by the Nazis; the hundreds of thousands who had died in the Blitz. Then, she realised it wasn't fair to ambush him in front of Grace. 'I'm going back to Bridgetown this morning. I'll see you before I leave.'

She left the table and swiftly made for her guest villa, where she vomited with gusto into the toilet.

Chapter 22

'Ooh, this is such fun!' Kitty yelled over the roar of the Rolls-Royce's engine. 'When you said you'd give me a ride, I wasn't expecting *this*!'

Her morning sickness had abated and she'd had no more abdominal cramping, thank heavens. Now, the warm sea breeze whipped her hair this way and that as Humphrey pushed the engine of the enormous beast of a car. With the top down and the sea glittering beyond the cane fields, this was a far cry from a journey down the Manchester Road with James in his Ford Anglia. She made a mental note to tell her fiancé all about it in a letter, which, this time, she would actually finish and send.

'I hope Ned will be all right for a couple of days,' Grace said, clutching her scarf to her head as though the wind might untie the knot beneath her chin.

'Never mind him!' Kitty turned back to grin at her new companion. 'Looks to me like he's been taking advantage of your good nature.'

With his arm resting on the driver's side door, steering nonchalantly with one hand, Humphrey glanced at Grace through his rear-view mirror. 'Poor Grace. Your heart is too big for your own good.' He turned briefly to Kitty, his hungover eyes only partly hidden by his sunglasses. 'Ned's got my legions of staff running after him. Don't worry, gals. Old Neddy boy's well provided for. I look after my chums.' He steered sharply into a tight bend and almost landed on Kitty's lap.

Kitty edged away from him. Humphrey looked the picture of Barbadian land-owning gentry – terribly dashing in his linen suit, cravat and sunglasses, driving this millionaire's motoring miracle across the Bajan countryside. It was hardly believable that he paid Ned to organise debauched parties with prostitutes at the plantation, turning the place into a gambling den and playboy's paradise. Yet, that was the cloth that Humphrey was cut from, she mused. He made an impression for all the wrong reasons.

'Oh, James. I wish you were here,' Kitty whispered to the breeze, hoping it would deliver her sentiments across the Atlantic. She realised that her annoyance with him was beginning to subside, leaving nostalgia and longing in its place. What would he make of her pregnancy? Would he be happy or angry? If it was the latter, would he blame himself or would he feel that she was responsible for the slip-up?

'Did you say something, Kitty old girl?' Humphrey asked, putting his hand on her knee.

Kitty brushed his hand away. 'Nothing. I didn't say a word. Keep your hands on the wheel, please.'

They came within sight of the cane-processing factory, and Kitty caught the delicious candy smell on the air. They passed the fields belonging to a neighbouring plantation and saw children playing in tall piles of cut cane, as their parents hacked away at what was left of the crop. They whizzed past shacks and donkeys and roadside stalls. Everywhere they drove, the locals paused to watch the car thunder by, as though it was the most remarkable thing they'd seen for months.

Before long, they scudded into the outskirts of Bridgetown and Humphrey was forced to slow the car's pace. This time,

Kitty took note of the ramshackle quality of people's homes – single-storey dwellings, clad in brightly coloured clapboard. The paint was often peeling, with no glass in the windows and corrugated-iron sheeting for a roof instead of slates. The children who played out front looked underfed, with no shoes on their feet. The adults were dressed shabbily, as though they wore hand-me-downs that were by far the worse for wear. These were not affluent neighbourhoods.

Nearer the centre, the stucco and paint on the grander, older official buildings were a picture of faded splendour, thanks to years of neglect and having to endure the vagaries of the weather – baking-hot dry seasons, hurricanes in the wet seasons, brine in the air. The citizens of Bridgetown sauntered, rather than walked. At home in Manchester, everyone seemed to scurry with their heads bent against the gusting wind or the driving rain – stooped, as though the heavy rainclouds were pressing down on them, washing the colour out and leaving only grey. Here, the people's bearing was more upright, their demeanour more open and friendly, the colours brighter. They looked better fed than their rural counterparts, but Kitty thought they still had an air of want about them – more so the Black folk than the mixed-heritage middle or white upper classes. Yet Kitty suddenly felt embarrassed to be British.

Humphrey pulled up outside Kitty's humble hotel, causing several pedestrians to stop and stare. He got out of the car and opened the door for her. Kitty took his hand and stepped onto the running board, into the dusty street. She withdrew her hand quickly.

'Thanks for the lift,' she said. 'And for your incredibly warm welcome.'

'At your service, ma'am,' he said, bowing ostentatiously and grinning.

Kitty noted with distaste that he didn't open the door for Grace. The tightness around Grace's eyes and the downward turn of her mouth said she'd registered the slight, too.

'I'll be back to see Ned before I leave,' Kitty said. 'Please keep him out of mischief!'

The Rolls-Royce swept away, leaving the two women alone.

'Is he always like that?' Kitty asked.

'Rude, you mean? Full of double standards?' Grace took out her handkerchief and wiped some dust off her sandals. She looked up at Kitty, raising her eyebrows pointedly.

Together, they entered Kitty's humble hotel.

'Will you sit in on the visit from one of the community elders?' Kitty asked.

Grace nodded. 'Where they coming from?'

'St Lucy.'

'All that way to meet you? I've got cousins in the north of the island. I haven't seen them in a couple of years, though. There's nothing up that way except – well, nothing. It's behind God's back! Fishermen's huts and fields. Certainly no nurses up there. Anyone with a decent brain and some ambition ends up moving to Bridgetown to find work.'

Kitty noticed that the clerk on reception was waving at her and smiling. He mouthed 'Visitor' and pointed to a middle-aged woman who was carrying a large package.

'This surely can't be her,' Kitty said. 'I was expecting an old lady.'

'Elder doesn't always mean old, when your country's life expectancy is low,' Grace said.

The woman, who made her way across the lobby to meet them, was shabbily dressed in an outmoded skirt and top that were too large on her. Kitty could see by the sinew and muscle in her forearms and calves that she wasn't thin, but lean and athletically built, as if she spent all day working in the fields or walking for miles and miles, carrying heavy loads. What had she brought with her in that bundle?

'Be you Nurse Kitty Longthorne?' the woman asked. Her accent was far stronger than Grace's.

Kitty nodded. 'The very same.' She smiled and greeted the woman. 'Are you Hope Philips?'

The woman nodded. 'Pleased to meet you.' She looked at Grace expectantly, clutching at her large bundle.

Grace pulled out a chair for her and gasped when she looked down at the bulky item Hope Philips was carrying. It was only as the woman took a seat and put the bundle on her lap that Kitty saw why Grace had seemed so startled. An opening in the rough cotton wrappings revealed a tiny little face.

'A baby!' Kitty said, putting her hand on her own belly.

Hope smiled, but the smile didn't reach her eyes. The uncertainty was audible in her voice. 'This be my grand-daughter, Nurse Kitty. Little Rose. She a beauty. But me got something to confess.'

'You're not here to help with recruiting nurses, are you?' Grace asked. She narrowed her eyes at the woman.

'Home drum beat first,' Hope said in response.

'I heard of you, Hope Philips.' Grace wagged her finger in an accusatory manner. 'You live near my aunty. I been over that way. You're no elder. You got ten daughters and no one to marry them.'

'Nine! And one of them be married all right! This *her* baby! And the elder that should have come, she drop down dead since this meeting arranged. We buried her last week! Hope Philips now be all the elder you need.' Hope glared at Grace and pressed her lips together. 'Anyway, me come here for help, not judgement. Me thought this English nurse, here, might have a good Christian heart beating inside her. Our little Rose – she not taking the breast. She not growing fat.' She looked at Kitty with imploring eyes. 'There be something wrong with her, and me can't afford no clinic doctor, standing there with his hand out.'

'Oh, dear,' Kitty said, imagining how desperate this woman must be to have travelled all that way, knowing it was under false pretences and might lead to disappointment. 'I'm not sure how helpful I can be. I've worked on maternity. I can *deliver* babies, well enough, providing it's a straightforward labour, and by all means, I can take a look at your granddaughter and see if there's anything obvious wrong with her, but I'm no paediatrician. I'm not even a paediatric nurse.' Kitty wondered fleetingly if she was cut out for motherhood at all, given how little she knew about babies, once they were out of the womb.

Grace leaned forward and stroked the cheek of the baby girl, whose enormous brown eyes had opened. She was now looking around in wonder, but her tiny face began to crumple. 'I used to work at the Bayley Clinic,' Grace said, drawing her eyebrows together and curling her bottom lip at the baby in sympathy. 'Aw, don't cry, little one!' The baby stuck her tongue out, but her tongue was an unusual heart shape. Grace turned to Kitty. 'They do surgeries and treatments for free if they think you really can't pay.' Then, she turned back to Hope Philips. 'And I know *you* can't pay. Why hasn't your daughter gone there and asked? Are her legs broke?'

'She got to work in the field. The baby won't feed from her breast, so me been trying her on a bottle of goat's milk or bush tea.'

'Goat's milk is no good for a baby. And bush tea won't fill her belly. If the baby won't feed from the breast, you need to find out why not. Get the problem fixed at the Bayley Clinic!'

Hope shook her head.

'Why not?' Grace asked.

'Don't like it in them kind of places,' Hope said, looking down at the baby and biting her lip. 'Me lost my one and only son in a clinic. My one boy out of eleven children. He got sick. They promised they'd save him for free, and it was lies. They let him die. Maybe if me been able to pay, he would have lived.'

'Your granddaughter needs medical attention, Hope!' Grace said, wearing a look of consternation on her face. 'When yuh 'en got horse, ride cow!'

'If me not paying, how me know they going to do a proper job of fixing my baby granddaughter? What if the same thing happens, like with my son? They make me fearful, all them doctors in those white coats, playing God. But me heard National Health Service don't cost a thing, anyhow.'

The wide-eyed pleading look she gave Kitty melted her heart. She held out her hands. 'Pass me the baby?'

Hope Philips passed the whimpering bundle to her. 'Be careful, now.'

'Of course. Don't worry.' Kitty unwrapped the child properly and looked her over. With the child on her lap, she wiggled her fingers in front of her eyes and moved them around to check that there were no problems with her vision. She felt her chest with the back of her hand and looked for rashes. The baby girl's ribs *were* prominent; her belly was distended and her head seemed overly large with those enormous eyes, bordering on the ghoulish. There was no doubt that Rose wasn't feeding properly, Kitty assessed. She tested the baby's reflexes, tickling her feet and checking she could hold Kitty's finger in a strong grip. 'There's no obvious signs of an infection; she's responding normally to stimuli. I can see she's painfully thin, though. She obviously isn't taking to the goat's milk, but it's breast milk she really needs – formula, if all else fails.' Kitty frowned at the disparaging sucking noise that Hope made. 'Could little Rose be allergic to her mother's milk? What sort of diet does your daughter have, Mrs Philips?'

A teary-eyed Hope opened her mouth to respond, but Grace cut in.

'Give that baby here!' She took the little girl from Kitty and tickled her neck so that she opened her mouth to giggle. Yet the sound that came out wasn't quite right. Grace stared intently at her tongue and smiled. 'This baby is tongue-tied.' She turned to Kitty. 'Have you got any medical equipment with you?'

'Only first-aid basics and a couple of other bits and bobs.'

'Surgical scissors and sterilising fluid?'

Kitty nodded. 'Why, yes. You're not planning on doing a procedure here, are you? Shouldn't a doctor do it?'

Grace chuckled. 'This is nothing! I used to fix problems like this all the time. What do you think the women in my village do when something goes wrong, and they need treatment in an emergency? Wait for an ambulance?' Her chuckle turned into laughter.

'We used to have a woman in St Lucy who was good with that sort of thing,' Hope said. 'But she moved to Bridgetown years ago, like all the rest. *My* girls – they useless! No nurses in the Philips family.'

The three women moved upstairs to Kitty's hotel room, and within a quarter of an hour, with Kitty holding the baby steady and Grace wielding a pair of freshly sterilised surgical scissors, little Rose's tied tongue had been snipped.

'She not even crying!' Hope said, grinning and holding her granddaughter close. 'Good girl. Clever girl!'

'Maybe she'll get an ulcer under her tongue for a couple of days while it heals, but she'll be feeding properly straight away, if your daughter's milk is still in, and the ulcer will go. These babies never seem to feel it.' Grace folded her arms triumphantly.

'Bless you, nurse!' Hope said. She turned to Kitty. 'And bless you, too. Both of you have saved my grandchild from starving to death.' She bit her lip again and sheepishly looked down at the baby. 'Sorry for lying. Lord forgive me.'

Kitty stroked the happily gurgling baby's forehead and smiled. 'You've got nothing to apologise for, Mrs Philips. I'm just glad we could help baby Rose. She's a darling.' She thought about the life that was almost certainly developing inside her and imagined holding a perfect miniature of either James or herself. Perhaps having a baby would be every bit as rewarding as being a nurse. Could it be that she was warming to the idea? She smiled and felt her cheeks flush at the thought.

They waved Hope off and Kitty turned to Grace. 'Now, I've got to go to the Bayley Clinic. The Matron, Winifred – I met her yesterday. She's arranging for a group of interested nurses to talk to me. Will you come with me?'

Grace's eyebrows bunched together. 'Matron? Lord Jesus, save me. Last time I saw her, I was handing in my notice. I'm not sure I'll be welcome.'

'Nonsense,' Kitty said.

'I'll come with you on one condition,' Grace said, holding her index finger up. 'You've got to come somewhere with *me*, tonight, Kitty Longthorne.' Grace's expression had an air of mystery to it. 'I'm going to show you the real island.'

Chapter 23

'Ha! All this time I thought it would actually be called the Bayley Clinic,' Kitty said, gazing up at the impressive 1930s building. The large sign outside declared that this was, in fact, the Diagnostic Clinic. It was nothing like the crumbling, faded grandeur of the old colonial buildings.

'Nobody calls it that anymore,' Grace said. 'Harry Bayley was campaigning for free healthcare before the NHS was even thought about. He's a genius. And he's the boss.' She'd wrapped her arms around herself, as though she were cold, though she could be anything but in the blistering heat of the mid-afternoon.

Kitty noticed that her friend's shoulders were hunched too. 'Are you quite all right, Grace?'

'Just . . . Matron.'

'Oh, don't be daft. Winifred seemed absolutely fine and dandy!'

'Winifred! Ha. That makes her sound human.'

They left the hot, dusty street to go inside, where the corridors were spotlessly clean and cool. Kitty announced herself at reception and, presently, Winifred – equally as formidable as Park Hospital's very own matron but somewhat more stylish, even in her uniform – strode towards them both.

'Nurse Longthorne! You made it. Good.' Winifred looked at Grace with undisguised curiosity and not a shred of recognition.

'I believe you know Grace Griffith,' Kitty said. 'She's offered to be my guide on the island. I'm hoping she might be my first recruit.'

Winifred's furrowed brow gave way to wide-eyed surprise. 'My dear! I didn't recognise you without your uniform. Oh, how very sad we all were that you left.' She treated Grace to a dazzling smile and then turned back to Kitty. 'If you get this girl on the payroll, the NHS will be extremely lucky.'

Grace blushed. She unfolded her arms and her shoulders relaxed. 'Tell the girls I miss them, won't you?'

'Well, you can tell them yourself. The ones who are on their break are waiting in the staffroom. The rest – well, it's a busy place. I'll take you round afterwards, and you can talk to the girls on the wards.'

They were ushered into a room that was crammed with nurses of all ages. Kitty noticed that the ones wearing sister uniforms were almost exclusively white or had the paler skin of mixed parentage. The regular and junior nurses were almost all Black. Regardless of the obvious racial hierarchy, where the senior nurses sat together at the front and the Black women stood in groups behind them, the welcome was warm. Kitty's wild-beating heart didn't slow, however.

She stood on a chair in a corner of the room, facing the sea of expectant faces. 'I-I suppose you're wondering why I'm here,' she began. *Come on, Kitty. You can do this. Just imagine you're showing a load of new trainee nurses the ropes*, she told herself. She pictured Matron commanding the attention of the quarrelsome senior consultants in the boardroom and felt instantly inspired. 'Well, I'm here to tell you how Britain's new National Health Service can change your lives for the better—' She looked over to Grace, who nodded encouragingly. Then Kitty began her speech in earnest.

The nurses listened intently, but it was not long before she was interrupted.

'What are the hours like?' one nurse asked. 'We be working round the clock, here.'

Another chipped in: 'And we not getting properly paid.'

A murmur of agreement rippled around the room. Even the sisters joined in.

'I can't afford to feed my family,' an older nurse said. '*When* I get to see them! I haven't left the hospital for *two weeks*, now! I been snatching what sleep I can on the ward, *if* there's a bed free.'

The murmur grew louder until the nurses were shouting over each other in vociferous agreement.

Winifred clapped her hands. 'Simmer down, ladies! Let our guest speak!'

The room fell silent once more.

'Well, part of the beauty of this recruitment drive,' Kitty said, pondering how gloriously rowdy and outspoken the Bajan nurses were, compared to her compatriots back at Park Hospital, 'is that your pay will be much, much better. If you're not at the standard already, as some of the more senior nurses will be, you'll be trained to State Registered Nurse level and paid accordingly. It's not a king's ransom, but it'll be better than what you get here, and you'll be able to send money home and train with the best of the best.'

She saw the women nodding at one another, murmuring their approval.

'You get your nurses' home digs for free,' Kitty continued. 'So there's no worry about finding accommodation. Our hours are long, but I've *never* had to snatch sleep during a shift. Never.'

Kitty felt the itch of a rash creep up her neck. Could the Bajan nurses see it? Did they somehow intuit she'd been operating on insufficient sleep for months, since the nursing shortage? Two hours here, three hours there . . . Was that any different from these women, catching forty winks in a side room?

The Bayley Clinic nurses grilled her for another half an hour or more, asking questions that, at times, she simply didn't have the answers to. When the presentation had descended into good-natured chaos, shouted witticisms and laughter, Winifred clapped her hands.

'Let's draw this talk to a conclusion, ladies. Nurse Longthorne has brought literature for those who are interested. I've put it on the table by the window and I'll collect completed application forms at the end of the week. Grab one as you leave. Now, back to work!'

Kitty watched with delight when a good proportion of those gathered took a form, thanked her and left the staffroom, chattering excitedly about the adventure they might embark on, care of the NHS.

'I told you this would be popular,' Winifred said, patting Kitty's shoulder.

Exhaling slowly and feeling the tension finally leach from her body, Kitty nodded. 'I'm glad. They seem a great bunch. I'm sure we'd be lucky to have them.'

Her eye was caught by the sight of Grace, talking with a group of her former colleagues. Grace's accent was so much stronger when she spoke to her fellow countrywomen, and they all seemed to be speaking mainly in a patois Kitty couldn't follow. It had a wonderful lyrical quality to it. Since Grace was brandishing a form, Kitty guessed she was imparting the news that she'd decided to take up the NHS's offer. Kitty certainly hoped so.

The rest of the visit involved speaking to nurses in twos

or threes on the wards. It was clear that, though the facilities in the hospital were top-notch and equal to anything
Kitty had seen back home, she sensed a bone-weariness and
dissatisfaction in the women. Many of them were keen on
the idea of starting a new life in Britain.

As they were leaving, Kitty turned to Grace. 'They seemed
so worn out. Do you think they actually enjoy their work?'

Grace looked back at the hospital and smiled wistfully.
'They live for their work. Problem is, they need to live for
their families, too, and being a nurse in Barbados – the hours
are so long, you got to choose between working round the
clock, here, or spending time with your kin. Nobody should
have to make that choice.'

Kitty registered an uncomfortable twinge in her womb
and thought about the sacrifices she was having to make
to have a family of her own.

'This is the sort of adventure I dreamt about,' Kitty told
Grace later, as they sat on her mother's veranda, sipping
pineapple juice and watching the evening skies streak with
orange and pink. Grace's many siblings were running riot
in the yard in front of their ramshackle traditional house,
taunting the neighbour's bony old dog.

'What? Being eaten alive by mosquitoes?'

'Yes. All of that!' Kitty chuckled. She shivered as she
watched a giant cockroach scurry across the stubby, balding
grass. 'You have a better class of insect over here. And I
like your family. They're full of fun and warmth.'

After their trip to the Bayley Clinic, Grace had taken
Kitty home. Kitty had met her newfound friend's family
and the people of her small community in a fishing village
further up the coast, between Bridgetown and Holetown.

She'd been given a warm welcome and the best food she'd ever tasted. The flying fish had been deep fried with its wings still on. She'd found it a little disconcerting, and it had looked nothing like the cod in Ada's chippy back home, but she'd persisted, not wanting to appear rude. There'd been a spicy stew of sorts and the most revolting thing she'd ever seen – barbecued pigs' tails. Happily, they'd tasted a darn sight better than they looked.

Now, Kitty was sitting with a full belly in the warmth of the early evening, marvelling that this very same brilliant sun would be setting on dismal old Manchester in just a few hours' time.

'What was Ned like as a little boy?' Grace asked.

Puffing out her cheeks, Kitty cocked her head and cast her mind back to her and Ned's childhood in Hulme, before the war. Their little terraced house had felt like a castle, even though they had slept together, top to toe in a single bed, covered in coats that served as blankets. Their bunk bed had been a luxury that came later, after their father had made some money from handling stolen goods. Back then, the old man had been careful to draw the line at getting involved in burglary and there had never been any trouble with the police. He and her mother had been loving and hopeful about the family's future. By and large, it had been a happy time, but the optimism and her father's self-discipline had not lasted. How could she distil the rise and fall of the Longthornes into a few sentences for Grace?

'Ned was always a charmer. Gift of the gab, he had. He got it off our dad. He had a brilliant imagination, too, did Ned. He'd come up with belting games. We'd build the best dens in the back entry from whatever we could lay our hands on – all the stuff nobody wanted. We drove our neighbour mad when he couldn't wheel his market barrow past us to get to his own backyard! Playing Cowboys and Indians and Shop with the other kids in the area . . . it was a lovely time. Just before Bonfire Night, we'd go round the streets with an old handcart, collecting firewood for the bommy – that's the bonfire, of course. Ned was artistic. He always made the Guy look like Mr Talbot from Number Fifty-four. Nobody liked Mr Talbot because he would never give you sweets and he always stank of onions. You could spot him a mile off from that string vest he wore morning, noon and night and those glasses that he had to hold together with a plaster, so he was perfect for a Guy.'

Grace wrinkled her nose. 'Guy?'

'Guy Fawkes. Blimey, all of this must sound like a foreign language to you. If you come to Manchester, how are you going to cope? All it does is rain. I'm used to it, and even I can feel the damp in my bones in winter. It's not like *this*, Grace. It's . . .' Kitty thought about how she might describe her hometown to a woman who was used to the sound of crashing waves and swaying palm trees. 'It's dark and cold and wet. The people are tired and desperate for change, but even now the war's ended, the good times never seem to roll. The houses are small and dirty and full of mould.'

'We've got roaches and spiders, big as your hand.'

'It's different. There's a heaviness to England. The light's bad. The food's grey. The people are grey.'

'Ned's not grey.'

There it was. *Ned's not grey.* Kitty was fairly certain at that point that Grace was sweet on her twin brother – inexplicably so.

'Ned's a pimp! My brother has strayed far from the righteous path. Tell me, Grace, are you a God-fearing girl?'

Grace nodded.

'Well, Ned left his soul in a Japanese prisoner-of-war camp, if you ask me. Honestly, don't get involved. You're gorgeous, like a silver-screen star. You can do better than our Ned. He's a tea-leaf – a thief. He's a liar. Don't ruin your life because of some romantic dream of taming the untameable and fixing the unfixable.'

Later that evening, Kitty met the young men and women of the village in the church hall. She told them that there were opportunities waiting for them in Britain, within the NHS, as long as they were prepared to work.

'We need auxiliaries,' she said, looking around at the young men in the audience. 'Manchester's got several excellent and large hospitals that service a population of a couple of million or more.'

The people in the audience inhaled sharply and started chattering among themselves. Kitty wondered if the idea of such a large concentration of people in one city was exciting or intimidating for island-dwellers.

'We already have a number of West Indians living and working in the city. Manchester's been home to Black people since the 1700s. But now, we need more people from the colonies to come over and work in our hospitals. Girls, if you're considering becoming a nurse, we can offer you the very best training and smashing prospects.'

For the first time in a long time, Kitty felt important, talking about the NHS in terms of 'we'. She wondered what James would think of her, standing on that little stage in the church hall of Grace's village . . .

Chapter 24

'My word, this is a far cry from Bayley's Clinic,' Kitty said the following morning, as she and Grace walked towards the single-storey sprawl of the Psychiatric Hospital in Black Rock. The windows were barred. The place looked ramshackle and run down.

'A world away,' Grace said, nodding grimly.

It had been an arduous half-hour's hike from central Bridgetown in the unrelenting sun, made possible only by the occasional breath of wind that came up off the sea. Kitty's dress was already stuck to her. Her sunburn smarted every time the heavy cotton fabric brushed against the backs of her calves, and her hot, swollen feet throbbed inside her wholly unsuitable leather shoes. Throughout the trek, she'd registered mild cramping in her womb, akin to those she might have during her time of the month. Was that normal for early pregnancy? She hadn't been plagued so much by the nausea in the last couple of days. She considered consulting Grace, but opted to remain silent.

Still, Kitty's discomfort was clearly insignificant in comparison with that of the Psychiatric Hospital's in-patients, judging by the shouting and wailing audible from the street.

She winced as a blood-curdling scream emanated from behind one of the barred windows. 'Psychiatric care isn't a field I'm familiar with. I have a feeling I'm going to be a bit out of my depth.'

'You get to go home at the end of this meeting, Kitty,' Grace said. 'Think of it that way. The nurses and patients aren't that lucky.'

'I must pull myself together. I've patched up the worst of the war-wounded, helped deliver babies and tended more gangrenous stumps than I've had hot dinners. I don't know why this should knock me for six. On with the motley!' Kitty stood straight and counselled herself to behave professionally and be inscrutable in the face of hardship. She was representing her beloved Park Hospital, after all.

Inside the hospital, Kitty and Grace were greeted by a stern-looking white senior nurse.

'Ah, good. You're here.' The woman looked Kitty up and down. 'I'm Sister Doris.' She spoke with the brisk tone of a gym mistress. 'It's lunch. We're very busy, so I don't have long.'

Kitty opened her mouth to speak, but Sister Doris had already sped off and was some way ahead of them, striding down a highly polished corridor with her wide bottom swinging to and fro, as though it had a life of its own. The hospital had something of a prison-like air to it. As they passed a number of doorways, Kitty glimpsed bone-thin patients, clad in straitjackets. They stared into the distance wearing glazed expressions, drool spooling from their mouths.

'Padded cells!' she said, looking askance at Grace. 'I've never seen one in my life.'

'I've heard about this place from other nurses,' Grace said, her eyebrows bunching at the sight of a patient wearing a helmet and repeatedly bashing his head against the wall as a nurse tried to offer him food.

'I can't look,' Kitty whispered, turning away. 'All the years of working in a general hospital, and I can't bear the sight of these poor mites, all trussed up and sedated.'

In the main dining room, patients whose conditions were manageable were sitting down to eat at tables, unrestrained. The nurses were spoon-feeding those who needed it. There were some spillages and tantrums, but the patients seemed happier in here. Kitty noticed that the nurses spoke to their charges in kindly voices and remained calm when a bowl of something was sent flying. She put her hand over her heart, where the vulnerability of the patients and the innocence in their eyes caused a discernible pang.

'You're in here,' Sister Doris said, snapping her fingers. She showed them to a side room, where chairs had been set out in short rows. 'The nurses who are interested will be arriving in the next five minutes.'

Before long, a group of women filled the room. As had been the case at the Bayley Clinic, those who wore the uniforms of junior staff all sat towards the back. The senior staff at the front were either white or fairer-skinned. Perhaps this rigid racial pecking order was why the island's nurses were prepared to sail alone to another continent, braving the unknown and the British weather. Maybe they naively thought it would be different in England!

Kitty explained what the NHS had to offer.

'How does this sound to you?' she asked uncertainly, trying to gauge the numbers of interested women.

They all murmured positively, looking at each other and nodding their heads.

'Truly?'

'Listen, dear,' one of the senior nurses said. 'We working seventy hours per week, every week, come hurricane or shine!

Black Rock's a tough place, looking after difficult patients. You seen the conditions here! It's hot. It's cramped. If we get a new patient bring a disease in – maybe their family's been treating it with bush tea and blind faith – the whole hospital community go down with a pernicious strain of it. You try nursing someone after lobotomy surgery when you feel like you gonna die yourself! You try looking after some six-foot-tall schizophrenic with the strength of a giant, the temper of the devil and the mental age of an eight-year-old – especially when he's sick with some fever. All the shock therapy in the world don't help some in here. And the pittance we earning doesn't sweeten the bitter pill.'

As the women took the NHS literature that she had brought from England, Kitty was privately agog that she'd managed yet again to command everyone's attention. For the first time in her life, she felt important and respected. She was gladdened by the thought of working with these talented nurses.

'I was so nervous about those presentations,' Kitty told Grace, once they'd left the Black Rock Hospital and marched up the road towards a roadside coconut stall. 'I didn't think I had it in me.'

'You did a good job in there,' Grace said. 'I know you British think us Bajans are in thrall to you, but I'll be honest, most of the time, we're looking for the lie in your fancy words. Especially us younger ones. We've had centuries of you coming over here, telling us what to do, making empty promises and leaving a mess for us to clean up. We've built your empires and ploughed your fields and cleaned your houses . . .' Irritation momentarily hardened her beautiful features, but then she smiled. 'I'm wandering! What I mean to say is, you went down well.'

Grace ordered two coconut milks from the man behind the makeshift stall, which was nothing more than a rickety bamboo table, covered in palm leaves and bearing a precariously stacked pyramid of fresh coconuts. With a machete, he hacked the tops off two fat, green coconuts, nothing like the sort Kitty had seen before.

'Are these really coconuts?'

Grace laughed. 'Of course. Why do you ask? Have you never seen one?'

'Yes. Yes, we get them at fairs, but ours are usually brown and hairy.'

'Do you eat them like that?'

The man handed Kitty her giant coconut and popped a drinking straw in the hole at the top.

'Of course not!' she said. 'They're a fairground attraction. We throw balls at them!' She drank the tepid 'milk', which was little more than fairly tasteless juice. It was refreshing nevertheless, and again, Kitty was reminded of what an adventure she was having. 'I wish my fiancé could see me!'

A look of horror replaced Grace's smile with such abruptness that Kitty gazed down quizzically at the spot that seemed to have transfixed her friend. She balked at the large bloodstain on her skirt. Only then did she realise she was standing in a growing pool of her own blood.

'No! No!' Kitty clutched her hand to her abdomen. 'This can't be happening. Help me, Grace!'

'What in the Lord's name is wrong?' Grace asked, helping Kitty to sit on the coconut-seller's wobbly wooden stool.

Kitty looked up at her through a veil of tears. 'I'm losing my baby.'

'Your *baby*? You're pregnant?'

Nodding, Kitty willed the life inside her to stay put, but

in her heart, she knew she'd lost too much blood for this to be a mere bump in the road. 'It's my fault. Walking for miles in the baking heat and gadding about the island as if—'

'Nonsense!' Grace said, cradling Kitty's head against her. 'You're not made of glass. The women over here dig in the fields right until the babies come out! How far gone are you?'

Kitty thought about the trip to the Lake District that she and James had cut short, thanks to her father's illness and her mother's blind panic. 'Couple of months. If that.'

Grace nodded. 'You of all people should know how common it is for a pregnancy to fail within the first three months. This is nature's way of telling you something wasn't right. It wasn't your time. I take it, it wasn't planned.'

Sobbing and shaking her head, Kitty looked helplessly down at the red mess of her dress and the blood trickling down her legs. 'I told James to be careful. He promised!'

'The road to hell is paved with good intentions. Your time will come, Kitty, but it's just not right now. That's good, isn't it? Better you marry your man and bury your father before you bring a baby into the world.'

Kitty held her hand and couldn't help but squeeze hard when a griping cramp overwhelmed her.

'You want to wash yourself?' the stall holder said, hacking the top off a coconut and offering it to Kitty. 'Use the coconut water.' He took off his shirt and gave it to her. 'Here, a cloth to soak it up.' He seemed unperturbed by the sight of a miscarrying white woman by the roadside.

Kitty thanked him absently, but she was so consumed by panic, looking on the dusty ground in desperation for signs of the foetus, that she spilled the coconut water over her lap. 'I've got to find it. I've got to—' She waved the shirt away. 'I don't want to ruin that. Take it back!'

'We need to get you back to the Bayley Clinic,' Grace said. 'Get you examined and cleaned up. They'll sort you out.'

'But Black Rock's just over the way.'

'That's no place for a woman in your condition to be.'

Grace turned to the stall holder and pointed to a donkey that was grazing in the field behind them. 'That your donkey? Can you take us to the Bayley Clinic?'

It took a matter of minutes for the stall holder to pack away and saddle his donkey back up to his old rough-hewn cart. The journey was not arduous, but it was the longest half-hour Kitty had ever endured. She sat on some coconut matting, clutching at her belly and covered in blood.

When they arrived, Kitty offered the sum contents of her purse to the coconut seller, though he wouldn't accept a penny. She was quickly ushered inside and put in a vacant side-room, at Matron Winifred's behest.

'You make yourself comfortable,' Winifred said, her brow furrowed with concern. She held out a sack. 'Put your soiled clothes in here and put on a clean hospital gown. I'll find you some spare clothes from lost property. And I'll send the doctor in as soon as I lay eyes on him.' She looked at her watch. 'When I last saw him, he was delivering twins!'

Kitty locked eyes with Grace. She felt tears threaten yet again. 'What will James say? How can I tell my fiancé that I lost our baby, all because I was selfish and reckless?'

Grace poured her some water and pushed the glass into Kitty's hands. 'You're dehydrated, in shock, traumatised. Stop beating yourself up! If your fiancé is worth marrying, he'll only be sorry he put you through all this to satisfy his own urges.'

Kitty nodded forlornly, contemplating James's reaction when he heard the terrible news. How could she begin to break it to him? *Hello, darling. I'm back. By the way, I was pregnant and killed our son or daughter because I put quenching my thirst for adventure before the baby's safety.*

'Miss Longthorne?' An ageing white man stood in the doorway, wearing a crisp white coat. He had formidable bushy eyebrows and thin lips. 'I understand you think you might be having a miscarriage.' His expression was stony. His tone was devoid of sympathy.

How Kitty wished she was being examined by another woman. How she hated having to explain herself and her out-of-wedlock pregnancy to a man in his fifties. 'I think so!' she said in a small voice.

Grace left the room and allowed Kitty to be examined by the doctor. He confirmed that she had, indeed, been in the very early stages of pregnancy and that she was, as she'd feared, miscarrying.

'Bed rest, if you can, Miss Longthorne. You'll be back to normal soon enough.' He smiled and glanced down at her engagement ring on her bloodied hand. 'And if I were you, I'd either abstain from sexual relations altogether or I'd bring my wedding plans forward. Unexpected pregnancies are generally a good deal easier to palate if you have the support of a husband. Miscarriages, even more so.'

Once Grace had returned and they were alone, Kitty wept for the baby, she wept for herself and she wept for all she had left behind in Manchester.

'I'm so homesick, Grace,' she said.

'I know.' Grace nodded sagely, wiping Kitty's hands gently with a clean, damp cloth. 'I would be too.'

'Take me back to Ned. Please. I need to see my brother, and then I want to go home.'

Chapter 25

Kitty and Grace hitched a ride back to the Buchanan plantation with a young doctor from the Bayley Clinic. He was travelling out to the cane-processing plant, where a lad had fallen into a molasses vat. Exhausted, Kitty offered her assistance but was relieved when the doctor politely turned her down and insisted on dropping them at Humphrey Buchanan's front door.

On arrival, the house's turmeric-coloured render seemed to glow an even brighter yellow than it had when she'd last seen it. The manicured gardens were a more florid green. The hibiscus blooms, red as sun-ripened tomatoes.

'This place looks flipping inviting now, after what I've just been through,' Kitty said, wriggling to readjust the lumpy sanitary dressing that Matron Winifred had supplied her with. She issued a silent prayer of thanks skywards that the lost-property clothing she'd been given was loose-fitting and in bright patterned fabric.

Grace rubbed Kitty's upper arm affectionately. 'Poor you. I bet you've had enough of the lumpy, bed-bug-ridden mattress in that hotel. Not to mention being top-to-toe in bed with me at my mother's house!'

Kitty chuckled. 'One night was enough, ta very much.' She rang the doorbell. Her spirits lifted at the thought of seeing Ned. Would he remember their argument?

'I hope your brother hasn't got a knitting needle stuck down his cast,' Grace said, peering through the glazed panel at the side of the door. 'He was itching like a madman when I left him.'

'Kitty, Grace! How lovely to see you both!' Humphrey's welcome was effusive, as the maid ushered them out to the pool area. Their host, wearing only swimming trunks, was sipping a cocktail by the pool. He was alone, however.

'Where's our Ned?' Kitty asked.

Humphrey gesticulated with a nod of his head towards the sea. 'The old boy's going stir crazy. I had my butler wheel him down to the cove. Why don't you go down and see him?'

In the stifling heat of the afternoon sun, feeling utterly drained and bereft but willing herself to carry on, Kitty clambered down a staircase hewn into the cliffs. She found Ned sitting beneath a copse of nodding palms right by the waterline. He was dressed only in a short-sleeved shirt, long enough to cover his modesty but leaving the leg that wasn't encased in a cast exposed to the sunshine. He was trailing his fingers through sand so pure white that the beach looked fashioned from refined sugar. The turquoise sea smacked playfully against the shore, sending ripples of foam up the beach to tickle Ned's fingers.

'I'm back,' Kitty said, taking off her shoes and padding barefoot towards him.

Ned turned around, smiled at first, then glowered at her, as though he was trying to keep his enthusiasm in check. 'So I see.'

'How's your bones?'

'Itchy and still broken. How was your world tour of Barbados?'

'I won a load of hearts and minds,' she said, sitting on the hot sand beside him. She decided to keep her own counsel regarding the miscarriage. Beyond the doctor who had examined her, the only man who had the right to know what had come to pass was James. She picked up a shell and marvelled at the mother-of-pearl interior, running her finger over its smooth surface. 'Kissed babies and had my photo taken by the *Barbados Advocate* and the *Beacon*. I'm thinking of giving up nursing and going into politics. They *loved* me!' She winked at him.

'Prime Minister Kitty,' Ned said, snorting with laughter. 'You'd get my vote.'

'Are we friends again?'

Ned studied her, long enough for her to wonder if he would ever break his silence. Then, he tutted. 'Course we are.'

She leaned over, took hold of his wet, sandy good hand and kissed him on the wrist. 'Good. Now, are you coming home with me? My ship sails in two days.'

Looking out to sea, Ned closed his good eye and exhaled heavily through the nose James had managed to fashion for him, against all odds. 'There's nowt to go back for,' he said.

'But Dad's dying.'

'Me and Dad . . . we've said all we need to say. Go home, Kitty. You belong in Manchester, but I—' He looked from one end of the palm-fringed cove to another. 'Tell Mam I love her.'

Kitty nodded, feeling tears pressing at the backs of her eyes but not wanting Ned to see that she cared so much. Damn him, with his gambling dens and his brothels and his stolen goods and his caring more for strangers than for blood. 'I'm taking Grace with me. Just so you know.'

Ned's face was pure thunder. 'You *what*?'

Kitty got to her feet, kissed her brother on the top of his sweaty head and walked away, amid Ned's furious tirade. She smiled, but her little triumph tasted distinctly bittersweet.

Chapter 26

'What did he say when you told him goodbye?' Kitty asked, as she and Grace stood on the starboard side of the *Tradewind*, waving at Grace's mother and older siblings below. 'Ned, I mean.'

Grace simply shook her head. 'I don't know what to make of your brother. He gave me the cold shoulder as if I was nothing more than a stranger.' She blew a kiss to her family. On the dockside, her openly weeping mother pressed a large handkerchief to her face.

'It's because he cares. He's upset. It's obvious.'

'Maybe he's just fed up he's got to go back to Bridgetown now and face the music.' Grace smiled, but there was a shadow of some other sentiment that flitted across her face. 'Well, I haven't got time to worry what your brother thinks. I've got my fortune to seek.' Tears welled in her eyes.

Kitty put her arm around her. 'Oh, Grace, whatever is the matter?'

Grace looked straight down at her family through a veil of tears and pointed. 'I'll miss them,' she said. 'When will I get to see them again?'

Shaking her head, Kitty had no answer. She knew the return fare was a king's ransom for a nurse. Had she not had her travel paid for, her own West Indian adventure would have been beyond her wildest dreams. 'Soon, I'm sure. My voyage from Liverpool was full of Jamaicans and Bajans, all going home to see relatives. They must have been able to put money by.'

'I'm going to be sending every penny I can to my mumma.'

'Where there's a will, there's a way. Something'll crop up. Maybe the hospital will help. Matron's really supportive. She's been belting when I've been up against it with my family circumstances. Try to look forward, not back.' *Was that a helpful comment?* Kitty wondered. Judging by Grace's crestfallen expression, she guessed not. 'You're about to start a whole new life. Everyone in Park Hospital is going to love you. Chin up!'

The journey back was rough. They hit squalling weather several days in.

'I feel like I'm going to die,' Grace said, vomiting into a bucket. She lay in her bunk, ashen grey.

Surprised by having found her sea-legs relatively quickly this time around – a mercy, given how uncomfortable and drained she felt otherwise – Kitty pressed a cool, damp cloth to Grace's brow and cleaned up her face. 'I'm going to get you some water. You're dehydrated. Maybe a plain cracker. We don't want you keeling over before you've even got a sniff of the Irish Sea.'

On the upper decks, second-class passengers were huddled together inside the dining room and the lounge, looking out at waves that must have been thirty feet high. They rose above the ship as ominous walls of grey before crashing down, engulfing the deck in rushing seawater and foam. Lightning forked down only yards away from the *Tradewind*. Thunder cracked overhead. As she tottered from the top of the staircase to the dining room, Kitty felt like the giant vessel was nothing more than a child's toy, fighting to stay afloat in the brutal rapids of a fast-flowing river.

'Oh, please let us get through this,' she muttered, gripping the handrail on the wall.

She clambered forwards, feeling a fast-incoming tide of nausea threaten to overwhelm her as the ship lurched from side to side. It was worse up here than in the windowless cabin.

A crew member jogged past her, as though coping with this storm was all in a day's work.

'Sir! Excuse me!'

He stopped and turned around. 'Miss?'

'My friend. She's terribly sick in our cabin. Any idea when this storm will blow over?'

He smiled sympathetically. 'We're in the Bermuda Triangle! But don't let the old wives' tales fool you. The weather's often challenging on this leg of the journey, and the *Tradewind* hasn't disappeared off the face of the earth yet! She's solid as a rock.'

'Yes, that's what they said about the *Titanic*,' Kitty said, balking at the news that they were in the midst of the infamous Bermuda Triangle.

'Don't worry, miss. The shipping forecast says the storm will blow itself out in a couple of days.'

'In a *couple of days*? My friend's going to be dead from dehydration by then. I need to see the ship's doctor. I need to get my friend some anti-emetics.'

'I'm afraid the doctor's fallen ill himself, miss.' He nimbly stepped to the side and righted himself as the ship listed violently to port.

'I'm a qualified nurse,' Kitty said, realising how desperate Grace's situation might become if she didn't find some medication to stop the vomiting. 'A senior nurse. Please, take me to the doctor's cabin so I can get the medication from him. I'll administer it myself.'

'It's highly irregular, miss, and you really mustn't go walking about the boat in this storm. You'll injure yourself.'

'She's going to die,' Kitty said through gritted teeth.

Finally, he relented and told Kitty which cabin she could find the doctor in. Stumbling around the ship, she eventually found him. Like Grace, he was lying in bed, ashen-faced, with a bucket next to the bed. The room reeked of the acidic tang of vomit.

Kitty held her nose. 'I'm so sorry you're ill, but I need something to stop my friend from vomiting. She's dangerously dehydrated.'

The doctor looked at her blankly. 'Do you think I'd be lying like a dog in a manger in here if there was some treatment I could give?'

'But I heard about the trial of Cyclizine a couple of years ago. The anti-emetic. Do you have any? I'm a nurse, you see. I can give it to my friend, if you've got an injection or some tablets.'

He shook his head and promptly vomited into his yellow bucket.

It was no use. Kitty would have to gather as many of the old-fashioned remedies as she could find from the dining room.

'Oh, please, God, don't let me get swept off the boat.'

Getting to the dining room necessitated running the gauntlet along the open deck. Kitty peered through the chunky, brine-smudged window of the door that led outside. Seawater was swilling down the deck, and the prow of the ship was pointed upwards at a terrifying angle as the *Tradewind* scaled a mountain of a wave.

Come on, Kitty. Now's your chance. Before the wave crests.

With the thunder crashing overhead and the lightning crackling all around the ship, as though she was in a theatrical production of *The Ride of the Valkyries*, Kitty made a dash for the door to the dining room. A swathe of seawater gushed down towards her, soaking her up to the calves. She felt the deck slippery beneath her inadequate leather-soled shoes. At that moment, the boat rolled unexpectedly to starboard and Kitty was knocked off her feet and swept several yards further down the boat, away from the safety of the door and the dry interior. Swallowing seawater and spluttering, she groped her way to the gunwale. Looking up, she saw that the wave the ship had been climbing was beginning to curl inwards.

It's going to crash down. You don't have time! Hold onto something!

Chapter 27

Kitty clambered as fast as she could to the railing and wrapped her arm around it. If she let go when that wave came down, she would surely be swept clean out to sea.

'Please, God, let me survive. Please carry me safely back to James and Mam and Dad. Please, please don't punish me for losing the baby.'

The wave hit with such ferocity that Kitty felt the freezing water as spiteful pincers, trying to prise her free of the rail. She could barely breathe. The saltwater stung in her nostrils, burning her sinuses. She coughed and spluttered, wincing as the seawater slapped against her exposed legs and face.

'Miss! Miss!'

Kitty heard a voice coming from somewhere. Where was it? She couldn't cling on for much longer. Just as she made out the crew member from earlier, shouting to her from the doorway, a secondary deluge washed along the deck. Kitty's fingers screamed with fatigue. She couldn't hold on much longer, and the boat was still tipping up, up, up at an untenable angle; the huge funnels looked like they might snap off and hurtle down towards her at any moment, dragging the lifeboats and other deadly flotsam and jetsam with them.

'Help! Help me!' she cried.

The crew member ran towards her. He was holding a rope – one end was looped around his waist, tied to some anchor point out of sight. The other, he flung towards her. 'Grab the rope and pull yourself up.'

Reaching out, Kitty tried to grasp the end, but there was a crack of thunder immediately overhead. She cowered and winced, missing the rope.

'Try again! Save me. Please!'

The wind was gusting, blasting her words away, but the lad threw the rope once more, and this time Kitty grabbed it. She pulled as hard as she could, getting to her feet and staggering her way up the deck, towards the door. With every treacherous step she took, she thought of James and gritted her teeth, determined that the Bermuda Triangle would not be the end of Kitty Longthorne.

'You made it, miss! Thank God.'

The crew member put a strong arm around her waist and dragged her into the dining room, where a small crowd had gathered at the rain-battered, steamy window to watch her struggle. When the door finally closed behind her and the squall was shut out, her fellow passengers cheered. Kitty stooped and grabbed at her knees, gasping for breath. Suddenly, overcome by a fit of giggles, she straightened up and flung her arms around the lad.

'You saved my life,' she said. 'God bless you, chuck.'

She released him from her ringing-wet embrace and staggered back on trembling legs. The lad looked flustered.

'I told you not to go wandering about, miss. You shouldn't be out in that. And you certainly shouldn't have gone out without a lifejacket on.'

'So sorry.' Kitty felt the heat in her cheeks. She'd need-lessly put this boy's life at risk. Thank heavens they'd both survived the elements. 'But I was desperate to get to the dining room. And here I am! I must get some bits from here for my friend. She's seriously poorly. If I die, it's my own stupidity. If she dies, it's neglect on my part. Will you help me? Please?'

Though they were both wet and starting to shiver, the lad took her to the galley. It was a gleaming, noisy and steamy cathedral of stainless-steel surfaces and white walls – it reminded her of the operating theatres at Park Hospital. Even in the midst of a storm, the cooks were preparing vast pots and pans full of steaming food for the passengers. The tilt and rock of the ship seemed not to bother them as they weaved their way around the place and chopped and stirred and dished up the delicious-smelling food.

Kitty was escorted back to her cabin, carrying a box full of homespun remedies for seasickness and dehydration.

'Thanks for everything,' she said to the lad as she stuck the key in the lock of her cabin door. 'I owe you my life.' She kissed him chastely on the cheek.

His tanned face glowed pink with embarrassment. 'Just you be careful, miss. England needs its nurses more than the Bermuda Triangle does!'

Inside the cabin, Grace lay on the bottom bunk, groaning. 'My stomach! Kitty, I feel like I'm being stabbed. I can't bring another thing up. It's just bile.' Grace frowned. 'Wait! You're ringing wet.'

'It's nothing.' Wrinkling her nose at the terrible, acrid smell, Kitty grabbed a towel out of their tiny bathroom, folded it twice and placed the thick wedge of fabric between her sopping-wet bottom and Grace's mattress. She set her box down on the blanket. 'Sit up, love. There's a good girl.'

She plumped up Grace's cushions and propped her into a sitting position. She took the lid off the box from the kitchens. 'Now, let's get some of this down you. Kitty's remedies.'

Grace's colour was even worse than before. Her eyes looked sunken and dry. Her lips were cracked. 'I've got a shocking headache. I feel so dizzy.'

'Ginger beer,' Kitty said, taking a bottle out of the box. She opened it and poured some into a glass. 'And I've got ginger biscuits and salty crackers, too. We need to get salt back in you. We need to get fluid in you, and we need to sort out your blood sugar.' Seeing Grace like this, Kitty was beset by guilt at having persuaded her to make the trip. She almost choked on the lump in her throat, but swallowed it down, remembering how terribly sick she'd been on the way out. Yet it had eventually passed.

'You're a saint,' Grace said, sipping on the beer.

Kitty took the bucket and cleaned it out in the toilet. When she returned, she considered Grace's words. 'I'm far from a saint, Grace. There's only one saint in this room, and I'm looking at her.'

Several days later, the storm finally abated and Grace's condition had vastly improved. The sun timorously emerged from behind the battleship-grey storm clouds and the two women stepped out onto the deck for some air. The West Indies were well and truly behind them. Britain lay ahead.

'My bittersweet adventure's coming to an end,' Kitty told Grace, as she held the rail at the prow of the ship and stared out at the blue expanse ahead of them. Seagulls wheeled overhead, squawking their approval that the weather had calmed. 'And yours is about to begin. Are you ready to change your life?'

Grace smiled and turned back to the south, where, some-where beyond the horizon, Barbados and all she'd ever known lay. 'Too late to turn back now. What about you? You glad to be going home?'

Kitty imagined the shores of her homeland and the liver birds beckoning her back to the North-west and the warm bosom of her loved ones. 'Home.' She conjured James in her mind's eye, waiting on that dockside. She was dreading telling him about the miscarriage, but her longing to see his handsome face and feel his warm embrace far outweighed any reticence she had about revealing the loss of their lovechild. Absence really did make the heart grow fonder, and her petty irritations from before were now forgotten. She pictured her long-suffering mother, standing in her cold scullery, wearing her old pinny while she made a meal from nothing. 'Home is where my heart is, Grace. I can't wait to get back.'

By the time Liverpool came into sight, Kitty was beside herself with worry that James wouldn't have forgiven and forgotten as she had. Would he be there to meet her? As the *Tradewind*'s engines went into overdrive in a bid to pull the ship alongside the quay, Kitty clenched and unclenched her sweaty hands.

'Are you all right, Kitty? You look unwell,' Grace said.

Kitty shuffled up to the rail with her case between her feet. 'Nervous. I've been away for a long time. I have no idea if my father's still alive. I have no idea if my mother's coping, and I certainly don't know what reception I'll be getting from my fiancé.'

Scanning the faces in the waiting crowd of family, friends and lovers who were standing on the drizzly dock, she couldn't see James or her mother.

'He's not here. They're not here. I should never have gone. Damn it. I had it all and I threw it all away on a silly principle.'

'If it's meant to be, between you and your man, it's meant to be,' Grace said, patting her shoulder. 'You told me you needed this trip before settling down. If he's a good man, he should understand that.'

Kitty nodded, but still, she couldn't spot any familiar faces in the crowd.

The passengers started to disembark. With a thudding heart and lips that prickled cold with dread, Kitty waited in the queue, gripping her cardboard case as though it were a lifeline. The biting Liverpudlian wind pummelled her and she donned her raincoat. It had been summer when she'd left, but now autumn had come to Britain. At her side, the skin on Grace's forearms was puckered with goosebumps. She looked thin and grey after a hard time at sea. Would Grace cope with starting a new life in a dark, cold, hard country that was still on its knees, post-war?

Again, Kitty wondered if she'd done the right thing.

They walked side by side down the gangway. Grace looked full of trepidation as she gazed at the tall buildings on the waterfront with undisguised wonder in her wide eyes.

'Oh, come on! Come on!' Kitty said beneath her breath. 'Please be here!'

They stepped onto terra firma after a month at sea, and Kitty almost swooned, surrounded as she was by strangers, all waiting to greet the weary travellers. Standing on her tiptoes, she tried to spot James's black trilby and her mother's floral headscarf, but there was a sea of black trilbies and women in headscarves.

Grabbing Grace by the hand, she dragged her through the crowd. 'Come on. Let's get away from the crowds and we'll see what's what. If they're not here, we'll find a caf and get you a nice hot brew to warm you up. Maybe a bacon butty, if I've still got enough English money in my purse.'

The dockside was emptying out, and so was Kitty's heart. There was no sign of James or her mother. Nobody was there to meet her.

'Yes. Kitty Longthorne. That's right. Oh, she was?'

The wind changed direction abruptly and carried a man's voice to her.

'James!'

Kitty turned around and around, trying to find him in the thinning crowd. Then she realised he was standing with the same crew member who had saved her from being swept into the sea in the Bermuda Triangle.

'James! I'm here!'

She left her case with Grace and ran towards him, wondering whether or not he'd greet her with glee.

'Kitty, my darling. At last.' James's voice cracked with emotion.

He scooped her up into a bear hug and swung her around in the air, kissing her repeatedly on the cheek and then setting her down and kissing her passionately on the lips.

'You're a sight for sore eyes,' Kitty said, taking in his chiselled features and dark good looks, marvelling that this prince among men was the man she was going to marry.

'And you're balm for my soul, Kitty Longthorne. I've missed you so much. I worried I'd never see you again.'

'I'm not home until you're by my side, James. I love you with all of my heart.' It occurred to her then that something was missing from her warm welcome. 'Where's Mam?'

The look on James's face was one of consternation. 'Ah. About that . . .'

Chapter 28

'Mam! What have you done with Mildred?' Kitty asked, barely able to contain the shriek in her voice.

Having dropped Grace at the nurses' home, where Matron had been on hand to help her settle in, Kitty had insisted that James drive her straight to her mother's place in the heart of Salford's Barbary Coast. Deciding that news of the miscarriage could wait, she'd tried to get some sense out of James on the way there, but his response had merely been, 'You'll see.'

Her mother had opened the front door with a harried expression on her flushed face. Her hair had been dishevelled, her apron covered in unmentionable stains.

Now, Kitty found herself in the parlour, looking at the makeshift bed that had been made for her dad on the settee, right by the radio. He was asleep.

'Jesus, Dad.'

'Don't blaspheme, Kitty, love!' her mother said.

'Taking the Lord's name in vain is the last of our problems,' Kitty said, looking down at her sleeping father.

The once-dashing Bert Longthorne looked reasonably clean, but the skin and the whites of his eyes had a yellow hue to them, which told Kitty that his liver wasn't functioning properly. She took his hand gently in hers and saw that his nails were starting to flake. She exchanged a knowing glance with James. Her father's kidneys were beginning to fail. Though he wore a mask that suffused his lungs with extra oxygen, by way of the giant canister next to the sofa, his breath still came short. He had deteriorated rapidly.

Kitty squeezed her eyelids tightly shut and two fat tears emerged. She wiped them away, opened her eyes and looked around at the parlour. 'Crikey! Look at this place, Mam! It looks like you've been burgled. And you! You look shocking. Are you eating? When was the last time you had a good strip wash and changed your clothes?'

Her mother didn't respond. She merely busied herself, stumbling over soiled bed linen and clothes, dirty pots and empty bottles of medication, in a bid to gather up the half-sewn piecework garments.

'Where's Mildred, Mam?'

'She was a right old battle-axe that one,' her mother finally said, speaking far too quickly. 'Like a sergeant major, telling us all what to do and how to behave and where to go. I didn't feel like my home was my own anymore. She had this place like a barracks, all tidy and a place for everything and everything in its blinking place! I could barely get to my Bert. The doctor came and said it was curtains.'

'Mam! Mam, slow down. What doctor?'

'Local doctor. Came and said your dad was on the slippery slope. Said to expect the worst. But that Mildred kept sticking your dad with needles, and your dad wasn't himself. No, he wasn't. So, I told that Mildred to take her casseroles and shove off out of my chalet!'

'What? You sent her packing because she was doing too good a job? Mam! She's a professional. She's being paid to do a top job.'

'She made me feel like a failure; like a spare part at a christening in my own home.'

Kitty collapsed in the old armchair but felt something lumpy beneath her bottom. She pulled it out and inspected it in the dingy light. It was one of her dad's vests. The sorrow and guilt and exhaustion were overwhelming. With shaking shoulders, she started to sob. 'I should never have gone.'

'Oh, Kitty, darling. I'm so very sorry.' James knelt at the side of the armchair and put his arms around her. 'I did check in on your folks a couple of weeks ago. I just couldn't find the time in my diary to swing by more than once a fortnight. Sorry. And then I found Elsie all of a two-and-eight.'

Kitty dried her eyes on the hem of her skirt and looked closely at her mother. She noticed the dark circles beneath her eyes, and the twitching of her right eyelid. 'When was the last time you slept?'

'Your dad needs me. My wants don't matter.'

'This ends now, Mam. I'm getting Mildred back, *if* she'll say yes.'

'But—'

'But nothing. This can't go on, Mam. You're thin. You need a good meal, a good tubbing and a good night's kip.'

Despite having sailed thousands of miles, and regardless of how the ground undulated beneath her from exhaustion, Kitty started to tidy up. She insisted her mother get in bed for an hour's nap, and she and James prepared a reasonable meal from the ingredients they could find.

'If only I'd brought back some spices from Barbados,' she said. 'I could have made a feast out of a few potatoes.'

James smiled at her. 'You'll have to track some down. I want to hear all about your adventures when we're alone.'

Kitty set her spoon on the spoon rest and looked towards the doorway, lowering her voice. 'He's not walking me down the aisle, is he?'

James shook his head. 'I'm afraid not.'

'I left a terminally ill man with only months to live and sailed off into the sunset. What on earth was I thinking?'

He encircled her waist from behind. 'Nonsense. You deserved that trip. Bert Longthorne has opted for a small life, cut short because of habits he chose to adopt. But you . . . every child deserves a blank canvas, Kitty. You have the right to fill yours with rich detail and colour. You're here – hang on. Why are you crying?'

Kitty was powerless to hold back the wracking sobs, though she tried her darnedest to stifle any noise with a tea towel.

James smoothed a stray lock from her forehead. 'Darling, what on earth's the matter? What did I say? Is it your dad?'

She shook her head and looked up at him. She tried to wrap her tongue around the difficult words once, twice. On the third attempt, she blurted out her confession with a sob. 'I was pregnant. And I lost it.'

The colour drained from her fiancé's face. 'What? Pregnant? I don't—'

'The Lakes,' she simply said.

She saw his pupils dilate as realisation dawned on him. He exhaled heavily and pressed his lips together, blinking slowly, digesting the ill-tidings.

Kitty's heart thumped violently. The blood rushed in her ears. How would he react? 'I'm so sorry,' she said in a small voice.

He shook his head and closed his eyes momentarily. 'It's me who should be apologising. Oh, Kitty. Can you ever forgive me?'

'What do you mean? It's me who went gadding about on a West Indian adventure, when I should have been taking it easy.'

'But you couldn't have known. How could you have known?' His chin dimpled. His eyes swam with tears. One rolled onto his cheek and tracked along his jawline. 'I made a promise to you that I'd be careful, and – you had to carry this burden and suffer that loss, all on your own, thousands of miles away.' He took her into his arms.

Kitty could feel from his quaking body that he was crying, albeit silently. She tried to pull away so she could reassure him, face to face, but he wouldn't let go. Sinking her nose into his strong shoulder, she drank in the smell of the spray starch on his shirt and savoured the warmth of his skin beneath. Relief supplanted the tension she'd been feeling, ever since she'd realised that her time of the month had been late. 'Thank you,' she whispered. 'Thanks for understanding.'

Finally, he released her from his embrace. The rims of his watery eyes and the tip of his nose were red. 'There's nothing to understand, Kitty.' He sniffed hard. He spoke slowly, as if trying to keep the sorrow from his voice. His lips quivered. 'A man should always assume responsibility for what happens in the bedroom. I wasn't careful enough. It was remiss of me, but it's your body that's borne the brunt of my lack of restraint.' He placed a hand on her belly and blinked a fresh tear away. 'I can't tell you how sorry *I* am. And I can't tell you how much I hope that—' He sighed and another tear fell. 'One day soon, once we're married, you'll have a pregnancy that's been properly planned, and we'll have a beautiful, healthy baby.' He took her hand into his and kissed her knuckles.

Kitty nodded fervently, thinking how she'd warmed to the idea of carrying a child. The bond to the life inside her had been surprisingly strong, after a matter of only weeks.

'I'd like nothing more,' she said. 'When the time's right.'

Chapter 29

'Did you sleep?' Kitty asked Grace, as her new recruit arrived at the bottom of the staircase in the nurses' home.

'Not really,' Grace said. 'My sleep pattern's all messed up. I didn't drop off until three in the morning! Up again at five for a bath.' Her teeth were chattering. 'I'm freezing.'

Kitty nodded. 'Me too. I was wide awake, thinking about my dad. I didn't expect to come back and find him as poorly as he is.' She swallowed hard, trying to keep her emotions at bay. 'Anyway, we'd better get some strong tea inside us, else we'll be dropping by lunchtime. Come on.' She offered her arm. 'Put your leg in bed, then.'

Grace looked at her with a confused frown.

'Give us a link. Link arms.'

Finally, the new recruit smiled. 'Ah. That!'

Together, they walked through the hospital site towards the main entrance. Kitty felt uncomfortable in her stiff, starched nurse's uniform after more than two months spent in her own clothes. The Davyhulme wind was bitingly cold, piercing through the fabric of her cape to gnaw at skin that had become accustomed to tropical sunshine.

She held her hand up. 'My tan's orange in this light. No – I look jaundiced like my dad!'

Glancing around at the people who scurried to and fro beneath the tall 1920s clock tower, Grace chuckled. 'I look

Black in this light. No – very Black.' She threw her head back and laughed.

People had started to notice the new arrival. Kitty spotted another nurse peering down from an upper-ward window at Grace. She turned away and within moments three more nurses had joined her to ogle the dark-skinned stranger. One of the senior doctors was walking from his car to the main entrance. He almost ploughed into the bushes, so intently was he staring at Grace.

'My word, Kitty,' came a voice from behind her.

Kitty turned round to find Molly Henshaw hastening along the path to catch up with them.

'Molly!'

'Look at the colour on you,' Molly said. She only cast a cursory look Kitty's way, however, and immediately turned instead to study Grace with undisguised suspicion. 'Though it's nowt compared to this one.' Molly stuck her hand out. When Grace extended her own to shake hands, Molly withdrew hers and wiped it on her skirt. 'Welcome to Park Hospital. I'm guessing you're the first of the colonials.'

Grace smiled sheepishly.

Kitty was flustered. She wasn't sure if the sleight warranted comment. Perhaps it was best not to cause a scene. Molly was difficult at the best of times. 'I'm just taking Grace, here, to get her sorted out with her contract and uniform. I'll see you later, Molly. I'm sure you'll extend a warm Park Hospital welcome to Grace on the wards, *won't you?*'

Kitty pulled Grace along and practically frog-marched her into the hospital to get away from Molly. Had Grace noticed the shoddy treatment and the pointed gesture? Should she comment on it?

'Molly's . . . er. She's like that with everyone,' Kitty said, wondering if this counted as excusing her colleague. 'Take no notice.'

Leading Grace to the personnel office, she introduced her to the secretarial staff there and presently met with the Home Sister, who was to finalise the recruitment process.

As Grace was getting a lecture about only running in the hospital if there was a fire or haemorrhage, Kitty took her leave and made her way to the lung ward. There, she found Mr Galbraith standing over a middle-aged man's bed, checking his notes and looking stern.

'Ah, Kitty,' Galbraith said. 'Welcome back! How were the West Indies?'

'I've never experienced anything—'

'Good, good. Now, the ward is busier than ever. Can I leave this gentleman in your capable hands? He's nil by mouth and needs preparing for theatre.'

Kitty nodded and drew the curtain around the man's bed.

The moment she'd hung up her cape, she'd become embroiled in giving a bed bath to the extremely reluctant patient who floundered around with some vigour, despite his being rail thin and hooked up to an oxygen supply. It was as though she'd never been away.

'Get off me, girl! Leave me be.' Her patient started to cough violently, putting Kitty in mind of her father. His hair even had the same stale cigarette smell clinging to it, and his index finger was the same dark amber colour from where, over time, nicotine had seeped from the tip of every cigarette he'd smoked, staining his skin.

'Now, now, Mr Wentworth. There's no need to panic. I'm hardly a girl! You can call me Nurse Longthorne. I've been at this a very long time, and you're in good hands, cocker. Mr Galbraith's a miracle worker.'

'Mr? Not even a bloody doctor?'

'He's a surgeon. Different title.' To distract her patient from his panic and embarrassment, Kitty explained how modern-day surgeons had derived their title from barbers, hundreds of years ago, who had been the only people skilled enough with a blade to carry out a doctor's surgical designs.

'Like Sweeney Todd?' the patient wheezed.

Kitty chuckled. 'You're thinking along the right lines, but you'll not be appearing in any steak-and-kidney pie today, Mr Wentworth. My fiancé is a surgeon. A plastic surgeon. We should all call him Mister, by rights, but our Chief Medical Officer came to visit years ago and kept getting his title wrong, so Doctor Williams just stuck. A bit of a joke, I suppose.'

She thought wistfully of James, holding his clinic on the other side of the hospital, or perhaps in surgery, treating his latest patient. He was taking her for dinner that evening on a proper welcome-home date, and she was looking forward to it in earnest. It was time to put the miscarriage behind her.

When Mr Wentworth was clean and gowned up, she made her way from bed to bed, introducing herself to each of the men. *How wonderful it is to be back*, she thought. Barbados had been an eye-opening and unforgettable experience, but fulfilling her duties at Park Hospital was as instinctive as breathing.

'And what's your name?' she asked a man in his fifties or early sixties, who occupied the bed at the end of the ward, closest to the large fireplace. He looked reasonably healthy, though the words seemed to slip away from him as he tried to speak.

'Trevor,' he said. 'Trevor Duncan.'

'Mr Duncan. What brings you in here, then? Let's have a look.' She took his notes from the end of the bed, wondering if he could possibly be yet another lung-cancer patient. Almost everyone she'd spoken to so far was afflicted by the terrible disease that was calling time on her own father's life.

'I had an X-ray the other day,' he said. 'I'm waiting on the results.'

Kitty nodded. Nothing had been reported yet, but she recalled having seen some paperwork relating to him in the office. She merely smiled and straightened his bedding. 'Not long till lunch. Have you got an appetite?'

'I could eat.'

'A good sign. I think it's fish and chips today.' She winked at him and made her way back to the makeshift sister's office in the bathroom. Leafing through the paperwork, she found the X-ray results for Trevor Duncan. Perhaps he would just have a nasty infection that could be cleared with penicillin. Or perhaps he lived by a main road and had developed asthma because of the noxious fog of exhaust fumes. In silence, she read the report and shook her head. She sighed just as the sister walked in.

'Sister Penny, how can it be that more than seventy per cent of our in-patients have got lung cancer? I've never seen anything like it.'

The experienced sister shrugged. 'I know, love. It's shocking, isn't it? It's like an epidemic. Galbraith reckons it's tobacco that's causing it, but I'm not sure. I reckon it's smoke from all the coal fires and those stinking bus fumes. I like a cig, me.'

'You smoke?'

Sister Penny nodded. 'I started smoking during the war. To calm my nerves and keep slim.' She patted her flat stomach.

For the first time, Kitty looked at her colleague's teeth and noticed that the insides of her lower incisors were stained brown. It had never occurred to her that a member of the nursing staff might smoke. She thought it unwise, but she didn't say anything.

'Anyway, the NHS is bringing more and more people to the doctor's surgery,' Sister Penny said, 'after they've neglected their health for decades, of course. So, by the time they get to us, it's too late. Such a shame.'

Later, after a hasty lunch of corned-beef hash in the nurses' dining room, Kitty made her way up to the staff-room, hoping to be asked about her Barbadian odyssey. Brimming with excitement, she opened the door, looking for James or Matron and, hopefully, Lily Schwartz. Instead, she found the place hot and fuggy with cigar and pipe smoke, devoid of her favourite compatriots. In the corner, by the radio, Professor Baird-Murray was holding court with the senior consultants, talking about the cricket – the commentary from some match or other just about audible on the radio. Nothing had changed.

Kitty coughed and wrinkled her nose at the stink. The air was a foetid yellow-blue with smoke. How had she never noticed that before?

'Oh, look, chaps!' Baird-Murray said, slapping his knees. 'It's Beryl, back from the West Indies.'

'Kitty, Professor. Not Beryl.' Kitty gave a timid wave to the consultants, though they all continued to chummer away about the West Indies' cricketing abilities and the likelihood of England winning the Ashes at any given time.

The professor beckoned her close. Kitty's cheeks flushed

hot at the attention from the most senior member of Park Hospital's staff.

'Now, Beryl. Matron informed me that you've been our emissary in the West Indies. Do tell us. Were your endeavours successful? Are we to be inundated with silly Jamaican junior nurses?'

'It was Barbados, Professor. And actually, I met some wonderful women over there at the Diagnostic Clinic and the Black Rock Psychiatric Hospital. The nurses are extremely well qualified. We had quite a few interested in coming over, and I brought—'

The consultants were no longer listening, however. On the radio, there was talk of someone hitting a six. Even the professor turned away. The men all cheered. Feeling rather disappointed, Kitty beat a retreat from the stinking staffroom and repaired back towards the ward.

I left my dad in the care of a stranger, she thought, balling her fists as she pictured her dying father on the settee in the parlour. *I abandoned my parents and my fiancé so I could gad about Barbados, waving a flag for the NHS. And now, that lot are puffing away like chimneys in there, without a care in the world. They haven't even got the good grace to acknowledge I'm in the same room as them, and all Baird–Murray can do is take the mickey out of those hard-working West Indian nurses, when it's them that's going to fish Britain out of the mire!*

The consultants in the staffroom put her in mind of Humphrey Buchanan and his land-owning friends at the plantation house, living high off the hog while the Black staff tugged their forelocks and catered to their boss's every whim. Kitty was no fan of Communism, but she felt strongly at that moment that the inequity between the rich and the poor needed addressing – more so than a few reforms by the new Labour Government. Had Baird-Murray not taken her seriously because she was a poor underling or because she was a woman?

One of the young doctors said something to her as they passed one another in the corridor, but Kitty was either so angry or so exhausted by the difference between Atlantic Standard Time and Greenwich Mean Time that she didn't hear him. *Maybe James hit the nail on the head*, she thought. *Maybe I should have stuck with my plan and left the hospital and nursing for good after my leaving party. Now, I've got to plead with Mildred Thorpe to come back and care for my dad, when I could be doing a better job.*

Kitty took a detour and found herself near the operating theatres. She came upon Mr Galbraith, scrubbing his arms in preparation for Mr Wentworth's surgery.

'You've got to ban smoking,' she said. 'In the hospital, I mean.'

'Nurse Longthorne. Whatever are you doing here?' Galbraith looked at her askance. 'Are you quite all right?'

'That staffroom is disgusting. If smoking tobacco is as dangerous as you say, you should take a stand. Did you know one of the sisters smokes? Women are doing it now!'

Galbraith looked at his soapy hands. 'All in good time, Nurse Longthorne. My paper hasn't been published yet, and even when it does come out, it won't garner many fans, I'm afraid.'

'Why not?' She was dimly aware that she was shouting, but she felt emboldened by her sleep deprivation.

'Well, for a start, tobacco products are highly addictive, so there's built-in resistance from smokers who are little more than addicts, before you even start on the dangers. Added to which the tobacco companies are extremely powerful and bring in a great deal of revenue to the country . . .'

'Stuff them! They've given my father an early death sentence. He's not up to much as a person, but I still prefer the old berk alive to dead. It's going to floor my poor mam when he goes.'

Galbraith sighed. 'Nurse, you really need to be back on the ward. Leave the politics to the politicians. Leave the science to the scientists. I fear my battle will be a long and dirty one. And there may well still be a fight to expose the ills of tobacco, even after I've retired. Perhaps after I'm dead and gone. Some things are entrenched – I say, Nurse Longthorne, are you quite all right?'

Kitty could feel herself sliding. Her focus was fading to grey. Then, everything turned black.

Chapter 30

'Kitty! Kitty! Wake up!'

Kitty opened her eyes to find Lily Schwartz looking down at her. 'Lily.' She tried to wave her friend away dismissively. 'I'm fine.' The intention in Kitty's head was clear, but she could hear her words coming out jumbled and indistinct.

'Come on. Let's get you to your feet,' Lily said.

Kitty's head was throbbing and she could taste blood in her mouth. 'Ugh. I've bitten the inside of my cheek.' Wakefulness started to return in earnest, and she agreed to be walked to the nearest ward, where Lily made her sit on a bed that had been remade in preparation for a new in-patient.

'Let's take your blood pressure,' Lily said, wrapping a fabric cuff tightly around Kitty's upper arm and squeezing a rubber bulb pump until it inflated. She felt for Kitty's pulse and kept her eye on the mercury. 'Ooh, your blood pressure's in your boots. Somebody's been burning the candle at both ends.'

'I'm fine. I missed breakfast.'

Lily frowned at her and looked in her eyes. 'Yes, yes. When did you last sleep?'

Kitty shook her head and shrugged. 'I can't tell up from down. I'm still on Barbados time.'

Sticking a thermometer under Kitty's tongue, Lily looked at the clock on the ward wall. 'James will be here in a moment.'

'Oh! You didn't call him, did you? He's in clinic!'

'He's practically your next of kin,' Lily said. 'Of course I called him. If you're going to go blacking out on us, he'll want to know. He can examine you himself. I said I'd do the preliminaries and make sure you don't get into any more mischief.'

Kitty was both irritated at being a nuisance and privately glad that James was coming to check her over. Would he be annoyed, though?

'Were you ill while you were away?' Lily asked.

'I puked myself inside out on the boat on the way there, and I got a bit sunburnt, but apart from that . . .' Should she say anything about her miscarriage? she wondered. Was it even relevant? No. Some things were too private to share.

At that moment, James walked briskly through the ward doors. 'Nurse Longthorne! I came as quickly as I could.' He made a note of the blood pressure reading and thanked Lily, but he only had eyes for Kitty. His brow was furrowed; his lips set in a grim line.

Pulling the curtains around the bed so that they were cocooned in a blue glow, James turned to her and perched next to her on the bed. 'My darling, what on earth happened?'

'I fainted. One minute I was talking to Galbraith, getting all of a dither over smoking. The next . . . There's no need to fuss, though. Really!' Yet despite her bravado, Kitty's heartbeat felt laboured and she felt too weak to get up off the bed. She looked at the stethoscope hanging around his neck.

Taking her cue, James stuck the earpieces of his stethoscope into his ears and helped her to loosen her uniform so he could press the cold metal diaphragm to her chest. His expression was inscrutable. Presently, he took the earpieces out and helped her to straighten her dress. 'Your heartbeat is a little erratic and your blood pressure is too low. I'm worried about you, Kitty. I want you to see a cardiac specialist.'

'Nonsense! There's nothing wrong with my ticker. I'm just – I've been travelling for a month. I'm just a bit over-wrought. I feel a bit worn thin.'

James smoothed the hair poking out beneath her starched nurse's cap. 'You need to rest. I insist you see our cardio man for a full check-up, but in the meantime, rest.'

'Matron will—!'

'Don't worry about her. I'll explain. See how you're feeling in the morning.'

'But we're going to dinner. I was looking forward to our first date since I got back.' She clasped his hands into hers and lost herself in his warm brown eyes.

'I'll bring dinner to you.'

Later, Kitty woke to find that the sun had gone down and long shadows stretched across her chilly room in the nurses' home. Somebody was knocking quietly on her door. Looking at her clock, she saw that it was just after half past six.

She pulled on her dressing gown and trudged to the door, her stomach growling wildly. 'James? Is that you?'

On the other side of the door, she heard her fiancé's voice. 'Quickly, before Matron spots me.'

Smiling weakly, Kitty opened the door to find James clutching a tray containing two plates, covered in tinfoil.

'You meant what you said!'

'Of course. Now, do let me in before we have Matron on the warpath.'

James shooed her into the armchair by the fireplace and set the tray on her lap. 'Cutlery for madam? A little *l'eau de* corporation?' He spoke with a strong French accent.

'Eh?' Kitty looked up at him bemused and then saw he was filling her glass. 'Tap water! Ha. Corporation pop, indeed! *Très* sophisticated. Yes, ta.'

Sitting at her side on her dressing-table stool, with his own plate on one of her thick nursing tomes, he pulled the foil away to reveal the surprise meal. '*Voilà!* Cook knocked us up your favourite as a special favour to me – steak-and-kidney pie and roast potatoes. I bought the meat myself when clinic ended.'

Kitty sniffed at the golden pastry of the pie. Gravy was oozing from the lid. After months of mass-catered fayre on board the *Tradewind*, which she'd often struggled to keep down, or else the spicy Bajan cooking she'd enjoyed on the island, it was comforting to be faced with a simple pie. 'Cook made *this*? It doesn't look anything like her usual stodge.'

She tucked into it. The meat needed at least another hour's stewing and the pastry was still raw on the bottom. 'It's lovely,' she said.

James grimaced as he chewed. 'Oh, dear.' He surreptitiously spat out a piece of gristle and left it on the side of his plate. 'I think Cook may have taken my braising steak home for her husband!'

'Maybe she swapped it with her dog's rations.' Kitty hadn't meant for such harsh words to come tumbling out, but when they did, they both started to giggle. 'Mind you, why would Cook know what to do with a nice cut of meat? She's probably cooked nothing but innards and rusk since 1939. You know, she's actually a worse cook than my mam, if that's possible. Poor Marge!' The giggles got louder, turning into loud guffaws.

There was a knock on the door – insistent this time.

'Kitty? Have you got a man in there?'

Kitty slapped her hand over her mouth in horror. 'Matron.'

James set his plate on her dressing table and answered the door to an indignant, red-faced Matron.

'Dr Williams!' she said, puffed up with self-importance. 'Whatever are you doing in the nurses' home?'

'My fiancée passed out this morning, and I thought it my medical duty to check on her and make sure she gets a hot meal.' He smiled winningly at Matron. 'I assure you, I'm behaving like a gentleman. Surely you wouldn't begrudge the NHS's very own West Indies recruitment star a bit of pie.'

Matron deflated somewhat. 'Very well, Dr Williams. I'm trusting you to . . .' Her eyes stared blankly out from behind the lenses of her glasses. For once, she was momentarily speechless. 'Get well soon, Kitty. I hope to see you on the ward in the morning.'

Matron flushed red and turned on her heel to leave.

'Did you meet Grace?' Kitty called after her. 'Matron! Did you meet our first recruit?'

'Yes.' Matron turned around. Her nostrils flared and she pressed her lips together. 'Park Hospital's going to be a changed place.' There was a sigh in her voice. With a pained smile, she walked away.

James closed the door. 'Well, that was odd.'

Kitty put her cutlery together. 'I think I've lost my appetite. Did you see that? What on earth is wrong with her? She was the one who made the recruitment trip possible. She's having regrets, isn't she?' She picked up a small roast potato with her fingers and popped it whole into her mouth. Chewing thoughtfully, she asked, 'Do you think Matron's prejudiced? Against Black people, I mean.'

Shrugging non-committally, James looked dolefully at his dinner. 'I really shouldn't have entrusted Cook with the meat, should I? I knew it was a mistake. Sorry.'

Was he changing the subject on purpose? Kitty noticed that he looked a little crestfallen. 'It's the thought that counts. I really appreciate the gesture, love.' Kissing him on the cheek, she drank in the smell of his faded cologne and the lingering odour of the hospital. 'You're a belter.'

For a few minutes longer, Kitty pushed her food around, but her appetite seemed to have left, along with Matron.

James cleared the plates away, tucked her in and knelt down to kiss her tenderly on the forehead. 'I'll see you tomorrow, darling. Get some rest.'

'I've got a horrible niggling feeling,' she said, reaching out to take his hand.

He frowned. 'What do you mean?'

'I think everything's changed by me going away, and I don't think it will ever be the same again.'

'I don't understand.'

Kitty propped herself on her elbow. 'The world's upside down, like it shifted on its axis or summat, by me sailing through the Bermuda Triangle.' She noted James's still-perplexed expression. 'I mean, my dad's dying. He was always big and strong and *there*, when I was a little girl, but he's going to be gone before the year's out.'

'He was already dying, my love.'

She stroked along the grain of his fingernails. 'And all those people who smoke . . . Suddenly, it turns out, they're killing themselves slowly, and Galbraith – to hear him talk, you'd think we're going to have another war brought to our door by the tobacco companies.'

'That's a long way in the future, Kitty. And the more

causes of cancer we discover, the more lives we'll save. It's smoking that's killing people. Not the research that exposes it, and certainly nothing to do with your trip!'

'But those new recruits from the colonies, coming to work at the hospital – we wanted their help desperately a couple of months ago, but I have a feeling it's going to drive a massive wedge between the staff. And I feel like I've brought the strife back with me from Barbados.'

'Is your friend, Grace, strife?'

Kitty shook her head vehemently. 'No. She's smashing. The opposite. She was so kind when—' She started to cry. 'I lost the baby out there, James! Our baby. I wanted an adventure of a lifetime. I was hell bent on it! Barbados granted my wish, but it took the baby in return. And now, everything else is going to the dogs.'

James held her gently, stroking her hair. 'There, there, darling. None of this is anything to do with you. If the old guard can't cope with progress, then, I say, bring in the new guard! And you didn't *lose* the baby, Kitty. You can't apportion blame for a biological process that's entirely down to nature. We're medical people, you and I. We know better than that, don't we?'

She nodded. Perhaps he was right.

'You're overtired and overwrought. Get some sleep, and this will all seem different in the morning.'

Surrendering to her exhaustion, Kitty pulled the blanket close and shut her eyes.

'I hope you're right, James. I pray to God you're right.'

Chapter 31

'Morning, Mr Galbraith,' Kitty said, as the surgeon entered the ward.

'Ah, Nurse Longthorne. I'm very pleased to see you back on your feet. Are you quite over your funny turn?'

Kitty nodded, shuffling her paperwork. James had been right. Sleep had been the best medicine, and now she felt able to tackle whatever lay ahead. She was standing in for the sister, who had been called away to a welcome meeting for some new nursing recruits from India and Malaya. It felt good to be sitting behind the desk in the sister's office, however makeshift.

'Yes. I'm fully recovered, thanks. I was just exhausted from my journey. I never realised the time difference would knock me for six like that.' She opted not to mention that it wasn't the first time she'd fainted of late.

Galbraith briefly reminisced about a surgeon's conference in Chicago that he'd been to in 1935, and then matters turned to the patients on the ward.

'Donald Wentworth's wife and sons are coming in this morning,' Kitty said. 'They want to speak to you about his prognosis.'

Galbraith's brow furrowed. 'Ah. Yes. Well, it's always very hard for the relatives to take that kind of news. One can never be truly certain what one is going to find until the patient is on the operating table.' He smoothed his moustache with his index finger. 'How is your father, by the way?'

Kitty looked down at her well-scrubbed hands. 'He's . . . we're making him comfortable. He's a permanent fixture on the settee in the parlour, driving my mam round the twist, when he's actually awake. So, still strong in spirit.'

'There will come a point when we make real advances in the treatment of lung cancer, Nurse Longthorne. I'm just very sorry that won't help your father. Very sorry indeed.'

Frowning but avoiding meeting his gaze, Kitty nodded and said nothing.

Out of the corner of her eye, she spotted a harried-looking woman who had entered the ward, flanked by two sullen adolescent boys. The woman made for Mr Wentworth's bed.

'She's here now. Mrs Wentworth. Shall I—'

Galbraith nodded curtly. 'Yes. Yes.'

Faced with one of the hardest parts of her job, Kitty took a deep breath and headed out of the office and onto the ward full of coughing, spluttering and wheezing men. Mr Wentworth was lying in bed, now surrounded by his grim-faced family. There was a pipe coming from under the covers, feeding into a large glass jar. The jar was filled with the pinkish-red fluid drained from his lungs. He was muttering fearful tidings to his family from beneath his oxygen mask. His grey complexion promised no hope.

'Mr Wentworth,' Kitty said, approaching the bed with a forced smile. She turned to his wife. 'Mrs Wentworth. Good to see you. Your husband's an absolute delight to look after.'

'Balls.' Mr Wentworth clearly wasn't in the mood for niceties. 'I can't wait to get out of here. You come in, they cut you open like a side of beef, and then send you home to die. They're a bunch of butchers.'

'Oh, now, now. Mr Galbraith is one of the best chest and lung men in the NHS. In fact, he's here to talk to you and your missus, right now.' She turned to his wife. 'Shall I take the boys to choose from a jar of humbugs in my office? Me and Sister Penny got given them as a gift, but—' She patted her tummy and looked down at the boys. 'We need help from some children or we'll never get through them.' She winked. 'Do you know of any children that can help us?'

The boys grinned at one another and peered hopefully up at their mother. 'Please, Mam!' they said in unison.

The chin of Mrs Wentworth dimpled up and the corners of her mouth turned down; her shoulders drooped and her head seemed to loll forwards as if all the air inside her was escaping. 'Aye. Go on, then. Don't get sticky hands.'

Kitty led the boys to the office, passing Galbraith as he approached Mr Wentworth's bed. They locked eyes fleetingly. Both knew all too well how the Wentworths would be feeling in five minutes' time.

When Kitty saw Grace standing at the entrance to the sister's office, looking lost, she felt some of the heaviness lift.

'Grace!' Just looking at the young Bajan nurse made her think of life-giving sunshine, turquoise seas and her fool of a brother. 'How are you settling in?'

Grace's shy smile subsided into something far more woebegone. 'Not too bad. Not too bad.' She bit her lip.

Kitty took her by the arm and steered her into the office. 'Homesick?' she asked.

'I suppose I am,' Grace said, wiping a tear from the corner of her right eye with her knuckle. 'I can't sleep. My appetite's gone. When I do eat, the food here's laying heavy all the time. And the change in water is playing havoc with my stomach.'

'Oh, poor you.' Kitty felt responsible for this girl. She'd dragged her from the bosom of her family and convinced her to sail through hell and high water to a wonderful new life in Britain. Judging by the tears that were standing in Grace's large eyes, her new life was proving anything but. 'It must be a culture shock. Look, we've both got a weekend off coming up. Why don't you come to my mam's for Sunday lunch? I know you're missing your family, but while you're settling in, you can treat my family as your own, for what it's worth. Adoptive, like.'

Grace looked at the pile of freshly laundered towels on the shelves behind Kitty and nodded unconvincingly. 'All right. That would be nice. Thanks.'

'Are you keeping up with the work? Getting on with the other girls? I see some women have arrived from India and the Far East.'

'Everyone's lovely. Honestly.'

Kitty felt that Grace wasn't being entirely truthful. She resolved to get to the bottom of it on Sunday. She hoped beyond hope that James would come to the lunch . . .

The lung ward was bedlam with two new chronic bronchitis admissions, but when Kitty had a short break, she made her way over to James's clinic to thank him again for his inedible pie and unfaltering support. When she arrived there, she found James attending the Jamaican Band on the Wall musician, Lloyd Chambers.

'Ah, Nurse Longthorne. Excellent. Do pass me some tweezers.' James reached out, opening and closing his hand in anticipation.

Lloyd was sitting in a chair, wincing. 'This ain't gonna hurt, is it, doctor?'

James smiled and shook his head. 'After your surgeries, this is going to be a cinch.'

Kitty took the tweezers from a tray of sterilised equipment to James. 'You're looking great, Mr Chambers.'

'Call me Lloyd.'

'Right you are, Lloyd. Dr Williams, here, has put your face back together. What a difference from when I first saw you in casualty! You'll have the ladies swooning when you next play on stage.'

Shying away as James came at him with the tweezers, Lloyd harrumphed. 'I'm not holding my breath.' He held up his hand and flexed his fingers. 'Main thing is, I can play my trumpet again. I was more worried about losing my livelihood than my natural good looks.'

'Oh, Lloyd, you are a wheeze!' James started to remove the stitches with care.

Kitty stood by and held a kidney dish to catch the waste. 'Tell me, Lloyd,' she said. 'I've got a nurse from Barbados who's just started working here. I recruited her myself. She's a lovely girl. Anyway, she's terribly homesick. Are there any organisations she could join? You know . . . where she can meet other people in the same boat?'

Lloyd seemed to be studying her. Was he trying to decide if she was somehow being judgemental or patronising?

'Moss Side,' he said.

'Really? I used to live in Hulme. I don't remember there being more than a handful of Black people around there, during the war.'

'Maybe you been looking in the wrong place.' Lloyd winced again as James cut and removed a stitch. 'Or maybe you not been looking at all. When I came last year, they already got a community in Moss Side. Africans owning houses. Man from Sierra Leone owns the house where I be renting a room. He told me they had the Pan African Congress in Manchester in 1945.'

'Oh, I think I read about that,' James said. 'There's an academic at Manchester University – an economist, I believe. Alfred . . . Albert . . .'

'Arthur Lewis,' Lloyd said. 'He an important West Indian man. Everybody heard of him. And we got a Negro Welfare Centre in Liverpool. They talking about building one here, in Manchester. We got clubs and churches and cafés where you can eat the best food outside Kingston. You don't think West Indians be organised?'

'I absolutely never—' Kitty was horrified by the insinuation that she might harbour anything less than respect for the new colonial immigrants.

'Joking!' Lloyd said, though the furrows in his brow said he was anything but.

'There's a lot of Black seamen live round my mam's way,' Kitty offered. 'They come in on merchant ships from the West Indies and then stay. Get work and that. But I didn't realise there were Jamaicans and Barbadians living just up the road from Hulme. Maybe my friend can find a little taste of home, there.'

'Cheetham Hill, too,' he said. 'But mainly Moss Side. When I first came to Manchester, my landlord in Ardwick kicked me out. Now I be living right up in the attic, in a big tumble-down old house in Moss Side. The only place where a Black man's rent money be good enough, and a musician can find a good party. Play till the sun come up. Nobody complaining!'

Kitty thought about Grace and imagined what sort of thing might make her feel more at home. She was a respectable girl from a churchgoing family who had fallen on hard times. Perhaps she'd like—

'You should give us the address of a Baptist church in Moss Side,' James said unexpectedly. 'Can you do that, Lloyd? I'm not really a churchgoer, myself, but perhaps Nurse Longthorne's friend will find a little corner of Manchester that feels like home in a church.'

'That's very thoughtful, Dr Williams,' Kitty said, standing back to admire Lloyd's reset nose and fixed eye socket.

'I'm not such a bad old stick, eh?' James said.

Lloyd looked in the mirror that James held in front of him and grinned at his reconstructed features. He primped the tight waves of his carefully styled hair. 'Looking good. You some kind of genius, Dr Williams. The ladies will sleep sound tonight, knowing Lloyd, the horn of Manchester, got his film-star looks back again.' He turned to Kitty, the relief and joy in his face lighting up the room. 'Hey, nurse. Why don't you ask your Bajan friend to come see me play at the Band on the Wall?'

Chapter 32

'Come in, love. Come in. We're not proud.'

'Oh, thank you. Pleased to meet you, Mrs Longthorne. Here. I brought this for you.'

'A plant? Lovey, you shouldn't have! Here. Give us your coat.'

From the scullery, where Kitty was peeling carrots, she could hear the exchange between her mother and Grace. There was the slam of the front door shutting; footsteps along the narrow hallway.

Wiping her hands on her apron, Kitty peered into the parlour, where her father was lying on the settee, snoring gently amid the hiss of his oxygen supply. James was sitting in the old armchair, reading the Sunday paper. When Grace walked in, he folded it up and stood to greet her.

'Grace!' Kitty wiped her hands on her apron and pushed James aside to embrace her friend. Her mother trotted past and into the scullery, clutching a spider plant. 'You found us. Smashing. How was the church?'

'Like going home,' Grace said, looking around at the dark, cramped parlour. 'There were a couple of men from St John in the north of Barbados. A few Grenadians. Lots of Jamaicans from Kingston. Mainly men, but—'

'Any handsome ones?' Kitty winked.

Grace shook her head and looked down at her shiny shoes. She laced her hands together. 'Oh, that's not why I went to church.' She chewed the inside of her cheek, her ebullience slipping away somewhat. 'I love singing. I wanted to sing hymns like the ones my mother sings and be among people my own colour and kind. Just for a couple of hours.' The bones in her slender neck rose and fell as she swallowed.

'Sounds wonderful,' James said. 'Shall I put the kettle on?' He turned to Kitty. 'Kitty, shall we make tea together?'

His meaningful nod towards the scullery told Kitty that James had something on his mind. 'Good idea, love. Grace, do sit down. Don't mind my dad. He's just having a snooze.'

Together, she and James repaired to the small scullery, where her mother was basting roast potatoes.

'Your guest seems very . . .' her mother said.

'She's lovely,' Kitty replied. 'And she's a long way from home and terribly homesick. Listen, both of you. If Dad starts acting up, I want you to intervene.'

'I hope she likes breast of lamb, because that's all I could afford,' her mother said. 'Do they eat that over there?'

'They eat all sorts, Mam. I'm sure Grace won't turn her nose up at a home-cooked meal.' Kitty could see James's expression sour and his lip curl at the mention of the fatty dish that always made a mockery of clean hands and freshly laundered clothes. She stifled a giggle, desperate to remind him how character-building having to endure another of her mother's 'roast lamb' dinners would be. 'Grace has got better manners than to complain.' She dug James surreptitiously in the ribs and then lowered her voice. 'What did you want to say?'

He glanced back towards the parlour. 'I wanted to ask, is she quite all right? She looks like she's struggling. She's lost an awful lot of weight in a short space of time. That dress is hanging off her.'

'It's a hand-me-down from Sister Penny,' Kitty said. 'Penny's much more robustly built than Grace.'

'Even so. She hardly looks like she's thriving. I'd say your new friend needs a little – comfort. More than just a square meal. A real shoulder to cry on. I'm wondering if we *can* introduce her to Lloyd. He's a top chap and he did say he was the horn of Manchester!' James grinned.

'Wash your mouth out with soap, James Williams,' Kitty whispered. 'Mam has ears, you know!'

Privately, she acknowledged that Grace was indeed looking frail since her arrival. As she buttered slices of only slightly stale bread for the table, she wondered if Grace was being treated with kindness by the other staff and the patients at the hospital.

'Elsie! Elsie! Who's this sitting in the parlour?'

A distressed voice interrupted her musings. It was her father. Over the past few weeks, he'd lost much of the power in his voice, but he'd lost none of the barb and bigoted intent. At that moment, Kitty realised she'd made a mistake in inviting Grace to her mother's table.

'Dad!' She burst out of the scullery, peeling knife in hand, and stood before her father, hands on hips. 'This is Grace. She's one of my nursing colleagues who came over with me from Barbados to work at Park Hospital. She's a guest in this country and a guest in Mam's house, so I'd be very grateful if you could show some respect.'

Her father coughed violently in response, lifted his mask and spat something foul and almost solid into a handkerchief. 'This is *my* house. I don't want her sort so much as setting foot over my threshold.'

Kitty smiled at Grace apologetically and turned back to her father. She lowered her voice and spoke quietly next to her father's ear. 'No, this is Mam's house. You're living here because she lets you. I know you're dying, Dad. We're all very well aware you're dying. But you've got no right to be nasty to my friend. So, if you fancy ending your days on a noisy hospital ward, instead of warm in Mam's double bed or on this settee, with the gee-gees on the wireless in the background, you'd best behave!'

By rights, her father should have been dead by now, given the advanced stage of his lung cancer and the secondary tumours that had made a mockery of his continence and dignity. Yet it seemed to Kitty that sheer bloody-mindedness and strength of spirit was keeping Bert Longthorne going, despite all odds.

'Make sure your mam smashes the cup she drinks out of.' The sneer was visible beneath his oxygen mask.

'You're having your tea in the back bedroom, Bert Longthorne,' Kitty's mother said, carrying a tray through from the scullery, containing a steaming tea pot, milk in a bottle, a higgledy-piggledy mix of chipped, jumble-sale mugs and buttered bread on a side plate. 'Any friend of Kitty's is a friend of mine, and I'll not have you showing this family up.' She turned to Grace. 'Take no notice of him, love. He's three sheets to the wind on strong medication.'

Grace sat primly on the sofa, gripping her handbag, as though it was a shield against Bert's charmless comments. 'He doesn't need to leave the parlour on my account.' She set her bag down and sniffed the air. 'Do you need my help cleaning your father up, Kitty?'

Kitty shook her head. 'Don't be daft. He's my problem, and you're off duty.'

Her father began to spew out a vile torrent of racial slurs, the likes of which Kitty had never even heard before.

James got to his feet. 'All righty. That's quite enough of that, Albert. Let's get you tucked up in the bedroom, shall we?' He mouthed a profuse apology to Grace.

Kitty helped him to hoist her father off the settee. Today, the old man wasn't wearing his prosthetic. He was dressed in clean pyjamas, but his thin, incomplete frame looked bedraggled in the too-roomy flannelette that he could no longer fill out. At that moment, Kitty had never loved or loathed her father in such equal measure.

'Come on, you mischievous old sod,' she said.

In the bedroom, she and James cleaned him up with a bowl of hot soapy water and a freshly laundered towel. They changed his pyjamas and the terry towelling arrangement that stood between him and indignity.

'Comfy?' Kitty asked, allowing James to shunt him up the bed while she arranged his pillows just so.

'Aye.' The old man patted her arm.

Kitty took his hand in hers and kissed it. His fingernails were still deeply grooved and peeling. 'You're a bugger up your back, Dad.' She adjusted his oxygen mask over his nose and mouth, now that James had wheeled the canister in from the parlour.

'Mouth on her like a docker,' he said, wheezing with laughter. 'That's my girl!'

Sitting on the edge of his bed, Kitty wiped his face with a clean, warm rag. She smoothed his lank hair from his yellow, emaciated face. 'What am I going to do with you, Dad?'

'Give us a smoke.'

'Don't be daft.'

'Go on. I'm dying. What difference does it make? Give us a cig.' The old man looked at the drawer of the bedside cabinet. 'I've got some Wills's Capstan in there.' He turned to James, his withered features full of pleading. 'Light us one up, will you, Jimmy Boy?'

James stood at the foot of the bed like a sentry. 'I'm afraid I can't, Bert.'

'How come?'

James smoothed his immaculate dark, Brylcreemed hair. He didn't meet Kitty's father's searching gaze. 'First, do no harm, Bert. Very soon, the general public will realise that cigarettes are nothing short of poison.'

'Stuff and nonsense!' Bert said. 'They're good for you.' He patted his concave stomach. 'Keep your weight down. Calm your nerves. Even pregnant women have started smoking them. If it was bad for you, they wouldn't be able to sit there with a cig and a bottle of stout, now would they?'

James sighed. He looked down at the candlewick counterpane on the bed. 'I'm sorry. Kitty will bring you a tray in when it's ready. We'll check on you. In the meantime, I'll leave you with the sport section of *The Times*. How about that?'

'Too many words!' Bert shouted. 'It's all bloody chit-chat.'

'Don't worry. There are plenty of photographs, too.'

Momentarily, James disappeared off into the parlour. He returned bearing the newspaper. He pointed to the back page. 'See? Told you! All the photographs a man could wish for. No cricket, though.' He sat on the edge of the bed and peered thoughtfully at Kitty's father, as if searching for the proper thing to say. 'Glad we made it to Old Trafford, Bert. Brian Close and Les Jackson put on quite a show, considering it was their debut.'

'They were rubbish. It was a draw. I was bored stiff. New Zealand went home laughing.'

'Oh, I don't know.' James smiled. 'Close scored forty-six

runs. He was only behind Hollies and Bailey. I rather enjoyed it, myself. A little son-in-law and father-in-law moment of sporting triumph.'

'Good seats. I'll give you that much.'

Kitty pulled James into the small hallway. 'I can't bear it.' She shook her head to clear it of maudlin thoughts. 'It was a mistake to get Grace over, when he's frail like this.' She rolled her eyes and looked up to the ceiling. 'Anyway, there's certainly nowt wrong with his foul tongue. Let's leave him where he can't hurt any feelings.'

The Sunday lunch progressed well, with Bert Longthorne tucked out of the way and, more importantly, out of earshot. Kitty's mother served a fine-looking lamb breast.

'Smashing gravy, Mam,' Kitty said, pouring the rich brown gravy over the hearty meal. 'I missed this when I was in Barbados.' She glanced at Grace and winked. 'They don't do Yorkshires like this in the West Indies.'

Grace battled to prise some lamb meat from the fatty mass and piled it onto her fork with some golden roast potatoes and overcooked cabbage. She chewed with an uncertain expression on her face. Then, finally, she smiled. 'Nicest meal I've had since the boat. God bless you, Elsie.'

Conversation soon turned to the hospital.

'How are you finding your new post, then, Grace?' Kitty asked. 'Is Molly treating you well on the mixed ward?'

'Fine,' Grace said. She gazed down at her Yorkshire pudding with studied interest.

It was only when a tear splashed into the hollow of the brown, crispy accompaniment that Kitty realised her friend was crying. ''Ey up, Gracie. What's the matter?' she said, rubbing Grace on the back. She could feel sharp shoulder blades beneath the fabric of her dress. 'Come on. Out with it!'

Grace took her paper napkin and started to sob into it. 'I'm sorry. I didn't mean for this to happen.'

'Spill the beans, love. What's wrong?'

When she had regained enough composure to be able to speak, Grace looked round at Kitty, James and her mother, as if trying to decide if they were trustworthy enough for her to reveal some terrible secret. She closed her eyes. 'Some of the other nurses.'

'Who?'

'I'm not a tell-tale.'

'What on earth are they doing to make you so upset?'

'Just being mean to me. Calling me names because of the colour of my skin.' She blew her nose loudly. 'And don't ask me to elaborate. I won't tell you them, they're so shocking. But I hear them in the office and on the corridors, the other nurses. They think I can't, but I'm Black, not deaf.'

Kitty put a supportive hand on her forearm. 'Oh, Grace. I am sorry.'

'I mean, it's not like I'm not used to prejudice. Barbados isn't perfect. The likes of Humphrey Buchanan think Black girls are just there to service his needs: clean his house, cook his meals, keep his bed warm.'

'Oh, Grace. Please don't tell me you've been maltreated by any of the doctors,' James said, his thick, dark eyebrows bunching with concern. 'Because they're intelligent men and they should know better.'

Grace picked her cutlery back up and then set it down again. She fingered a single piece of red coral that hung around her neck on a gold chain. 'I've been made to do all the menial jobs. I'm a qualified nurse, Kitty, but the sister on my ward has got me sluicing bedpans with the trainees and mopping floors, when I could be administering penicillin and putting on fresh bandaging.'

'Really?'

Nodding, Grace sighed and held her hand to her brow. 'This isn't what I came here for. You know that, don't you?'

'That's certainly not why I came out to Barbados,' Kitty said. 'I didn't travel thousands of miles to tear skilled women from the bosom of their families and make them false promises. If that's what's happening, we need to do something about it.' She was looking at James. 'I'll have a word with Matron tomorrow. She'll fix it. She'll right the wrongs.'

'Don't be so sure,' Grace said.

'What do you mean?' Kitty felt her innards twist into knots.

'Matron's no ally. Not my ally, at any rate.' With the tines of her fork, she poked absently at a pile of overcooked mashed carrot and swede.

'How so?'

'I'm being paid the wages of someone far more junior, Kitty.' Grace locked eyes with her. 'I'm supposed to be earning the same as a State Registered Nurse, but I'm not. It's a fraction of what I'd been promised.'

'I'm sure there must be some clerical error,' James said. 'Surely the NHS is no thief. And I know Kitty was acting in good faith.'

Grace closed her eyes and spoke with calm conviction. 'Dr Williams, my money's short and I'm being treated like dirt. The bad treatment is one matter. Maybe that's down to one nasty group of prejudiced women. But if I'm short-changed in my pay packet, week after week, you can bet that's come from above. Somebody, somewhere, has decided to bring thousands of colonial workers here under false pretences, to plug the gaps in your labour market and empty your hospitals' bedpans at a knock-down price. And if that's something that's come from the Department of Health, or whoever came up with the idea to send nurses like Kitty, here, out to the West Indies and India and the Far East, you can bet that the likes of Matron know exactly what's going on.'

'I can't believe it,' Kitty said, pushing her plate away. 'Matron's always been so honest and even-handed in her dealings.'

'Maybe she is – for you. But not me, Kitty. Not when her skin is white and my skin is Black. I hate to sound paranoid, but I think I've been brought over here under false pretences.'

Chapter 33

'Ah, Kitty. There you are,' Matron said. She was sitting at her little desk in her room in the nurses' home, rifling through some paperwork. 'Sister Penny has contracted a pernicious stomach bug. Until she returns to the ward, I want you to be in charge.'

Kitty stood in the doorway, pulling her dressing gown tightly shut against the early-morning cold of the home's corridors. Her toes were freezing and leaden inside her carpet slippers. She leaned against the architrave, inhaled sharply and clasped her hand to her chest. 'Really? Me?'

Peering at her over the top of her tortoiseshell spectacles, Matron's stern expression betrayed little, though Kitty was sure there was a glint in her eye. Even at half past five in the morning, she was fully dressed in her perfectly starched uniform, concerned only with hospital business. 'If I didn't want you to be acting sister, Kitty, I wouldn't have asked you, now would I? Are you up to the job?'

Kitty nodded enthusiastically. 'I'll say.'

'Good. That's that. I'll drop by the ward at the start of the shift to tell the other nurses that they're to do your bidding at my say-so. It really is time you applied for a sister's position, Kitty. Whatever is holding you back? Is it Dr Williams and his romantic—'

'Matron, I really appreciate your faith in me. You know I always have. When my dad passes, I'm going to be taking a view on everything, I promise.' She watched Matron's features immediately soften into a half-smile. 'Now, do you think I can have the new West Indian girl, Grace, doing her probationary period on the lung ward?'

'Why?'

'I think she's unhappy on the ward where she is currently. The other girls are being less welcoming than they should, I'm told.'

Turning to her paperwork, Matron picked up a pen and started to fill in a form, as if Kitty had already left.

'Matron.'

'Very well. Keep an eye on her. See that she works hard and doesn't shirk.'

'Why would she? Matron, do you know that Grace is the equivalent of a State Registered Nurse back in Barbados?'

Matron continued to write. 'I am aware of all the nurses' qualifications and abilities. New recruits *and* existing staff. I am the Matron.' Finally, she turned to Kitty and treated her to a cold, hard, beady-eyed stare. 'It is my job to know each nurse's strengths and weaknesses.'

'Did you know Grace is being asked to sluice bedpans and mop floors? She's earning far less than she was promised.'

Matron turned around to face Kitty and laced her hands together on her lap. Again, she peered over the top of her spectacles as though she was an aggrieved school ma'am, trying to explain something relatively simple to an obstinate pupil who refused to listen. 'Ours is not to question why, Kitty. There is an edict from the powers that be that the new colonial recruits can't be employed in positions higher than that of State Enrolled Nurse. Naturally, SENs are paid less than SRNs. You do see the predicament, don't you?'

'That's not fair.'

'And neither is colonial skin. We have a nursing shortage, but these women are not yet tried and tested over here. They're guest-workers, trained to different standards. I don't make the rules, but I do run a tight ship and I do decide which girls deserve to progress and which girls still need to prove themselves by mopping floors and sluicing bedpans. These colonials may turn up with a sheaf of certificates under their arms, but they're not worth the paper they're printed on, as far as I'm concerned. These people live in shacks. They can't be bothered to pave their streets.' She waved her hand dismissively and wrinkled her nose. 'I hear they'd rather sit drinking rum all day.'

'You sent me to the West Indies, Matron! I've seen what it's like with my own eyes. Britain has left it to rot. The coffers are empty for all but the plantation owners. People work themselves to the bone, but they're still starving.'

'God helps those who help themselves, Kitty. You, of all people, should know that.' She slammed her hands sharply down on the desk. The conversation was at an end, and she clearly aimed to have the last word. 'No. The likes of Grace will have to work harder than local girls to earn *my* respect.'

Kitty bit her tongue, desperate to stick up for her friend. She wrapped her arms around herself against the chill in the air, emanating not from the open window but from the matron herself. Matron, who had always been her champion and the member of hospital staff whom she'd looked up to the most, had suddenly shown a side of herself that was far less than palatable. 'Well, I appreciate the opportunity to stand in for Sister Penny. I hope I don't disappoint.'

'I have every faith in you, Kitty.' Matron turned away and took up her pen.

Trudging away and trying to turn her focus to getting a good strip wash before the other girls started queuing for the bathroom, Kitty was disappointed that she had failed Grace, and that the woman she had put on a pedestal for all those years was fallible and petty, like everyone else. Her body felt leaden and her feet felt too clumsy in her slippers to drag along the hallway.

'Oh, and Kitty!' Matron shouted after her.

Turning around, Kitty sighed. *What now?* 'Yes, Matron?'

'I don't suppose there's any harm in you taking Grace under your wing. I suppose if you judge her to be diligent and honest – well, then, perhaps she'll shine under your supervision.'

'Thank you, Matron.'

She felt as light on her feet as Ginger Rogers, then.

'Right, Molly,' Kitty told Molly Henshaw, as the shift began. She beckoned Grace forward. 'I want you to show our new recruit the ropes on the lung ward, while I attend Mr Galbraith on his rounds. We don't know when Sister Penny's going to be back in, so just imagine I'm her, for now.'

Molly put her hand on her hip and screwed up her doughy features. 'Says who?'

'Says Matron.'

Though it clearly pained her, Molly managed a show of teeth in response. 'That makes me second in command, then.' She turned to Grace. 'Let's get cracking on those bedpans, shall we?'

Kitty noticed that Grace was shaking slightly. 'A word in the office before you start, please, Grace.'

Once they were alone, Grace sat in the visitor's chair on the other side of the makeshift desk. Her shoulders drooped. 'It's really kind of you to get me moved, but—'

'But what?'

'Bedpans? Is Molly going to be as bad as the others? Can't you do the rounds with me?'

'I'm acting sister, Grace. I've got to oversee the ward and do the day-to-day managerial stuff; liaising with doctors and that. I'm not going to be walking the ward every minute of the day, but I can't just leave you to it, either. You've not been here long enough. Listen, Molly's a good nurse, but if she starts, she's got me to answer to,' Kitty said. 'If anyone calls you names or you think you're being unfairly treated, don't be afraid to let me know.'

Two weeks went by and Kitty became more confident with every passing day.

'You seem to be made for a position of authority,' Galbraith told her, as they finished the rounds – later than usual, thanks to an emergency admission. They stood together just outside the doors to the ward, peering in. 'Jolly well done, Nurse Longthorne – or should I say Sister? You run a tight ship. If you weren't due to walk down the aisle with Dr Williams, I could easily see you as matron one day.' He saluted her in jest and clicked his heels. 'At your service, ma'am!'

Kitty felt a rash of embarrassment itch its way up her neck and flush her cheeks. 'Oh, go on, Mr Galbraith. You are a charmer.'

'I'm not one for hyperbole, as you know. My particular specialism doesn't lend itself to uncalled-for levity, either.' He pressed his lips together. 'Speaking of which, I notice the young Black nurse is terribly subdued. Is she shy?'

Kitty glanced through the window to see Grace fashioning hospital corners from a flat bedsheet on a newly vacated bed.

'I think she's struggling to settle in. These recruits from the colonies have been promised the earth and have come over here, only to find they're getting crumbs from the table.'

'Damn shame,' Galbraith said. 'Still, I suppose they're earning enough to send money back home. And that girl will be learning new skills.'

'Not unless you count mopping.'

Galbraith scowled. 'Oh? Well, I'm told most of the nurses from the West Indies are being sent to work in psychiatric hospitals like Prestwich, so your girl should count herself lucky, if truth be told.'

The grim memory of Black Rock Psychiatric Hospital flashed before Kitty's mind's eye and she shuddered. 'I can't help but feel responsible. I brought Grace over here.'

Patting her on the shoulder, Galbraith sighed. 'You're a good girl, Kitty Longthorne. But you have to disengage from what goes on in a day's work, or else you'll lose your mind and have that big heart of yours broken. Don't get too involved.'

Kitty thought about his words of advice throughout the rest of the morning, though she was busy updating the notes of the patients and organising patient transport to X-ray and down to theatre. There was so much more responsibility as a sister, and given that Sister Penny had been diagnosed with a nasty case of gastroenteritis, it was unlikely she'd be back for another week or two – a state of affairs that suited Kitty well, given that she desperately needed to be distracted from her father's decline. The issue of Grace, however, could not be shelved, no matter what advice Galbraith had given.

Marching along the ward, Kitty took her friend gently by the elbow and steered her away from the pile of fresh bedding. 'That can wait. Come with me.'

Molly emerged from behind a curtain that surrounded a patient's bed, carrying a kidney dish and a used syringe. She drew the curtain back fully with her free hand, casting a judgemental glance Kitty's way. 'I asked Grace to get the beds made for two new admissions,' she said. 'And she's got to give Mr Fenton a bed bath and deal with his bedsores.'

Kitty appraised the puffed-up figure of Molly. 'Thanks for your contribution, Molly. Now, get on with your own work. In fact, I suggest *you* sort out Mr Fenton's bed bath and bedsores yourself. Grace and I have other matters to attend to.' She turned to Grace and winked. 'Come with me.'

Grace looked at her askance. 'Where are we going?'

Kitty led her towards the exit and out of Molly's earshot. 'Lunch.' She pointed to the clock. 'There'll be nothing but Cook's bullet dumplings left if you leave it any longer, and you look like you need a break. Lord knows, I do.'

Together, they made their way to the nurses' dining room, where there were few seats free. Kitty hadn't broken bread with Grace since she had joined them for the fraught Sunday lunch at her mother's.

'You go ahead,' she said. 'Get yourself something to eat and find us a table, will you?' Grace didn't need to know Kitty's intentions.

Grace nodded and went up to the servery, where a dinner lady was replenishing the cabbage. Kitty observed how the dinner lady's smile faltered as Grace doled a child-sized portion of corned-beef hash onto her plate.

Is this how everyone treats her? Kitty wondered.

She hung back as Grace made her way to a table where there were two free places.

'Mind if I sit here?' Grace asked one of the nurses, whom Kitty recognised from the maternity ward.

The nurse looked up at her blankly. 'Yes. It's taken. Sorry.' She moved her pudding bowl into the spare space adjacent to her own place setting.

Yet there was nobody else standing around or queuing for food in the entire dining room.

Grace moved to the next table where there were also two free spaces. The same episode unfolded, this time with several junior nurses chipping in.

'Oh, we're saving those spaces for friends.'

'Sorry. Those places are taken.'

'No. You can't sit there. Why don't you find somewhere else?'

Kitty had seen enough. Aware that Grace was standing helplessly by the second table full of unfriendly faces, clearly wondering what to do, she marched up to the first table.

'Are these two places taken, Clarry?'

The same nurse who had refused Grace moved her pudding bowl. 'Take a seat, Kitty. Or should I say, *Sister* Kitty?'

'Shame on you!' Kitty said.

She moved to the next table, where the junior nurses were openly and audibly sniping about Grace for her skin colour and her status as 'colonial cheap labour' – seemingly without an iota of guilt.

'Can I sit here, ladies?' Kitty said, pulling out a chair expectantly.

'Course you can, Nurse Longthorne,' the nurses said deferentially and in unison.

'But aren't you waiting for friends?'

The young nurse who had rejected Grace shook her head. 'Not at all. We'd be honoured if you sat with us lowly junior nurses, wouldn't we, girls?'

Kitty set her tray down and beckoned Grace over. 'Then you won't mind if my colleague Grace sits with us, will you, *girls*?'

The nurses' mouths hung open as Grace took her seat beside Kitty in silence. She squeezed Kitty's arm.

Setting her cutlery on her plate, loud enough for the young nurses to hear her and look up, Kitty said, 'If I catch any of you bad-mouthing any of our new arrivals or commenting on their skin colour or coming out with claptrap about them being different or inferior to the British, I will personally tell Professor Baird-Murray and you will be disciplined, possibly dismissed. Do I make myself absolutely clear?'

The junior nurses nodded and muttered their apologies. One by one, they took their trays and left, casting panicked glances at one another.

Kitty exhaled and turned to Grace, smiling. 'I'm glad they've buggered off. We can enjoy our boot-leather stew in peace, now.'

Grace put her hand over her mouth to conceal a wide smile. 'You're so much like Ned.'

Kitty raised her eyebrows. 'Not quite. I haven't got Brothel Keeper on my curriculum vitae.' She gobbled down a few forkfuls of corned-beef chunks and stewed potatoes, then she turned to Grace. 'Out with it. You've been late eight out of the fourteen mornings I've been in charge of the ward and you barely say a word. What's the matter?'

'Nothing. I told you. I've never taken to snitching.'

Putting a supportive hand on Grace's shoulder, Kitty sighed. 'Well, you'd better start, or you're going to end up on a boat back to Barbados with a bad reference. Come on, Grace. I know you've got excellent nursing skills. I saw you in action in Barbados, and I've been watching you when Molly's turned her back and let you get on with it. You're clinically highly competent and you've got a great way with the patients. Some of them love you! Heck, you even managed to find a vein in Mr Tavistock's arm to get a blood sample. Nobody else managed that! I've been keeping my eye on the other nurses on our ward, and I haven't spotted anything beyond Molly being her usual flippant self. So, come on. Out with it! What on earth is going on?'

Grace pushed a potato around her plate. 'It's the nurses' home.'

'Eh?'

'I do my washing, they take it out of the machine and dump it on the floor. I put my clothes on the drying rack. They take them off and dump them on the floor. I put milk in the refrigerator for a cup of tea. They leave it out on the side so it curdles. I try to get in the bathroom for a bath, they push past me, saying I'm going to contaminate the bathtub with a ring of black grime.' Tears rolled silently onto her cheeks, but she forked the hash into her mouth as if nothing at all was unfolding at their table beyond a friendly chat. 'Molly's the ringleader, but she's by no means on her own.'

Kitty rolled her eyes. 'They're all bullying you. How did I not see this?'

'You go in early. You come home late, because you see James or visit your family every night. I'm not the only one putting up with this either. The three Indian ladies and the girl from Malaya are having the same problems.' She pushed her plate away. 'Kitty, they make fun of our accents all the time. I love to laugh, but not when I'm the butt of the joke.'

'This is – crikey, I had no idea. I'm so sorry.' Suddenly, Kitty had lost her appetite. She could understand ignorance and prejudice in uneducated people like her father – particularly the older generation, who rarely saw anyone who wasn't white. It was harder to accept the same level of intolerance in her colleagues, who were skilled and literate. They knew enough about the world to understand that their behaviour wasn't acceptable. Kitty blushed, mortified and angry as she was. 'What about being late, though? You realise that just fuels their fire, don't you?'

Grace looked around the dining room ruefully. Her judgemental gaze came to rest on those nurses who lived in their nursing accommodation. 'You try getting up on time when you've not slept a wink most of the night. At first, I didn't sleep at all. Lately, I finally drop off at about four in the morning. When my alarm clock goes off, I just don't hear it. I'm exhausted. That's why I'm late.'

Kitty closed her eyes, digesting the terrible tale. 'Nobody should have to put up with this sort of treatment. Least of all a good soul and diligent worker like you,' she said. 'Leave this with me.'

Chapter 34

'Can I see you in the office a minute, Molly?' Kitty asked the following day, careful to ensure that Grace was otherwise engaged at the far end of the ward, taking a patient's blood pressure and temperature.

Molly treated her to a bright smile. 'Of course. I'm just going to sterilise these syringes and—'

'*Now*, if you don't mind.'

Molly blanched. Her pallor gave way to the beginnings of a scowl. 'I suppose I'll have to just set these aside and wash my hands, then.'

As Kitty walked back to the sister's office, certain that the temperature on the ward had just dropped by a couple of degrees, she thought about the conversation she'd had with James at the end of his clinic, when she'd told him about Grace's maltreatment in the nurses' accommodation and in the dining room. His response had disappointed her initially.

'Kitty, darling, you simply mustn't be seen to tread on Matron's toes,' he'd said. 'It sounds like she made her position entirely clear.'

'I felt like she was just saying that, though. The matron I know has always stuck up for—'

He'd steepled his fingers together, closing his eyes when he'd spoken, as though he'd been espousing some patronising pearl of wisdom to an apprentice. 'I know since that squalid debacle with Sister Iris and Lily Schwartz you've loved nothing more than to fight for the underdog, and that's admirable. But really, some issues are too big and dirty to wage war on by yourself – especially without proper authorisation. We can't have a nurse turning renegade.'

She'd sat on the edge of his desk, looking not at her fiancé, James, but at Dr Williams, the consummate politician and member of the hospital's elite echelon. A gulf had seemed to open up between them at that moment. 'Like that, is it? I'm just a rebellious little girl who won't toe the big-boy's party line?'

'I didn't say that, Kitty.'

'Oh, but you did. A nurse turning renegade. There was a time, James Williams, when you would have supported me in speaking out against bullies in the hospital. But now, it's just a "squalid debacle" to you. I don't even know what debacle means, but I can tell from your high-and-mighty tone that you see what went on with Iris and Lily – what's going on now with Molly and Grace – as just squabbling women.'

'Kitty, I—'

She'd got to her feet and backed away towards the door. 'If you're not going to stand up and be counted – well, I hope you can sleep at night. Because I'm certainly not going to stand idly by and allow a young Barbadian nurse be treated like dirt by her professional equals, just because they're British and she's not.'

James had got to his feet and hastened after her as she'd crossed the empty waiting room. 'Wait!' he'd said, grabbing her by the elbow. 'Wait! You're right. I'm being a pompous, selfish idiot. I really shouldn't denigrate Grace's suffering – especially not since I used to be on the receiving end of some pretty nasty treatment when I was a young doctor, progressing up the ranks.'

Though her heartbeat had started to slow, Kitty hadn't let her stony expression soften. 'Actions speak louder than words, James.'

He'd nodded and rubbed her arm affectionately. 'I'll bring the matter up with Professor Baird-Murray at our next board meeting. I swear. But promise me you won't go rushing in, all guns blazing, to sort this matter yourself.'

Having James on her side had felt like a small victory. Kitty couldn't twiddle her thumbs and watch Grace suffer, however, while he courted the support of the board. She'd resolved to tackle the matter of Molly alone. And now, she was thoroughly looking forward to flexing her muscles as stand-in sister to nip injustice in the bud.

'Close the door,' Kitty said, positioning herself behind the desk. 'Sit down.'

'What's this all about?' Molly asked. She sat stiffly in the chair, hands on knees. She tittered nervously.

Kitty cleared her throat. 'Why do you think it's acceptable to bully Grace and the other new recruits?'

Molly shook her head and smiled. 'I have no idea what you're talking about.'

Smoothing her fingers along the desktop, Kitty held her voice steady. 'I've heard you've been taking Grace's washing out of the machine and dumping it in a wet pile on the floor. I've heard you've been nicking her milk; whipping up the other nurses to tittle-tattle behind her back and make her life a misery.'

Molly was red in the face. 'I don't know what you're talking about. It's all lies. If Grace has told you that, then she's a big fat liar. I've been nothing but friendly to that girl.'

Chewing the inside of her cheek, Kitty frowned. She hadn't been expecting Molly to deny Grace's allegations. How naive she was! 'So, it's your word against hers, is it?'

Examining her fingernails, Molly slowly, nonchalantly rolled her gaze across the makeshift office and onto Kitty. She raised an eyebrow. 'Have you got any proof?'

'You've had her doing menial stuff. Bedpans and mopping.'

'Instructions from Matron.' Molly's nostrils flared and her eyebrows shot towards her hairline – a picture of righteous indignation. 'And I don't know where you've got your other information from, but that's slander in my book, and I'm not taking that lying down, Kitty Longthorne. No one slags off Molly Henshaw and gets away with it. She's nowt but a stirrer, that Grace.'

The enormity of how completely her confrontation had unravelled dawned on Kitty. She felt the blood drain from her face and shivered. 'I've seen how the other girls treat her with my own eyes. In the dining room, she—'

'Maybe they just don't like her,' Molly said. 'There's no law says you have to like everyone in Park Hospital. She's a bit uppity, if you ask me, coming over here and expecting to be treated like one of us. She's not earned her stripes yet. The girl's arrogant. Turns up late to work and thinks she can get away with it because she's new. If any of us did that, Matron would have our guts for garters.'

Standing and scraping the legs of the chair along the linoleum, Molly straightened her dress over her stomach. 'Matron's going to hear about this, Kitty. You mark my words. You might think you're sister, but you're not. And you're out of line.'

When she'd gone, slamming the door behind her, Kitty slapped her hands to her face. 'What have I done? Why couldn't I have kept my big mouth shut?'

It was no surprise to Kitty that she was called into Matron's office later that evening.

'Explain to me why I've had Molly Henshaw sobbing in here at teatime, Nurse Longthorne.' Matron tapped out each syllable on the desk with her index finger. She might as well have been shooting flames from her eyes, as she glowered at Kitty over the top of her spectacles.

'I-I can explain.' Kitty bit her lip and scratched her chin.

'Stop simpering and sit down!' Matron's raised voice felt like a sharp slap.

There was no friendly pep-talk in the offing; no glass of sherry by the fire to calm Kitty's feverish spirits. She could feel an icy and brutal storm was upon her. She had never had the strength or the inclination to stand up to Matron before. This was the first time they had ever clashed over anything, and Kitty felt bile rising in her throat.

'What have you got to say for yourself?' Matron had changed from being Kitty's rock and surrogate mother-figure to being Mrs Danvers in *Rebecca*. How could the woman she admired most take a tumble from such a high pedestal?

'I've heard that some of the other nurses have been bullying Grace and the other new recruits. Molly's the ringleader. According to my source.' Kitty inhaled deeply and held her breath for a moment.

'And who's your source? Grace Griffith, by any chance?'

Kitty nodded. 'Yes. She told me she's having a terrible time of it, and it's stopping her from sleeping.' She related the litany of unfair treatment to her superior, just as Grace had described it to her.

For too many tense moments, Matron sat in silence, studying her through narrowed eyes and tapping the desk top. Finally, she spoke. 'Might I remind you that I asked you to *stand in* for Sister Penny? You are *not*, in fact, a sister. You are Molly's equal, yet you saw fit to rebuke her, as though you had some jurisdiction over her.'

'I thought she was being cruel, and it broke my heart to see Grace—'

'The Barbadian girl is a new arrival, Kitty. A colonial worker, who will, no doubt, return home when she feels she's wrung out all she can from the British experience and the NHS. Molly is your long-standing colleague – a nurse who does an excellent job and whom everyone holds in high esteem.' She rolled her eyes. 'Whatever possessed you to take the side of some West Indian girl over a British-born nurse? This Grace character can't even be bothered to show up on time for her shift.'

Kitty's cheeks were ablaze. The fear of being given a dressing down was subsiding and giving way to irritation that Matron, of all people, was tacitly condoning bullying, just because of the colour of Grace's skin. Kitty felt betrayed. '*You* sent me to Barbados. *You* wanted me to bring Grace back. I coaxed her away from her family and her home and everything she'd ever known with the promise of a bright future in Manchester, and she can't even wash her smalls in peace!'

Matron removed her spectacles and polished them on the hem of her dress. 'The hospital needs these nurses. The NHS needs cheap labour to swell its ranks. But you need to decide where your loyalties lie, Kitty. Do they lie with foreigners – strangers – or with your long-serving colleagues?'

As Kitty stood there in Matron's office, surrounded by her medical manuals and myriad files, stacked on the desk and on the shelves, and the austere trappings of a spinster's life – photos of nursing colleagues and long-dead pet dogs and perished parents and the sherry bottle on the mantel-piece – she realised that the woman she'd always admired so much had chosen to love an organisation instead of a family. Somewhere along the way, Matron's warm, beating heart had hardened, and now, there was only strict discipline and the abstract love of a job where once there had been passion and empathy for people. 'Have you finished?' she asked.

'I beg your pardon, young lady.'

'Is that it? Molly makes a penniless young West Indian nurse feel like she has no place here, and I'm given – what? The order of the boot? A demotion? A telling-off.'

Matron slammed her meaty hand on the desk. 'Enough! I will not tolerate this insubordination, Longthorne. You were supposed to leave three months ago to get married. It was you who begged me to let you go to the Caribbean. You wanted an excuse to keep nursing. I gave it to you because I don't want you to waste your potential and throw away your nursing future to become a housewife. You wanted a palliative nurse for your father. I arranged it for you because I didn't want to think of your poor mother trying to juggle everything, or to put too heavy a burden on your shoulders. I have always been on your side, girl. Do *not* use me as your whipping boy because you're torn between marriage and your career, Kitty Longthorne. Don't think being engaged to a doctor on the board gives you the right to talk to your superior without proper respect, either. Now, I suggest you get to bed early and start your shift with your head screwed on straight, Nurse. One more word from you, and I'll be escorting you off the hospital campus myself!'

Kitty left the matron's office and ran back to her room. The moment she closed her door, the tears came.

Chapter 35

'Kitty! Kitty! Are you awake?'

Kitty had been drying her eyes when the insistent knocking at her door had shaken her out of her self-pitying reverie. It was Grace's whispered voice behind the door.

Shivering, she wondered how she could have let the fire go out. 'Grace? Whatever is the matter?' She threw her ugly man's dressing gown over the uniform she still hadn't changed out of and opened the door.

Grace was standing in the doorway, beaming. 'I just met your Dr James coming out of the hospital. He told me to tell you to get your glad rags on and meet him by the car.'

'My glad rags?' Kitty craned her neck to catch sight of the clock on her mantelpiece. 'It's nine o'clock in the evening. Curfew's at ten!'

Grace nodded. 'I know. Exciting, isn't it? He said he's taking us *both* to see some live jazz. He said it was to cheer us up.' She bounced on her toes. 'See you downstairs in ten minutes?'

'Not likely,' Kitty said. 'Everyone will see us going out! No. Come back to my room when you're ready. I'll show you how we sneak out. Make sure you've got your dressing gown over your dress. Bring your lippy with you in your handbag.'

Grace hared off along the landing to her own room, leaving Kitty quite bemused at the prospect of sneaking out.

It had been a wholly dreadful day. She was intensely frustrated at Matron. What better way to dispel her melancholy fug than to flout the rules and let her hair down for once?

She donned her best dress, which her mother had made for her. As ever, the fabric was a pair of chintz curtains Elsie had found at a jumble sale. Kitty was no longer embarrassed by such things, however, especially since this dress was so very reminiscent of Dior's famed 'New Look' – a figure-hugging bodice that nipped in nicely at her waist, with a longer, full skirt. Her mother had even fashioned starched underskirts from the neighbour's old net curtains! Brushing her hair and hastily rubbing her teeth and gums with a rag dipped in soot from the back of the fireplace, she glanced in the mirror and deemed herself fit for an elicit night on the town.

Ten minutes later, Grace knocked again, and she pulled her friend inside, pushing the door to.

'Now, we go out through the first-floor bathroom, because there's a flat roof beneath the window and nothing but the door to the coal hole below. We come back in through the kitchen. There'll be nobody around to see us, gone midnight. The lock's broken and there's a grit salt box to climb on.'

Grace was wide-eyed but still smiling. Kitty's heart was thumping. It wasn't as if she was a stranger to sneaking out these days, but with women like Molly, who were prepared to run with tales to Matron, it wasn't without risk.

'Come on!' Kitty said, checking the coast was clear.

They crept along the hallway, breathing a sigh of relief when they found the bathroom vacant. In silence, Kitty opened the frosted window wide and gave Grace a leg-up onto the ledge. Grace scrambled out onto the flat roof, beckoning her outside. With nobody to help her climb,

Kitty wedged her foot against the sink to boost herself up to the ledge. When she heard the familiar click-clack of Matron's low heels on the parquet of the hall below, she froze. Matron came to a halt. Kitty didn't even dare breathe. She prayed her superior wouldn't come upstairs to investigate a cold draught or the sound of someone scrambling noisily on the coal hole's roof.

A young nurse called out to Matron on the other side of the nurses' home, and mercifully, Matron marched off, away from Kitty and Grace's subterfuge.

'Blimey, that was close!' Kitty whispered, as she led Grace across the grounds, grateful for the cover of darkness. 'Matron nearly copped us, you know.'

'What would have happened if she had?' Grace was shivering in the shadows in a Sunday-best dress that had been made for rather better weather.

Kitty shrugged. 'Docked pay? A sharp ticking-off? A bit like a bad cold or stomach upset. Unpleasant, but neither would kill you.' She giggled at her own daring.

James was waiting for them by the Ford Anglia, looking at his watch expectantly. 'Ah, at last. I'd given you up. Thought you'd gone chicken on me, Longthorne.' He winked and opened the passenger door for her.

Grace took a seat in the back. 'Oh, I haven't done anything this exciting since Ned—' She seemed to think better of sharing her anecdote, but Kitty caught her reflection in the rear window, grinning out at the Davyhulme night.

'Where are we going?' Kitty asked.

'I happen to have a patient playing at the Band on the Wall, and we're his guests!'

Kitty inhaled sharply. 'The Band on the Wall? Isn't that rough as a badger's bum? You're talking about Lloyd, aren't you? That's where he got beaten to a pulp, wasn't it?'

James chuckled. 'Fear not, my dear. I'm told it's just an evening of dancing to good jazz. It's not a Saturday night, so I think it should be reasonably tame.'

'Whatever has come over you, James Williams!'

'You've both got a couple of days off from tomorrow, haven't you?' He overtook a bus and sped down the main road into Trafford. The lights of the city centre twinkled ahead of them. 'I thought it would do you both good.'

Kitty frowned. 'But we've got to drive down to your parents' in Berkshire in the morning.'

'I promise to have Cinderella back before the clock strikes midnight.'

In spite of James's optimism, the club was crowded. The moment they entered the cavernous space, Kitty was hit by the humidity from the writhing clientele who jitterbugged and jived to the music. She had expected to see the band on a stage at the far end of the club, but burst into delighted laughter when she realised that the house band was literally performing on the wall – albeit on a cantilevered stage that protruded from the wall.

'Oh, this is wonderful!' She clapped her hands together. 'And there's Lloyd! James! Look!' She pointed to the Jamaican trumpeter – cheeks puffed out and eyes screwed tightly shut as he blasted out a solo. His efforts were being admired by a group of earnest-looking young men who were standing near to the stage. They clapped enthusiastically as he finished with a long, loud toot, and the solo focus switched to the double bass player.

At her side, Grace's face had lit up. She held her hands clasped to her chest.

'Is this all right, Grace? Not too rowdy for you?' Kitty shouted above the din.

'Oh, no. Not at all. I'm loving it!' Grace started to sway in time to the music. She turned to James. 'Would you be a dear and get Kitty and me a rum and Coca-Cola, please, Dr James?' Without waiting for a response, she grabbed Kitty's hand and led her into the throng, leaving the flustered-looking James to negotiate the crowded bar. 'Let's dance!'

Kitty felt the strain of the day seep out of her tight muscles as she swivelled her hips and feet from side to side and twirled. The beat of the drums seemed to have a primal force, drumming away her doubts and disappointments. James soon returned with the drinks, having gingerly navigated his way through the revellers. Kitty had never known him to do anything but waltz before.

Thirsty and hot, she downed her sweet drink in two or three gulps. Grace followed suit.

'Are you going to dance, then, James?' Kitty asked her fiancé.

James was standing stiffly in the midst of so many of Manchester's young people, having a ball on a Friday night. 'Oh, I, er . . . Not sure if, er . . .' He looked at his drink and swilled the contents of his glass. 'Oh, twist my arm!'

Before long, Kitty, James and Grace were all dancing with abandon to the music, as if they'd been regulars at the club all of their adult lives. James kept the rums coming, and the band played on.

'I feel such a bohemian,' Kitty said, giggling at her hedonistic efforts as she twirled beneath James's outstretched arm. 'What would your mother say?' She could hear that she was slurring her words just a little. She hiccupped loudly and clasped her hand to her mouth.

'I think she'd say you're a real-life Tallulah Bankhead and are to be avoided at all costs!' James encircled her waist with his strong arm and pulled her to him for a kiss.

Kitty mused that she'd have to bring him dancing more often. Their argument about Matron seemed mercifully forgotten.

The band reached a crescendo and stopped, announcing an interval. At this point, Lloyd lay down his trumpet, climbed down off the elevated stage and picked his way through the crowd towards them.

'I can't wait to introduce you,' James told Grace.

Kitty was surprised by Grace's sour expression, but she did note a glint in her friend's eye as she observed Lloyd approaching.

'Dr James!' Lloyd said, embracing James as if he were a long-lost relative. 'I'm so glad you came. How you enjoying it?'

'It's rather good fun,' James said, mopping his brow with a big white handkerchief. 'I'm quite tuckered out, old chap. These ladies, here, have put me through my paces.' He turned to Kitty. 'I believe you know my fiancée, Kitty.'

'Of course! Of course! From when you took my stitches out. I remember!' Lloyd clasped Kitty's hands between his.

'You're looking very well, Lloyd,' Kitty said. 'And you played beautifully.' She turned to Grace. 'We're having a ball, aren't we?'

James turned to Grace. 'Allow me to introduce Kitty's colleague, Grace Griffith. She's from the West Indies. Just like you! Grace, this is Lloyd Chambers, a former patient of mine.'

Lloyd took Grace by the hand and kissed her knuckles. He spoke with a much broader Jamaican accent, now. 'Very pleased to meet you, Grace. Me never seen no hibiscus in Jamaica as beautiful as you, girl. Where you be from?'

Grace withdrew her hand. 'Barbados.'

'Then the Bajan girls must be drinking sweeter water and eating riper fruit than the Jamaican girls, because—'

'My mumma told me never to trust a smooth-talking man from Jamaica. She say, "Gracie, egg ain't got no right ay rock-stone dance!"' She turned her back on him and spoke to Kitty. 'Shall we powder our noses?'

As they started to walk away, Lloyd called after Grace. 'Hey! Bajan Princess! James tell me you like to sing. Any time you want to try out for the band, you know where to find me. Lloyd will fix you up.'

Grace curled her lip. 'If I want to sing, I'll sing in my church choir. Thanks all the same.'

'Where your church? Maybe I come see you.' Lloyd was grinning, clearly taking her hostility for flirtation.

Even in her drunken state, Kitty was sure she could discern a half-smile on Grace's lips, though the sucking noise she made with her molars and cheeks and the tone of her response said otherwise.

'Wait till you trough put an' bubble in it, Lloyd Chambers.'

By the end of the night, Kitty had never laughed so hard or consumed so much alcohol. On their return to the nurses' home, she stood before the kitchen window, staring at it in confusion.

'The window's moving,' she said.

'It's not moving,' Grace replied. 'You're drunk. You're swaying!'

Kitty stepped forward and tried to push the window upwards. 'It's stuck.'

'Let me try.' Grace pushed and pushed, to no avail.

'Someone's only managed to lock the flipping thing.' Kitty grabbed a large lump of coal out of the coal hole.

'What are you doing, Kitty? No! You'll wake the matron!'

With sooty black hands, Kitty lobbed the coal at the window. There was a frightful crack and the crash of broken glass landing on the floor inside.

Matron's thunderous voice was the first thing she heard as she poked her head through the jagged hole.

Chapter 36

'I say, Kitty, you're terribly morose. Do cheer up.' James stole a glance at her as he pushed the Anglia hard along the empty road.

'Don't you feel absolutely dreadful? I feel like I've got a woodpecker inside my head. I haven't felt this bad since my voyage to Barbados.'

James laughed and patted her forearm. 'My darling, you're hungover. Too many rums for you. Relax. It will pass. We can stop at a café, if you like. Get a good breakfast to soak up the booze.'

Kitty's stomach lurched. 'Ugh. I feel sick just thinking about all that grease! Not to mention Matron's face when she ran outside to see who'd smashed that kitchen window. If she'd spotted me and Grace, hiding behind the laurel bush, she'd have had our guts for garters. I can't believe she didn't call the police.'

'Oh, dear. Kitty, whatever possessed you to smash the window?'

'Rum. Rum possessed me. It's not called "Dutch courage" for nothing. And fighting spirit. I was feeling rebellious.' She fell silent and stared straight ahead in a bid to quell her car sickness, watching the Berkshire countryside unfold before them through the windscreen. 'It took us nearly an hour to sneak back in. I'm surprised we didn't die of exposure.' The sun was shining and made her squint. 'Did we really have to trek all the way down here for the weekend? I've got enough on my plate as it is.'

She caught James rolling his eyes, not quite surreptitiously enough. 'I haven't seen my parents in months. My mother said they had some news when she wrote, but she didn't elaborate. Darling, I know they're stuffy old so-and-sos, but they are my family. We do spend an awful lot of time with yours.'

Toying with her best lace gloves, Kitty pondered why James's words rankled so. He was right, after all. Perhaps it was because she simply didn't like his mother and father. When both sets of parents had met for tea at the Midland Hotel in Manchester, James's father had hewn a gulf between the Williamses and the Longthornes with a few sharp words about Kitty's own father's spell in prison. Or perhaps it was because she was nervous at the prospect of visiting James's family home for the first time. She had no idea what to expect.

'Is it a very posh house?' she asked, spotting the sign for Windsor and swallowing hard.

'They don't live at Windsor Castle, if that's what you mean. Ha ha.' He squeezed her thigh in a show of support. 'My mother might have been a debutante, but she's not one of the princesses. It's just a nice house, not an ancestral home!'

Before long, Kitty abandoned her troubled thoughts of her father's dwindling life, Grace's predicament and Matron's betrayal. James had turned onto a long driveway in the middle of a well-heeled suburban idyll that bordered the rolling Berkshire countryside. She focused her attention on the sprawling mansion that was visible behind large beeches, clad in autumn gold and beaten copper. 'Flipping Nora,' she said. 'Just a nice house, eh? What a pile!'

'It's Arts and Crafts,' James said. 'A Lutyens, actually.'

'Oh, aye? We had one of those, and the wheels fell off!' Kitty puzzled over what a Lutyens was – another thing for her to learn, no doubt.

James chuckled. 'You are a wheeze, Kitty.'

The driveway widened and the trees thinned to reveal the house in its full, unobscured glory. Kitty gasped, taking in the intricate patterns of the huge knot garden at the front, fashioned from low box hedging. Beech leaves fluttered down on the breeze, as though it was snowing gold. It was a semi-rural idyll like those she'd seen in the upmarket society and fashion magazines that Violet used to read – similar to the Buchanan plantation house in grandeur, but so very different for being on British soil. There was no call of tropical birds – only the coo of wood pigeons. There were no banana palms and hibiscus – in their place were large hydrangea bushes beneath the windows, still covered in enormous blue and lavender flower heads. This was no maisonette on Salford's Barbary Coast. Kitty felt shabby and grey, surrounded by so much brilliance and beauty.

James brought the car to a standstill and switched the engine off.

'Do I smell like a distillery?' Kitty breathed heavily in his direction. 'I don't want to show you up.'

He smiled. 'You smell of mints and you could never show me up. Stop worrying!'

With her heart hammering away in her chest, Kitty snatched up the flowering pot plant that she'd brought all the way from Manchester and stepped out of the car onto the gravel.

Her future in-laws were already standing at the door, dwarfed by the steep gables and tall chimneys above them.

James's mother was wearing a fully fashioned twinset and pearls. His father was wearing slacks and an argyle sweater. They were both the picture of upper-middle-class sophistication. A dog bounded to meet them. Kitty had no idea what breed it was, but James greeted it with more affection than he'd shown anyone apart from her, as far as she knew.

'Rufus. You beautiful boy. Yes! Yes, that's right. You're a big furry beastie. What's Daddy got in his pocket?' He wrestled with the auburn furry giant for at least a minute, giving it treats and kissing its snout. Then, he greeted his parents with a reticent peck on the cheek for his mother and a shake of the hand for his father.

'James.' His father didn't smile.

'Darling. You look . . . frayed around the edges.' His mother fixed Kitty with a steely gaze, though she spoke to James.

'I brought you this,' Kitty said, pushing the flowering plant towards her. 'I think it's an ivy, but I couldn't be certain. House plants are a mystery to me.'

Her future mother-in-law raised an eyebrow. 'Amaryllis. At this time of the year? It'll be dead by Christmas.' She walked off with the plant, click-clacking in her low heels on the parquet floor.

'G and T, old bean?' James's father asked. He turned and marched off into the wood-panelled hall, shouting and raising his arm, as if he was a tour guide in London. 'Margery says lunch will be ready in the fullness of time. You know what the dotty old bat's like. Come through to the orangery!'

Kitty followed James through the glorious oak-panelled hallway, with its grand, ornate staircase and jewel-coloured rug beneath her feet. On the walls were old oil paintings in heavy gold frames – portraits of James's ancestors, perhaps.

'Looks like you avoided the worst of the Blitz,' Kitty said, fleetingly thinking of how her own family's two-up, two-down and all the neighbouring houses and terraced streets in Hulme had been reduced to rubble by the Luftwaffe, rendering hundreds of families homeless.

James's father didn't look back. He kept walking into the next room, shouting, as though he were talking to two hard-of-hearing pensioners. '*Quam fortuna me favorit*, eh? Yes, Jerry left Windsor alone, for the most part. I understand Hitler gave the order to leave the castle intact. He rather fancied it as his pad, if they'd invaded. Bloody Hun!'

The next room had a grand piano as its centrepiece. Kitty mused that her mother and Ned would have chopped the thing up for firewood during the hard winter of 1947, if they'd been fortunate enough to get their hands on such an enormous thing.

'Do you play?' she asked James.

'A little. Badly.' He smiled and took her hand. 'It's mother's forte. She studied at a conservatoire until she married my father.'

As they were marched through to the back of the house, Kitty glimpsed a library through a large open doorway, where the fully laden bookshelves stretched right the way up to the high ceiling. She tried to imagine her own father, lounging in some fine leather easy chair, reading improving books and writing correspondence, seated at some grand leather-topped desk, using an old gold-nibbed fountain pen – Bert Longthorne, a man of no letters whatsoever, who only ever looked at the pictures in the paper. Kitty almost burst out laughing.

There were no oranges in the orangery, it turned out. Kitty still marvelled, however, at the sight of the tropical plants that flourished in pots in the warm, south-facing room. Above them, a large glazed lantern gave a view of the blue skies. Generously sized picture windows and French doors onto the breathtaking manicured back garden made the place feel like a Victorian botanist's glass house. Margery, her future mother-in-law, entered with some flourish, bearing a tray containing four gin and tonics, with some little puff-pastry snacks arranged on a fancy platter.

Kitty grimaced at the sight of the gin.

'Vol-au-vent?' Margery asked, offering James the platter first. 'I made them yesterday. They're quite delicious.'

What on earth was the brown mush inside the pastry case? Kitty wondered. 'Lovely. I'm . . .' She tried to think of something upper class to say. 'Famished.'

'So, James,' James's father began. 'How's the world of plastic surgery?'

A good half-hour's worth of chat ensued, and not once did either James Senior or Margery ask Kitty anything about herself. The old man blathered on and on about the inadequacies of the NHS.

'It's no good if you teach a layabout that he can continue his feckless ways, dear boy, by giving him all the things he ought to earn, fair and square. A roof over his head. Food on the table. Healthcare. By Jove! What has the world come to that the state simply gives these things to every man, regardless of how competent and diligent he is?'

'That's not the point, Father. Many are too sick to work, especially after the war. Men came home badly wounded, suffering with their nerves. A lot of people have breathing difficulties because of the poor air and diet.'

'Nonsense!' James's father slapped his knees. 'His Majesty didn't award me a CBE for services to the Navy for knowing nothing about the men who served under me. They were proud and able and willing to give their lives.'

Margery put her hand on her husband's shoulder. 'Now, now, darling. I'm sure we don't want to get into a political broo-ha-ha before our starter.' Finally she turned to Kitty. 'He'll curdle the soup, won't he, dear?'

Kitty tittered nervously. 'I'm sure he—'

'Now tell me, Kitty. Why are you brown like a navvy? It's most unladylike. James tells us you've been gadding about in the West Indies. Are you trying to become like them?'

'Mother!' James said. 'That really is uncalled for.'

Clearing her throat, Kitty chose her words carefully, for James's sake. 'I caught the sun in Barbados. I was lucky enough to be chosen to represent the hospital over there in our new recruitment drive for nurses.'

'It's very fetching, Kitty,' James said. 'You look healthy and outdoorsy. Nothing short of a miracle for we medical folk, eh?'

Kitty smiled. 'Exactly.' She turned to her future in-laws, wondering how James could have come from such people. 'It's in the high eighties or even the nineties every single day out there. Maybe hotter.'

Margery cringed visibly. 'Couldn't you have used a parasol?'

'It was hardly practical, riding through the countryside on buses with no windows and on donkey carts.'

'Donkey carts!' the old man wheezed with mirth, taking out a fat Cuban cigar and lighting it up. He filled the orangery with foul-smelling smoke. 'So this is why you two have been dragging your heels with regard to the wedding.

So that Kitty, here, can gad about on donkey carts! Good Lord. James, dear boy, I bet you're the laughing stock of the hospital board.'

'Kitty's doing a sterling job, Father. Without the new recruits, the NHS simply can't fulfil its mandate to offer top-quality healthcare to everybody.'

His mother curled her lip. 'They're workshy sorts, aren't they? The West Indians.'

'I see no evidence of that,' Kitty said. 'They're highly skilled, hard workers. It was an honour to go.' She turned to James's father. 'You're a man of the world.'

'Indeed.' He chuffed on his cigar. 'I've done my fair share of sailing the seven seas.'

'Then you should appreciate the finer points of our colonies. Britain would be nothing without them.' Kitty dug her fingernails into the palms of her hands, amazed at her own daring. In truth, she felt too ill to put up with the Williams's prejudiced nonsense and ridicule.

Margery got to her feet, glaring down at Kitty, gin glass in hand. 'I'm going to serve lunch. I do hope your Bolshevik notions won't make my gravy lumpy.'

'Mother!' James stood up, glancing down at Kitty with an apologetic look on his face.

'I hope you two Bolsheviks are still eating pork.'

The dining room was vast and cold, at the north-facing front of the house. Kitty wasn't used to sitting in such fine surroundings. She stared down at the array of cutlery, wondering where to begin. It was like a less enjoyable take-two of the dinner at Humphrey Buchanan's plantation house, with dusty velvet curtains that made everything feel sombre and wintry instead of colonial shutters that were clean and bright.

'Help yourselves to foie gras,' Margery said, smearing what looked like liver pâté onto a bun. She turned to Kitty. 'Now, do tell me, dear, why you've been gallivanting in Barbados when you should be married and trying for a baby. Violet, who was a very elegant young lady with skin like porcelain' – she took a dainty bite of her bun – 'she was *already* at the altar. She understood everybody's expectations of a woman. She didn't need to be nagged.'

James Senior drained his glass of white wine. 'Ah, well, Violet wasn't a racy sort like Kitty, here,' he said, leaning uncomfortably across her place setting to help himself to soup. He dripped some onto Kitty's thigh and tried to wipe it away. 'Oops. Silly me!'

Kitty batted his hand away and blushed. She fixed him with a disbelieving stare, agog at his ungentlemanly manners. Had James noticed that his own father had put his hand on Kitty's thigh? 'I'm *not* racy.'

The old man put his face close to hers and sniffed her. 'You both reek of stale booze.' He turned to James. 'You look like you haven't slept in a year. Where were you both last night?'

'Dancing, if you must know,' James said, gripping his spoon with a slightly shaking hand. 'We went to see a live jazz band. For the first time ever, I hasten to add. One of my patients plays the trumpet rather well.'

'A likely story, Margery!' his father said, guffawing. 'Our James has been jitterbugging into the small hours. See?' He nudged Kitty and winked; took another slug from a fresh glass of wine that Margery had poured for him. 'Racy! Drinking till all hours with dockers and floozies, no doubt.'

James threw his napkin onto the table. 'Really, Father. You're the limit! I have to question why I drove Kitty and myself down here on our precious day off to listen to this kind of nonsense. It's very . . . very . . .'

'Bad manners?' Kitty uttered the words before she could deem them respectful for future in-laws.

Margery's face reddened. She opened and closed her mouth twice, clearly searching for hurtful words. Then she seemed to happen upon the ultimate insult, pointing to Kitty's engagement ring. 'You know, that's not the ring James's future wife was supposed to have. It had always been my intention for James to give my mother's two-carat solitaire to my daughter-in-law to be. It's flawless and has an exquisite setting. And he *did* – give it to his fiancée, I mean. Well, his first fiancée, at any rate. Violet still has that ring, and in many ways, though she was cruelly jilted by our implacable, over-indulged son' – she scowled at James – 'and, seemingly, will never be the daughter-in-law I'd hoped for, I feel she is the better woman to wear it. *You* don't have the breeding to carry off a ring of that pedigree, Kitty. So, it's fitting that you should get something that looks like it was bought from Woolworths.'

'Mother! I say!' James set his spoon down on the side of his bowl with a loud clang.

Is that all James has got to say to the old witch in my defence? Kitty thought. She felt hot tears threatening to emerge. Her head was throbbing harder than ever. She threw down her napkin and stormed out of the house, no longer sure what sort of future she had ahead of her. At that moment, it certainly didn't feel like she and James would be Dr and Mrs Williams any time soon.

Chapter 37

'Well, aren't you going to say anything?' Kitty asked, looking intently at James's face in profile as he drove.

He never took his eyes from the road. 'I don't know what to say. I'm mortified. I just don't have the words.'

'No. You don't, do you?' Kitty's hangover had gone now but had left in its place anger she simply couldn't quell.

'What's that supposed to mean?' Finally, he shot a glance in her direction. His dark eyebrows hung low over weary-looking eyes.

Kitty tried to express her disgust and hurt with poise and clarity, but all she managed were hot tears and a hiccupped response. '*Mother! I say!*' Kitty mimicked his understated, middle-class disdain in a high-pitched voice. 'That's what you said! That's *all* you flipping well said. Really, James, was that the best you could do to defend the woman you love against your mother's despicable . . .?' She shook her head wildly while she searched for the right word. Suddenly, it came to her. 'Slander!'

James pursed his lips. He inhaled, ready to speak. Then, he closed his mouth again. Inhaled a second time, perhaps thinking of a different response. 'I can only apologise for my mother's shocking behaviour. Honestly, Kitty. I'm as outraged as you are.'

'Oh, I sincerely doubt it, James.'

'He closed his eyes momentarily. 'No, I am.' The tendon

in his jaw flinched. 'The whole thing was dreadfully embarrassing. My parents are ogres. We never should have gone.'

'No, we bloody well shouldn't have.' Kitty's voice wobbled with emotion, much to her chagrin. She took a handkerchief out of her handbag and scrubbed her wet cheeks dry with it. 'I don't want to see them again until the wedding. That's if you still want to marry me. If you can bear to be with a drunken floozie who lacks any kind of breeding.'

'Of course I still want to marry you!' James brought his gloved hand to his lips and shook his head. 'The breeding thing was indefensible – what my mother said about the ring. I'm so, so sorry, Kitty.'

'She talks about me like she's weighing up a dog at Crufts or something. It's like . . . it's like she's putting you out to stud and only the best brood mares will pass muster. I'm surprised she didn't measure the circumference of my head or the length of my legs, for God's sake.'

'Take no notice.'

'Tell her to apologise!'

'No.'

'*What?*' Kitty stared at James in disbelief. 'Are you willing to set a precedent where your parents think it's fine to talk to me like I'm dirt? Is that how she's going to speak to our children?'

'Don't be ridiculous. Our children will be well mannered and sweet natured because *we*'re good people. You'll be a wonderful mother, Kitty. Warm, giving . . .' He rubbed her shoulder encouragingly.

She brushed him off. 'What if she drips poison in our children's ears? Tells them they're low born and worthless, or praises them and says their good points are all down to you? What if—?'

'I wouldn't let her.'

'Oh? You'd say, "*Mother! I say!*"? Is that it? Because I don't think that's defence enough to protect our children from horrible comments about Black people and declarations of what a penniless scrubber I am.'

'Kitty! You're being ridiculous.'

At that moment, their argument was interrupted by a police car, travelling at speed, hot on James's heels. Kitty saw the flashing lights bouncing off the rear-view mirror of the Anglia, reflecting on James's alarmed face.

'I don't believe it. Good Lord. They're going to feel my collar for being over the limit. I just know it. Damn that gin and glass of wine. We should have fronted it out and stayed overnight.' He pulled into a layby with the police car slowing behind him. 'I should never have got behind the wheel.'

Feeling the blood drain from her face, Kitty hastily slipped James a mint. 'Play it cool. Don't let them smell the guilt on you.'

The memory of her father driving them all home from the pub after a neighbour's wedding, without a licence and in a stolen, untaxed car flooded back to her. She and Ned had only been about ten at the time. Bert had been pulled over, six pints of ale down. Kitty remembered her father's placatory words to her mother. *Don't worry, Elsie. Watch this! I'll just play it cool.* Her mother, however, had been less than supportive. *They'll smell the guilt on you a mile off, Bert Longthorne. It's seeping out of your pores.* Her father had had the keys taken from him and had narrowly avoided arrest by concocting some cock-and-bull story about having borrowed the car to get home in an emergency to his dying mother. Kitty could still smell the foetid stink of the rag-and-bone cart that had given them a lift back home. Embarrassment had overwhelmed her then, as it threatened to overwhelm her now.

'Men! They're all the same,' she whispered beneath her breath.

James had rolled down his window. He smiled at the policeman, who leered at them both. 'Good evening, officer. What seems to be the problem?'

At least he sounded sober. How much had he drunk at lunch? Kitty couldn't remember. He'd certainly drunk way too much at the Band on the Wall.

'You've got a rear light out, sir. Passenger side.'

'I'm terribly sorry. I had no idea.'

The policeman leaned in further and scrutinised Kitty. 'And you were driving ten miles over the speed limit.'

'Really? Oh dear.' James's voice started to falter.

Kitty willed him to keep strong. She spun her engagement ring around so that it looked like a wedding ring. 'It's my fault, officer. I'm expecting, see.' She patted her stomach. 'I've got a dicky tummy and we were miles away from any conveniences.'

James's hand began to tremble as he gripped his steering wheel. He lowered it onto his lap, out of sight. 'Yes, officer. There was nowhere to pull in. It seemed a rather dangerous ploy just to stop the car on a single carriageway, with twilight not far off. I suppose I must have unwittingly put my foot down.'

'Have you been drinking, sir?' the policeman said. He was in his mid-fifties, Kitty assessed, and with his bulbous red nose, he was certainly no stranger to the smell of alcohol.

'I had a G and T at midday, before a heavy meal. I'm sure it's out of my system now.'

'Can I see your driving licence or some form of identification, please, sir. And step out of the car.'

Kitty closed her eyes, resting her hand on her belly where there was no longer any baby – only the queasy remains of a hangover and some undigested vol-au-vents.

James got out of the car and took out his wallet. Kitty saw him offer the policeman his hospital identification.

'Williams. What do you do for a living?'

'Consultant plastic surgeon. We were just at my parents' in Berkshire and we had to leave early because we received a call that my father-in-law has taken a turn for the worse and is on his death bed, in Manchester. Lung cancer, poor chap. Obviously, I'm a little shaken and desperate to get my wife home to see him. What with the baby and all.'

The policeman nodded slowly and handed the identification back. 'Walk in a straight line for me, Mr Consultant Plastic Surgeon, there's a good lad. Just up and down the layby, if you will. Should be easy for someone of your intellect.' Here was a man who was unmoved by status or perceived respectability.

Kitty gulped, willing James not to lose his nerve. She felt responsible for the dramatic turn of events that had led up to this excruciating confrontation with the police. Would James get struck off the medical register if he was arrested for driving under the influence? She'd seen men in far worse states at the wheel, driving much faster and far more recklessly. She'd observed the carnage resulting from car crashes when badly injured motorists had been rushed into casualty.

Craning her neck, she watched her fiancé walking up and down confidently enough.

There was a hushed exchange and James got back into the car. Kitty turned to look out of the back window to see the policeman finally retreating to his own vehicle.

'Well?' she said.

James exhaled heavily. 'Fine and dandy. He told me to get my light fixed. Good Lord, Kitty. That was a close shave. I shan't make the mistake of driving under the influence again. I thought my heart was going to give out back there.' He watched the police car pull away and waved at the grumpy-looking policeman. Then he kissed Kitty on the cheek. 'Shall we try again? This time I'll go slower, on account of the baby.' He winked.

Was he secretly hoping their cross words had been forgotten? 'We've not finished our conversation, I'm afraid,' Kitty said.

'Ah, yes. About that. Look, I'm dreadfully sorry, Kitty. If there's a next time, when my mother behaves appallingly, I will be firmer with her. I promise I won't let her speak to you like that again. But you have to realise, darling.' He reached over and squeezed her hand. 'I can't afford to get on the wrong side of them to such an extent that they sever ties. I need their money for my experimental surgeries on those who can't afford to pay.'

'But the NHS—'

'It doesn't cover everything. And you saw the pile my parents live in. I'm loath to wave goodbye to my inheritance. It will put our children through school and university. It will set them up in the professions of their choice.'

'If my mam or dad ever talked to you like that—'

'You've got considerably less than me to lose, darling. That's all there is to it. My parents can be utter pigs, but I – we – can't afford to alienate them. And once upon a time, of course, I loved them and they loved me. Mother wasn't always so aloof. They've both become set in their ways. Age has turned the old buggers to stone. But I want them in our lives – a very small dose of them, perhaps every other Christmas and the odd Easter!'

Kitty exhaled hard and stared dolefully out of the window. She held her hands up. 'Fine. I'm not driving a wedge between you and your family. I've never been manipulative or demanding like that and I'm not going to start. But you have a word with your mother and tell her she's to treat me with a little more respect. I won't put up with it, James. I mean it.' She toyed with her handkerchief. 'Listen, do us a favour. Can we drop by my mam's before you take me back to the nurses' home? I want to check on Dad. I've got a funny feeling.'

'Upset tummy?' James grinned.

'Don't start.'

As they crossed the boundary between Cheshire and Manchester and headed down the road towards Salford, Kitty realised that she and James might always clash over his parents.

'We're from two different worlds, me and you,' she said, looking out at the cramped brick terraces that were now in darkness but for pools of sulphur-yellow streetlight.

'It's what makes us a great couple,' James said. He stopped at a junction. The lights glowed red. He leaned over and kissed her tenderly on her cheek. 'We'll make our own world, darling. James and Kitty's world, filled with love, light and happiness – and open minds and broad horizons. You're not marrying my parents and I'm not marrying yours. Let's just remember that.'

The roads were empty by now. As the Ford Anglia pulled into her mother's street, the strange sense of foreboding that Kitty felt grew stronger.

'Oh, I do have a queer feeling,' she said. 'I hope they're all right.'

'I'm sure you're just tired. It's been a long and fraught day.'

She knocked on the door and heard footsteps beyond. Her mother opened the door, looking drawn and puffy-eyed. Kitty could hear another man's voice emanating from the parlour.

'Oh Kitty. I am glad you're here. I sent word to the nurses' home but nobody knew where you were.'

'Me and James drove down to—'

'Father Patrick's here from St Joseph's. He's come to – you'd better come in.'

Hastening through to the parlour with an icy dread creeping along her spine, Kitty gasped when she saw the priest sitting on a low stool by the settee, administering the last rites to her father.

Chapter 38

'Oh, Dad,' Kitty said, clutching her father's thin, gnarled hand as he slept on the settee. 'I wish I'd looked after you myself. I wish I'd come over last night, instead of dancing like a berk till all hours.'

James stood at her side, stroking her hair. 'There, there, Kitty. We weren't to know, were we? And you've had bonus time with your father, since he came out of prison. Happy memories of him driving your mother to distraction, eh?'

Through her veil of tears, Kitty smiled. She cast her mind back to her father tracking her down at the nurses' home; how he'd persisted in pursuing her mother for a second chance, hanging around at her mother's digs until the two of them had been forced to move into a slum because the old landlady couldn't bear Bert's malingering presence any longer. Then, the printing-press fiasco. Kitty reflected that her father had been at his very best over the last couple of years. His disability had kept him out of the pub, and for once, he'd been a father and a husband instead of a liability. 'Poor Dad.' She looked at the amber hue of his forefinger. 'What a waste.'

'Here,' James said. 'Your mother's seeing the priest out. Why don't you go and put on some tea? I'd like to look Bert over, if I may.'

Feeling at a loss and wishing more than anything that Ned was there, Kitty nodded and set her father's hand down gently. She made her way to the scullery and found it in disarray. The pots were unwashed and stacked high in the sink. The mess of meal preparation from dinner had not been cleaned up. She filled the pan and set it to boil on the stove. She was just about to tackle the washing-up when her mother appeared at the kitchen doorway.

'Oh, Kitty, love,' she said. 'I'm all of a two-and-eight.' She was trembling and looked frail, as though she'd aged by several years in the space of a week.

'Come here, Mam. It's going to be all right. I'll look after us.' Kitty wrapped her mother in a tight hug and drank in the smell of carbolic soap and her unwashed hair. It had been a long while since she'd been to have it washed and set. Kitty determined to do it for her as soon as time allowed. 'I wish to God you hadn't sent Mildred away. These last few weeks have been too hard on you.'

Her mother freed herself from the embrace and started to pull a motley collection of chipped mugs from a cupboard. She took a bottle of sterilised milk out of the larder. 'You know precisely why I sent her away. I sent her away because grief is private. Your dad dying . . . looking after him . . . that's a job for family, not strangers. If your dad had wanted Uncle Tom Cobley and all prodding and poking him, he wouldn't have kicked up such a fuss about breathing his last in a busy hospital ward.' She wailed and clutched the milk bottle to her chest.

The pan of water began to steam and hiss. Kitty turned the light out underneath it and gently took the bottle from her mother. 'Sit yourself down, Mam. Let me look after you, for a change.' She poured milk carefully into the three clean mugs, then spooned some tea leaves into a teapot that needed a good scrub but would do.

Her mother slumped onto a chair at the little Formica table. 'It's funny. I wasn't sure I ever wanted to see him again, when they banged him up.' She gazed wistfully at the rising steam as Kitty poured the boiling water from the pan into the teapot.

'Remember when he came out? He nagged his way back into our lives. He was like a dog with a bone, showing up at my nurses' home! Getting his feet right back under your table.'

'Aye. He always was a handful, my Bert. But we've had a good run, these last couple of years.'

Kitty set the lid on the pot and sat beside her mother at the table. 'I think when Dad lost his limbs, he also lost the part of him that made life a misery for the rest of us. He's still a bugger, but it's been a joy, not worrying if he was going to get his collar felt for some new scam he'd dreamt up down the pub.'

Her mother started to sob anew. 'Oh, Kitty, I wish our Ned was here. I wish your father could live to walk you down the aisle.'

'I'll send Ned a telegram straight away.'

'I sent him one weeks ago, love.'

Kitty looked at the band of white skin beneath her engagement ring that had avoided the strong rays of the Caribbean sun. 'I told him when I was in Barbados. I said to him that he needed to follow me home as soon as possible. He told me he was waiting to get up and about, what with his broken arm and leg and all. But – I don't know if he'd even have had his plaster off by now. We've no way of knowing—'

Rising from her place at the little table and marching through to the parlour, she found James talking in soothing tones to her father. Her father's eyes were open – wild and staring.

'He's awake? He looks distressed. Dad! Are you all right? Can you hear me?'

Her father didn't respond. He merely looked at her, or rather, looked through her.

'Try not to worry, Kitty,' James said, adjusting the old man's oxygen mask. 'He's just confused, I think. He woke up in pain, so I've given him a shot of morphine. The district nurse had noted his last dose as being two days ago, so he must have been sleeping fitfully.'

Kitty sat on the edge of the settee. Her father's emaciated frame took up hardly any space at all. 'But the priest? Don't you get the last rites at the very end?'

'Perhaps your mother and the priest didn't know. It's always hard to tell. He could go tonight. He might have a couple of days in him yet. In any case, it's a jolly good job we did come back from Berkshire.'

James put his arms around Kitty, and Kitty could have sworn her father smiled.

The three of them spent the night taking turns keeping vigil beside Bert. James was first awake.

'Kitty, darling. I've got to go to clinic to read case notes for next week. I'm so sorry.' He was shaking her gently by the shoulder.

Kitty looked around the parlour and then remembered that she'd fallen asleep in an armchair around four in the morning. Yawning and stiff, she reached up and stroked James's stubbled chin. 'Absolutely. You go. But please let Matron know what's going on. I can't leave Mam. I'm staying till the end, now. She'll have to understand.'

James gathered his coat and his hat from the pegs in the hall and stood at the threshold to the parlour. 'You'll need to top up his morphine when he needs it. I'll come back as soon as clinic is over, providing there's no emergency surgeries to perform.'

Glancing over at her sleeping father, Kitty nodded and padded over to see James off. She kissed him tenderly. 'I'm so sorry about throwing a tantrum yesterday. It's not like me.'

'None of it was your fault. I'm sorry my parents spoke to you that way. Can you forgive my lily-livered behaviour?'

'Think nothing of it. Least said, soonest mended.'

James was just about to head out of the door when he paused and turned to Kitty. 'I've thought of a quicker way we can get to Ned. He won't get back to Blighty in time to say goodbye to your father, but at least we can tell him what's going on, *if* he's still there.'

'Where?'

'The plantation. The one where you stayed.'

'The Buchanan place?'

'Yes. I'll find out the number and try to get Ned on the telephone. I'll call from my office!'

'Brilliant idea!' Kitty said, flinging her arms around her fiancé. 'You're a smasher!'

The day seemed at once to drag and, conversely, whizz by. While her mother enjoyed a few hours of much-needed sleep, Kitty washed, dried and put away the dirty pots, cleaned the kitchen and tidied as best she could, with all of her father's medical regalia littering the parlour. She called the Co-op's funeral director and was alarmed to discover that her parents hadn't made any provision for their burial whatsoever. Balking at the cost of even a simple funeral, she nevertheless committed to one that she felt she, her mother and Ned could just about afford between them. Imagining her father lying in an open coffin in the parlour was a grim thought that she tried her best to bat away.

Her father slept for the most part, save for when he woke needing morphine. It saddened her that he couldn't speak. His eyes opened, but he didn't seem to see her. *When will it end?* she wondered. *If I sleep, will I miss the chance to say goodbye?*

Her mind was a blizzard of heartbreaking thoughts, arrangements and memories of her childhood. When there was a knock at the door just after lunch, with her exhausted mother still in bed, Kitty rushed to answer, grateful for any company at all.

'James! I thought you were reviewing your cases.'

Her fiancé stood on the doorstep. He took off his trilby, but it was clear he wasn't staying. The Anglia was parked outside, its engine still running. 'I am. I allowed myself an hour's breather. Look' – he kissed her fleetingly on the lips – 'I can't stay. I just wanted to tell you that Buchanan—'

'You got through to the plantation? To Humphrey?'

'Yes. I called before clinic started. I woke him up, I'm afraid! It must have been the small hours out there. But Kitty, darling, it's not encouraging news, I'm afraid.'

Kitty felt her broken heart sink. 'Go on. Has Ned been arrested?'

'Nothing like that. No. Apparently, he left the plantation some weeks ago to have his casts removed. Buchanan hasn't seen or heard anything of him since. Not a whisper.'

Frowning, Kitty tried to imagine how Ned could possibly have lost touch with his own personal goose that so reliably laid the golden egg. 'There's something funny going on. Oh, I do hope Ned's all right.'

James put his hat back on. 'Look. I have to go. I'll be back this evening, I promise.'

As he opened the driver's side door to the Anglia, Kitty shouted after him. 'Did you speak to Matron?'

'Yes. All sorted. Don't go back in till after the funeral,' she said. Compassionate leave and all that. You mustn't give it a moment's thought. Ta-ta!' He blew her a kiss and drove off.

Kitty retreated into the hall and closed the door, feeling grief descend on her like a suffocating, rough blanket. How she wished she was on the ward with Grace, carefree and only having Molly Henshaw to worry about.

'Morning, Kitty, love!'

Her mother was finally awake. Kitty made her way through to the parlour and found her standing beside the settee, gazing down at her father.

'Do you think he's in pain?' her mother asked. 'His breathing's very noisy. He's rattling.'

Kitty shook her head. 'I doubt he's in pain. That rattling's just mucus in the back of his throat. He can't swallow.'

'Do something for him! I can't bear it!'

Kitty put her arms around her mother. 'I can't. Just let nature take its course, Mam. It won't be long now.' How dearly she wished at that moment that she could just give her father a little too much morphine and send him gently and swiftly on his way. She looked down at the syringe, which she'd sterilised for its next use.

'Please! Make the noise stop!' Her mother held her hands to her ears.

'Go in the kitchen, Mam. Make some tea and butter yourself a slice of bread. Keep busy. I'll look after Dad.'

With her mother otherwise occupied, Kitty looked again at the syringe and the bottle of morphine. She pondered her feelings and conscience with regard to ending the suffering of the sick and dying. All the nurses had heard tell of doctors slipping cancer patients a little too generous a dose of morphine to ensure they just drifted away in peace.

'I know you've only got a matter of hours – maybe a day at most, Dad. I should leave you be, but I can't stand seeing Mum so upset,' she whispered to her father. She encased his thin hand in hers and felt his yellowed skin, still warm but only just. His major organs had all but stopped working. There was no turning back, so would easing his passing really hurt so much?

From beyond the closed kitchen door, her mother sobbed as though the world was ending.

Kitty's hands were shaking as she loaded up the syringe. She squirted out some of the morphine and looked at her father, biting her lip as she mulled over her options. The Bert Longthorne she'd always known had already gone, leaving but a shell. Where once he'd hefted her onto his shoulders with powerful, hairy forearms and well-developed biceps, his accident and the cancer had left him with but one bony arm. Could she do the unthinkable to lessen his suffering?

Her mother's sobbing grew louder. 'Make it stop! Let him go, God!' she heard her saying over and over again.

Steeling herself to administer the final jab, Kitty brought the syringe closer to the only vein she could see. *Stop this lunacy, Kitty! First, do no harm! How can you kill your own father? It's murder, if you do it!* She was torn. She gently took hold of his arm and was poised to send her father out on a cloud, when there was a knock on the door.

'Jesus wept!' she cried, placing the syringe back in a dish.

She marched to the front door, expecting to see James on the doorstep. Perhaps he'd forgotten something. When she opened it, however, she almost fainted with shock.

Chapter 39

'Ned!'

The prodigal son had returned, and in the nick of time. Kitty didn't pause to tell her brother how she'd been on the brink of overdosing their father. She grabbed him by the shoulders and pulled him in for a hug.

'There's no time for questions. Dad's on his last legs. Get in here!'

Kitty crept past her father on the sofa, leaving Ned to stand, open-mouthed, looking at the shell of a man that their father had become. She knocked on the scullery door and went in. Her mother had stopped crying and was sipping tea, staring blankly at the 1949 calendar pinned to the wall.

'Mam! You'll never guess who's here.'

Her mother fixed her with swollen, red eyes. She frowned. 'I'm not in the mood for guessing games. Is it Father Patrick again, asking for funeral-service details?'

Kitty shook her head. She retreated to the parlour, grabbing Ned by the sleeve of his coat. She pulled him into the scullery.

'Ned! My Neddy boy! Oh, Jesus, Mary and Joseph!' Her mother stood so abruptly that her chair fell backwards onto the floor. She flung herself at Ned, covering his disfigured face with a flurry of kisses. 'If there's one silver lining to all this, it's that our Neddy's home!'

Kitty's mother held her arm out to encompass the three of

them in one warm embrace. Squeezing Ned tightly around the waist on one side and rubbing her mother's back on the other, Kitty felt bolstered by the togetherness of their little family. Ned might never know it, but he'd unwittingly stopped her from going against everything she believed in as a nurse.

'James tried to get you on the telephone at Buchanan's plantation this morning, would you believe it?' she said once their huddle had broken apart and Ned was seated at the table with a cup of tea.

He took a slurp and dribbled only slightly from his surgically reconstructed mouth. He looked at Kitty with his one functioning eye. 'I set sail a couple of weeks after you left. As soon as I could get my casts off. You told me Dad was dying. I did everything in my power to get here in time.'

'You should have asked James to pick you up from Liverpool.'

'I didn't want to put anyone out, and besides, I wanted it to be a surprise.'

Kitty swilled her tea around her mug, in a bid to encourage the jam at the bottom to dissolve. 'If you'd come tomorrow, you'd have been too late. Save your grand gestures, Ned.'

'Would you rather I'd stayed in Barbados? I'm risking my neck showing my face back here, you know.' Ned raised his one good eyebrow. He looked over his shoulder at the window as if someone might be staring in at him. 'I'm still wanted in connection with the counterfeit coupon job.'

'Oh, stop being melodramatic, Ned! Dad's dying. Mam's spent months nursing a terminally ill man. It's not all about you.'

'You think the police won't still be on the lookout for me?' He took out a packet of cigarettes and put one in his mouth. 'I bet every grass in Manchester's waiting to make a bob out of spotting me back in town.' He struck a match.

Grabbing the cigarette from between his lips before he could light it up, Kitty crumpled it in her fist. 'No smoking! That's what's killed our dad, you berk. I told you in Barbados. Don't you listen?'

Her mother slapped the table so abruptly that they both jumped. 'Enough squabbling, you two. Show some blinking decorum.'

Kitty and Ned exchanged glances. Ned extended his hand by way of a truce and she took it.

'I'm glad you're back,' she said. 'Will you stay?'

He looked up at the ceiling where it had discoloured from regular blasts of steam from cooking pans and the ensuing mildew. 'I might do. It depends.'

'On what?'

'How's Grace settling in?'

It seemed like her brother was trying to change the subject, Kitty mused. Knowing Ned, he'd almost certainly fled bad debts and his terrible reputation in Barbados, sailing to England with only the coat on his back. 'Where's your suitcase?'

'I didn't bring one.' Ned turned to his mother. 'Have you still got my old gear, Mam?'

Their mother nodded. 'All boxed up on top of my wardrobe. I knew my Ned would come home one day!'

The truth dawned on Kitty. 'You've not come back for Dad, have you? No suitcase? Nothing but the clothes you're standing in. This was a spur-of-the-minute decision, wasn't it? You've been chased out of town, haven't you? By God, Ned Longthorne! Do you never learn?'

Ned opened his mouth to deliver some sharp retort, no doubt, but their bickering was interrupted by an ominous rattling noise coming from the parlour – even louder than before.

'It's Dad,' Kitty said.

She hastened to her father's side and perched on the edge of the sofa, holding his hand. His eyes were shut, but the rattle at the back of his throat told her this was more than sleep.

Ned and her mother knelt beside her: her mother, stroking her father's hair and kissing his brow; Ned reaching over to put his hand gently on his father's chest.

'Take his mask off,' Kitty said. 'Here. I'll do it.' She removed her father's oxygen mask so they could see his face properly.

Without warning, her father took one deep breath in. The rattling stopped. He exhaled slowly and peacefully.

'Oh, my Bert!' her mother said, stroking his cheek. 'I'll always love you. Thanks for everything.'

'We had some fun times, Dad,' Ned said. 'You've been the worst teacher and the best pal. I love you, Dad.'

'Goodbye, Dad,' Kitty simply said. 'Be at peace, now.'

And with that, Bert Longthorne, one of Manchester's most infamous living legends, died.

Chapter 40

'Leave it to me, Mam,' Kitty had said once her mother's sobbing had subsided. 'If you can't face it, I'll speak to the undertaker and make all the arrangements.'

Kitty had known as soon as her father had breathed his last that the bulk of the burden of burying him would fall to her, and she'd been right. No sooner had the undertaker collected her father for preparation than Ned had drained his cup of tea, retreated into the bathroom and emerged smelling of cologne, wearing an old suit that his mother had stored.

With their distraught mother in bed, he was now standing by the sideboard, rifling through the bits and bobs in the old red-glass vase where he knew she kept, among other things, spare coppers. The coins clinked in his hand as he counted out several shillings.

'Dad's not cold and you're already thieving off Mam?' Kitty asked. 'Don't you think she deserves some respite from Longthorne men poncing off her?'

'There's no need to be like that, our Kitty. I was going to ask if you've any idea where I can find Grace.'

'Where do you think?'

'The hospital?' Ned looked hopeful, as if he hadn't witnessed the passing of his father only hours earlier.

Kitty started to pack away the oxygen apparatus and tidy the various unused lotions, medications and equipment from months of palliative care. 'Leave her be, for heaven's sake. She'll be working a shift. The last thing she needs is her long-lost boss turning up drunk and bursting into tears on the ward, snotting and weeping all over her clean uniform.'

'What makes you think I'd do that? What makes you think I'm taking Mam's loose change to buy booze?'

'A leopard doesn't change his spots, our Ned.'

'I might have designs on buying Grace some flowers.'

'And I might eat my hat. Look, I've not seen you really shed a tear over Dad, yet. But you will. And Mam needs you. Just sit tight, and be a decent son for a change. You've literally just got off the boat after years of not sending so much as a postcard, let alone birthday cards or Christmas presents.'

'I had to keep a low profile after the printing-press business. The Old Bill were after me. What if somebody had seen a card?'

Kitty stood up straight, satisfied that the apparatus was all ready to be picked up by James later that evening. 'Then you can't go to the pub, can you?' She pointed to his face. 'You'll stand out like a sore thumb. Do yourself a favour, Ned. Just stay put and help me look after Mam. Grace doesn't need you driving her mad. Anyway, she's got a feller now, I reckon. She doesn't need you cramping her style.'

Ned dropped the coins back into the vase. 'Oh aye?' Even with his ruined features, it was clear from his good eye and eyebrow that he was scowling.

'A musician. Lloyd, his name is. Nice chap from Jamaica. Plays the trumpet at the Band on the Wall.' Kitty could see that the mention of Lloyd rankled, but Ned's sensibilities were the last thing on her mind. She couldn't get the memory of her father's dying breath out of her head.

When James finally turned up, once his clinic and his various meetings had ended, Kitty was relieved. He appeared on the doorstep bearing an enormous bouquet of white lilies for her mother and embraced Kitty the moment he set foot over the threshold.

'Oh, darling. I'm so sorry for your loss.' He kissed her forehead. 'Bert really was one of a kind. Such a character. I'm glad to have had him in my life.'

'He thought you were such a toff!' Kitty said, taking the flowers for her mother.

'How's Elsie?'

'Bearing up. She's listening to the wireless. The horse racing, of all things! I don't think she knows what to do with herself. The place feels empty and dull without Dad. But there's someone else to drive us mad . . .'

James and Ned shook hands formally and took a seat at opposite ends of the parlour – Ned on the settee next to his mother and James in the armchair at Kitty's side. The tension was so thick in the air that Kitty could almost bite down on it.

James clearly felt the same. 'I say, Elsie. How about Kitty and I go and get everyone a fish supper?'

'Oh, I was going to make some tater hash,' her mother said, leaping off the sofa and smoothing her apron down, as though James was a sergeant major, assessing her readiness to do battle in the kitchen.

'Nonsense. I won't hear of it. Cod and chips do?'

Elsie smiled half-heartedly. 'I don't feel much like eating, to be honest.'

'Got to keep your strength up, Elsie,' James said. 'Doctor's orders.' He winked.

'Oh, I don't know.' Elsie patted her stomach. 'I feel like

I've got a big hole in my stomach without my Bert here. I feel right queer.' The tears welled in her eyes.

'You can share with me, Mam,' Kitty said.

'I'll have a large cod, large chips and mushy peas, me,' Ned said, leaning back and crossing his legs. 'Go easy on the vinegar. There's a good lad.'

Kitty and James exchanged a knowing glance with one another and hastened out of the front door.

'He's intolerable,' she said, once they were some way down the street. The dockland wind whipped around her legs.

'You were desperate for him to come home yesterday.' James held his arm out for her to link. 'Look, I know he's trying. He's always been like a miniature version of your father. Baby-Bert.'

Kitty giggled, though her laughter was tinged with grief and exhaustion.

'All I'm saying is, just try to humour him until after the funeral. He's bound to be on the first boat back out to Barbados as soon as Bert's in the ground. You've got . . . how long?'

'A fortnight. The church is booked. The plot's being organised in Southern Cemetery.' She pulled him close. 'Thanks for offering to help with the cost.'

'Not at all. It's the least I could do. Can't have the old bugger going into a pauper's grave, can we?'

As they stood in the queue at the chippy, Kitty cast her mind back to the way she and James had bickered in the car on the way back from Berkshire. Now that her father had gone and James had stepped in to make a decent funeral a possibility, Kitty could hardly believe she'd ever been so petty or discontent. *You've got a bobby dazzler, there, Kitty Longthorne*, she mused, staring into the glazed heated cabinet above the fryers. *Don't you dare take him for granted. Don't be a berk all your life.*

Four days dragged by and, cooped up in her mother's place with Ned, sleeping on the settee where their dad had breathed his last, Kitty could not bear being on compassionate leave any longer.

She woke just shy of five in the morning, watched the sun come up and resolved to go back into work.

'By heck, our Kitty,' her mother said, fastening her green dressing-gown belt around her waist. She yawned. 'You're up with the larks. Where are you off to?'

'Go back to bed, Mam,' Kitty whispered, kissing her mother on the cheek. 'Get some kip. I'm going to the hospital to do a shift. If I stay here any longer, watching our Ned scratch himself and break wind like a chimpanzee, I'll go insane.'

'But the arrangements!'

'All taken care of. I'll be back tomorrow night. I just need a breather.'

She slipped out into a city that was just waking up, hitched a ride on a milkman's cart and eventually found her way back to the nurses' home.

Grace was leaving to begin her shift just as Kitty put her key in the door.

'Grace!' Kitty said. 'You're a sight for sore eyes.'

'I haven't seen you in a week,' Grace said, clasping Kitty by the hands. 'Matron told us about your dad. My condolences. Should you be here?'

Kitty shook her head. 'Not really, but I'm climbing the walls at my mam's. The funeral's not for another nine days. I can't bear sitting around, twiddling my thumbs. Mam's got company . . .' Should she tell Grace about Ned? Kitty thought about the social life Grace was beginning to enjoy at her church and, now, with Lloyd. At least outside work, Grace was flourishing. Kitty could see it in her eyes. The last thing her newfound friend needed was Ned hogging her attention as if he were still her boss in the Holetown brothel, ordering her around and sapping her vibrancy from her. No, news of Ned's arrival could wait. 'So, I thought she wouldn't miss me for a day or two. It'll take my mind off Dad.'

Making her way up to her room, Kitty changed into her uniform and felt immediately calmer. There was comfort in routine and rules and responsibility. As she pinned her nurse's watch to her dress, she looked down at her family photo, smiling at the image of her father when he'd been well. 'I hope I'll always remember you like that, Dad,' she said, stroking his face. 'Big and strong and full of mischief. Bert Longthorne: cock of the walk; Manchester's best bad boy, eh?' She chuckled and wiped a tear away.

Her beloved Park Hospital was busy, even at that hour. She entered the lung ward to find breakfast being served. Matron was standing by the office, chatting with Mr Galbraith about some patient's post-operative care.

'Kitty! My dear girl,' Matron said, wide-eyed at the sight of her. She approached and rubbed Kitty's upper arm affectionately. 'Should you be here? I told Dr Williams you weren't to show your face until after your father's funeral.'

Kitty looked down at her highly polished, sensible shoes. 'It's very kind of you.' Clearly, Matron hadn't worked out that she and Grace were behind the broken kitchen window. Guilt gnawed at her. 'But I needed some time to myself, away from my family. A bit of routine and a change of scenery.'

Matron nodded. 'As you wish. You're under no obligation to be here, should you find things start to get on top of you.'

Mr Galbraith smiled sympathetically at Kitty. 'I'm so sorry to hear the news, Nurse Longthorne. Cancer is a thief. It's a pity there wasn't more I could have done for your father.'

Nodding, Kitty thought about the cigarettes her father had never been without, as long as she'd known him. 'Just you make sure everyone gets a read of that study that's getting published next year,' she said. 'The world needs to know they've been throwing their hard-earned wages at the tobacco companies for nothing but poison. They need to understand that smoking kills. Maybe you can save younger men from the cruel fate my dad met.' She willed herself not to cry – not here; not on the ward in front of Matron and a senior consultant surgeon. *Hold it together, Kitty. You're made of sterner stuff.*

She forced herself to smile, spotting Grace at the far end of the ward, drawing a curtain around a patient in readiness for a bed bath. 'If you'll excuse me, I think Nurse Griffith could do with a hand.'

'You're a little overqualified for giving a bed bath, Nurse Longthorne,' Matron said.

'So's Nurse Griffith. And besides, I need to be doing something undemanding today, if you don't mind. Just a spot of back-breaking graft. Is that all right? Just for now, to take my mind off – you know.'

Matron nodded. 'Do what you must, dear girl.'

Kitty made her way down to Grace, ignoring the cutting glances of Molly Henshaw, who was injecting something into the man in the bed opposite.

'I've come to help,' Kitty said. 'Many hands make light work, eh?'

'Here you go, Mr Bridges,' Grace said. 'Now you've got *two* women fussing over you. Nurse Longthorne's a senior nurse, too. There's nothing she doesn't know about making patients comfortable. Aren't you lucky?'

Mr Bridges wheezed his assent through the hiss and whine of his oxygen mask.

In companionable silence, she and Grace tended to the elderly man and dressed him in clean pyjamas.

When they'd finished, he pulled his mask aside and grabbed Kitty's hand with weak, bony fingers. 'This one has got the voice of a nightingale, you know.' He inclined his head towards Grace. 'Cheer an old man up, will you? Get her to do a little turn for us lads one lunchtime, will you? I like all those hymns she sings.'

Grace hid a broad grin behind her hand, then waved the compliment away. 'Oh, you're such a charmer, Mr Bridges. I'll have to watch you!' She fixed the old man's mask back into place. 'Nightingale, indeed!'

As they tidied breakfast away, changed beds and applied clean dressings for those who had had surgery, Kitty began to feel almost cheery. She followed Grace into the storeroom and started to stack clean towels that had just come up from the laundry onto the shelves.

'I'm nothing without a sense of purpose,' she told Grace. 'Just being here, I feel like a cloud's lifting. It was a nightmare at my mam's, what with—' She bit her tongue just in time to avoid letting slip about Ned's return. 'All the arrangements and that.'

Grace nodded sympathetically. 'I know what you mean. I was the same when my father passed away. Keeping busy chases the blues away. Listen, talking of blues – I've got to go to an audition at the Band on the Wall when shift's over.'

'With Lloyd?' Kitty nudged her and winked.

Grace merely rolled her eyes. 'Will you come with me?'

'Of course.' Kitty was aware of the sensation of guilt, gnawing away at her at the thought of leaving her mother to spend the evening with her grief and nothing for entertainment but Ned's half-truths about Barbados. Nevertheless, she knew she needed just one night to herself, lest she throttle Ned over dinner. 'All right, then, Gracie Nightingale. You're on. Let's go into town. I'll be your chaperone. Make sure Lloyd doesn't get any ideas!'

When the shift ended, they changed out of their uniforms and hitched a ride into town with one of the young doctors. In the early-evening chill and steadily falling rain, Kitty's breath steamed on the damp air. She pulled on her hood, stuck her hands deep into her coat pockets and tried desperately to bat away memories of the rattle in her father's throat at the end.

'We'll have to make some toast when we get back in, else we'll starve,' she said, as they marched up Oldham Street from Piccadilly and rounded the corner. 'I could do without this rain. We're getting soaked.' She could already feel the encroaching wet around her toes.

'You should see it rain in Barbados,' Grace said, tying her scarf tightly around her chin. 'This is nothing.'

The Band on the Wall was apparently shut.

'Are you sure we're supposed to be here now?'

'Yes.' Grace glanced at her watch and frowned. 'Lloyd said. Maybe we should go round the back. I think there's a musician's entrance.'

'Ah, that will be it,' Kitty said.

Arm in arm, they gingerly made their way up a dark cobbled alley at the side of the club. Sure enough, there was a double gate at the back, where the brewery's trucks would undoubtedly unload barrels of beer during the day. It was slightly ajar. Kitty stopped in her tracks, balking at raised voices above the pitter-patter of the rainfall, coming not from within the club's yard, but from inside the neighbouring Smithfield Market.

'Wait! Something's going on.' She approached, beckoning Grace to follow. She pressed her index finger to her lips, heart thudding. There were heavy doors at the back. Kitty tried them and was surprised to find one of them unlocked. She cracked it open, just enough to hear what was being said.

Men were shouting. Arguing. She heard a familiar voice – English spoken with a lilting Jamaican accent. There was the dull thud of someone being punched, then a groan.

'Lloyd,' Grace whispered.

Kitty looked at her friend and, together, they pushed their way inside. She took her wet hood off to take in her surroundings. The cavernous market hall was in darkness, but for moonlight that streamed in through the glass of the giant vaulted lantern above, pooling on the cobbles below. Initially, she saw nothing but empty stalls. The smells of rotten cabbage and damp were pungent, tickling Kitty's nostrils. Was that the acrid tang of rat urine she detected beneath the rot? She shuddered, imagining fat, disease-ridden parasites scurrying over her wet shoes. Just as she was instinctively about to retreat, she heard Lloyd cry out again.

'No! No! You got it all wrong. Let me go!'

Grace grabbed her hand and squeezed hard.

Pull yourself together, Kitty! she told herself. *Lloyd needs help.* Kitty patted Grace's hand encouragingly. They crept on into the deep shadows, where the voices were coming from.

When she collided with something solid that made a rattling noise, Kitty froze; held her breath. Reaching out to touch the barrier that blocked her path, she realised she'd walked straight into a giant stack of large wooden crates. What did they contain? Bottles, perhaps? Dim light shone through the cracks between the crates. The men were on the other side. Mercifully, they were too busy shouting to have heard her.

'We saw you with the white girl,' one of the men bellowed. 'The blonde cutie in the red dress that *I* got my eye on.'

Kitty and Grace edged their way to the corner of the stack, until they had a clear view of the grim gathering – lit by a solitary paraffin lamp that had been perched on one freestanding wooden crate. Lloyd was pinned to the stone of the market-hall wall by a white man, whose hair hung lank and loose over his forehead. Despite the cold and the pouring rain that battered the vaulted skylight, he wore only a grubby-looking vest and trousers that had seen better days, held up with rope. He spoke with a Canadian accent. 'What did we say about keeping your hands off *our* girls?' He looked to the other man, whose knuckles were bloodied, for confirmation.

'You got it all wrong,' Lloyd said. He was staring at his attackers with wild, terrified eyes. His lower lip shone, as though it was slick with blood. Sure enough, the wall bore a dark spatter mark, where Lloyd's head was pressed up against the pale stone. 'She asked me something about the band!'

The second assailant pulled back a balled fist. 'I'm gonna finish the job we started in the summer. I'm gonna break your new face, you lousy, lying cockroach.'

It was Morgan and Jim – the Canadian ex-servicemen who had been sent to Park Hospital, along with Lloyd, from the Royal Infirmary! Kitty would recognise those man-mountains anywhere. She knew she might be the only thing standing between Lloyd and another trip to casualty, or perhaps, given the size and the determination of his attacker, even the mortuary.

'Wait!' she called out, stepping forward into the light.

The man's fist was already moving with force towards Lloyd's face. In that split second, Lloyd locked eyes with Kitty and jerked his head to the side, but the Canadian's fist kept going. There was a sickening crack.

The Canadian cried out and hopped backwards, clutching at his hand. Lloyd pushed him aside and started to run towards Kitty and Grace.

'Run away! Call the police!' he cried.

Grace, however, had other ideas. 'How dare you lay hands on my friend, rasshole!' she shouted, barrelling into Lloyd's attacker with a ferocity that surprised Kitty.

Might us two girls actually fend off a couple of brick outhouses like these? Kitty wondered.

All at once, however, the scene took a turn for the disastrous. Lloyd lost his footing on the slick, uneven cobbles and plunged headlong into the wall of crates. As he did so, Kitty felt strong arms grab her from behind.

'What's a white girl like you hanging around the likes of him for?' It was the other Canadian. The biggest of the two. He pressed his sweaty face up against Kitty's cheek and licked her.

'Get off me, you pig!' She tried to wriggle from his vice-like grip but he was strong.

He hefted her into the air and shook her as though she was a doll, laughing like a madman.

'Let go!' Kitty yelled, trying to kick her heels backwards into his shins.

Across from her, Grace had been wrestled onto an old handcart by the other Canadian. He was unzipping his flies. At Kitty's feet, Lloyd was sprawled on the ground, groaning. The delicate balance of the stacked crates had been compromised. The upper layers were teetering ominously . . .

Kitty saw their ruin unfold in slow motion: the top-most crates tipped too far and tumbled onto the crate below that held the paraffin lamp. The bottles inside smashed. Kitty felt the splash of their medicinal-smelling contents against her skin. Fumes stung her sinuses – vodka!

'No!' Kitty yelled.

Too late. The flaming paraffin ignited the vodka with a *whump*. The rest of the crates exploded in a lethal, billowing cloud of shattered glass, splintered wood and furious flame. It engulfed everything, filling the air with searing heat and blinding light.

'Help!' Grace shrieked. She locked eyes with Kitty through the hungry flames, springing up from the vodka-soaked ground.

Kitty screamed and screamed, but it was in vain. There was nobody to hear them in that empty market hall. They were trapped with two violent men behind a wall of burning fury.

Chapter 41

The flames were sucking every bit of oxygen out of the air. Gasping, Kitty wriggled and struggled with all her might to free herself from her captor.

'Let go!'

Suddenly, he began to screech in an ungodly manner. Kitty was abruptly dropped on top of Lloyd. Scrambling to her feet and looking up, she saw that her captor's hair was ablaze. He was desperately trying to smother the flames with his bare hands.

Even in the midst of the mayhem, Kitty tried to remain calm, as she'd been trained to do in any emergency. She yanked Lloyd up by his braces, and caught sight of a set of double doors beyond the flames.

'Come on, Lloyd! We've got to get Grace and get that cart!' she yelled above the noise of exploding glass.

Grace's attacker lay on the ground, surrounded by shards of glass, his head bleeding heavily. Was he unconscious?

'Kitty!' Grace was standing by the cart, clutching the neck of a broken vodka bottle in her right hand. Her eyes were glazed and staring. She was in shock. Kitty had to reach her, but a wall of fire stood between them.

Taking off her ringing-wet coat, Kitty flung it over both her and Lloyd, covering their heads. She put her arm around his waist. 'On the count of three, run through the flames. One, two, three!'

They sprinted through and made it to the other side unscathed.

'All right?' Kitty yelled. 'Now let's grab this cart and ram it as hard as we can against those doors.' She was sure she could hear the bells of a fire engine ringing in the distance, growing closer and closer, but still not close enough.

Grace was still standing in a daze over her attacker.

'Snap out of it, Grace!' Kitty grabbed her friend's wrist and shook the bottle neck loose.

Lloyd was already manoeuvring the cart so that it faced the double doors. 'We got a good run-up.'

'Grab a handle!' Kitty shouted to Grace.

Grace coughed. She shook her head, as if she'd just woken from a nightmare. 'Yeah. Yes. Sure thing.'

'Now, push!' Kitty heaved the cart with all of her might. It moved forwards at speed, but one of the wheels seemed to get stuck between the cobbles. It stopped abruptly, yet the three of them were still moving forwards. Kitty yelped as the edge of the cart hit her in the ribs. Winded but determined, she grabbed her handle anew. 'Again!'

Together, the three of them yanked the heavy cart backwards.

'Now, push!' she cried.

This time, they got the cart going, and it met no resistance, ploughing into the doors. Yet they wouldn't give. They merely wobbled on their hinges.

Kitty noticed that the wood around the hinges had splintered, though. 'Third time lucky!' she yelled.

Exhausted, coughing and fighting for breath, the three backed up once more and heaved the cart forwards. This time, the hinges were ripped from the wooden architrave and the doors shot open, smashing down onto the pavement outside. A gust of freezing wind and now-driving rain blasted into the fiery market hall, dousing Kitty's boiling skin with icy water.

They were out, just as the fire engine swept up to the kerb.

Kitty sprinted through the rain to the fireman standing by the bell. 'Quickly! There are two men still inside. One's on fire; the other's out cold.'

'Leave it to us, miss,' the fireman said. 'Stand back!'

Gathered together in a huddle in the doorway of the Band on the Wall, Kitty, Grace and Lloyd watched the firemen unfurl their hoses and begin to douse the inferno.

'We need to call the police,' Grace said. 'And an ambulance.'

Lloyd reached out to touch the scratches on Grace's face. 'You're hurt.' He turned to Kitty. 'Both of you.'

Grace pushed his hand away. 'Not for me, you ass. For *you*! And those rassholes in there!'

'I don't need no more doctors,' Lloyd said. 'I got a split lip, is all.' He turned to the doors of the Band on the Wall and started hammering on them. 'Landlord got a telephone.'

Kitty touched her own cheeks and saw that her fingertips were bloodied. 'Must have been scratched by flying glass when the crates went up.' She prodded carefully around the area but mercifully could feel no splinters beneath the skin. 'Surface wounds.'

They had all been lucky.

'Who's there?' A gruff voice came from behind the club's door. 'Who's making such a bloody racket?'

'Lloyd, boss! It's me. Open up. The market be on fire.'

Ferocious barking came from within. Then there was the sound of several bolts shooting back, and the door finally opened to reveal a middle-aged man. Heavy set and tall, the landlord cut an impressive figure, though he was only dressed simply, in slacks, with shirtsleeves rolled up. The dogs emerged from the hallway behind him in a barking, growling, snarling flurry of fur and teeth, but they came to heel the moment he clicked his fingers. He stared at the trio, but his scowl quickly gave way to a look of pure bafflement. 'Fire? You what?'

Lloyd jerked his thumb in the direction of the fire engine, and the landlord leaned out to see the rain-soaked high drama that was unfolding outside the neighbouring market hall. The firemen were dragging Morgan and Jim out of the club, still alive by the looks of it. The din of more emergency vehicles approaching was carried to them on the wind.

Kitty narrowed her eyes and made out not only an ambulance, but also two police cars with lights flashing. She coughed. 'Looks like we're in for a long night.'

An hour later, and Kitty, Grace and Lloyd had finally finished giving witness statements about the attack and the ensuing fire. Kitty and Grace had cleaned up Lloyd's and their own cuts and grazes, using the landlord's first-aid kit. Now, they were sitting with the landlord and Lloyd's fellow band members around a card table in a backroom of the Band on the Wall, drinking neat spirits to revive them.

The landlord sipped at a whisky. 'So, I takes those flaming Canadian idiots in, gives 'em a roof over their heads, and they repay me like this?' he said. He slammed his glass down on the table. His lounging dogs immediately sat up, twitching their ears forward and licking their chops. One emitted a low growl. 'Robbing my vodka delivery and trying to sell it on under my nose?'

Lloyd nodded. 'Me come out of the auditions for a breath

of air and get chatting with this girl at the back.' He addressed Grace. 'Nice girl. She was going to try out for the band, like you.' He turned back to the landlord, speaking hesitantly, thanks to his split lip. 'Anyway, me notice Jim and Morgan doing a deal – counting a wad of money from some guys who turn up with a truck. Except they start arguing over the price and a fight break out. The men drive off, taking their money with them. Morgan and Jim spot me and the girl, watching. The girl didn't hang around. Good Lord, no! She scared of Jim. He too familiar, you know?' He looked around at his bandmates, who murmured their agreement. 'And then Jim and Morgan decided to blame *me* for their deal falling through. Start accusing me of all kinds.' He shrugged. 'But Grace and Kitty, here – they save the day.'

His bandmates cheered and clapped, congratulating Kitty and Grace on rescuing Lloyd from certain death.

Kitty blushed and smiled, but next to her, Grace was looking down at her fingernails. Her shoulders drooped.

'Hey, Gracie,' Lloyd said, topping up her rum. 'Why you look so sad?'

Grace pressed her lips together. 'All I wanted to do was sing.' She coughed and thumped her chest.

The landlord clapped his hands together. 'I can't sit idly by and watch a heroine being disappointed.' He lit a cigarette and blew his smoke towards Lloyd, pointing at him with the glowing end. 'Set the audition up.' He raised his eyebrows and nodded at the other band members. 'Go on, lads.'

'Yeah. No problem. We will.' Lloyd smiled at Grace. 'Maybe later in the week.'

The landlord shook his head. 'No. Not later. Now.' He tapped emphatically on the table. 'I've got hundreds of paying punters coming in this weekend, and you lot need a singer.'

'Now?' Grace and Kitty said in unison.

One of the band members, whom Kitty recognised as the lead guitarist, flicked cigarette ash into the ashtray in the middle of the table. 'Why not? Gear's all set up. The club's shut. No skin off my nose.' He turned to his colleagues. 'We don't mind, do we, lads?' Then, back to Lloyd and Grace. 'If you're feeling up to it, like.'

Kitty put her hand on Grace's arm. 'Is your chest all right? 'Cause I don't know about you, but I feel like I've got a tonne of bricks on mine, what with inhaling all that smoke.'

Grace coughed and cleared her throat. 'I'm not too bad. I think I could sing.'

The decision was made.

'Are you quite all right?' Kitty asked, touching Lloyd on the cuff of his jacket. She pointed to his lip. 'Will you be able to play trumpet with that?'

'No problem,' Lloyd said, dabbing the wound with a handkerchief. 'Nothing get in the way of Lloyd blowing his trumpet! I be the horn of Manchester, remember? Ha ha.'

Grace folded her arms tightly over her chest, looking around at the cavernous, empty dance hall as though she were grading it for decor and cleanliness.

'It's so cold in here without all the people,' Kitty said.

Lloyd lifted his trumpet reverentially out of its case. 'On with the audition,' he said. He turned to Grace. 'You be the last singer we trying out.'

'Last but not least, eh?' Grace said.

'Let's see!'

Lloyd helped Grace up a step ladder and onto the elevated stage. Kitty leaned on the bar, watching from below. Even with a couple of rums inside her, Grace's demeanour was stiff. It was clear she was nervous as hell.

'Break a leg, Grace!' Kitty shouted. 'Not literally, mind!'

When the band struck up and Grace started to sing into the silver microphone, her rich, soulful voice came through the speakers as though she hadn't spent the evening fighting off violent men and escaping a blaze!

Kitty cooed with delight. The band members were grinning at one another, too. *If the sweetest jar of honey had a sound,* she thought, *this would be it. That patient was right. She does have a voice like a nightingale!*

Without realising why, tears started to well in Kitty's eyes. It was as if the music – a Billie Holiday song – had divined all the pain and grief and regret inside Kitty, and now, here was the physical manifestation of that heartbreak, rolling onto her cheeks in the form of fat tears. She wiped them away, smiled up at her friend and clapped enthusiastically when the song ended.

'Bravo! Incredible!' she shouted. 'More!'

Beside her, the landlord wolf-whistled his approval.

It was then that Kitty noticed the scabbing on his knuckles for the first time. Something dawned on her. She sidled closer to him. 'You know Lloyd has already had a couple of surgeries to put his face back together, after those two Canadian fellers beat him to a pulp?'

'Aye.'

'And now his face is all busted up again, thanks to the very same bullies. He's in more danger in the backyard of his employer than he is on the street.'

'Aye.' The landlord pointed to his broken nose. 'Occupational hazard of working in a club, love. If I had a shilling for every drunk I've had to turf out on a Saturday night because they couldn't keep their hands to themselves . . .' He chuckled and rubbed his scabbed knuckles. 'Listen, love. This area's full of tough men, spoiling for a fight.' He pointed to Lloyd. 'If it wasn't my cellar boys, it'd be the barrow boys from Smithfield Market. Lloyd's one of them what's got a mouth on him. Always wise-cracking and trying to charm the ladies. Local lads – they take the hump because he doesn't know when to button it.'

'I'm sure his charm isn't why he keeps getting beaten up. I wasn't born yesterday.'

The landlord merely shrugged. 'My cellar idiots are gone. They're dead to me. Lock the buggers up and throw away the key, I say. Better still, I hope they get put on the first plane back to Canada. So, they won't be starting with him again in a hurry. I can't do nowt about the barrow boys from the market, though. Lloyd's got to learn when to keep his gob shut. This isn't some Jamaican fishing village where it's all palm trees and rum. This is Manchester.'

Kitty thought about how her own twin brother had spent years ducking and diving in a bid to avoid the wrath of the city's thugs. If Ned, a local boy, had sailed across the Atlantic in fear for his life, what chance did Grace stand of keeping out of harm's way? 'My friend, Grace – she's a nurse and a respectable girl. I don't want her getting tangled up in anything else that could get her hurt or jeopardise her nursing career.'

The landlord shrugged. 'She's got a lovely voice, your pal. The best of all the birds they've auditioned today, by far. I'm sure the band will welcome her with open arms, and

I'm happy, as long as folk keep paying to listen to her and part with their wages at my bar. I'll keep an eye on her if she gets the gig. I like her. She's got pluck. But you've got to remember – I'm a busy man and I'm not her dad.'

Sighing at the lot of the new West Indian immigrants, trying to make a new life in a once-rich city that had bet everything on industrialisation but had lost its shirt, thanks to two world wars and the Great Depression, Kitty thought about her own father's illegal antics. Bert Longthorne had become a luminary among the city's bad boys, preferring to burgle, rob and swindle on an industrial scale rather than claim dole. He'd left his family with a legacy of poverty and a bad name, but still – oh how she missed him.

She swallowed down a hard lump of grief, not wanting the landlord to sense her sorrow. She visualised the bleak funeral, only days away – black-clad mourners singing dirge-like hymns in a cold church. Sobs punctuating the priest's hellfire and damnation by a wind-swept, damp graveside. Then, something occurred to her.

'It doesn't have to be like that, Dad,' she whispered. 'We can do better for you than that.'

Chapter 42

'The flowers are flipping lovely, sweetheart,' a woman said, digging her nails into Kitty's shoulder.

Kitty turned around to see an older platinum-blonde woman who was heavily made up and showing rather too much wrinkled cleavage for a funeral. She wore a mink coat, gold rings on almost every finger and was sitting next to a man in an expensive-looking Crombie overcoat, with a scar running down the side of his face and blurry blue tattoos on both hands. Kitty forced herself to smile. 'Ta. Thanks for coming.'

The couple gave her a sympathetic smile.

'Your dad was a cracker,' the man said. 'We were in Strangeways together. Good lad was Bert. Solid as a rock.'

Nodding in silence, Kitty turned back to the front and squeezed her mother's hand.

'I don't know how they all found out,' her mother whispered. 'I'm here to bury my husband, but I'm that ashamed, I wish I could throw myself in the hole after the coffin.'

'Don't worry, Mam. Let's just get through the next few hours, and then it's just us.' She hadn't the heart to tell her mother that idiot Ned had put an obituary in the newspaper, giving the time, date and location of the service. He'd booked the upstairs of a large pub, not far from the cemetery. The wake was going to be a cramped affair.

James leaned over Kitty and whispered, 'We'll still be here for you when that lot have gone, Elsie. *We're* your family. We're not too disappointing, are we?'

'No! No! You two are my saving grace. God bless you, son,' Elsie said, her watery eyes betraying the tumultuous mix of anguish and gratitude she was undoubtedly feeling.

Kitty hadn't dared to look back at the crowd that had amassed in the church in the last half-hour, but there had been a constant stream of well-wishers coming down to the front to shake their hands, none of whom she or her mother knew, but all of whom Ned greeted as though they were long-lost friends. She could tell from the uncharacteristic warmth of the church and the hubbub, however, that there was a hundred-strong throng of mourners sitting in the pews behind theirs.

'This isn't the send-off I wanted for him,' her mother said. 'I wanted something dignified.'

Ned snorted with derision. 'Dad would have loved this. You're forgetting, he didn't have a dignified bone in his body, and he'd rather have bought this lot a round in the pub and been Mr Popular than have brought a regular pay packet home to us. Me dad was a lot of things, but dignified wasn't one of them. This is exactly what he'd have wanted. All his old friends; a wake to remember with a hangover to forget.'

Kitty could see Ned was smiling. Even in the midst of grief, with his father's coffin in his eyeline, he was being mischievous and contrary. She'd been feeling guilty about keeping her surprise a secret, but now she was glad she had. It was almost time.

The priest came over, gathered up his vestments and squatted on his hunkers with cracking knees. 'We'll be starting in five minutes. Everybody has an order of service. I've just one question. What's this music you've arranged, then?'

'It's a choir with some accompaniment,' Kitty said.

'"Ave Maria"? That sort of thing?' the priest asked.

'Not quite. You'll see.'

Kitty's mother shot her a concerned glance but then rolled her eyes at Jesus, nailed to his crucifix, suspended high above the altar, as though he'd sympathise with her plight.

Presently, the priest climbed into his pulpit and began. He spoke sombrely and at length about Bert Longthorne as though he'd known him all his life; as though Kitty's father had been a good Catholic and regular church attendee, when nothing could have been further from the truth.

The congregation prayed for Bert's tainted soul. Kitty took the time to stare blankly at the huge mullioned windows behind the crucifix. The Luftwaffe's bombs had robbed the church of its once-glorious stained glass, and now, drab, semi-opaque reinforced security glass, threaded with prison-like bars, was installed in its stead. At a funeral peopled with hardened criminals, the irony of her father failing to escape the baggage and trappings of an ex-convict, even in death, was not lost on her. Her gaze settled on his coffin. Kitty tried to imagine his body inside, dressed in his best suit, which had become many sizes too big for him. Ned had insisted on putting a bottle of single malt in with him, shoving a packet of Capstan and a lighter into the inside pocket.

Closing her eyes, Kitty said a prayer for Galbraith and his colleagues. Their research on smoking would be published the following year. *Please, God, let the findings save someone else's parent, so they don't have to go through this at the age of twenty-eight.*

As if sensing her sorrow, James put his arm around her. She felt bolstered by his touch. This experience had taught her the most important thing of all – James was her rock.

The priest cleared his throat. 'Kitty. Kitty! I believe you had some words you wanted to share about your father.' How long had he been trying to catch her attention? She blushed.

'Of course.'

Taking to the pulpit, she pulled the folded piece of paper out of her jacket pocket. Her hand shook as she smoothed it out. She could barely see the words through the veil of tears, but a sobering glance at all those mourners, who filled every pew right to the back of the church, focused her mind.

Swallowing hard, she began.

'My dad, Bert Longthorne, was always the biggest man in the room. Even when other men towered over him, he had the loudest voice and the funniest jokes and charisma that just pulled you to him like a magnet.'

There was a murmur of approval from the congregation.

Kitty looked at her mother. 'My mam, Elsie, loved him her whole adult life – whether he deserved it or not, because, let's face it, he gave her a run for her money.' There was a smattering of laughter. 'Bert Longthorne was like a force of nature that couldn't be tamed. He always had some grand plan. Even when I was little, he'd pick me and my twin brother, Ned, up in his big arms and tell us how the Longthornes were going to conquer the world.' She swallowed hard at the painful memories of all the bits she hadn't put in the speech – the agony of his boozing, his philandering, his temper tantrums, his crimes and his incarceration. Some things were better left unsaid, especially in a church and particularly when most people knew those stories anyway. She locked eyes with Ned. 'When we were young, he loved me and my brother with the same ferocity that he loved life – and our mam. We were his and he was ours, and it was us against the world.' She sighed at the sight of her silently weeping mother. 'My dad was a legend – for all of the right reasons and some of the wrong. But his logic was sound. Whatever cockamamie shenanigans he got involved with – and he excelled at shenanigans, probably in cahoots with many of you in here, today, by the looks of you . . .' More raucous laughter rippled around the church. Kitty felt like a performing monkey, but this was not a crowd to disappoint. 'He always did what he did for us. His plans never amounted to anything but a holiday at His Majesty's pleasure and the loss of two of his limbs, but I know in my heart that he meant well.' She bit her lip. The truth that he had been a demanding and utterly selfish narcissist roiled around her stomach like a poorly digested meal. She looked at James and knew from the softness around his dark eyes that he understood perfectly what she was going through. Her voice started to falter.

'The last couple of years, since Dad had his accident, brought us all closer together – me, Mam and him. He'd lost some of his hard-man swagger, and in its place, we found the softer bits. He didn't like needing us, but I'm a nurse, and my mam's one of life's givers—' She inhaled deeply, willing herself not to break down. 'So, caring for him was our pleasure and our honour.

'Bert Longthorne hasn't really gone.' She smiled at her mother and at Ned. 'He lives on in his family. He lives on in all of our memories. He's just waiting for us, either up there' – she pointed to the vaulted roof of the church – 'or down there.' She pointed to the cold marble flags of the floor, unwilling to look at the smiling mourners who had enjoyed more of her father's company than she, her mother or Ned ever had. 'He'll be propping up some celestial bar, telling bad jokes to the angels and the saints – or maybe to the Devil himself.'

Her mother crossed herself. In Kitty's peripheral vision, she caught a glimpse of a very disgruntled-looking priest, who was pointedly tapping at his watch.

'Knowing my dad, wherever he is now, he'll be having a beano. So, don't you worry about him. But do keep a little corner of your heart for his memory, like a dedication on a park bench. He'd like that. Because my dad loved people and he loved life and he went too soon. Too soon for a man so full of life to die. I'll miss him, the mischievous old so and so. I'll be keeping a corner of my heart just for him.' She pointed to her chest. 'Right here. This is for you, Dad, for all you were and all you should have been.'

She folded the paper back up, letting the tears drop freely onto it so that it became transparent. At the back of the church, she saw the singers, gathered and ready for her cue. The priest was approaching the pulpit from the right.

Holding her hand up, she addressed the congregation. 'I've arranged some music. I wanted something that would make this service feel like a celebration of Dad's life. So, I hope you'll enjoy it.'

Grace, dressed in a floor-length green robe, as were the others, marched down the aisle with her fellow singers, all carrying tambourines. There were some twenty choir members from her church, accompanied by a large, fearsome-looking woman who took her place at the church's old upright piano.

The piano struck up and the choir began to sing hymns with such beautiful and complex harmonies that a shiver ricocheted down Kitty's spine. Grace was the lead singer, belting out the verses and punctuating the choruses with such incredible power.

At her side, Kitty felt her mother's shoulders rise and fall as she sobbed heartily.

'It's so beautiful,' her mother said, when the performance neared its end. 'Thanks, love. Your dad – he would have adored this, if only to see the looks on everyone's faces! It's not every day you get this kind of thing in a Catholic church!'

Kitty felt uplifted by the music. The church didn't seem such a drab place, after all. What surprised her most, however, was not the jubilant reaction of the white Catholic mourners to the Black Baptist choir, but the way that Grace was beaming at Ned with undisguised love in her eyes.

Kitty looked at her brother to see his reaction.

Ned was beaming right back at Grace with his hand placed over his heart.

Chapter 43

'Well, that was quite a wake,' Ned said, slumping in his chair at the small kitchen table. He was wearing his father's old dressing gown and pyjamas. The sheen of sweat on his face and the smell of stale alcohol emanating from his every pore bore testament to the fact that he hadn't rolled in until the small hours, after a night of hard drinking.

Kitty wrinkled her nose. 'I'm glad James drove me and Mam straight home after the cemetery. All those hoodlums under one roof! I can't think of anything less fitting. Dad grassed half of Manchester's criminals up to avoid prison after the coupon fiasco. That lot only showed up to his funeral so they could dance on his grave.'

Ned merely shrugged. 'Dad was more popular than you give him credit for. Honour among thieves, and all that.'

'Honour? Pull the other one! It's got bells on.' Kitty smeared margarine on a doorstep of toast. 'Was it a lock-in, then?'

'I'll say.' Ned belched quietly and rubbed his scalp. 'Dad's old pals know how to let their hair down.'

'I'll bet there was a fight,' their mother said ruefully, pouring dark brown tea into Ned's cup from the black ceramic teapot that never showed the tannin stains.

There was an impish glint in Ned's good eye. 'Course there was a fight. Gilbert McMahon punched Harry Brown's lights out, and then their boys piled in.'

Kitty's mother inhaled sharply. 'They always were rough, those two. I hated my Bert knocking around with that sort. I hope they paid for any damage.'

'Don't worry, Mam. It's taken care of.'

'You've been exiled in Barbados for two years because your dad dragged you into his dodgy dealings. Should you be rubbing shoulders with ex-cons the minute you're back, son?'

Kitty noticed how this morning, her mother's skin was grey. It was as though the funeral had drained any joie de vivre out of her. Her eyes had a haunted look about them. She looked as empty as the house felt. No Dad. No medical paraphernalia now that James had driven everything back to the hospital. No flowers now that they'd all been left at her father's graveside. Only a handful of mawkish lilac sympathy cards remained on the mantel.

Ned seemed oblivious to the emptiness. 'I'm a big boy, Mam. It's the coppers I've got to keep an eye out for.' He took a bite out of the black pudding that their mother had fried for him and spoke as he chewed. 'They've got long memories.'

'Do you really think they're still going to want to talk to you, two years on?' her mother asked, sipping her tea. She'd pushed her toast away with a pained expression. 'With all your dad did for them? In a city already full of swindlers, burglars and thieves?'

'I can't take any chances,' Ned said. 'I've been running the gauntlet as it is. Especially putting that obituary in the *Evening News*.'

'So, is that it?' Kitty asked. 'Are you going back to Barbados?'

'What choice do I have?' Ned drained his tea.

'Won't you be leaving something precious behind?' Kitty asked, raising her eyebrow archly. She remembered the way

Ned had looked at Grace during the funeral service. Hadn't Grace stood by his side as their father's coffin had been lowered into the ground? Kitty had seen how the two had surreptitiously entwined their little fingers together. Small wonder that Grace had rejected Lloyd's advances.

Even with a face that was covered with so much scar tissue, it was clear that Ned was blushing. 'I don't know what you mean.'

Their mother, who had been gazing mournfully at Bert's empty chair, suddenly slammed her hand down on the table, hard enough to make them both jump. 'For God's sake, boy! Stop fannying around, as if you've got all the time in the world to start a family and all the girls falling at your feet. Grace is clever, respectable, beautiful. If she's daft enough to have you, grab her hand and make something of your life!'

Ned opened and closed his mouth, searching for a response. His forehead was now almost the same shade of pink as the rasher of bacon on his plate.

'Mam's right,' Kitty said. Then she cocked her head to the side and paused for thought. She pointed at Ned with the corner of her toast. 'In fact, no. Maybe Mam's wrong. Maybe she's not seeing the full picture. Grace is far too good for you. Maybe you *should* go back to Barbados and leave the poor girl be. Maybe she'll find herself a nice doctor at the hospital. Or who knows? She might come round to Lloyd, the Jamaican trumpet player in the band she's just started singing with. He's definitely got designs on her, and he's a good sort, he is. Hard grafter and straight as a die.'

Her words had the intended effect on Ned. He straightened up in his chair, frowning. 'Lloyd? A bloody trumpet player? Who the hell does he think he is? I fell for Grace years before he ever laid eyes on her. He can go and blow his horn elsewhere. She doesn't even like Jamaicans!' He folded his arm across his chest.

Kitty reached out and squeezed her brother's arm. 'If you've got feelings for Grace and she feels the same, getting on the next boat back to Barbados isn't going to do you or her any good. Grace is here. Now. In Manchester for the foreseeable.'

'But the police—'

'You're using that as an excuse. They never had any evidence against you, did they?'

Ned shook his head. 'One of the others on the job told me the coppers wanted to question me.'

'Hearsay,' Kitty said. 'If they'd wanted to arrest you, you'd never have made it out of the country. They got Dad. He brought the whole house of cards down. It's over. Chip-wrappings.'

Their mother rose and started to clear away plates. She paused to stare at their father's empty chair and then her sorrowful gaze drifted onto Ned. 'If I'm prepared to learn to live alone again, son, you've got to learn to let yourself be loved.'

The following day, Kitty returned to work. Dressed in her freshly laundered uniform and free of the damp smell of her mother's place, she felt a little better. When she entered the ward, she spotted Grace in the bathroom-cum-office, nodding enthusiastically as Sister Penny, finally returned from her bout of gastroenteritis that had dragged on longer than expected, went through the roster with her. Both were engrossed in their activity.

On the ward, Kitty saw that every single bed was occupied. With the colder weather setting in, it was hardly surprising.

Freezing fog and the acrid smoke billowing out of chimneys everywhere always proved life-threatening – especially for those suffering from bad asthma and bronchitis.

At the end of the ward, next to the large open fireplace, a junior nurse was standing on a chair, hanging Christmas decorations on a beautiful pine tree. She looked Indian – clearly one of the new colonial recruits. For the first time in a while, Kitty felt ready to look forward to the months ahead. Christmas was coming and the hospital was evolving to meet the NHS's needs. A new year, a new decade and more medical discoveries were just around the corner . . .

She started to pad along the ward, intent on saying hello to the new recruit, all the while checking who was a familiar face and which patients were new.

'Good to have you back, Nurse Longthorne!' Molly called out to her. She was changing the dressings of a post-operative patient.

Kitty was bemused at her friendliness. 'Thanks, Molly. Nice to see you, too.' She approached the bed and checked the notes of the new patient. 'Who have we here? Mr Crossland, is it?' Smiling at the elderly man, she glanced surreptitiously at Molly Henshaw to determine if any sarcasm had been behind her greeting. The last time they'd spoken, Kitty had admonished her for her treatment of Grace. But no, it seemed Molly was at least *trying* to greet her with genuine enthusiasm. *That's a turn-up for the books*, Kitty thought. *Maybe she feels sorry for me because Dad died.*

Kitty straightened the blankets on Mr Crossland's bed and replenished his jug of water, while Molly checked that his chest drain was flowing correctly. 'Molly's taking smashing care of you, I see.' It wouldn't hurt to offer her colleague an olive branch.

'Aye. She is that.' The old man wheezed, scratching his nose with the amber index finger that was characteristic of a heavy smoker. 'I had that Black one looking after me, but I complained. I don't want one of *them* touching my wound. Now, I've got lovely Molly, here.' He grinned a brown-toothed grin.

Holding her breath momentarily, Kitty clung onto her irritation. *Things will get better,* she counselled herself, *he's just old and set in his ways.* 'You don't need to worry, Mr Crossland,' she said. '*All* the nurses in this hospital are first class. You're in safe hands.'

Kitty was about to move on, when she heard Matron's voice.

'Nurse Longthorne! May I have a word?'

Matron beckoned her back towards the entrance of the ward. Remembering how, the last time she had spoken to Matron alone, their relationship had soured over the issue of Grace's allegations against Molly, Kitty swallowed hard.

In silence, she followed Matron into the storeroom. Matron closed the door and turned towards her.

'Is everything all right?' Kitty asked. 'I came back as soon as I could. I just needed a couple of extra days after the funeral to help my mam sort out all Dad's—'

Matron held her hands up and closed her eyes. 'Don't give that a second thought.' She opened her eyes. Behind the lenses of her tortoiseshell spectacles, they looked big and searching.

At that moment, Kitty felt certain that if it had been possible to dissect a person by sight alone, Matron would surely be a top practitioner in the discipline. 'Is this about the—?' Where should she start? The insubordination? Had she finally discovered the truth about Kitty and Grace's breaking of curfew? The drunken coal-throwing and wanton window-smashing at two in the morning?

Matron chuckled. 'My dear, you look as though you're about to faint.' She awkwardly took hold of Kitty's forearm, seemed to think better of it and let her go. 'I'm very sorry about your father. I hope your mother is coping.'

'She is. Yes. She's made of stern stuff. She just needs to remember that and she'll be right as rain. Thanks again for sorting us out with Mildred. That was really thoughtful.'

Nodding, Matron laced her fingers together. 'About our little debate – Molly and Grace.'

'Oh.' Surely Matron wasn't going to pursue some kind of formal disciplinary action?

'I've been thinking.' Matron pursed her lips. She took her glasses off and her eyes returned to their normal size. 'You were right. I was being unreasonable in defending Molly and I've since had words with her. We need these colonial workers, and though I can't do anything about their pay and status, they absolutely deserve our respect.'

Kitty opened her mouth to say something but Matron beat her to it.

'Kitty, my attitudes are that of a much older woman. I realise that. I just haven't been in step with the brave new world.' She inhaled, then exhaled slowly. 'And it's because of that that I'm retiring.'

'What?' Kitty blinked hard.

'Yes. I think it best to let the new generation move up the ladder. Kitty, we need women like you in top nursing positions. This is what I wanted to say to you.'

'Th-thank you. That's very kind.' Kitty wasn't sure how to feel about the revelation that her long-standing mentor was moving on.

'The new matron will be chosen from one of the sisters.' She looked down at her impeccably clean, short fingernails. 'Consequently, there's to be a vacancy. I'd encourage you to apply for that sister's job, my dear – when it comes up for grabs. I will give my recommendation to the board. If you want the job.'

'Me? A sister?'

'Why ever not? You're ready for promotion. I told you it would be all but guaranteed after your recruitment trip to the West Indies.'

Kitty thought about how she was also finally ready to walk down the aisle with James – a commitment that was utterly at odds with being promoted in a profession that precluded married women. She bit her lip.

'I – I don't know what to say. Thanks so much.'

'Take your time to think about it.' Matron put her spectacles back on and smiled fleetingly. 'You've got until the New Year to make your decision.' She took Kitty's hand and patted it affectionately. Then, she turned on her heel and left the storeroom.

Alone among the clean towels, gowns and boxes of dressings, Kitty looked out at Sister Penny, who had just emerged with Grace from the office. She tried to imagine herself wearing the sister's uniform and wielding her authority on the ward in an official capacity – not just acting in an incumbent sister's absence. Kitty could barely stifle a grin.

Whatever would James say?

Chapter 44

'Right. I've greased and lined the tins,' Grace said, tying her pinny around her slim waist. 'And we've got all the ingredients, thanks to that whip-round for food coupons from the other girls.' She unfolded the recipe that her mother had posted to her. The paper looked old and fragile, as though it had been handed down through the generations.

'Yes. There's a small fortune sat here on the side. They were right generous. Even Molly chipped in, and she's always been tight.' Kitty eyed the bags of dried fruit, the sugar, the butter, the flour and the coveted ground almonds that the other nursing staff who worked on the lung ward had contributed towards. She looked over the prized fresh brown hens' eggs that James had sourced from his favourite indebted farmer in Cheshire. Finally, she cracked open the half-bottle of Jamaican rum that Lloyd had kindly contributed and inhaled its heady aroma. 'This'll put hairs on the patients' chests.' She set the bottle down and scratched her head. 'Now, what do you want me to do? I told you, I'm about as good at baking as I am at changing a car tyre.'

Grace placed the scales in front of Kitty. 'You can be my assistant. Get weighing things out, first.'

Taking the softened butter from Kitty, Grace started to cream the brown sugar into it with a wooden spoon. 'God bless you, Kitty. This was a lovely idea. Those patients had better like it! Grace doesn't bake her special Bajan black cake for every Tom, Dick and Harry.'

Kitty clumsily measured out some flour and started to sieve it into a separate bowl, inadvertently covering everything next to it with a veil of white. 'Oh they will. This should be a rare treat for them. We've all known nothing but years and years of strict rationing. And most people have never had rum in a Christmas cake before. Someone gave me a piece while I was in Barbados, but I can't wait to try yours!'

She started to slice some fat prunes into quarters and cast her mind back to the previous Christmas, when her mother had made a bland Christmas dinner. James, as an unmarried doctor with no children, had drawn the short straw and had worked the entire day. Her father had still been able to sit up in his armchair and had eaten his meal from a tray on his lap. Her mother had tried her best to make the occasion feel as festive as possible, hanging tinsel from her cheese plant as they couldn't afford a tree. Together, they'd listened to the wireless. It had been a threadbare affair, but at least her father had still been with them. Contemplating this first Christmas without the man she'd loved and resented in equal measure was a painful prospect.

'Are you all right?' Grace asked, soaking the dried fruit with a liberal portion of rum. 'You look like you've lost a shilling and found a penny.'

Kitty shook her head. 'I'm just nervous about tomorrow. I don't think James can cook, you know. He's as bad as me. How is he going to cater for me, you, Ned and my mam? How are we going to fit in his tiny little bachelor pad!'

Grace threw her head back and laughed. 'Oh, Kitty! You worry about everything.'

'So did you only a few weeks ago.'

Her friend nodded and started to whisk the eggs together in a bowl. 'That's true. Everything's come up smelling of roses.'

'You're learning all the local lingo, too, I see!'

'Why not? When in Rome . . . If it wasn't for you speaking up for me, I'd still be picking my damp washing off the floor and sluicing bedpans.' She started to add the egg. 'I think I'm finally starting to settle in, you know. I've got my church, I sing in a band on my day off and I'm making friends, at last. I've even learned to like pie and chips.'

Kitty laughed. 'Don't you miss home? Your family? Your friends?' She thought about the chemistry she'd sensed between Grace and Ned; the surprising way in which Grace clearly favoured her disfigured, problematic white brother over the handsome, charming and easy-going Lloyd, who shared her West Indian heritage. 'Our Ned sets sail in the first week of January. How do you feel about that?'

Grace paused and sighed. 'Let's get some of that flour and ground almonds into this mixture. Look! It's curdling!'

Whatever was going on between those two, Kitty could see that Grace wasn't going to volunteer any information.

'Thanks, Nurse Longthorne. You're a good'un. Merry Christmas, love, and thanks for all your kindness and care!' Mr Barker, a chronic bronchitis and emphysema sufferer and the ward's longest-standing patient, was wearing a broad smile on his weary face, as he looked down at his Christmas stocking-filler – a hearty slab of the home-made Bajan black cake, which Kitty had wrapped and tied with a bow.

'My pleasure! Me and Nurse Griffith made it ourselves,' Kitty said. 'Or rather, she did all the clever stuff and I just weighed things out and did the washing-up. I'm no cook! I could burn water, me!'

Her patient laughed and wheezed and coughed. 'You're a little belter. You all are, you girls. I don't need to wait for heaven to see angels. This hospital's full of 'em!'

Amid the freezing Mancunian winter, Kitty felt like a summer sun was shining its warm rays onto her heart. How could she leave this profession, on the cusp of promotion, to marry?

'Let's hope the New Year brings you better health,' she said, patting Mr Barker's arm.

'With emphysema?' He shook his head. 'I'm not daft, love. I know that every time I come in here, it's like you're just putting a plaster on a leg that's been chopped off.'

'Medical miracles happen all the time,' Kitty said, feeling guilt tighten around her gullet, trying to squeeze the truth from her that progress was slow; that there was little to be done for the sufferers of emphysema and chronic bronchitis who packed out wards across the country.

Perhaps it was time for change. Perhaps, if she applied for the promotion, she could ask to be transferred to another ward, where broken limbs could be fixed and infections could now be cured. The lung ward reminded her too much of her father. It was suddenly harder to be among these men, stripped of their vitality and gasping their last, than it had been to nurse young soldiers who had lost limbs on the battlefield. Was this grief? Had watching her father die robbed her of her ability to shove her feelings in a box whenever she tended a dying middle-aged man?

'Are you crying, love?' Mr Barker asked.

Kitty shook her head. 'Just something in my eye! Enjoy your cake.'

She needed to speak to the one person who would understand what she was going through. She needed to find James.

*

On Christmas Eve, James's plastic surgery clinic was empty.

'Have you seen Dr Williams?' she asked his secretary, Florrie.

Florrie looked at the clock on the wall. 'He went into an emergency surgery about an hour ago. If he's not still in theatre—'

'Staffroom?'

Florrie nodded. 'Professor Baird-Murray will be cracking open the brandy and mince pies for the consultants, I should think.' James's portly, always cheerful secretary stifled a yawn. Even her brightly coloured floral blouse couldn't cheer her pallid complexion up.

'I think we all need a break.' Kitty held out a piece of the Christmas cake. 'Here. A little festive something from us nurses. Rationing and waistlines be damned.'

Florrie took the gift and inhaled deeply. She narrowed her eyes. 'I can smell rum! God bless you, love. You and Dr Williams have a cracking break. Maybe 1950 will bring wedding bells . . .'

'Maybe.' Kitty kissed her on the cheek and started to walk away.

'Oh, by the way. Sorry for your loss.'

Unwilling to turn around to let Florrie see the look of sadness on her face, Kitty merely waved. 'Merry Christmas.'

She found James at the sink in the operating theatre, scrubbing blood off his forearms under a steaming tap.

'Did you win?' she asked.

He looked up and beamed at her. 'I certainly did. A horrific facial injury on a little girl, no less. I think with a couple of extra surgeries, I can have her smiling again.'

'My hero!'

James raised an eyebrow. 'We must remember never to let our children play with a neighbour's vicious fighting dog.'

Kitty balked. 'Ouch. Thankfully, I don't think there will be many fighting dogs in Hale. If that's where we end up.'

Drying his hands and arms on a snowy white towel, James leaned against the sink. 'So, you'll come house hunting with me in the New Year?'

Looking around to check that they were alone, Kitty realised that it was time. She could put off the conversation no longer.

'Listen! I've got to tell you something.'

'Let me guess. You don't want a pink bathroom suite?' James put his arms around her waist. 'You'd prefer pistachio.'

Kitty pushed him away gently. 'Matron said there's a sister's position opening up. She wants me to apply.' Her heart was pounding too fast. The floor beneath her seemed to undulate.

Now it was his turn to back away. 'But we're getting married! I thought we'd agreed. New decade, new path in life together.'

'Oh, I want to, but Matron said—'

'I thought there was just you and me in this relationship, Kitty. If I'd known at the start that Matron would hold sway over every decision we made—'

'You'd what?' Kitty felt tears prick at the backs of her eyes. This wasn't the Christmas Eve she'd envisaged at all. The claustrophobic feeling she'd had in the Ford Anglia travelling back from Berkshire was upon her again. 'You'd have stuck with Violet?' The words spilled out of her, hot and acidic. She had no way of stemming their flow when she saw James look down at his feet. 'Oh, yes. I see I've hit the nail on the head. You and Violet would have had one, maybe two children by now, wouldn't you? Boys, I'd bet. Little strawberry-blonds with solid legs, toddling round on a perfect lawn. But no. You chose me. Workaday Kitty, with her bargain-basement family and her professional dedication. It always did stick in your craw that I believed so passionately in nursing; that it's not just something to busy myself with till I walk down the aisle with my handsome doctor.'

'That's not fair.'

She stormed out of the operating theatre. No. This wasn't at all how she'd hoped the conversation would go. This was nothing short of a Christmas disaster. Even Grace's Bajan black cake couldn't sweeten the bitter taste she'd just left in her fiancé's mouth.

Chapter 45

'Come on, Mam. It's time to go.' Kitty was already waiting at her mother's front door, carrying the heavy Tupperware container that her mother had borrowed from a neighbour. Inside, peeled carrots and prepared Brussels sprouts sloshed about in water.

Ned pushed past Kitty, carrying a swinger of potatoes. He was dressed in the same linen suit he'd worn on his arrival from Barbados. The smart woollen overcoat was one he'd pilfered from James.

'So, Grace is meeting us there?' His breath steamed on the cold Christmas morning air.

'Yes. Where on earth is Mam?' Kitty knew there was irritation in her voice. She also knew it was down to the argument she'd had with James in the operating theatre. What sort of a reception could she hope to receive when they showed up at James's place?

Finally, her mother emerged, wearing her best knitted beret and a jumble-sale coat. She carried a large pudding basin covered in foil. 'I hope he remembered to put that turkey in at the crack of dawn.'

'I'm sure he will have done.'

'Lucky that him two doors down is a black cab driver,' her mother said. 'We would have had a right old time of it, trying to get all the way out to James's neck of the woods on Christmas Day, if I hadn't promised him two doors down that I'd babysit his four tiny tots come January. His wife turns thirty, you know.'

The bulk of the black Austin cab, parked just along the street, moved towards them slowly.

'Here he is!' Elsie waved at her neighbour.

The taxi came to a halt, they all wished each other a merry Christmas, and they pulled away, full of chatter about the first Christmas they'd ever spent in another household, where somebody else had cooked the turkey.

'Are you all right, our Kitty?' Ned asked, as they turned into James's tree-lined road. 'You look green, like you're about to be sick.'

'I'm fine.' Kitty treated him to a curt smile, but she knew her twin had sensed her unease. It was true. She did feel queasy. It was undoubtedly nerves.

Finally the cab stopped in front of James's bachelor pad. It was on the first floor of a rather grand 1930s privately owned block of purpose-built flats. Outside, the front gardens were well tended and attractive, even in winter.

Kitty pressed the buzzer.

Grace answered. 'Oh, Merry Christmas, everyone! I just got here myself. James says you should all come up.'

They marched in and climbed the Art Deco staircase. James was waiting at the door for them, wearing an apron over his slacks and shirt. He held his hands high. 'Merry Christmas, Longthornes. I'm afraid I have pigs-in-blankets hands, so I won't give you my usual effusive greeting. Ha ha.' He locked eyes with Kitty. 'Perhaps my wonderful fiancée could come and help me in the kitchen. Ned, dear boy, would you pour some sherry for everyone?'

Kitty could feel the heat in her cheeks. She felt suddenly coy as she followed her family inside. Clutching the Tupperware container full of vegetables to her bosom as though it would protect her from heartbreak, she padded across the parlour. So unlike her mam's, it was a stylish but spartan affair, showcasing a sideboard and a glazed book cabinet of the curved walnut Art Deco variety, two boxy white-leather settees with tubular steel frames that ran along the outside and two black-leather and steel armchairs that looked more like sculptures than furniture. James said they were Bauhaus pieces. Kitty still wasn't sure what that meant but she'd always intended to replace them with something more comfortable and feminine-looking, when they furnished a family home together. If James was harbouring a grudge about their Christmas Eve exchange, however, she was sure she'd never get the opportunity to replace those unforgiving leather settees!

She stood at the doorway, biting the inside of her cheek. 'Are you still talking to me, then?'

James washed his hands under the steaming-hot tap and dried them on a tea towel. He was smiling but the tendon in his jaw was flinching and he was blinking hard, as he always did when he was considering a tricky response.

He slipped behind her, closed the door and took the Tupperware container, placing it on the side. Turning around, he took hold of Kitty's hands. 'I owe you an apology,' he said. He rubbed her knuckles with gentle fingertips.

'It's the other way round, isn't it?' Kitty asked.

James shook his head. 'No. It really isn't. Look, you and I – we've been at sixes and sevens over the past few months, what with your father dying and the trip to the West Indies and the miscarriage and me pressuring you to name a date.'

'It's been horrible. So much loss. All the arguments.' Kitty felt a tear of frustration leak onto her cheek. 'I didn't want any of that. I was just trying to juggle—'

'I put you under pressure unnecessarily, Kitty. I was selfish and I'm happy to admit that.' The Adam's apple in James's neck moved up and down. 'Nobody ever asks such things of a doctor. We just set out on our career path and thunder along. Family aspirations fit into our jobs, not the other way round. And yet, I made thoughtless demands of you to give up nursing and settle down before you were ready.'

Kitty sighed deeply. 'You weren't thoughtless, James. You were trying to build a life for us at the pace people normally go at. You didn't account for a bluestocking as a fiancée, but it turns out, I am a bit of a one!' She smiled uncertainly.

When he gently used his knuckle to wipe her tear away, she turned to kiss his hand, resting her cheek against it.

'Look, I love you, Kitty Longthorne,' he said. 'I want you to be my wife, and I understand that there's a mismatch between the rules and regulations of nursing and the life of a married woman in 1949. But I hear rumblings of change being just around the corner. We're about to start a new decade, and it's possible that nurses will soon be able to stay in the profession, regardless of their marital status.'

'What are you trying to say?' Kitty was puzzled. She cocked her head to the side. 'Are you trying to un-propose to me? Are we going to live over the brush until they change the rules, like bohemians?'

'Well, sort of.' James grinned. 'I still think we should buy a house and set up home together.'

'How can I when I'm contractually obliged to live in the nurses' home?'

He shrugged. 'If you apply for the role of sister, you should insist on your freedom to live where you like. If they want you enough, they'll accommodate you. Baird-Murray and the rest of the board know we plan to marry.'

'It's just not going to work, James.'

He looked crestfallen; his colour drained. James got down on his knees and took a small box out of his trouser pocket. He opened it. Inside was an enormous solitaire diamond – almost certainly the ring that had been his mother's and the very same ring that Violet had kept after he'd jilted her at the altar.

'What's this?' Kitty covered her mouth, wide-eyed and wondering what on earth James was doing. 'I've already got a ring.'

'I got my mother to get this off Violet. After the Berkshire debacle, I was determined that you shouldn't be side-lined by my parents. I can only apologise. Kitty, Mother's behaviour was outlandish when we went to visit. I don't know how you put up with me.'

'Er . . . you've met my family!'

He got to his feet again, took off her smaller ring and put on the much, much larger one. It glittered in the wintry sunlight that streamed in through the windows. 'I like your family, for all their foibles. I wish my parents were half the loving, straightforward, plain-spoken sorts that your parents are – were—' He shook his head. 'You know what I mean!'

Kitty looked at the facets of the flawless blue diamond in the ring's setting. 'It's out of this world. But you don't have to give me a bigger ring. When you proposed to me, you thought you were getting one thing, and you've ended up with another.'

'You thought you were getting some knight in shining armour, who fixed the faces of the poor and needy, but now, you find you're engaged to a workaholic who spends half of his time in board meetings or giving debutantes smaller noses and ridding rich old ladies of their eye-bags and jowls.'

Kitty giggled. 'You're not doing yourself justice, James. I'm very glad you're a doctor and not a car salesman. We'd never eat!'

He pulled her into a warm embrace, resting his chin on her head. 'You still want to marry me, though, don't you? You still want children?'

'I do. I just don't want to be rushed.'

'Then we both want the same things. I confess I was pushing you to name the date because of everybody else's expectations, and I'm sorry. I'm sorry for everything. For being a pig about you going to Barbados and not standing up to my parents when they were beastly. But they were in the wrong. I was in the wrong. You're still young and you only get one shot at life. If gunning for the sister's position means so much to you, we can still start a family in a couple of years' time, if that's what you want.'

Pushing him away so that she could study his expression, Kitty frowned quizzically. 'Are you sure?'

'Absolutely. Let's make our own rules and not care two hoots what other people think. You're the girl for me, Kitty Longthorne. Never doubt it.'

A smile crept across Kitty's fraught and pale face, warming her cheeks until they glowed pink. 'Does that mean I can still get rid of your horrid bachelor furniture when we buy this new house? Can we get something I'd actually want to sit on?'

He laughed and took her face in his hands. 'I'll put my horrid bachelor furniture in my study. How about that?'

'It's a deal.'

They kissed passionately and only broke apart when there was a knock on the door.

'Kitty? James? Can I come in and put the Christmas pud on to steam?' It was Kitty's mother.

345

'Course, Mam.' Kitty opened the door. 'Come on in. We were just wrestling with the pigs-in-blankets.'

At two o'clock, as Kitty helped James to put out the steaming dishes of potatoes, vegetables, stuffing, bread sauce, the gravy boat and the gigantic roasting dish that contained the turkey and pigs-in-blankets, she mused that coming to his flat, rather than eating Christmas dinner at her mother's place, where her father's absence would be so acutely felt, had been an excellent idea.

'Ooh, hey! What a spread,' her mother said. 'It's like rationing's over!'

James winked. 'It helps if you've got an "in" with a friendly farmer. Last Christmas, I was working. This Christmas is worth pulling out all the stops for.' He popped the cork on a bottle of real champagne and started to fill everyone's glasses until they fizzed right to the rim with effervescent bubbles.

Kitty looked around the table and saw that, despite the empty chair that marked their loss, her family was happy. Now that she was able to get out of the house, the grey hue of her mother's normally drawn face had given way to a brighter complexion and shining eyes. Ned . . . *Ned's happy as a sandboy*, Kitty thought. *He looks like the cat that's got the cream, sitting there next to Grace.* Kitty wasn't listening to what Ned was saying, but she could hear the animation in his voice. There was laughter at that table, and the Longthornes hadn't truly laughed for a long, long time.

Sandwiched between Ned and her mother, Grace looked positively radiant. She leaned into Ned, giggling at his jokes. They locked eyes, as though some hidden meaning passed between them, like the lovers she suspected they were.

'Are you really going back to Barbados, Ned?' Kitty asked.

Ned grinned at her without answering. It was clear that he was mulling over her question. His grin faltered somewhat. He frowned, as if deep in contemplation. Then, he grinned anew. 'No. No, I'm not. I've decided. It's time to stay put, face my demons and put down roots, here in Blighty. I'm turning over a new leaf. I'm on the straight and narrow.' He turned to Grace and took her hand in his. 'If you'll have me, gorgeous Grace, I'm yours.'

Grace squealed and covered her face with her hands, but it was clear she was delighted. She threw her arms around Ned. 'I never met a man with a heart as big and as true as yours, Ned Longthorne.' She planted a kiss squarely on his mouth.

A flustered, red-faced Ned looked around at the table's occupants. 'Well, what can I say, folks? If a beauty like Grace Griffith can love a beast like me, love is definitely blind!'

Kitty clapped her hands in delight. 'Ooh, I love a happy ending!' She poked at Ned. 'You'd better look after my friend, here, Ned Longthorne, or James will have to do another surgery on the good side of your face!'

Ned saluted her. 'On Dad's memory. I swear I'll do right by Grace – for once in my life.'

With dinner on their plates, James raised his glass.

'To absent friends,' he said.

A murmur of agreement rippled around the table.

Kitty's mother wore a contemplative expression. 'Yes. To my Bert. Wherever you are,' she said, barely audible. 'I hope you're behaving.'

James cleared his throat. 'To enduring love, to family – and to a brave new decade, just around the corner. May we all enjoy good health, and may our dreams come true.'

Kitty clinked glasses with him and they kissed. 'Merry Christmas, my love.' Her stomach rumbled. 'Now, let's get stuck in before I starve to death. I tell you what, James, for a man who says he can't cook, this dinner looks out of this world.'

'Well, I might have had some expert guidance.' He nudged Kitty's mother and winked.

While Kitty ate, she observed her fiancé, sitting at the head of the table, pulling Christmas crackers with the others and laughing at his own and Ned's terrible jokes. Beyond the bounds of Park Hospital, the serious and often severe Dr James Williams was a warm, funny man and a generous host. She imagined him presiding over their own family table in the comfortable home that they would one day share as man and wife: a proud father regaling their children with anecdotes from the hospital – the sort of irreverent tales of guts and goo and gouty old professors that children would love, all told with a healthy dose of self-deprecation and absurd flourish. The thought made her smile.

For all 1949 had brought grief, strife and agonising decisions, Kitty realised that the last year of the 1940s had also bestowed upon her adventure, new friends and a deeper understanding of how very lucky she was. She knew that the care of others would always be in her blood, but she knew that James Williams, the family they would create together in the future and the family that she'd known her entire life, sitting around that table in James's flat, would always be the reason for her heart to keep beating.

Epilogue

'This is a song for Ned,' Grace said. 'And all you young lovers out there.'

The Band on the Wall was so packed that even though it was freezing outside, Kitty had had to peel every layer of her thick woollen clothing off until she was down to a light cotton summer dress. Lloyd had warned them that the club would be busy on the eve of a new decade, and he'd been right.

Kitty stood on her tiptoes and craned her neck to see her friend lean into the microphone. To her right, James took her by the hand. To her left, Ned wolf-whistled at Grace – not a nurse with flat shoes and a well-scrubbed face tonight, but a beautiful Barbadian songstress, glittering in a sequinned dress and holding the entire club in her thrall.

'Care to dance?' James asked, kissing Kitty's hand.

'I could dance all night,' she said. 'Especially with a devilishly handsome doctor who has two left feet!'

'Your wish is my command!' He held his arms out, beckoning her to him. 'Shall we?'

The band struck up, and the other couples on the dance floor all grabbed each other just a little tighter as the men started to whirl the women around in time to the music. James was certainly no Fred Astaire, but Kitty was content to sway with him on the side-lines, cheek to cheek.

That night, she was certain she could feel magic and optimism on the air, along with the cigarette smoke and beer fumes. A new decade was about to begin, hopefully leaving war, suffering and despair consigned to history.

'Do you think things will be better?' she asked James, shouting above the music.

'I'll say. We're at the start of an entirely new era.'

She was sure she could see a bright future reflected in his large brown eyes. 'I wish Dad had lived to see what comes next.'

James looked up at the balloons that were gathered inside a vast netting hammock, suspended above the dance floor. 'He's probably looking on with bated breath.'

'So what do you think the highlights will be?' she asked.

Pursing his lips, James frowned momentarily. Then, his face softened. 'Well, Galbraith's research on smoking is coming out. That will put the cat among the pigeons, all right. I think we'll finally see an end to rationing, and I can't wait for that! Digging for Britain isn't the easiest when you're in a first-floor flat and work round the clock most days.'

'I know,' Kitty said. 'If I see another powdered egg or grey sausage, I think I'll scream!'

They swayed along to the music without speaking for a while.

'I think Ned and Grace will tie the knot before we do,' Kitty said. 'There's no way Ned will give a woman like that time for second thoughts!'

'Ah, yes. Your brother's certainly landed on his feet. I'm not entirely sure what Grace sees in him.'

'It's the Longthorne good looks, of course,' Kitty said, pinching James playfully on the waist.

'Yes. Of course. Though Ned has me to thank for his!'

The band finished the song and Grace exchanged words with the guitarist, who nodded over at the landlord.

'Ladies and gentlemen,' Grace spoke into the microphone, 'it's nearly midnight. Will you join me in counting down to 1950?'

The crowd on the dance floor and drinkers by the bar all cheered their assent.

'Here we go, folks! Ten, nine . . .'

Everybody joined in with the countdown.

James held Kitty's face in his hands. 'In the new year, can we at least set a date for our big day, darling?'

'You bet,' Kitty said. 'How does a Christmas wedding suit you, 1950s style?'

'Three, two, one. Happy New Year!'

The balloons descended from the netting like giant rainbow-coloured confetti, landing on the heads of the dancers. They started to pop all around, as if fireworks had been let off inside the club. The band started to play 'Auld Lang Syne', and everybody linked arms as if they were old friends, singing along with Grace. Only Kitty and James stood on the dance floor together in an embrace, gazing intently at each other.

'I see the future in your eyes, Kitty Longthorne,' James said. 'And I'm ready to embrace it.'

'Well, that's a good job, James Williams, because everything I want is already in my arms, and I'm not letting go!'

Author's Note

Dear Reader,

With so many books vying for your attention and pennies at any one time, let me take this opportunity to thank you for choosing to read *Nurse Kitty's Unforgettable Journey*. For those of you who enjoyed my first story in this series – *Nurse Kitty's Secret War* – I hope you've enjoyed this second tale just as much. I'm chuffed as mint-balls (as we say up North) at the reception my debut has got from readers. If you're just dipping your toe into the waters of the 1940s with this second book, however, I hope you fall in love with the characters in Kitty's world as much as I did when penning them! Do go back and read the first story.

I had already written about the end of the Second World War and the start of the NHS in the first book, and it was quite a challenge to choose a period in Kitty's life that would be as interesting for book two. Research is my joint-favourite part of writing, along with the magic of creating that scruffy but promising first draft. Consequently, I enjoyed spending weeks poring over clips from Pathé News and various archives, as well as casting my mind back to what I can remember of the late forties and my own mother's reminiscences.

With the NHS still in its infancy, 1949 was a really interesting time for a young nurse. There were two big issues that really jumped out at me. The first was the dawning realisation that smoking tobacco products was linked to lung cancer . . .

Smoking came to Britain hundreds of years ago, when Sir Walter Raleigh brought tobacco back from Virginia. Yet it was in the early twentieth century when pipes, cigars and cigarettes really got a grip on the world. Men were already hooked on nicotine, but women had started to smoke, too, finding that cigarettes helped to keep them trim. Smoking was made to look glamorous on the silver screen, and I can remember going to our local 'bug hut' at least three times per week to see the latest Hollywood films, as well as the latest Pathé News. We children even had our own anthem and merrily used to sing that we were the 'ABC Minors'! But I digress. Most actors and actresses smoked. It gave them an air of sophistication and glamour. The women looked emancipated and positively racy with a cigarette holder between their fingers. As medical science progressed, however, it soon became clear to some doctors that the golden leaf might well be taking the public's breath away, quite literally. Hospital wards started to fill up, not just with TB sufferers, but also with those gasping their last from emphysema and lung cancer.

The first study into the link between smoking and lung cancer was published in 1950, so it seemed fitting that I should involve Park Hospital's finest fictitious cardiothoracic surgeon, Mr Galbraith, in his own fictitious global study into the ills of tobacco. Why not also show tobacco's human cost to Kitty's family, since her father, Bert, is such a heavy smoker? My own mother, my cousin, my aunty *and* my great-uncle all died of lung cancer. Sadly, I was able to portray the agony of losing a relative to the Big C faithfully. I used to smoke, too, and stopping was a right trial, I can tell you! I did it in the end, though, and I did it cold-turkey, would you believe? I've never looked back. It heartens me that young people are smoking less and less nowadays. That's the kind of progress I like, and I'm sure Kitty would be delighted to hear that this dirty habit is finally burning itself out.

The second, and perhaps the most important, thing that started to happen at the end of the forties, was the *Windrush* generation's arrival in Britain from the Caribbean. The popularity of the brand-new NHS was immediate – unsurprising, given the shocking health of the nation, post-war. In fact, demand was so high for the new health service that there was an acute shortage of all manner of medical staff – nursing staff, in particular. The Government looked to the colonies to fulfil that need, with the overwhelming majority of nurses coming from the Caribbean islands of Jamaica and Barbados. It was clear to me that I should send Kitty on a wonderful recruitment journey to Barbados, where, coincidentally, I had left her twin brother, Ned, at the end of the first book. Yet, writing about the colonies and the racial prejudice that the *Windrush* generation endured when they arrived in Britain in the late forties and fifties has been a rather tricky challenge for me. I'll explain why . . .

During lockdown in the current pandemic, there has been much debate surrounding issues of empire and colonialization. The Black Lives Matter activists who dominated the headlines following the murder of George Floyd in the US, famously – or infamously, depending on how you view it – tore down the statue of slave trader Edward Colston in Bristol and threw it into Bristol Harbour. There followed a national re-examining of the ethics of keeping many statues, street names and other homages to slave traders – perhaps, most famously, the debate surrounding the removal of the statue of Cecil Rhodes from the façade of Oriel College, Oxford.

Men like Edward Colston and Cecil Rhodes, who were seen as philanthropic bastions of the British Empire but who made much of their money from the brutal trade of African slaves, are now seen by activists as symbols of white supremacy and the oppression of Black people – hence the call to remove their images and names from public property. Oriel college *still* has some of Cecil Rhodes's money in its coffers. It is not alone as an institution, though. Britain's wealth and power as a modern-day, first-world nation has its former empire to thank, and the slave trade was a major nasty by-product of that imperial might. Black or white, whether we want to or not, as British citizens we *all* indirectly benefit from that historical wealth, power and exploitation. A conundrum, indeed, and definitely one to be discussed sensibly.

So, what's the right way to talk about empire, now that so many are aware of the truth about our inglorious past? Well, some would prefer that terms like 'West Indies' were left in the past and replaced by words like 'Caribbean' instead – Caribbean has no colonial connotations and therefore cannot cause offense. As with the statues of those slave traders, there are those who believe that old-fashioned terminology should be stripped out of modern-day vocabulary. Out of sight, out of mind, you might say.

There is another school of thought, however, and one which is applicable to authors, like me, who are writing historical fiction: retain and explain. It is very difficult to write accurately about the past without walking the line between potentially causing hurt to some readers and being faithful to the era and the stories of the sort of real-life people your characters represent. In 1949, the British-ruled islands in the Caribbean were still referred to as the West Indies. In Barbados, there was an enormous gulf between the white plantation-owning classes and the Black population. Black nurses like Grace were well-trained professionals, but senior nursing posts were usually held by white or mixed-race women. Most doctors were white men. That is simply historical fact.

When nurses like Grace came to Britain, they would have faced terrible racism. They were called all sorts of horrible names, though I made a decision to leave those particular words out of this story. You might be wondering why I've also referred to Grace as 'Black', rather than choosing to use the historically accurate term 'coloured'. Well, this is because today 'coloured' is regarded by many as highly offensive, though it was still in use as a polite term as late as the seventies and early eighties! Us oldies might think that, ironically, it's not dissimilar to the more recently coined, acceptable term 'people of colour', but then we're all learning every day, aren't we? It's good to change with the times. My generation has much to learn from our youngsters, but the younger generation would do well to absorb some of the wisdom of their elders and to respect their accounts of their own lived experiences, too – 'twas ever thus!

Anyway, I have tried to portray at least *some* of the racist behaviour that Grace's contemporaries would have met on arrival in a very white Manchester. I felt it was necessary to show to a certain degree how women and men like her would have been treated and how that suspicion and shoddy treatment would have made them feel, thousands of miles away from their home and their loved ones. It's really important that we keep truth and honesty in our historical fiction, however unpalatable, so that terrible atrocities like the Amritsar Massacre and other murderous exploits of the British Raj, like the slave trade, and crimes against humanity like the Holocaust, are not forgotten and will not happen again.

This is a heart-warming story about Nurse Kitty, her fiancé James Williams, her dysfunctional but lovable family and the fledgling NHS, however. It's not meant to be an academic thesis about racial politics or an opinion piece about smoking, but I do hope you understand, during these times of great change and ideological upheaval, why I have explained my thinking to you, dear Reader. Words have power, and I only want to use mine for good!

So, let me thank you once again for reading *Nurse Kitty's Unforgettable Journey*. At a time when millions have died globally from COVID-19, let's all keep appreciating what our NHS has done for our country and the grand job that our nurses, doctors, hospital staff and, of course, medical researchers do for us every day. They're risking their lives to save ours, and that's something worth celebrating. Right, I'm going to sign off now, make myself a nice brew and start thinking about Kitty's next tale . . .

Yours truly,
Maggie Campbell

Acknowledgements

It is never just an author lurking behind a good story. Bringing a novel to publication requires a team of talented professionals, who work in tandem to support the author. First, they help the author to turn a flabby first draft into a tightly plotted manuscript that sings, and then, hey presto, with more publishing magic, that manuscript becomes a lovely-smelling, tactile book that you can buy in a shop or an e-book that gives you hours of enjoyment at the swipe of a fingertip.

The following people have been of tremendous help to me during the writing, editing and publication of *Nurse Kitty's Unforgettable Journey* (which was a joy to write), so I'll say thanks to:

Caspian Dennis, my agent, for his unfaltering support and friendship, and to the rest of the crack team at Abner Stein – especially Sandy, Felicity, Ray and Amberley.

My editor, Sam Eades, for commissioning the *Kitty* series in the first place and for agreeing to let me write this compelling story of migration and medical research in 1949. Thanks also to Zoe Yang, Sarah Fortune and my new editor, Rhea Kurien.

Sarah Benton, the Deputy MD at Orion, for taking time out of her extremely busy schedule to engage in a thoughtful conversation about the representation of ethnic diversity in historical fiction.

The savvy saga readers who have really got behind *Nurse Kitty*, leaving absolutely wonderful reviews online, and also my colleagues, Gill Paul and Kitty Neale, for saying lovely things about the books before publication.

Finally, thanks to my family, for putting up with me when I have a deadline brewing. I couldn't write without their love and encouragement…or maybe without their constant interruptions, I'd write a darn sight more! Who knows? I love them anyway.

I'd like also to apologise to my poor garden which has been sorely neglected in favour of delivering my edits. I *will* give those weeds what-for before the Autumn's out, I promise!